'Amalric's tale is of a glass ma[____] the human soul. Each window [____] vivid, colourful images which p[____] As I journeyed through each [____] moved by Amalric's life to ref[____] brought Amalric's world to life in full colour.'
Rev Jason Powell, Greater Manchester

'*Life of Glass* plunges the reader once again into the life and times of Amalric, a fourteenth-century artisan glazier, and the inhabitants of his village, Warren Horesby. The narrative is both captivating and immensely readable while offering highly researched insights into coloured glass window artistry and the medical knowledge of the time, set as it is against the menacingly real threat of the Black Death. The world beyond the village never seems far away, and turmoil in Church and State is engagingly depicted. Above all, the author's deep and empathic understanding of human relationships and the frailties that affect them enhances a vivid portrayal of her characters, imbuing them with cares of faith, love, health, sustenance and superstition in a way that I find intensely moving.'
Jane Townell, retired counsellor and member of Woodhall Spa Library Writers Group

'In *Life of Glass*, Andrea weaves her way around the daily routines, habits and culture of fourteenth-century England – scarred by the legacy of the Black Death. She knows a great deal about the making of medieval stained glass and medical reactions to the Great Plague and uses this to shine a light on the gap between the past and the present. Taking history out of the archive and personifying it into her hero, master glazier Amalric Faceby, she plots a journey through the travails of pestilence-torn England set against the background of ecclesiastical politics.'
Carolyn Bayley, history teacher

LIFE OF GLASS

Can Amalric finally make peace with his past?

Andrea Sarginson

instant
apostle

First published in Great Britain in 2023

Instant Apostle
104 The Drive
Rickmansworth
Herts
WD3 4DU

British Library Cataloguing-in-Publication Data

A catalogue record for this book is available from the British Library.

This book and all other Instant Apostle books are available from Instant Apostle:

Website: www.instantapostle.com
Email: info@instantapostle.com

ISBN 978-1-912726-69-1

Printed in Great Britain.

... using every means to learn by what skilled arts the variety of pigments could decorate the work without repelling the daylight and the rays of the sun.

Theophilus[1]

---

[1] John G Hawthorne and Cyril Stanley Smith, *On Divers Arts: The Foremost Medieval Treatise on Painting, Glassmaking and Metalwork,* (NY: Dover Publications Inc, 1979). Originally published by University of Chicago, 1963, translated from De diversis artibus: Theophilus (Roger of Helmarshausen), twelfth century.

Author's note

The setting of *Life of Glass* is inspired by events of mid-fourteenth to early fifteenth century England when a terrible, recurring disease devastated the population and challenged society, the Christian Church, medicine and the use of coloured glass.

The location is based on the ruins of a long since abandoned medieval village and abbey – Warram Percy and Meaux Abbey, both in East Yorkshire.

The *Life* is that of Amalric Faceby, a fictional master glazier.

Historical details

References to York, Beverley, medicine, the Church in England and windows are based on facts but the story is a work of fiction and I apologise for any inaccuracies.

Included are some famous characters of the time, Geoffrey Chaucer, John Wyclif and John Thornton of Coventry. I have fictionalised their connections to Amalric Faceby, his village and Meaux Abbey. John Thornton, however, *is* recorded as the master glazier of the Great East Window of York Minster, dated 1408,[2] but references I have made to his inspiration, life and character are purely conjectural.

---

[2] For example, Sarah Brown, *The Great East Window of York Minster: An English Masterpiece* (London: Third Millennium Publishing, 2018).

The pestilence

Dates given for the pestilence, now known as the Black Death, are as accurate as I could make them, there being many recorded. It seems the first pestilence (I refer to it as the Great Pestilence) reached the south coast in 1348 and swept through Britain, reaching Scotland by 1350. Further major episodes occurred around 1361, 1369, 1374-79 and 1390-93 and recurred until the mid-seventeenth century. Theories and cures were many and various. All were ineffective.

Window glass

The technique of coloured glass window-making used in medieval times is still practised in a very similar way today. It was described in a twelfth-century treatise by a German monk known as Theophilus.[3]

After a small sketch, an accurate drawing was made onto a whitened table with thick lines representing leading. Then, coloured pieces of glass were cut to shape using a hot metal cutting point and refined into the final shape by chipping with a grozing iron. Details were added with paint made from one-third each of powdered copper, ground green glass and blue glass, then all three ground together with wine or urine. The decorated glass was fired so that the paint and glass fused together. The glass pieces were then surrounded with H-shaped lead strips called cames, the glass fitting neatly into each side of the H. Each shape was joined to the next with solder and made up into a panel. Several panels would make a whole window.

By the fourteenth century, silver stain was in use, painted and fired onto glass, giving a pale lemon to dark amber colour which could be used for shading or changing the colour of the original glass. It is from this that the term 'stained glass' arose later and is not used in this story.

---

[3] John G Hawthorne and Cyril Stanley Smith, *Theophilus: On Divers Arts: The Foremost Medieval Treatise on Painting, Glassmaking and Metalwork.*

In *Life of Glass*, Amalric works in a small workshop tagged onto his own home, but in the fourteenth century increasingly window-making was carried out in large workshops attached to the great new churches being built or extended. Apprenticeships lasted from eight to ten years.

The candle-holder mentioned was inspired by one made for a church in Rochdale in 2017 by a stained-glass artist in Todmorden, West Yorkshire.

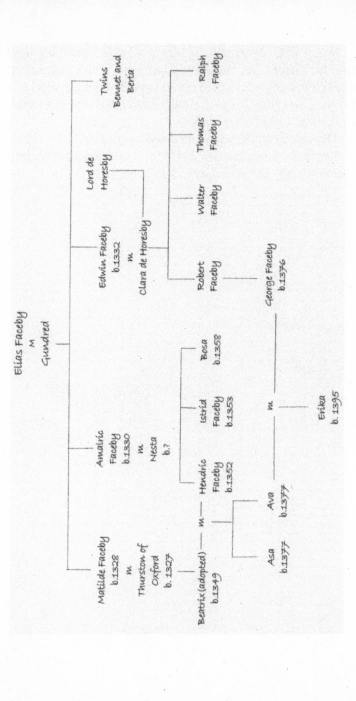

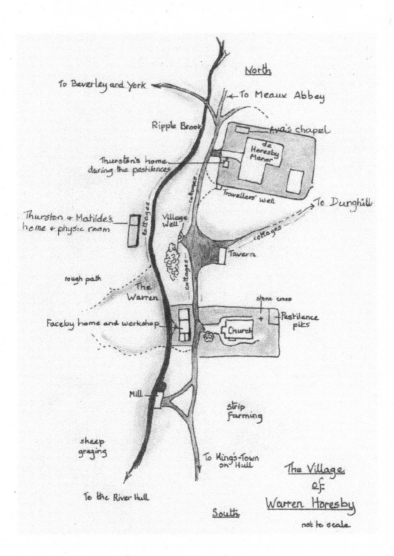

North

To Beverley and York

To Meaux Abbey

Ripple Brook

Ava's chapel

de Heresby Manor

Thurston's home during the pestilances

Travellers' well

To Dunghill

cottages

Thurston & Matilde's home & physic room

Village Well

cottages

Tavern

rough path

The Warren

cottages

stone cross

Faceby home and workshop

Church

Pestilence pits

Mill

strip Farming

sheep grazing

To King's-Town on Hull

To the River Hull

South

The Village of Warren Horesby

not to scale

The Faceby Home and Workshop

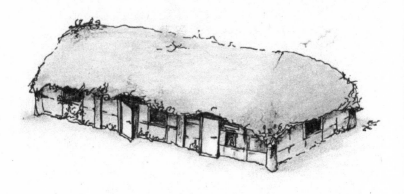

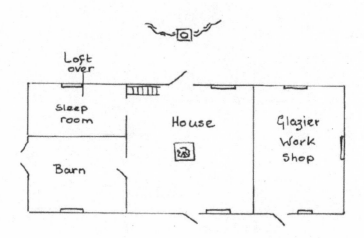

Loft over

Sleep room

House

Glazier Work Shop

Barn

Prologue

The days of our years are threescore years and ten; and if by reason of strength they be fourscore years, yet is their strength, labour and sorrow; for it is soon cut off, and we fly away.[4]

It is autumn in the year 1408. Amalric Faceby, a master glazier, has put aside his glass cutter and grozing iron, stored his few remaining glass sheets in the rack and closed the shutters on his coloured-glass window business. Now, he is about to take a journey. At the end of it, he will know whether or not he has achieved his long-held creative ambition.

On the journey, he will have the opportunity to reminisce. He will be free to doze, as an old man does, to look back on a life that changed abruptly when the Great Pestilence, the first showing of a horrific disease, arrived in East Yorkshire in 1349.

For Amalric, the Great Pestilence and its immediate aftermath was like a doorway separating his life into a before and an after. Before, he lived a regular life: an apprentice with a loving family. Then the Great Pestilence came, causing the death of family members and an act of villagers' recrimination that left his own legs burned and scarred. It shut off his past life like a great door slamming. Afterwards, he faced a new world, forcing him to become a confident, skilled artisan.

In his dozing and remembrances, it is the long years *after* this first devastation that will return to him most clearly. He will turn

---

[4] Psalm 90:10, KJV.

over his memories like the crisp leaves of a manuscript, the happenings that shaped him and the people who shared his life: those he loved and those he tolerated. There will be chapters and paragraphs, but on every page there will be the shadow of the recurring pestilence, like a palimpsest, ever present, ever disrupting his long-held dream.

And always, Amalric has a faithful companion – a dog. As an old one dies, another young one comes along, unbidden but welcomed. He names them all 'Noah'.

Part One
Love

~~~~~~

Chapter One

1408 Warren Horesby
Autumn
The coming journey to York

Amalric Faceby settled in his chair. The age-loosened wooden joints shifted slightly, causing it to strain to one side, but he'd learnt to compensate and didn't mind the familiar bother of it. He adjusted his position to correct the leaning and let the chair hold him with its arms and high back. He felt as one with it; like him, its legs were scarred with burns and it creaked the wear and tear of years. He sighed. Older than his allotted three score years and ten, he felt weary at the mere thought of the journey he was about to take. While it excited him for what he would finally see, it could not be the fulfilment of his dream.

He held his hands in front of the central fire and gazed into flames struggling to circumnavigate a log balanced precariously on a block of peat. The small flames lit up blemishes on his sinewy fingers, the result of handling glass for years. How long had it been, something more than seventy years of working with brittle, transparent colour? Now, bony nodules, stiffness and shaking had finally put paid to the work. The last time he looked in his workshop, it was cold and dusty.

Looking back, when he'd been an idealistic youth apprenticed to his father and excited about the possibilities of glazing with coloured glass, he was secure in this same house, with love and warmth. Then the Great Pestilence had stormed into his life. Loved ones could not be protected. It had changed almost everything he was familiar with.

Yet, despite the hard times, some things had carried him safely through the years: family, friends – and his dogs. Here beside him was one of them, the latest Noah. Amalric put his hand down to his side and felt a soft, silky ear. The dog's head lifted and he licked the gnarled fingers. Amalric smiled, noting how growing flames intensified the colour of the smooth golden coat, which would soon become shaggy. The discovery of him a year ago slipped easily into Amalric's memory.

He'd just buried his most recent dog near the churchyard gate, by the side of the huge yew tree. These days he couldn't recall how many Noahs he'd buried there. Each dog had been so much like the others that they were now all one in his mind. They had been, he assumed, the progeny of Samson, whose master, Ned, the glazing workshop assistant, had been the first villager to die of the Great Pestilence. Samson had drowned in the mill pond, but not before fathering a pup in his image who had sauntered up to Amalric when the disease had retreated, demanding companionship. This had continued; when an old dog passed on, a new dog appeared looking for a master. Amalric had always obliged, naming each one Noah for simplicity – it meant rest, it was biblical – Noah a protector of animals and birds. A dog to keep away foxes and rats, a guardian of chickens. But the death of the last-but-one Noah had been different; no young dog had appeared. For one moon's passing, Amalric had felt lost and abandoned.

He gazed now at the flames and recalled a certain orange/red sky that had enclosed him when out for an evening stroll. He'd stopped to lean on the church gate opposite his own home, alone, sadly watching the church stone walls change from cream to pale amber, then deep pink, and the flitting bats, like little angels in a hurry. It was then he'd heard a small whimper, otherworldly in the clear air. In the diminishing light, he followed it to a bed of blown leaves and dry grass under the great yew tree. He gently pushed the leaves away. The whimper came again. His heart was pounding – more so than usual, fearing a rat or some such would dart out. His back ached from bending. Then, the last of the sun glinted on two eyes looking up at him. Amalric recalled the effort to push additional leaves away with his hands. It became clear that below the autumn coverlet was a small, trembling bundle of ginger hair. Further behind was the still, slumped, fly-blown carcass of an adult female dog.

Amalric had ached for the little orphan. He scooped up the shivering form into his arms with a gentleness that surprised himself and was unexpectedly enveloped in a feeling of pure love; a warm sense of both giving and taking. He nuzzled his cheek to the little snout. A small piece of wet leaf was transferred from the pup's nose to Amalric's own. He rubbed his nose now and recalled the delicious feeling of the puppy's softness on his flesh as he put him inside his tunic and under his undershirt. He had once done the same with a babe.

Amalric came out of his reverie. 'Eh, lad. That were a year ago,' he said, as if the dog had seen into his mind. He glanced around. Istrid was working at her household duties, moving in and out of the barn and the sleep room, both leading from the large room called 'the house'. Her skirt was pushed into her belt so she could easily climb the ladder to the loft to collect things – Amalric couldn't see what. Even though all the shutters were open, the light didn't penetrate all corners on such a grey autumnal day. He heard her mutter hopes for better weather for their journey. She descended, then climbed another ladder resting on a rafter above the fire where he sat.

'No need to move, Da. I just need to get the ham. You'll be safe there.'

Amalric wasn't convinced as he visualised a black leg of pig plummeting onto his head.

'Good, it's well and truly smoked,' she said as she descended. 'At least, it should be, it's been hanging over the fire for long enough. I'll lop chunks off so it'll see us through two to three days on the way to York, especially if we can buy bread on the way. It'll be a slow journey.' There was a thump as the joint landed on the table.

'Now Da, before I carry on with preparing for our journey, I've to make food for today. I'll sit by you and prepare some vegetables.' She loosened her skirt from her belt. 'You can tell me what you've been dreamin' of just now.'

'Oh, nothin' much.'

'That's not true, Da. You've nearly let the fire go. Been back in the past again, have you? You've a grim look on your face.'

It was true – his dozing and dreaming, remembering times gone by, was his chief occupation these days. Amalric looked up at his daughter from his chair and watched her poke more life into the fire. 'Well, lass, it was about Noah, but I would've got round to your mother, as I often do.' A slight feeling of guilt nudged his thoughts. 'I think I could've been a better husband.'

'Nay, Da. She loved you.'

'Aye. Well, it cheers me to remember our wedding day.'

Istrid took root vegetables from the table, secured them in her apron and lowered herself onto a stool by her father. She began to peel the rough skin off them ready for the pot. Amalric knew by her soft sigh she was humouring him, listening to a tale he'd told many times before.

'Aye, reet pretty she was. I felt the luckiest of men. On our wedding day she had a fuzz of hawthorn blossom tucked into a plaited coronet of her lovely hair. The spring sun had lightened the ends to the colour of cream. I thought it was a shame that bein' married she'd have to cover it.'

Istrid touched her own stiff wimple and Amalric noticed

annoyance as she scratched her forehead at its rim. She'd spent most of her life without one, having married late.

'Anyway, the berry juice she'd used to tint her cheeks was unnecessary,' he went on. 'She had a glow about her.' Istrid forced her knife through the tough skin of a parsnip. He saw her mother in her thick arms and strong fingers and her determined facial expression softened by an upturn of nose and a splash of freckles. 'You favour her.' Amalric stared into the increasing flames. 'She carried a bouquet of bluebells. There we were, standing in front of the east window, the one I'd made that gave me my Guild Master's Certificate in coloured glass. I remember being distracted by the purple-blueness of the flowers and wishing I could find glass of the same colour.'

He clearly saw in his mind the church. Behind himself and Nesta stood his ginger-haired friend Thurston in his cleaned-up physician's gown, and beside him Amalric's sister, Matilde, cradling little Beatrix, their adopted daughter. Amalric had felt real joy at the union of his friend and sister after all their troubles of the Great Pestilence. As for his brother, Edwin – always remembered with a sinking feeling – it had been a source of regret that he hadn't been at the ceremony, but that wasn't unusual; *he* could only be relied upon to be unreliable when it came to family doings, usually claiming something important to do at the manor.

Amalric refocused his eyes on Istrid and forced a cheeky grin on his face. 'Ee, I remember how I looked forward to the night to come...'

'I know, Da, *a crisp, clean bed and fresh herbs on the floor to be crushed by your bare feet and the dried lavender and sweet violets on the bed scattering as you fell onto it, clasped together.*'

Amalric grinned mischievously at her.

'So... there's still passion in those old bones,' smiled Istrid.

He felt his cheeky grin delight her, but his memories of Nesta were not all good. 'Aye, thoughts of your mother still make my heart beat quicker.'

Istrid threw vegetables and the most tender peelings into the family pot for the ongoing stew and gathered the remaining peelings in her apron for the pig. A blast of cool air entered the room before she could dispose of them outside.

Beatrix stood in the doorway. 'Hello, it's just me.'

Just me! There was no *just* about it. Amalric felt a surge of love for his now ageing adopted niece. She was taller and slimmer than the stocky Istrid. She had married Amalric's own firstborn child, Hendric, Istrid's brother. They'd had twins: Ava, who he would see tomorrow with her daughter, Erika, and Asa who, like his father, practised physic but somewhere else in England.

He waved a welcome and noted her excited breathlessness.

'I've just popped in to say we're all set for tomorrow.'

'Hey, now, Beatrix lass, I reckon that means you've sorted the glazier cart for the few days away? It's stable enough. If you get me a few cushions I'll manage reet well. It's a pity these bad old legs of mine'd never cope on a horse.'

'Well, Uncle, there's good news. We've arranged a princely ride for you. Uncle Edwin has loaned us…' she smiled broadly, '… he's loaned us Clara's litter with two horses. Istrid will mount the lead horse.'

Amalric was appalled. Borrowed from his brother! A litter! His wife, Clara's, litter at that, given to her many years back as a wedding present by her father, Lord de Horesby. He knew almost for certain that it would still have old frippery about it. Clara had ever been a person inclined to daintiness. Her favourite mode of transport had probably lain untouched since she died. Added to which, Amalric didn't like to feel beholden to his brother. Too much mud had been trampled underfoot over the years for feelings to be good between him and Edwin at this late stage.

'Ee, lass, I'm not sure about that. It's a bit – well – old, and probably still fancy.'

'Oh, come, Uncle. You deserve a comfy ride.'

'Aye, well, I'm used to the trundle of my old cart and don't fancy the side to side of a litter. I might be sick. An' you know how horses can stumble on rutted roads, and I could topple out.'

Undaunted, Beatrix carried on. 'Now then, Uncle. Nothing of the sort. Your Istrid will make certain it's comfy and safe for you.'

'It'll be overflowing with cushions.' Istrid's voice came from smoky shadows.

'Aye, she's a good lass, our Istrid,' said Amalric, forcing himself to be resigned to the gifted litter. 'Reet capable, like her mother.'

'She's repaired the old roof cover. It'll be like a royal procession from Warren Horesby to York. All the villagers will be there to wave us off. Maybe even Uncle Edwin. He's being kind.'

Amalric smiled cynically, recognising her goading with the mention of his brother to spark up his thoughts. It had almost become a joke. 'Aye, reet kind. Now let our lass get my food.'

'Very well, Uncle. Rest a while before it's time for Istrid's thick stew to land in your gut with the weight of a stone!' Beatrix's laughter spread through the house. Istrid playfully threw a peeling at her cousin. Amalric was warmed by their good-natured banter born of their different characters: Beatrix, the healer with a creative talent; Istrid, the practical carer and homemaker.

Amalric raised his palms to the central fire, felt the heat and gazed at revived flames.

Peat glowed. The smell, mixed with that of the stew, was intoxicating. His hand went down to his side where he found the soft ears of Noah.

Chapter Two

1408 Warren Horesby
Start of the journey

An autumn sun shone through the gaps in the shutters. By the quality of light, Amalric knew a hoar frost would be covering the garden. He rose with a trembling anticipation in his chest.

'I'm too old for such excitement,' he said to Noah, as the dog stretched into wakefulness.

Thin drifts of smoke crept into the sleep room from Istrid's early cooking fire, wafting over clothes laid out for him at the foot of the mattress: his best shirt, leather jerkin, woollen hose. His woollen surcoat hung from a nail. 'What would I have done all these years without our lass, Istrid?' he mumbled as he put the clothes on over flesh that had been bathed in warm, herbed water the evening before. He smoothed back his short, thin, white hair and rubbed his hand over his smooth chin, cropped with a specially purchased obsidian blade: volcanic glass, the sharpest, hardest glass he knew, with an impenetrable depth of dark colour.

He walked fully dressed, into the house. Thicker smoke gathered over the pot on the fire and swirled to the roof. Bread was on the table but Istrid was nowhere to be seen. He guessed she would be sorting things for travel. Almost without thinking he went to the front door, opened it and stood in the doorway. His cottage, the largest in the village of Warren Horesby, was the only home he had ever known. Almost every day of his lifetime he'd stood there and looked up, assessing the day's weather. Weather mattered to a man of glass. Changing light could alter colour tones and the cold make fingers drop the precious material. Winds made the installation of a window hazardous. In this part of the country, they blew cold from the east beyond the sea thrashing the Holderness Plane, desiccating the soil or soddening it, and whipping bog water. From the west and north they blew rain clouds over the dip slopes of the Yorkshire Wolds. It was a delight when they blew more southerly from beyond the Humber Estuary and the marshes where the birds descended in their hundreds and the eels squirmed. Amalric's work with coloured windows had largely been spent within these windswept boundaries.

He took his cap from a hook by the house door, then his fulled wool cloak and flung it over his shoulders. Istrid had done her best to disguise the fraying edges with fine stitching and it looked good. He then took his two walking sticks that leaned against the wall.

A slight, cool breeze rustled faded, frosted grass. The sky was pale blue with streaks of pink and gold. Distant hills were a warm grey. For him, life always had colour. Sometimes it hit his eye like a dart, sometimes, like this day, it settled on his eye like a feather.

Amalric walked stiffly across the rutted road with Noah padding behind. Warren Horesby's small church stood resolutely planted in its own long history, while gates and fencing shut off its grounds to troublesome sheep, indicating its more recent past. Just inside this perimeter, the great ancient yew tree quivered slightly. He reached out to the leaves, some shiny and light green with new growth of the past summer, and some dark with old life. He ran his hand over them and felt the odd sensation of both an end and a beginning. In the graveyard beyond lay his family – some of them in the pestilence pits.

In slanting light, the zigzag carving of the Norman arch was in high relief; the porch behind it was untouched by sun and therefore dim; the venerable oak door was darker still. Amalric pushed against the weight of it, anticipating the metallic moan of the black hinges. Inside the church, he lowered his thin backside onto the cold stone ledge that ran around the Saxon nave. Noah, though tense with youth, settled on his master's feet, warming them with gentle heat.

Amalric felt the mixture of balm and slight contempt that comes with familiarity, yet he was at home here. For some seventy-eight years he'd known this place. He'd even put his own mark on it with two coloured windows. He was, though, not entirely at peace with the once bright frescos that were mellowing into faded uncertainty after a hundred years – a jumble of figures telling the story of the Christian faith – the suffering and the triumph.

He turned his gaze to the west wall, the most recent to be painted and the brightest. It illustrated the Last Judgement – the end of the human story – an admonition to worshippers as they left the service, clearly depicting their fate if they failed to give up their wicked ways and repent. The fresco rose from the floor to the roof. It's meaning had been horribly heightened when the Great Pestilence was approaching; it was then seen as a timely warning to curb excesses which might, the clergy believed, be the root cause of the disease. High above was a figure of Christ, and below, St Michael, weighing souls on scales, separating goodness from evil. The peasant was there with his dreary short tunic, the rich landowner in furs, the alewife with her apron and huge jug and even a glazier in leather apron and thick-soled boots for protection from glass. It amused Amalric to think it might have been inspired by his own great-grandfather. Bodies of the sinful were seen falling to hell on the left, while the righteous were being hauled up to heaven on the right.

This huge, grim portent of doom was meant to stay in the minds of the congregation, but conversely, the artist had introduced notes of comedy in many of the gestures of figures writhing towards hell, to the extent that hell seemed more interesting than a tedious heaven.

Such things had always confused Amalric. It was here that he had first become aware of life's contradictions; what ought to be contrasting with what was. A long life had not made things clearer. Even his own favourite saint, King Edmund, on the north wall, had become more identified with the Great Pestilence than his death by Viking invaders, being painted semi-naked in his underhose, with arrows prophetically piercing where the great, angry buboes arose. The saint's face showed no emotion in his agony: another contradiction.

'Master Faceby!' A priest had come through the door and was walking swiftly towards him, a new-looking pale-grey habit swishing about his legs, wafting the clean odour of a monk. He was youthful, stocky and lively. 'I'm your new priest. Father Everard I'm named now. Here, my friend, let me take your arm lest you fall as you stand.'

Amalric was startled for a moment, but recovered. The face was familiar. Who was this new priest? 'Same as the others, I expect,' he thought, with dismay rather than malice.

'I've been so busy settling in I've not had time to meet you again. I've met only your daughter as I passed your home. She's a fine, capable woman. Not unlike my own mother was, of course. I believe you're off to York today. I'm settled as a priest at Meaux Abbey but glad to be released to help the parish of Warren Horesby.' He chatted rapidly. 'In fact, I told your daughter of two nuns' priories on the route. I hope you will find safety and comfort there overnight.'

Father Everard's chat left Amalric slightly winded. Who was this man? His old mind struggled to identify him.

'So, what were you doing in church?' continued the priest as they left. 'I see from the rushing about of the womenfolk over the road and the mounting sacks of journey provisions by the door that you should perhaps be there rather than here.'

'Just revisiting the past, Father. I'm of an age when I want to stay in touch with it and remember those buried nearby.'

'I understand. Come, I'll see you safely home. I'm eager to hear your many stories, Master Faceby. I'll look forward to your return. I regret I've not visited your home yet since I was last here.' Father Everard pointed across the road and smiled wistfully. 'Aye, your old home, looking almost part of the land. I remember the house room in the centre with the welcoming fire, the barn there to the left and your glazier workshop to the right with its glass window.'

Amalric wondered what on earth he was talking about. Last here? When? The question evaporated as Father Everard's arm wrapped around him. He allowed the young priest to assist him across the narrow road back home as if he was incapable, and bent to rub Noah's ear with a conspiratorial feeling of a shared jest. But it was true he had a lot of stories to tell.

'Here we are, then, Master Amalric. Back home.'

He felt as if he was being spoken to like a child. 'Thank you, Father Everard,' he said sullenly.

Istrid rushed towards them with unnecessary, excited breathlessness. 'Come on, Da, it's time to have breakfast, then go.' She almost dragged him inside.

'I hope your journey will be a good one, and safe,' Father Everard called through the doorway. 'I hear that in many parts the trees have been cut back to prevent bandits from hiding close to the road edge. God speed.' He stood as if thinking, then said, 'The journey *can* be treacherous, and your party *will* be small... Mm... Soon, I need to go to the Cistercian monastery in York; there are new manuscripts I need to catch up with. I wonder if I could make the journey with you? The more of us the safer, don't you agree? Yes... I could pack my bag and be with you as you reach the top of the village.' His face was all smiles.

'That would be wonderful,' said Istrid, then turned to her father. 'Break your fast quickly, Da.'

Full of food, Amalric emerged outside.

Istrid was brandishing a strip of home-woven cloth as if it was a garrotte. 'Don't forget your muffler. These lovely autumn mornings can turn chill later. You might need this sheep's offerin' to keep the cold off that thin neck of yours.'

Amalric was now certain that his life was being completely organised by others. Aggravation rose in his throat. He was usually tolerant of his daughter's fussing but it was irking him today. 'Thin neck! So what? Do you want to strangle me?'

Istrid ignored the outburst. 'It's new, Da. I wove it especially for this journey. See, I know your love of colours.' Istrid draped the soft, thick cloth around him. The blues, greys, purple, yellow and green colours of Yorkshire moors made him smile despite his mood. He loved the heathers and gorse.

A sound diverted Istrid's pampering. 'Oh look, they're coming,' she said. A litter swayed down the road with a manor servant leading a horse harnessed to the front, with a second horse to the rear.

Amalric's mouth gaped. 'Nay, lass, this litter's not fittin'.' He sighed with dismay at the old frill-edged, fabric canopy which would hardly keep off rain, with ribbons of cloth at each corner and abundant colourful cushions beneath. He guessed Istrid had been at the manor the day before adding new finery to make it both comfortable and respectable. He saw her face fall and tried to make amends. 'Well, it's reet grand… but no one else in York'll be so fancy.'

Istrid recovered. 'Oh, they will. It's a celebration day for York – and for you it's *really* special.' Her eyes glowed with love.

Ava followed the litter, driving the glazier cart packed with journey essentials – drink, food, bedding and changes of clothing. Her daughter, Erika, tripped at the side, trying to disguise her adolescent excitement with adult poise under a red velvet cloak. Beatrix came next on a small horse.

Istrid's excitement got the better of her. 'Oh, Da, doesn't Beatrix look grand on the palfrey' They both knew her new long, blue riding surcoat hid swollen knees. 'And look at Ava! My, how elegantly that dark-grey wool shows off her figure. You'd never guess she's in her middle years. Beatrix, Ava and Erika – mother, daughter and granddaughter, how well they look.'

Amalric felt a little sad that Istrid herself was dressed inelegantly in coarse-weave brown wool with a wide skirt suitable to straddle the lead horse of the litter.

Finally, mounted on a fine-looking horse, came George, Ava's husband and Erika's father. Neither Ava nor Erika paid him any heed. Amalric pushed down a feeling of distaste for him in his fashionable leather and multicoloured woollen clothing but managed a nod of his head.

Further sacks were added to the glazier cart, and with much excitement and laughter, Amalric was then heaved onto the litter and settled onto a bed-like softness of wool and feather cushions. He had not properly settled when George suddenly shouted 'Ho!' and the procession began to slowly heave into movement. The litter began to sway a little.

Amalric looked anxiously back at his home. A servant lass and an ageing glazing assistant stood in the doorway. Behind them both, shadowed by the low doorway, with his hands on their shoulders, was the big, rough man who was Istrid's husband. The Faceby home was in good hands. Amalric's anxiety transferred to the young dog who stood on the ground in front of them with his head tipped to one side, stepping from front foot to front foot, clearly not knowing what to do.

'Here, Noah. Come boy,' called Amalric. 'Come and join us.'

'No, Da, not today,' said Istrid turning round in the saddle, clearly annoyed and refusing to stop. 'He'll have fleas! I don't want fleas in all the cushions and blankets!'

'Yes, today,' said Amalric firmly. 'My dogs have always been faithful to me, and after our trip, they'll be known long after I'm gone.'

'Da! Your mind is getting ever more addled. Who will remember your dogs?' She made a show of being irritated by flapping her skirt as if to rid it already of fleas.

'Wait and see.'

Beatrix, having heard, smiled at her uncle knowingly.

'The dog deserves to be with me. See, I've treats in my pouch.' Amalric pulled out a piece of dried meat. 'Come, Noah. Come, boy.' The dog trotted forward, wary of the horses, and leapt onto the litter, but was immediately unsettled by the softness. He padded unsteadily towards Amalric and gently took the titbit, swallowed and looked with eyes of joy at his master. It always surprised Amalric that dogs could gain such pleasure from a show of appreciation. He rubbed a velvety ear. It was soft and warm; the dog's head leaned into the ecstasy of it, then he turned in a circle, padded a cushion and settled with a snuffling noise and his head on his master's knees.

Chapter Three

1408 Warren Horesby
The journey

The little procession moved off with George leading, arrogantly holding his horse's rein with one relaxed hand and a whip in the other. Afterwards came Ava on the glazier cart, with Erika having clambered to her side, then Istrid on the litter's lead horse with Beatrix at her side on the little palfrey so they could chat.

Amalric clung to the litter's side to lessen the unfamiliar sway. Unexpectedly soon, Father Everard appeared at his side. He was pleased to see the monk – whoever he was – for distraction from his impending nausea.

'I didn't expect to catch you up so soon,' said the monk. 'The churchwarden came into church and I was able to tell him of my absence without having to seek him out.'

Only the monk's head was able to be seen over the edge of the litter. Amalric raised himself a little and looked down at him. 'My goodness, Father, what is that you're riding?'

The priest sat astride an animal with thick, grey, untidy hair and long, pointed ears. Large brown eyes stared ahead. Father Everard's legs dangled indecorously down either side of the animal from a withered saddle. His feet, which hung a mere hand's length from the ground, were kept warm with incongruous, crinkled, copiously darned red socks. Amalric wondered how his lower limbs would look if it had been the height of summer and their rather bandy nature left bare.

Father Everard reached down to pat the animal's neck. 'This is Dorkas, my donkey. She's patient and faithful but not quick-footed. Still, she's adequate for a slow journey such as this. Christ rode a donkey, so it's no hardship for me. My bags are light. But are *you* comfortable? This village road is in poor condition.' Father Everard looked ahead with sympathy at Ava negotiating the glazier cart around a rut, and at Istrid just in front, pulling the litter's lead horse to one side to avoid the same. 'Master Faceby, I wonder if, while we're passing homes, you could perhaps tell me of the people who live or have lived here so that I may know my flock? So far, I know few.'

'Of course. But call me Amalric.'

Villagers stood by their doors and waved cheerily as the little procession rumbled up the main street. A few small children ran at the litter's side, jumping to try to catch the ribbons as they fluttered. Noah barked, disturbed by their antics.

Amalric pointed out Lord de Horesby's tenants and homeowners, the poor and not so poor. He told how, after the Great Pestilence, he'd persuaded Lord de Horesby to help him become a master glazier one year early, in order to obtain contracts for windows and provide work for the village. The families of the blacksmith, carpenter, mason and haulier had thus managed to hang on and, as a result, so had the weaver, the honey gatherer, the ploughmen and the alewife at the tavern. But now, after many years of struggle, numerous homes were unoccupied and boarded up. Like most villages, the recurring pestilences had caused Warren Horesby to lose folk in one way or another; if not to the awful disease, then to the lack of local work both in trade and on the land. Their resilience had diminished, like his own; many had prematurely died, sought better lives elsewhere or watched their few children leave for the increasing work to be found in big towns.

'And to whom did that belong?' asked the priest, pulling down his mouth in disgust at a stink.

They were partway up the village looking at a building far more ruined than any other empty home. Voracious weeds and a whole tree grew in the empty space once covered with heather thatch. Robbed of precious wooden beams, the collapsed building was hardly discernible as a small cottage at all, except for a single, rotting shutter hanging precariously on a tottering piece of damp, mouldy wattle and daub.

'Ah.' Amalric leaned towards the priest. 'In 1349, it was tenanted to Myrtle Ashe, a spiteful widow-woman who believed only in superstitious nonsense. She hated my mother who had refused to help rid her daughter of an unborn bastard child. The girl died in childbirth but the child lived. Myrtle cursed my mother and persuaded the villagers to believe that my family was responsible for bringing the pestilence to the village. Our home was set on fire. My legs were burned as I went in to save a valuable manuscript. Myrtle was seen shortly after, suffering from the sweating and swellings of the pestilence. No one would go near her. She was never seen again. It's believed her skeleton is still in the ruined house, grappled by tree roots and brought to pure whiteness by devil rats. It's feared she left a curse behind her, clinging to the ruins of her home. No one dares go near at all, especially on All Souls' Night, but sometimes brave young lads throw rotting vegetables and worse – whether to appease the devil rats or taunt 'em, I know not.'

'So that's why rotting parsnips and cabbage leaves litter the roadside. And stink.'

'Aye.' Amalric turned away from the priest to glance at Beatrix on the palfrey behind him. He saw her stare at the building. He went on, 'No one knew what happened to her bastard grandchild, but as Myrtle disappeared, a baby was mysteriously left at our household's door when I was ill with my leg burns. Our village priest arranged for her to go to the nuns of Swine Priory.'

'Swine Priory? I know it well!'

Father Everard's sudden exclamation surprised Amalric; he hadn't expected such an enthusiastic response but decided not to ask the reason, it was his own business. He carried on. 'Months later, the child was adopted by Matilde, my sister, and her husband, my good friend Thurston of Oxford, Doctor of Physic. Beatrix is the child.'

'Aye, the pestilence has made many an orphan.' The monk looked sad then cheered. 'I've heard of Thurston. We have some of his texts at Meaux Abbey. They're full of observances and common sense.'

'Here at the top of the village is their home. Beatrix lives there still.'

'The house is large, like yours.'

'Aye. It still has the physic room where Thurston and Matilde kept their medications and curatives. Beatrix followed her mother's skill in midwifery and still uses it, though she has always yearned for creative things.'

'Well, children are created.'

'Aye, well, I mean the artisan type of creation.'

'Ah yes – sorry, my Cistercian leanings slipped out.' Father Everard grinned roguishly.

Amalric began to really like this man.

The hill began to flatten out, and after the rough village houses came a neat, enclosing stone wall, beyond which was a jumble of buildings. The largest of these was a two-storey, stone-built, tiled-roofed manor house. Behind it was a great barn with its haylofts and threshing floor. Other roofs marked the necessary adjuncts to manor life: stables, dovecotes, an ox house. A collection of carts was to one side, some clearly in need of repair. There was also a small stone chapel which was the only building without a slight air of neglect. The signs of decline disturbed Amalric, as did the deep-throated growls of mastiff guard dogs that came from behind the buildings.

A figure could be made out, leaning on a gate in the wall that closed off the path to the house. Increased anxiety niggled in Amalric's breast as it always did when he knew he would have to come face to face with his brother.

Edwin leaned with both elbows on the gate while nonchalantly sucking on a stem of grass. One soft leather-booted foot casually rested on the other. Still fashionable, despite being more than his allotted three score years and ten, his gaudy clothing both fascinated and repulsed Amalric. His green top-coat fell open, showing a very fine fur interior; a sumptuousness that Amalric felt was marginally above his brother's station. Edwin was always on the fringes of conformity. Beside him on a leather lead was a thin, long-limbed, pointed-snout young female dog. Amalric guessed she was owned simply to follow fashion traits. Around her neck was a studded metal collar. Noah stared awhile at the fragile, trembling creature ahead of him, then turned away, uninterested.

George stopped the procession and sat unspeaking on his horse. Ava nodded to Edwin, her husband's grandfather, passed by and stopped the cart with sufficient room for Istrid to guide the litter to the gate, forcing the aged brothers to speak.

Amalric lifted himself on his elbows and clutched the side of the litter. Goaded by Edwin's smirking silence, he spoke first. 'I thank you, brother, for the loan of this litter. My daughter has added cushions to aid my comfort and warmth.' He hoped Edwin would recognise the slight slur suggesting that the comfort he was able to provide had been minimal. 'A fur covering would have been beneficial.'

'No bother,' replied Edwin, unmoved. 'It's been in a stable since Clara died. It has a rather feminine look, I'm afraid, but no doubt suitable for you.' He made a sucking sound with the grass stalk.

Amalric's eyes screwed at the jibe.

'It will be a great day for you, when you arrive in York,' Edwin continued. 'Well, perhaps not as great as you would like. But I wish you well.'

Edwin had a knack of speaking truth in ways that hurt. Yet it was true, Amalric mused, the day in York would not be as good as it might have been if pestilences had not intervened so extensively in the past. He offered a weak smile. 'Brother, I have fought a good fight, I have finished the course, I have done my best for my family, the village and, I hope, my faith. It is enough.

I'm a happy man.' Amalric knew he would recall the biblical words often forced upon them in church worship[5] but, unlike Edwin, he felt he'd always cared more for other people than himself. The realisation of his own shameful conceit struck him.

Edwin looked at him with mild disdain, then picked at an invisible mark on his sleeve and stroked the soft wool. Amalric perceived that behind his brother's habitual bravado and heartlessness was a sadness, of sorts. Emotions began to prickle between them. Amalric felt the need to mollify the situation.

'Aye, it would be nice to have you with us today.'

Edwin laughed jokingly. 'What, me support an artisan? Go against the wood grain?'

'Way back, you paid me to put coloured windows in the manor house to show your stature. That was support for me, an artisan.'

'Maybe – but they're not quite my taste. The shields our father crafted before you are fine, but *your* screwed-up faces and flowers do not please me.'

Istrid, having heard, looked astonished. 'Uncle Edwin, the windows in your manor house are the envy of Yorkshire! Why, only yesterday when I was up here decorating the litter, someone came to see about having some similar. He'd taken the advice of a master glazier in Beverley. Such things in wealthy houses are growing in popularity.'

Amalric remained silent.

Edwin looked down. 'Aye... well... anyway, be away now. The weather favours us all for a while. I've sheep being delivered from the fells. I need to have 'em protected from the weather over the coming months. Watch out for 'em on the road.' He threw the grass stalk down with annoyance, turned away before either Istrid or Amalric could respond and walked back to the manor, slightly swaying.

'More sheep!' said Amalric. 'His lust for wealth from wool is a stupid interest in his old age. He'll take over common land and

---

[5] 'I have fought a good fight, I have finished my course, I have kept the faith' (2 Timothy 4:7, KJV).

leave villagers even more destitute with no more thought than which fur to line his cloak with.'

'Aye, but he walks poorly,' commented Beatrix from behind. 'I believe he's not well. His skin is pale.'

The end of the manor boundary wall marked the end of the village. The half-dozen children who'd kept following stood on a small hillock and waved, shouting goodbye. It gave Amalric a feeling of finality, of going into the unknown.

His mind quickly returned to Edwin. He wished they'd been friends but they were as unlike as sheep and cows. His brother had blighted his life.

Chapter Four

1408 Warren Horesby
The journey

The road widened as the procession moved towards the plane. By the road on either side lay hedges of growing and tweeting things. Tangled stalks and berries had replaced decorous summer flowers. On it all, the dawn dew still sparkled.

'Master Faceby, if I seem to pry, ignore me, but I detect a poor relationship between you and your brother.' Father Everard had returned to the litter's side.

Amalric momentarily wondered whether or not he should confide in this man a little more, then threw his caution to the soft autumn breeze. 'Our difficult relationship is, in part, down to my own manufacture. The Great Pestilence left many dead. Lord de Horesby lost his wife, two sons and most of his servants. He'd only a spirited daughter, Clara, and himself to manage his estate. At the time my younger brother, Edwin, was troublesome. We'd lost both our parents and young twin brother and sister. He was no help, caring nothing for coloured glass work nor the drudgery of farming that kept us in food. We had to let our family sheep go.' He sighed with the contrast of Edwin's present belief in sheep. 'Knowing Edwin's predilection for hunting and the richer side of life, I took a risk and successfully asked for a place for him with Lord de Horesby, hoping his recklessness would be calmed with work he loved. It did. He married Clara and eventually became reeve. But he became grasping and we never saw eye to eye.'

Father Everard had no time to respond.

'Hey up!' hollered George.

Suddenly, a confusion of sheep released from the confined space of a narrow bend came charging towards them. Amalric gripped the side of the litter. They surrounded George on his horse, leaping on top of each other to get to freedom, and flowed around the glazier cart. Erika was screaming and clinging to her mother, but Ava managed to keep hold of the reins, and the old horse kept its ground despite its rearing head and snorting annoyance. The sheep were then destined to pass either side of the litter. The horse at the front of the litter reared up. Amalric saw Istrid fall. Noah barked furiously and leapt about. The litter side broke away and Amalric found himself hitting the ground. Someone began immediately rummaging through the tangled blankets and cushions that had plunged him into darkness.

'Oh, Uncle Amalric! Are you hurt?'

'What?' Daylight hit his eyes as a blanket was pulled away by Beatrix.

Baas and bleats filled the air. Noah added to them with even more frenzied barking.

'Are you hurt?' persisted Beatrix.

'My limbs seem to be in one piece. I think the cushions broke my fall. I've had worse. What happened?'

'The sheep surprised the horses. They reared and you fell out onto the bank, fortunately with hardly any distance to fall.'

'I think I'm alright. I seem to be on a grass hummock.' He wriggled to ease himself. 'What of yourself and the others – my Istrid?'

'Istrid is shaken after falling but uninjured. Father Everard helped her from the ground as she shouted obscenities at the shepherd. She's still seething but calming the front horse now.'

Amalric smiled at this typical picture of his daughter. 'The litter remains attached to the horses, but the side is off. Father Everard's donkey was unperturbed, and he's unhurt. Ava and Erika too are fine. My horse kept calm and Noah, though noisy, shows no inclination to harass the sheep, thank the Lord.'

George trotted up almost as if nothing had happened, even though his horse's eyes had something of a wild look. 'It's that stupid individual to blame,' he said, pointing his whip to a man in rough clothing walking towards them.

The man clearly recognised George but ignored him in favour of Amalric, to whom he tipped the curved end of a shepherd's crook to his forehead. 'Master, I'm reet sorry.' He wiped his weathered, sweating face with the wide sleeve of his overgarment. 'We met at a bad point. Yon sheep were crowded as the road narrowed afore the bend, and they come out into the wider road in a rush. These are your brother's sheep. I'm bringin' 'em down from the fells to the manor. There'll be good wool on 'em but more good tenant land'll be goin' to feed 'em, I reckon.'

Disapproval was evident in the shepherd's tone. As he turned to follow his sheep, he noticed Istrid pacifying the snorting horse still harnessed to the front of the litter. 'Master, yon animal is wrong for the front of that litter. I know 'im. He needs to be at the back. The other horse goes at the front. No wonder he tossed yer.' He saw the litter. 'An' that thing is too old.'

Istrid and Beatrix looked at each other. Amalric knew they were thinking, as he was, that Edwin would have known those things. George too would likely have known; he was still sitting astride his horse, now apparently appalled but, Amalric reckoned, probably feigning. Ava appeared too upset by her husband's callousness to even glance at him.

Istrid moved towards George, her face contorted with fury. 'Father could have been killed. You...' Amalric feared she would attack George with her horsewhip – she was as strong as any man when roused. Beatrix grasped her arm to hold her back.

Amalric intervened before the situation worsened. ''Tis no matter!' he shouted, anxious not to have strife throughout the journey. 'I'm old but of strong bones.' He rubbed his elbow. 'I've bruising only.' He turned to the shepherd. 'Go your way, man, or you'll lose your flock.'

The shepherd raised his crook in acknowledgement and turned to follow his sheep.

As Amalric looked with dismay at the litter, Father Everard appeared with a beaker of ale. 'To ease you, Master Amalric. Don't you worry, I have skills and simple tools that will repair the litter. I'm Cistercian, remember.'

The horse's positions were exchanged and the side put back firmly on the litter. 'It's safe to get in now, Da,' said Istrid.

'George, help me get into the litter,' demanded Amalric of his granddaughter's husband. Their heads came together as George heaved him up. In the closeness, Amalric said, 'You dare allow something like that again and I'll not bring a halt to the consequences.'

Amalric found it hard to settle in the litter. His nerves felt ragged and he needed the comfort of Noah; the dog had not bounded in to him. Looking over the edge, he saw him sniffing around Dorkas' legs. She lowered her head and pushed her nose to his. Her ears twitched. Amalric smiled and wondered if this was the beginning of a friendship.

'Here, boy. We must continue our journey. Your feet will tire. Come.' Noah leapt obediently into the litter. Amalric's stiff wrists and finger joints, which had begun to bother him when drawing on glass, now ached from protecting himself as he fell. 'Come here, boy. Put your head on my lap and let me put my hands under that young neck to warm 'em.' Noah obliged.

Istrid came to his side, tutting her condemnation of George. 'After all that you'll need a nap, Da. We have a long journey. We'll arrive at Nunburnholme Priory by early evening and stay for the night.' She pulled a blanket close around him and, after slight hesitation, around Noah. The little procession moved off and, save for the clatter, creaks and clomps of movement, grew silent.

The sun was rising high and the crisp day was warming. The song of a skylark, rarer at this time of the year than summer, filled the glassy, transparent sky. Other birds seemed to be gathering for their winter flight. Amalric idly wondered where they went every year and contemplated their flight high over the fells and moors and their swooping down into the valleys and over the sea. A slight breeze brought the smell of stagnant water and rotting vegetation from a clogged drainage ditch as they turned into a bend. It drifted away.

Amalric's nerves still jangled from the sudden fear that his journey had ended almost before it had begun. But the skylark song, the dappled sunlight and the wafting colours of the litter's ribbons worked their magic on him: amber, green, purple... Amalric melded into the past.

Chapter Five

Amalric carefully lifted a thin sheet of glass from the storage rack and held it up to the light. An intensity of purple was revealed. It reflected from the smooth, gently undulating surface onto the white table. Yes, it was perfect for a saint's long robe. This is what he loved: colour.

At roughly twenty-one years old, he was a master glazier with his own business, inherited from his father. Way back, when religious orders had begun to fully realise the advantages of window glass for both practical and spiritual purposes, Old Elias, his grandfather, had seen opportunities, especially at the Cistercian abbey at Meaux, nearby. He learned the skill, tagged a workshop onto the end of his home and taught the trade to his son, Amalric's father. The Faceby family was thus raised from peasant to artisan class; they became free men.

Amalric had been apprenticed to his father and continued the work of Faceby glaziers at Warren Horesby, making windows in the same workshop. Now, with the Great Pestilence gone, he was enjoying life. The future looked bright. In fact, he even admitted to himself that he'd become confident and rather smug.

Noah barked at the door. Nesta stood on the low step. Behind her, a low sun shot rays through pale frosted air, framing her in light.

'Master Amalric, a Mistress Yarrow has come to see you.

She's in the house.' After a few moments thought she added, 'And she's well dressed.'

Nesta had one hand on the latch and the other holding a large wooden spoon. It was the tool she wielded at Amalric from time to time to emphasise her point of view: her strong point of view. Amalric guessed that she had been stirring the large pot on the central fire and, on seeing the woman at her door, wiped the spoon on the cloth that tucked into her waist – he could see gravy marks – and brandished it as both a comment and a weapon, should one be needed. He was amused.

'Oh, a Mistress Yarrow, eh? Is she pretty?' he said provocatively, and carefully placed the glass sheet onto the chalk-whitened table, careful not to smudge the drawn design upon it. He ran his fingers over his short-cut beard, spat on his fingers and smoothed down his untidy black hair with unnecessary care. Then he passed his hands down his leather apron to even out the creases from his bending. He polished the front of one leather boot on his wrinkled hose-covered calf and then the other.

All the while, Nesta stood, irked at his taunting delay. Once she would have smiled but he could see by her sullen expression that his humour had begun to hurt her; he knew this attention on him from a higher-born woman was raising her hackles. Her lowly upbringing would always be... not a shame, but an embarrassment. But there was no doubt in his mind, he loved only her. She was beautiful in her small, plump, freckled, upturned nose kind of way, especially now since his comment had brought a deep pink to her cheeks. Wisps of hair, sun-bleached to cream, escaped her thick, long, mouse-coloured plait. He grabbed it, pulled her close and bent to kiss her on the lips. She leaned into him. The situation was saved.

'Give over,' she said as she pulled herself away, straightening her plait and smiling. 'She awaits you.'

'I'll come now.'

Amalric followed Nesta into the house and saw her disappear straightway into the shadows. He halted in the doorway and looked for his visitor. He was surprised to see a woman of taut beauty sitting at the table, whose age defied his guessing. Her married woman's wimple sat back a little on her head, revealing a low, dark, curving hairline framing stern, unsmiling, refined features. She stood when she realised he was there, disclosing to him the effort she had made to impress; sweet-smelling, clean clothing was pulled in slightly, revealing a tall, slim figure. Amalric found it hard not to compare her elegance with the ruffled homeliness of Nesta.

There was a sniffing sound. At the woman's feet, among the copse of table and stool legs, Amalric saw a small child sitting, quietly picking at tapes of fresh straw that covered the compacted earth. His small features suggested he was a boy no more than a year old. Thick wetness dribbled from his nose.

'This is Cuthbert,' said the woman.

'Please sit,' said Amalric. He felt important; he had an inkling of what this visit was about. 'Mistress Yarrow, I believe?' She nodded.

Nesta came forward with two beakers of ale, which she thumped onto the table, and returned to the shadows.

'What are you doing here, Mistress Yarrow?' Amalric's eyes fixed on the visitor. Hers met his audaciously.

'Well, Master Faceby...' Her chin jutted forward in a haughty manner. He guessed she was younger than himself. 'I grew up near here. My brother still resides in the same cottage, over at Dunghill. I married three years ago and have lived south near King's-Town on Hull. My husband inherited his father's tenancy when he died; killed, fighting the Scots for his lord of the manor.'

Her accent was certainly of this area of East Yorkshire. He tried to place her brother. 'Err... who...?'

She was not allowing questions.

'The pestilence came and my husband and his mother died. I had death duties to pay. Though an impoverished widow, I refused to marry the lord of the manor's choice for me – a filthy, drooling old man – and so the lord ended the tenancy. Folly, if you ask me; there's no one capable in the village after the Great Pestilence to take up the tenancy. The cottage remains empty.' She sighed, indicating the foolishness of such an act. 'I have but this one child. I wish to be near my brother and his wife, even though they barely have room for me – their home is small and their income paltry. But family is family.'

'Mm. That is a tragedy for you. What can I do to help? Who is your bro…?'

'Marry me.'

A strangled 'humph' came from a dark corner of the house. Amalric tried to cover it up. 'Err… marry?'

'Yes. You'll think me too forward. But many women are in my position and we must do what we can to find a husband quickly. But not just any man. You are a busy master glazier, unmarried, and my brother says both unmarried and widowed village women are lusting after you, looking after finding a man because so many died of the pestilence here. I had to come quickly. Out of all those women, I believe I'm most suitable for you.'

Amalric found it hard to hold back a smile – this woman's presumption was astounding. More sighing accompanied by the clatter of a broom came from the shadows.

Mistress Yarrow continued. 'I believe you lost your mother and twin brother and sister from the pestilence. Your elder sister is disfigured from the disease. Your father died in an accident and your brother works for Lord de Horesby.'

Mistress Yarrow coughed and took a gulp of ale. She sat silently for a few moments, holding an erect posture. Then she looked at him with dark, determined eyes. 'If you marry me, I'll be a good, faithful wife and will satisfy you.' She hesitated; the first indication of discomfiture. 'My husband never complained.' Her head bent to look at her own clasped hands around the beaker. 'I'm not of the servant class.' She gave a slight glance back into the room where Nesta had begun sweeping vigorously.

Amalric was aghast. Mistress Yarrow had certainly done her

research. This was no sudden decision but something well thought out. He felt uneasy; he found himself an object of desire for two women!

'I cannot marry you. The pestilence changed everything for all of us. I'm afraid my heart is already taken. I'm reet sorry.' He was a little sorry… in front of him was a fine woman.

'But necessity overrules heart these days, don't you think? I married beneath me. My parents were formerly upper peasant class, but father wasted his land, I prefer not to say how, and we descended — but not before my mother had taught me airs and graces, though not my brother, alas.' She cleared her throat. 'You have an artisan trade. I have enough about me to bring your status closer to that of your own brother. He will one day be reeve to Lord Horesby, will he not? I'm a good cook and can produce a good table. There are rabbits out the back, I see, in the warren. If the trend is followed, it will soon be under control of the estate, and you will need a strong woman to barter for your share.'

Nesta drew closer with her broom. Dust rose up and wafted to the table. Amalric was momentarily amused by the wily ways of women to get their point across and then alarmed that neither woman had thought of the child on the floor in the middle of the dust storm. Mistress Yarrow glared at Nesta and fanned her hand over her face.

Amalric saw the necessity to intervene. 'I'm sorry, Mistress Yarrow. My heart is truly taken. I'm betrothed. It will not change.'

He heard a sigh of relief from Nesta. From Mistress Yarrow, a sigh of despair.

'Some people are reduced to marrying servants,' she remarked pithily, 'when they could do better.' She placed her hands on the table and heaved herself up.

Amalric was not surprised at Nesta's response to such an insult. Her broom was thrown to the floor and again she grasped the spoon and brandished it as a threat. He placed himself between the two women and felt the spoon in his back.

'Thank you, Mistress Yarrow. I value your offer but cannot accept.'

Nesta huffed behind him.

'Very well. I'll leave.' Mistress Yarrow bent to pick up the child. 'I'm afraid he's a little unwell. It was damp and cold where we lived.' The small boy's skin looked pale; his eyes were sad and tinged with pink as they gazed at a stem of straw in his hand. Dust rested lightly on his lashes.

'No, wait!' Nesta was suddenly by Amalric's side and he couldn't help but put his arm about her. 'Am…' He guessed she had deliberately used the familiar abbreviation as she looked up at him. 'Your sister needs help. Matilde's adopted child is takin' up a lot of her time. She might accept Mistress Yarrow with Cuthbert, as home-help.'

Nesta's impetuousness, he knew, had been because she was moved by the plight of the malnourished child, but from Mistress Yarrow's dismal expression, it was clear the work of lowly servant to his sister would not be acceptable.

'Aye.' He turned to the proud woman having rapidly constructed a more attractive proposition. 'My sister is not of low status but married to a physic doctor. Surely you've heard of Dr Thurston of Oxford who works in this village and throughout all of East Yorkshire? My sister is a midwife. Her child is Beatrix, an adopted child left from the pestilence. About a year and a half in age. It would be a most interesting position.'

Mistress Yarrow's face illuminated. 'Oh. Would you introduce me?'

'Surely. Who is your brother, by the way?'

'Colin Scarthe.'

Colin Scarthe! Amalric was shocked. His mind reeled. Even before the Great Pestilence and though not living in Warren Horesby but the nearby village of Dunghill, he was known to be a man who would act dangerously and think later. Once he had threatened to harm Amalric with a scythe on the mistaken belief that Amalric's family had brought the Great Pestilence to the village. One swing of the scythe would have taken his legs off.

Yet the man had suffered; the disease had subsequently seen off most of his family, except his wife and this sister.

Amalric gave a reassuring nod to Nesta as he left their home with Mistress Yarrow. He noticed Nesta was biting her bottom lip. Her heart had opened to the child but he wondered if she was now regretting it. Mistress Yarrow's elegance and obvious intelligence was easy for Amalric to admire, but he strongly suspected that to Nesta, she would always be an adversary.

Amalric and Mistress Yarrow walked up the gentle hill to his sister's home in silence. Matilde appeared at the door with a tousled, harassed look and the small Beatrix clinging to her leg.

'Amalric! Forgive my appearance. This child gives me no rest. *Ma, ma, ma.* It really stretches me. Oh, who is this?'

'Mat, this is Mistress Yarrow and Cuthbert. Mistress Yarrow is Colin Scarthe's sister,' said Amalric, emphasising the latter words. 'She's looking for a position.'

Matilde beamed, either not recognising the inference or ignoring it. She invited Mistress Yarrow and the child in. The children looked at each other impassively.

Amalric made his way back to Nesta with misgivings, hoping that Matilde would not employ Mistress Yarrow. But he knew she would. He had now unwittingly brought his own family into contact with the brutish, resentful Colin. He was a man to cause trouble!

In the house, Nesta remained agitated. 'I told you, didn't I? A while back. I said there'd be women after you, an eligible man with a trade.'

'A man with burn-scarred legs.'

'A free man who is an artisan. A man who could have healthy children.'

'But I love *you.*'

'Well, as *she* hinted, I'm low born from a high fell farm with poor grazin' and crops, mud and moraines. Not a good catch; a servant, as your mother was always quick to point out.'

'Nesta, you have no need to fear. It's you I love. What say we marry soon?'

For a moment she was silent, then her eyes teared. 'Oh, Amalric, it would mean a child, and I'm afeared. Bearin' a child is full of danger. Your sister, Matilde, has told me of the things she has seen when called to her women. As well as that, I dread the pestilence has left me cursed.'

'Nesta, that's your fell-hamlet superstition. You didn't even catch the disease.'

'No!' She childishly stamped her foot. 'It may be what *you* call superstition but *I* know awful things happen, even when you're only *near* the devil's work.'

He chuckled, disregarding her fear. 'Well, if you want to stop widow-women lusting after me, marriage is the only way.'

One year after their marriage, Nesta gave birth easily to Hendric, proving to Amalric that her fears had been unfounded. The time with his firstborn was happy, clouded only by his wife's inbred anxieties. Ignoring her concerns, he stubbornly refused to countenance any further superstitions about the devil and childbirth.

Chapter Six

Outside, frost skimmed the ground and edged leaves. Inside, Amalric shivered and paced the house. He glanced at their new servant girl cowering in her dark sleep corner, fearful of being given jobs she didn't know how to carry out. He smiled at her, relieved to find someone as scared as himself. Thankfully, little Hendric was being cared for by Mistress Yarrow who'd become a valuable, if discordant, employee of the Thurston household.

Moaning came from the sleep room towards the back of the house. Beyond self-control, Amalric rushed to Nesta and dropped to the floor by the mattress. She breathlessly pleaded to the Virgin and St Margaret to help her at this time of travail. Her second child was taking an agonisingly painful long time to come.

'Am, go away,' said his sister, Matilde, rubbing her hands on the rough woven apron that covered her short-sleeved undergarments and saved her day-gown from mess. A close coif tidied away her hair.

Amalric feared the worst. Life had taught him that many marriages ended with the loss of both mother and child, but till this moment, he'd ignored such a truth. Now, the fear in Nesta's eyes was almost more than he could bear. She began to weep. 'Am… hold my hand!'

Matilde was adamant. 'No, Am, you must leave. Fathers aren't allowed at the birth. In all my work, I've never had a father present.'

Nesta clamped his hand.

'I'm stayin', Mat.' There was no better midwife in the area since his mother had died, but his love for Nesta knew no conventional boundaries. 'I've seen enough animals born to know what can happen. I'm stayin',' he said fiercely.

Matilde gave in. 'Very well. Put one arm under her shoulders and your face close to hers. Hold her.'

Quicker than he expected, the little body appeared and Nesta slumped back on Amalric's arm. He thought she was dead. Fear surged in him. Then Nesta opened her eyes.

'A girl! Am, Nesta, you have a daughter,' cried Matilde, excitedly.

'She's Istrid,' gasped Nesta, 'after my mother.'

It had never occurred to Amalric that his wife would long for her own mother at a time like this. He was suddenly aware of his own selfishness; Nesta had feared pregnancy and she had not once left him to seek the comfort of her own mother-love in her hilltop home. Her second perfect child was put to nuzzle in her arms. 'Istrid is a fine name, my love – old and venerable, like Hendric. Mat – what's wrong?'

Amalric had seen his sister's face lose its smile. Strands of her greying hair had escaped from her coif and stuck damply to her glistening forehead. Her brow became furrowed. Amalric knew all was not well. He suddenly became aware that Nesta's arms had relaxed, leaving her child in danger of falling. He grabbed at the little bundle. 'Nesta!' He knew there would be no response. Blood was oozing onto cloths and he felt the rawness of the animal births he'd seen.

Creeping into his mind came a similar scene from the past, when Matilde lay in the same room in agony as the Great Pestilence ravaged her body with grotesque buboes. Thurston in desperation had pierced them to let out foul pus. Nesta helped him. His sister's life was saved, and he hoped passionately that Nesta's too would be saved. But his sister's survival had been at the expense of scarring to her neck, armpit and groin. Her head had remained pulled to one side, as did one breast, her lopsidedness now clearly hampering her work this day with Nesta. Would Nesta be scarred for the rest of her life too? The irony of the situation struck him. Matilde's disease and scars had led to a hidden heartbreak; she was unable to conceive her own child, and here she was now, trying to save Nesta from a fate she would never have to risk suffering herself.

The newborn child in Amalric's arms moved. He realised she needed to be kept warm. He opened his jerkin and undershirt and slid her inside. Love flowed out from him to the soft, mewling bundle. Unmeasured time passed as he rocked back and forth, humming to the child for the comfort of both of them. Then he heard Nesta moan and ask for water.

'I think it's alright now, Am,' said Matilde warily. 'Lay the child down and get ale with honey for Nesta. Make sure the fire is topped up.'

Amalric reluctantly lowered little Istrid into a box crib and covered her with soft cloths the servant girl had warmed by the fire. He put his hands on the crib edge. The colour and smoothness of the old oak spoke to him of its long-gone maker: his talent and love of wood, and the many babes it had held. The servant girl pattered around him, seemingly happy to follow his orders for jobs she could cope with.

The door opened and Thurston's head peered gingerly around it. Amalric saw his face change from cheeriness to concern.

'Oh, my friend,' said the physician.

'Come in,' said Amalric, still standing by the crib. 'I saw it all, Thurston. See, I'm trembling. I thought Nesta was going to die. This is Istrid.'

Thurston glanced at the child then peered into the sleep room and nodded silently to his wife, who was hunched over Nesta. 'Come, sit a while, Am. Nesta looks quite grey. She must have lost a good deal of blood. You'll need a woman's help in the house until she's strong again.'

'Aye, well, there's not much about.' Amalric dropped onto a stool. 'We all must cope as best we can till the village has come up to strength after the pestilence.'

'True, but I'll get Mistress Yarrow to come and help a while. I'm sure Matilde will agree. Hendric can stay with us. He'll have Mistress Yarrow's Cuthbert and my Beatrix for company. Matilde and I will cope without Mistress Yarrow for a while.'

Amalric faced Mistress Yarrow with mild trepidation as she glided into his house with an air of entitlement and exaggerated good breeding. He was sitting by the crib.

'Move away from there. The child needs swaddling. Where are the bindings? No good comes of mollycoddling. And keep that dog away.'

Noah had seized the opportunity to squeeze inside past Mistress Yarrow's legs as the door had opened. It made Amalric smile, but he had immediately obeyed her instructions and pushed the offended dog outside. He sought out the swaddling bindings.

'Where's the mother?'

'*Nesta* is in there,' he said, forcing his wife's name on her. He pointed towards the back of the house and the narrow doorway of the sleep room.

The age-darkened, wooden doorframe obviously gave Mistress Yarrow some concern as she rubbed a finger over it and looked at the dust it had picked up. 'You could have woodworm here,' she said scathingly. 'I'll have to clean up this place. Girl, put water on to boil.'

Amalric had the distinct impression that Mistress Yarrow was pleased to have found a way of exerting authority in his household. It was at the same time mildly amusing and worrying. She was, after all, a servant but clearly thought she ought not to be. Even without seeing, Amalric felt Nesta's bristling response to being called *the mother.*

Mistress Yarrow's implacable efficiency enabled Nesta to rest and recover and avoid the need for a wet nurse. Amalric was glad of her immaculate care of his wife and child but she seemed to have little concept of human warmth. His own natural comforting of their new child came at the expense of her cold, disapproving stares. *A child is a small adult, that is all*, she was fond of saying. Amalric was intensely pleased when Matilde, for his sake, insisted that the woman return to her own work with the Thurston household.

Alone at last with their children, Amalric was able to resume his old companionship with Nesta. But in time, after Istrid was weaned, to his dismay fear once again gnawed at their happiness. Nesta kept saying she was cursed. Amalric failed to see how this could be, especially as they had two perfect children. She finally reminded him that the dead village troublemaker, Myrtle Ashe, had laid a curse upon his mother for not using her midwifery skills to end Myrtle's daughter's bastard pregnancy. Nesta feared that the same curse had subsequently been passed to Amalric at his mother's death and thus to herself, his wife. She decided not to have more children; she didn't want to leave a newborn child motherless or, worse, tainted by the devil.

Amalric was angry. Frustrated. The marriage bed was for begetting children, the Church strongly said so. Not to partake in intimacy was wrong. Amalric held in his anger, never mentioning it to Father Luke at confession in the village church, fearing the celibate priest would never understand. Instead, he watched his wife become joyless and withdrawn, even refusing to attend the raucous village fertility festival that she had once found an annual delight: a day of freedom from constant toil.

Amalric forced himself to be patient and eventually, with gentle coaxing, on rare occasions he found their passion for each other delightfully overcame her superstition. Amalric would put his hands on either side of her face and gently lean down to kiss her. Nesta would put her arms around his muscular neck and allow him to carry her to the sleep room.

1358

Amalric saw the look of fear in Nesta's eyes.

'Am, I'm with child again.' She cried in his arms.

Amalric's emotions swung wildly through love to fear. Nesta took no precautions, hoping to lose the child while it was still very small, but it was not to be disturbed from its course. He watched broken-hearted as his wife prepared for death. His eyes followed as she frequently visited the church across the way to confess her sins before Father Luke. She washed and folded burial cloths and arranged for help with Hendric and Istrid; Mistress Yarrow would be available, she reluctantly asserted. Amalric could hardly bear it.

'When the time comes,' Matilde said to Amalric and Nesta, 'Thurston and I will both be here with you. We'll do what we can.'

Three weeks early, as snow drifted onto the village, a little boy slipped effortlessly into the world. All of them could hardly believe it. They named him after a saint of York, Bosa.

'He's a gift,' said Nesta. 'Look, he's like an angel.'

He was indeed perfect.

'Brother! I'm here to see my new nephew!' Edwin pushed open the house door, causing it to clatter against the wall. Amalric was startled and looked up from his wooden platter of bread. A horse snorted outside. His brother was framed in the open doorway standing with legs astride, showing off his fashionable travel garments: a fine leather cloak over one shoulder, revealing a short, tight leather jerkin, leather hose, and satchel and whip. Amalric was amused to think that there was so much fine, smooth leather about him that man and rider would be difficult to tell apart − except for the flamboyant, glass-like colours of silken trim frothing profusely at his neck. A perfume of herbs and rosewater wafted from him.

'Still a stinking, smoking hole I see,' said Edwin of his family home, his mouth in a sneer at the stink of freshwater fish laid out ready for the meat-free Friday pot. 'The walls need whitewashing.'

'Yes, well, it needs time and money to do that and I have little of either.' Amalric had long lost the will to bandy pleasantries or otherwise with his brother. 'It's early. What's the need for this visit? I'll call Nesta if you wish a beverage. She's outside with the children.'

Edwin smiled. 'Ah. No need. I'm on my way to Hull to do business for Lord de Horesby and have beforehand been admirably breakfasted. The old man is too doddery to go himself. He's a fool when bargaining.'

'Aren't you being a little disrespectful? He's enabled you to have a good life.'

Edwin ignored the pithy repost. 'It's a matter of purchasing wine and very fine glass goblets for his table. The Hull warehouses have had recent shipments from the east.'

Amalric knew this was a taunt at his own trade. While the expensive vessels his brother spoke of were made of remarkably clear glass with precise gold and silver decoration within it, *his* window glass was full of colour and myriad imperfections that added texture and reflections. He knew his brother had not the sense to understand such haphazard beauty.

Edwin poked with his whip at the pottery bowls on the table, the crude jug and wooden platter, the horn beakers. 'Oh, brother, you're a peasant at heart, despite being a master of your trade.' A beaker toppled over. It rolled to the table edge. Amalric caught it before it fell to the floor. 'You may not believe it, but I wanted to see how your family fares – brotherly love and all that; to acknowledge my new nephew.' He craned his neck, looking through the smoke of the central fire past the crib where Bosa slept, and towards the far outside door. 'I wondered how you and Nesta are coping.'

'We're coping admirably, thank you. How are your four boys? I hear they've had a childhood complaint.'

'Aye, spots. We thought it was the pestilence but your physician friend said it was something going around. They're a little weak but almost well now. Good food helped heal them. Plenty of meat.' This was another taunt at the peasant quality and variety of food on the table; as well as fish, there was oat gruel and apples. 'You eat too much fruit. Clara has procured a new cookery book that everyone's talking about. Lots of recipes for venison, birds and...'[6]

Amalric could bear the high-minded talk no longer. Desperate to change the subject, he blurted out, 'So... you've begun to take common land from the villagers, I hear.'

'Not taking, just changing the use. Putting more sheep on it. I predict in years to come there'll be lots of money to be made from wool. The religious orders are doing well already.'

'And what will the villagers get out of it, seeing that they'll lose farming strips and common grazing?'

Edwin shrugged his shoulders and the corners of his mouth turned down. 'Believe me, Am, this will become widespread in years to come. The Great Pestilence left us too few peasants to work the land, and a lot of it is still idle.'

'It's resting land. It's good land and the village numbers are slowly increasing. It's their land, a common right. If impossible death duties weren't demanded, maybe more peasants could stay and continue to work it. The Great Pestilence is over. Things will recover.'

'No, brother. The peasants are already starting to ask too much in return to work it.'

'So you and Lord de Horesby profit from the land. You especially.'

'Oh, Amalric, are you suggesting I'm dishonest?'

'Now would I do that?'

Edwin carried on unruffled. 'And some even now shamefully demand wages instead of the usual remunerations. They're restless and need controlling. Fortunately, the King's Statute of Labour helps a little, to maintain the old order.'

'Perhaps we need a new order.' Amalric was growing angry. His brother irked him almost beyond reason, but before he could put his thoughts into words, Hendric came into the house through the back door from outside.

'Hello, Uncle Edwin,' the small boy said cheerfully, and

---

[6] This date of 1358 is conjecture, but from 1390 a collection of recipes was known by the Master Cooks of King Richard II. Samuel Pegge, in the eighteenth century, transcribed them and named the book, *Forme of Cury*.

stood by his uncle's side.

'Hendric, my boy. Good to see you. Nearly a man, I see. You'll soon have a beard.' He slapped the little lad on the shoulder and laughed.

Hendric was nearly seven years of age and Amalric was struck, not for the first time, by an increasing similarity between the two; it was beginning to eat away at him. Hendric insisted on gathering his same black hair into a high tail at the back. Edwin had done it too, flaunting what their father had called an ass' backside. There were also the same narrow eyes and a figure destined to be of moderate height, slim and elegant, not like himself – tall, thickset and clumsy.

Nesta, still wan from the birth, followed Hendric in. She glanced at Edwin and blushed; he responded with a leering grin.

Amalric saw and became uneasy. 'Goodbye, brother.'

Edwin took in the message of curt dismissal and left in a contemptuous swirl of expensive cloak.

'Da – why did you send Uncle Edwin off? We don't see him often, do we, Ma?' said a puzzled Hendric.

'No,' said Nesta quietly.

Amalric went into the workshop and slammed the door behind him. Fired by Edwin's leer at Nesta, his mind searched for a logical reason for Hendric's strong similarity to his brother but found only distasteful ones. He thumped the table with a clenched fist and turned to an older but easier resentment – Edwin's apparent disregard for his valiant and successful attempt to persuade Lord de Horesby to employ him after the Great Pestilence. It riled Amalric that, as reeve, his brother cared little for the needs of the peasantry, disdaining the tradition of loyalty, of give and take, within the social order. True, Edwin had to mitigate the effects of growing unrest if he could, by taking advantage of opportunities that presented – but surely not if they included exploiting Lord de Horesby, who remained grossly dispirited after the Great Pestilence?

He thumped the table again. What made it all worse was that he could not help but admire Edwin's determination to thrive.

Chapter Seven

1361 Warren Horesby
Spring

It had been a strange start to the morning. The sun had only just risen above the church roof when, instead of the day getting ever lighter, it grew darker. The sun dimmed.[7] Amalric, having just risen, was perturbed. Birds flew back to their night-time haunts. An owl hooted. Spring flower petals that had begun to open closed again. Outside their houses, petrified villagers forgot previous similar occasions and muttered that at the very least it heralded another pestilence – another monstrous disease, one which this time might mean the end of the world, as the Bible foretold. And indeed, to Amalric, it did look as though the sun was ill and failing. Father Luke and Thurston were both away and could not be consulted, but in the past Father Luke had put it down to the sins of men, while Thurston said it was to do with celestial bodies.

Nesta visibly quaked, wringing her hands in front of her husband. Finally, the sun regained its strength and Amalric was relieved. Nesta took longer to regain her normal composure, fearing she and her children could be snatched away by a gigantic black bird. Amalric had shaken his head at her irrationality but wondered if the sun might really die one day.

By mid-morning the village had calmed and Amalric settled to leading up a window panel with no thoughts other than

---

[7] Early in May 1361, a partial eclipse of the sun occurred in England.

which piece of glass to fit next into lead cames. Gradually, breaking through his concentration came a change to the workaday background noise: a distant frenzied honking of disturbed geese, a clattering-creaking of wheels and a tinkle of little bells. He looked up. Keeping his hand on a piece of green glass so as not to knock it off the table, he strained to look out of the one workshop window that gave sight of the road uphill.

Coming into view below the manor was a cart pulled by an ageing, weary mule. As it progressed towards the green, the cart swayed precariously with each rut of the rough road. A shaking superstructure of half-circle, thin wooden bands was partly covered by a murky cloth of weathered red, yellow and blue stripes. Pliant sticks of willow waved thin strips of fresher colours from each corner of the cart.

Amalric tipped his head towards the sound and recalled, rather than heard, a familiar song, sung more huskily than usual.

Here's old Wyler for your delight,
A healer of ills which catch, you might.
A healer of pestilence, the fright.
Hey ho, hey ho.
I make the devil's ill to go.

Hendric's voice came from outside. 'Come on. It's the pedlar.' The boy darted around the workshop corner followed by Istrid. Their young legs carried them as fast as they could go up the hill.

Amalric left his workshop and went to the back garden to find Nesta, acknowledging it would be a welcome distraction for her. He saw her coming towards him with a bunch of herbs in one hand and little Bosa clinging to the other. She looked efficient; her peasant practicality showing in her clean linen apron, rolled-up sleeves and fresh wimple covering her hair. But her superstitious fear of the sun-dimming still showed in her pale and anxious face. She went into the house and came out with a shawl about her shoulders, saying, 'He's early this time, usually it's after high sun. He must be going on to King's-Town on Hull when he leaves here.'

Amalric knew Nesta loved to see the curios that the pedlar would reveal: large, dried corns from a sufferer's foot, an amputated withered hand, amulets, relics of saints, and things to buy — cloth, wooden bowls, woven baskets, little carved figures and, especially, cure-alls with mysterious ingredients in precious little bottles and pots. Wyler had visited the village many times before, and though Amalric was dubious of his wares, nevertheless, they were always worth a look. The man's exotic garments and his knowledge accrued from far beyond the East Yorkshire everyday lent him an exciting air of mystery hard to resist. Amalric's friend Thurston, of course, had advised against buying anything from such a charlatan, but today he would be on his way back from Beverley and was not there to cast his disapproving eye.

'I must tell the children,' Nesta said. 'It's been two years or more since he was last here.'

'They've gone already, love. You'll have to run to catch them up.'

'Will you come too, Am?'

'Aye, but I'm not spending money on stuff we don't need.'

'Course not,' grinned Nesta.

Amalric went back to close his workshop shutters; magpies and jackdaws had been known to fly in and take small pieces of glass and lead, creating mayhem with their flapping wings and foul droppings as they did so. Noah often stayed behind to scare them off, but on this occasion of family fun, the dog was allowed to follow.

At the lower part of the green, Amalric pushed through the gathering crowd to join Nesta and Bosa at the front. Hendric and Istrid were at the higher part near the back of the crowd, having joined Beatrix, Mistress Yarrow and Cuthbert. Matilde, it seemed, had not been tempted. Amalric waved across to them. Beatrix waved back enthusiastically. At twelve years of age he knew she would be fascinated by anatomical curios and artistic things such as little icons. His own children seemed interested in just about everything, while he'd noticed that Cuthbert's attention was drawn by anything that spoke of battles or part of a knight's attire: arrow points and colourful fletches. Amalric glanced at Mistress Yarrow to find her gazing at him. It was unnerving.

The morning sun-dimming was surprisingly forgotten as the crowd watched Wyler produce tiny stuffed birds from the wide sleeve of his silk damask overgarment. He placed them for display on the rim of the cart and the sun caught iridescent feathers. Then he fumbled again in the sleeve and slowly, with dramatic effect, withdrew his hand, clasping something. His fingers uncurled. 'Now see here…' On his palm nestled a small metal object. He looked very seriously at the intense faces before him. 'The darkness this morning was a sign.' He looked upwards. A murmur arose as folk remembered. 'I have here medals of St Thomas, like this one from Canterbury. Buy them and wear them to save yourselves when the end of days comes.'

Amalric felt Nesta go tense. He wondered where Father Luke had gone. Would he approve of Wyler's assertions? He felt little angelic Bosa move between himself and Nesta, excitedly hopping from one plump foot to the other. He saw the pedlar lift his rheumy eyes to Nesta and watched him smile ingratiatingly.

'So… is it that long ago, Mistress Faceby, that since I was last here your little son has grown from a babe so splendidly? His name is…?'

Nesta smiled. 'Good day, Wyler. He's called Bosa.'

Amalric knew she would be proud to be remembered among all the women gathered there.

'Ah, yes, a good saint of York. Come here, lad,' said the pedlar.

Little Bosa looked at Nesta for reassurance; the man had food spattered on his plaited beard, and mud splashed from hem to waist almost hiding the colourful, intricate pattern of his long overgarment. Nesta gave a nod. A wariness rose in Amalric. Yet he hesitated to act as Bosa stepped steadily over to the man. Noah followed his little master and sniffed the pedlar's soiled hem.

From further inside the extensive folds of his garment, Wyler pulled something that glinted in the light. 'Here, laddie, squint your eyes at this. It's special.' He held out a little glass phial with a small fragment of something rattling inside. 'That is part of the bony skull of St Thomas à Becket, brought all the way from Canterbury. See...' A grimy fingernail pointed at the inside of the bottle. 'There is a drop of his blood dried upon it.'

Bosa gazed reverently through the glass, but Amalric was wary. 'Sir, my child is too young to know of such things. Don't touch it, Bosa.'

'No, let him,' said Nesta, unusually disobeying her husband. 'He's old enough.'

Amalric turned to her, speechless.

Bosa grabbed the phial then suddenly let out a cry and dropped it. The phial shattered on a stone and a small, curved bone fragment shot sideways, to lie resting on bright green moss, the too-bright blood stain uppermost. Folk sharply drew in their breath. Noah nosed the object and turned away. Bosa rubbed his hand.

Amalric's speech returned. 'Wyler, what did you give my boy? You necromancer!'

Still facing Bosa, Wyler's eyes widened at the accusation. Small black discs peered out from pink watery seas. Sweat broke out on his pale forehead. He became agitated and, breathing deeply, was caught unawares to cough. Spittle landed on Bosa's face and a smattering on his jerkin. The boy cried out and, while wiping away the slime with his hands, ran to his mother and hugged her knees. She wiped his hands and face clean on her apron, her expression taut. Amalric felt disgust. He tried to pull Nesta and Bosa away from the scene but his wife would not move.

Wyler wiped his damp lips on the edge of his cloak. 'No matter,' he fawned and turned away from the little boy to face the astonished gathering. 'I take no heed,' he said to them all.

With a dramatic look of sad piety on his wrinkled face, he took a grubby cloth from his sleeve and bent to pick up the bone and broken glass. With infinite gentleness, he wrapped the cloth around the pieces before returning them to the dark inside of his cloak. 'A little accident,' he simpered, which served to magnify the crime. Then, as if nothing had happened, he turned back to his silent audience. 'I have cures for all your ills.' He picked a sack from his cart and rummaged inside. 'Come forward, children, and I will show you.'

The children stayed, held by their parents, so Wyler moved towards them. Bending down to their height and using his hands with elegance, he showed a jewelled box. He spoke to them as if in secret. 'In this special box is an ancient miraculous cure. It's recently been delivered to me from Jerusalem; a potion containing frankincense and myrrh. An efficacious nostrum.'

Parents began to look with interest, forgetting past inefficiencies of such remedies amid new fears generated by the sun-dimming. Nesta, too, became fascinated again.

Wyler lifted the lid of the small glinting box. Inside, a pottery phial nestled on golden cloth. 'Only a tiny drop is needed. Hold out your hand,' he said to a boy no more than ten years old. Wyler held the boy's hand. He took the bottle and let one tiny, oily drop fall onto the smooth skin.

'Smell the wonderful perfume.' The boy's eyes lit up as he put his nose to the back of his hand. 'Let your mother sniff.'

The child lifted his hand to his mother's nose. She breathed in. 'Oh, 'tis wonderful!'

'Of course. How could such a gift to Christ at His birth be any less? Such a scent can only do good. It is blessed by heaven.' Wyler turned aside to cough. 'You may use the potion to make a cure-all or heat over the fire for perfume, like incense. Only just before coming here did I sell a phial to Mistress Clara at Horesby Manor. A sensible, knowing young woman; we had a long chat before she had to attend to her duties – her husband is away. She bought it for her sons' safety. I saw two of them. Fine boys. Like me, she suspects the sun-dimming was a portent

'– of pestilence, maybe.'

Amalric felt sick. His brother's wife and their children had been mentioned and Nesta was bound to be impressed. He could see she had become enthralled – and not without reason; her birth-home had seldom been visited by pedlars and she had not learned the art of discernment when it came to charmed talk. Amalric, however, had been enlightened by his friend Thurston and had come to see men such as Wyler as cheats, fooling good wives into spending money with false warnings of pestilence. Yet he too felt slightly influenced by the holiness of frankincense and myrrh. He saw Nesta move towards Wyler with her hand out to him, and struggled with knowing what to do. Should he follow Thurston's dispassionate physician's opinion and pull her back, or should he allow her to believe in charms with a Christian origin – just in case it worked? He decided.

'No, Nesta! It's a false remedy. Perfumes don't cure. Let's go home.'

She glared spitefully at him.

'Be gone! Be gone!' A sudden shouting came from up the hill and everyone's head turned. Thurston was running towards them, his grey travel robe open and flying to either side, his long black garment visible beneath. His boots splashed through puddles in the ruts of the road. Dogs, cats, chickens and geese scattered. 'Be gone, I say!'

The crowd knew Wyler had met this authoritative man before, one who held no liking for the pedlar's promise of cures. Folk shuffled expectantly, mildly excited at the thought of an entertaining confrontation. Thurston drew close and stood to catch his breath.

'What is my presence to do with you, physician, I may ask?' Wyler's eyes narrowed.

'It is to do with the fact…' the doctor took a deep breath, '… that the pestilence is in York.' A collective gasp came from the crowd. 'I heard about it in Beverley today and know that the magistrates refused to allow you entry there, knowing you had come from York. Begone with your mangy mule, your filthy clothes and your...' he sought for words, '... your foul remedies.'

Frankincense and myrrh, foul! Is that blasphemy? wondered Amalric. But more fearful was the news that the pestilence was in York! The Great Pestilence had been there twelve years before and had spread to Warren Horesby a short time after. And this morning, the sun had nearly died! He turned to Nesta and saw the fear that he felt inside etched on her face. She turned abruptly from him and walked away, dragging Bosa by the hand.

'Nay, my friends,' the pedlar pleaded, 'I have cures. Frankincense and... See, I am well.' He strangled a cough and glared at Thurston as the crowd shrank away.

Amalric walked to the other side of the green, to Hendric, Istrid, Beatrix and Cuthbert as they stood with sullen faces of disappointment watching the pedlar fitfully tugging dull red brocade over the cart's baskets and satchels. Mistress Yarrow left them, stomping off, uttering, 'Pah!' and leaving Amalric to wonder what she meant.

Thurston joined them. 'Thank goodness he's going,' he said. They all watched the pedlar trundle from the green, down the slight hill, past the Faceby home and the church opposite and away towards King's-Town on Hull. 'That man is dangerous. He's probably mortally ill, and not only are his nostrums useless, they may even be poisonous.'

'But it was frankincense and myrrh,' said Amalric, almost apologetically.

'Aye, maybe in his sample but not in what he sells. And...' he turned his face away from the children, '...he may be spreading the pestilence, though I've only theories as to how. I hope your children didn't get too near him, for this time it's affecting the young more than adults, especially boys, it seems. I can't account for it.'

Amalric's mouth fell open. An old panic gripped his chest. He looked appealingly at Thurston. 'Wyler gave Bosa a glass phial to look at which contained a relic. The lad dropped it. He coughed in Bosa's face. Nesta wiped the slime off with her apron.'

Thurston eyes widened. 'We must go to your house.' He turned to the children. 'Beatrix, did any of you go near the pedlar?'

'No, Father. We were all on the far edge of the green. Shall Cuthbert and I go to Aunt Nesta with Istrid and Hendric now?'

'No!' said Thurston sharply. 'Go home with Cuthbert to your mother and Mistress Yarrow. Take Hendric and Istrid with you. They must stay there. Go!' The children wandered away, with puzzled frowns playing on their faces. 'Come, Amalric,' he demanded.

Thurston walked rapidly to the Faceby home. Amalric had difficulty keeping up. Noah, detecting urgency, ran ahead. Without ceremony, the physician burst through the door with Noah pushing in at his side and Amalric behind. Nesta jumped with surprise. Amalric saw the spattered jerkin and apron in her hand ready to add to the wash-pile on the floor by the back door. Bosa came through the gloom with his arms out to the dog.

'Come to the light, lad,' said Thurston.

Bosa, sensing something serious, obeyed. Standing before the window opening, Bosa's hair shone golden in the sunlight. His little chest stuck out manfully, and his face glowed from a scrubbing. He stood trustingly as the tall man cast his eyes all over him. Amalric stood back, wondering, not for the first time, if those pale eyes could see through skin into the depths of a body. Bosa began to scratch the back of one hand with the other.

'What ails you? Show me.'

Bosa obediently lifted his hand. Scratching had broken skin around a small raised red area.

Amalric watched Thurston's face; he had come to know Thurston's many expressions. The one he had now was his physician's face – calm, without emotion. It often disguised alarm.

'Ah yes. You've had a little bite from an insect. Nothing to fear.'

Amalric knew better. That filthy old devil Wyler had body lice and fleas! He was ill! Oh, why had he not realised the significance of that sooner? Twelve years ago, he had been at Meaux Abbey following delivery of glass sheets for a new window. Ned, the workshop assistant, and a lay brother had been unpacking a crate when fleas sprang at them from fearfully smelling, damp old clothing used as protection. Both Ned and the lay brother were horribly bitten by the starving fleas, and had died within a few days. Amalric had not been bitten. Nausea now welled into his throat.

Nesta stood by, unable to move. She mouthed, 'No!'

'Now... no one knows the cause of... there's every reason to think nothing will hap... Nesta, Amalric, you must watch this little one.' Thurston turned away. The calm face began to collapse. Muscles began to pull at his jaw. Anger seethed in him – Amalric could tell. Thurston left without a further word.

Bosa toddled outside to the back garden with Noah to look at the newly hatched chickens. Nesta turned to Amalric, her eyes glaring at him and her finger pointing up into his face.

'You should have let me have the nostrum. The frankincense and myrrh. 'Tis the smell we have in church on special saints' days. It kept the Christ child alive. And Wyler is still alive, isn't he, so it must keep the pestilence away?'

'Yes, but you might have found it to be something different when you'd bought it from that twister.'

'No, I would not. Wyler is honest. What if Bosa has caught...? We've only ordinary curatives: honey, rue, rosemary, marigold and whatever Matilde and Thurston have in their cupboards. Wyler's nostrum would've worked. It's heaven blessed. Thurston has admitted before that it has some healing power.'

'Yes, but nothing for the... Thurston says nothing will cure the... You know that.' Amalric's raised voice lowered to

70

convince his wife of the truth. 'And it would have been most expensive – for nothing.'

'So… money! Expense against our child's life. Clara bought some.'

'Well, she has money to waste.'

'Waste!' Nesta looked astounded. 'If Bosa becomes ill with the… I'll hate you.' She turned swiftly and went out of the back door, slamming it behind her.

Amalric slumped onto the bench by the table, his head in his hands: What she meant was, *If Bosa dies.*

Chapter Eight

Three days later, Bosa sneezed over his morning bowl of food, sending some of the dryer contents into the air, an explosion that normally would have caused laughter but which this time caused both Nesta and Amalric to look at him in alarm. Nesta put her hand on his forehead. 'He's hot, Am, he's very hot. Bosa, do you hurt anywhere?'

He nodded and put his hands to his neck. Nesta pulled them away and parted his long, gleaming hair. 'He has swellings in his neck.' Her face contorted. 'If only I had some frankincense and myrrh,' she said pointedly. 'Go to Thurston, Am, and tell him.'

Though hot to the touch, Bosa began to shiver. 'I'm cold, Ma.'

Amalric, distraught, ran out and up the hill to Thurston's home. Matilde came to the door. Beatrix and his daughter, Istrid, were by her side.

'Hello, brother, you look agitated. What's wrong?'

'Bosa is ill. Nesta wants frankincense and myrrh.' His face contorted in pain. Matilde pushed the girls away. 'Go inside, my loves.'

'Mat, where's Thurston?'

'He's in his physic room. Go!'

Amalric went quickly to the room at the side of the building and opened the door without knocking. The smell of a hundred tinctures, unguents and curatives hit his nostrils. Reflected light glittered from glass flasks, manuscripts jumbled on shelves, leeches swam in a glass bowl of water. Thurston barely looked up from a table where shiny new instruments were laid out. He seemed pleased that his friend had walked in.

'Ah, Am. Come see my new purchases. Even physicians such as myself are now expected to perform the cutting arts. These ones cut, these probe, these hold the tissues open, this one is interesting, it...'

'Thurston!' The physician was at his most annoying – distracted by the science of his trade. 'Come, please, to see Bosa. Nesta wants frankincense and myrrh.'

'Bosa? He is ill?' Thurston's face became rigid.

'Yes. Hot. Headache. Swellings in his neck. I've seen these things before, Thurston. I should have let Nesta have the frankincense and myrrh!'

'No, my friend, they're only good for old-age swollen joints, if they're good for anything at all, that is, but not for what I expect this to be. However, I keep a little in my store. I'll bring it to satisfy Nesta.' Thurston packed a satchel with phials, bottles, pots, cloths and charts.

'Hurry!'

'Am, be calm. Little will be gained by panic. You need to be strong.'

Amalric was grateful for Thurston's switch to his physician's ways and became less agitated.

Nesta had made up a bed for Bosa near the central fire when Thurston pushed open the door of the house. She had hauled his mattress down from the loft and was laying him gently onto it. 'Ma,' he groaned.

Nesta's tearful face looked at Thurston. Amalric saw the helplessness in her.

'I'm here to help, Nesta,' said the physician gently, putting his satchel onto the table. 'Here's some frankincense and myrrh unguent. Rub it onto his buboes.' He held it out to her.

'It's too late,' shouted Nesta. With a sweep of her hand, she sent the little jar flying into the fire. They all looked on, horrified. The jar cracked, the ointment sizzled and a strong perfume started to waft around the room.

'Nesta!' cried Amalric.

Nesta sank to her knees and cried bitterly.

'No matter. The perfume will be efficacious,' said Thurston, without conviction. 'I must look at Bosa.'

Amalric put his arms about Nesta but she shook them off. He tried to soothe her but it had no effect. He too needed comfort before he heard the inevitable words from Thurston, but she ignored him.

'It's the pestilence, Am,' said Thurston softly. 'There's little I can do except give you something to relieve the little lad's pain. This will not be the only case in the village after that evil man so recklessly travelled through. I will, no doubt, be visiting others.'

'But Hendric and Istrid? They're still at your home.'

'Aye, and they can stay there. They had no contact with the man. The contagion may well escape them. I won't go near them. I'll stay in my physic room. I'll sleep there until I see how badly it spreads and maybe move on to even more isolated accommodation. I can only think that this disease is somehow driven by contact with others who have it. During the Great Pestilence, I observed that, mainly, those not in contact with the disease escaped it. There were just a very few others who escaped after being in contact – like myself, you, Nesta, Edwin and Lord de Horesby… but unlike Matilde, hardly any at all survived having succumbed to it. This time, it is the young… See to your little boy, Am. I hope you and Nesta can reconcile.'

'I'll pay you back for the special unguent.'

'No, Am, it's a gift. The perfume will disguise the stink of… it *will* ease you. Farewell.'

The smell of incense persistently pervaded their home, diminishing the stench of pestilence; a reminder of Amalric's failure. He watched Nesta care for their son. She held Bosa to keep him warm and when his body became too sore for her to even cradle him, she heated stones to lay along his body on the bed. Then when he was hot, she stripped his clothes and wiped a wet cloth along his limbs to cool him. All she had learned from the Great Pestilence twelve years before, she put into practice again. She refused to speak to her husband and kept him away from his son. Only when Nesta could not help but fall asleep, did Amalric hold Bosa's little hand.

He appealed to his friend as they chatted a distance apart. 'Thurston, there must be something you can do. What about all your manuscripts?'

'There have been no advances in physic to deal with this. The pestilence has simmered on abroad for a while now, with physicians trying to find a cure, but our different languages are a barrier; we need translations. In this new bout we are no more able to help than at the first one. Some advocate bleeding to remove the excess heat and bad essences, but I refuse to do that: your little lad is too small. I would hardly find a place to do it, and in any case, it would only add more insult to his painful body. Sometimes consideration of the humours can be efficacious – the imbalance of blood, black and yellow bile, phlegm as well as hot and cold, sweet and sour considerations, but this disease makes a nonsense of them all.'

'But your charts of the heavens?'

'Such as the recent sun-dimming, you mean? Useless when the predicted disaster has arrived. In all honesty, there's little to be done; when any of the buboes in Bosa's neck, armpits and groin become swollen and taut, I can use poultices to draw the evil matter from them and watch for signs that I might prick them to release the poison as I did with Matilde – and you know the outcome of that. I may try applying leeches to the buboes to suck out the poison, but generally, that sort of thing is not to their taste. It's blood they want. Really, the only useful thing I can do is to keep the pain away.' Thurston moved closer and put his hand on Amalric's shoulder. 'My friend, there is nothing. You will need Father Luke.'

In less than two days, after Father Luke's ministrations to ensure a good and proper death, black spots appeared on Bosa and all was lost. Nesta and Amalric watched Bosa slip away. A thick, tearless, exhausted silence lay between them. A gift of food from Matilde lay uneaten on a shelf. A jug of ale remained half full. The central fire went out. The house was cold. The servant girl retreated to the barn with the milk cow. Noah detected the sorrow and sat in a corner with head on front paws, quiet. Not a sound did he make.

The following day, the day of the funeral, little Bosa lay on the table in the cool house. Nesta stood back after securing the final fold of his grave wrapping. Her tears and nose dripped and then flooded. Amalric moved to comfort her but she turned on him through spluttering wetness. 'If we'd had Wyler's cure, he would have lived. Am, I hate you. I hate you.'

'I… I don't believe it would have worked. Thurston said…'

'Thurston, Thurston! Your mother said he had too much learnin' from that university. What this village needed was practical folk like Wyler…'

'Wyler, Wyler… You shouldn't have been close to him! He's a filthy, stinking necromancer! A quack, a fake, trading on women like you!'

'Like me? You mean poor, low-born, simple-minded. Not educated like you were at the abbey. What would speakin' Latin be to me? Wyler was one of us simple folk. Scrapin' a livin', learnin' from doin' things. I cured your legs, didn't I, after their burnin' in the fire? Used maggots on your moulderin' burns like on sheep sores?' Nesta stamped her foot. The childish remnants in her character broke through as they did when anger got the better of her. Her wimple slipped. Small hairline curls escaped, darker now that the sun seldom reached them. Amalric wondered how it was that women could make men feel chastised so effectively. Normally, he found her endearing at such moments, but not this day with Bosa lying still. On this day, her anger settled very deep within the shell of him.

To Amalric's relief, Bosa was not buried alone in a new pestilence pit, but in the family plot. During the burial, he looked through a clinging Yorkshire mist to see the shadow of the old Saxon cross. Once, he had appreciated the fine carved image on its shaft of Jesus healing the blind man. The artistic beauty of the healing had struck him as something wonderful, but now it was obscured by lichen and both the beauty and healing were gone, covered up, impotent. He bent to grab a clump of grass, still seeded from last autumn, and threw it with a handful of wet soil into Bosa' grave, hoping it would grow to represent resurrection, new life. After all, you didn't give up on your faith when every other thing you loved had slipped away. Isn't that what faith meant? he asked himself.

Nesta and Amalric walked back to their home together. He reached out his hand to find hers and found the small fingers held tight against her palm. All he could do was hold her wrist as if she were his reluctant captive. He wondered if she would ever forgive him. Over the years since the last pestilence, he had learned to control the lump of grief in his chest; now he felt it return in nauseating turmoil.

Chapter Nine

The morning after Bosa's funeral, outside in sunny warmth with Noah at his side, Amalric leaned on the workshop wall by the only glass window in his home. It was a colourful scene of an angel telling shepherds of Christ's birth. Birth and death. God understood those things; He'd birthed and lost His own Son. The workshop window now acted as a comfort. It had been Amalric's first apprentice piece and as such had faults, but his father had been proud to have it displayed to signify the glazing work of Faceby and Son.

Through his melancholy, Amalric became aware of a figure coming up the hill who subsequently went into the church across the road. It was Colin Scarthe; an unusual event, since he was never one to enter church unless he had to.

Amalric waited with curiosity. Eventually, Colin came out and stared menacingly across at him before going back down the hill. The silent confrontation was unnerving.

Shortly afterwards, Father Luke came out. 'Oh, I'm pleased to see you, Am. There's apparently a commotion down in the woods beyond the mill. You may be interested in it.'

'Normally, Father, I would, but my heart cannot raise interest today.'

'I fully understand, my friend, but I think the matter is related to the trouble of your heart.'

Amalric looked at him quizzically.

'Come.'

Amalric was unable to glean any further information but accompanied the priest as he rushed down the hill. Noah trotted, unbidden, behind.

Even before arriving at the site, Noah's attention to a filthy cloth by the roadside that had once been brightly coloured brocade confirmed to Amalric that something was very wrong. Further mystery was added as he realised that the clattering mill wheel was not turning, allowing the unimpeded sound of the mill stream's gurgles to be heard. Even so, the watery noise failed to overcome an excited chatter of village voices from ahead.

Father Luke pressed on. Amalric followed. A putrid stench hit their nostrils as they reached a small clearing by the roadside full of people. Village faces turned to them. Amalric saw some women had a small child on their hip, or in a cloth on their backs. Men were dressed for their daily work and some with tools in their hands, as if they had left their work in a hurry. Mistress Yarrow stood at the edge of the group. Her young son, Cuthbert, leaned sullenly against her, and Colin Scarthe, her brother, stood next to her.

'Now, what's happening here?' said Father Luke, trying not to retch. Men shrank away a pace or two, revealing a body slumped with his back against a tree trunk. Damp grey hair covered the eyes and a ruffled plaited beard hid the chin and neck. A long outer garment of silk damask with wide sleeves was held around the chest with unmoving blackened hands. Vomit had cascaded over it all. Noah trotted forward and sniffed loosely shod feet, splayed out inelegantly like a drunkard's.

'Noah!'

Noah turned to his master with a look of resentment and stood his ground, unable to relinquish the interesting aromas.

'May his soul rest in peace,' were the only words that Father Luke could summon in one breath.

''Tis Wyler,' said Colin Scarthe assertively. He stepped towards the priest and Amalric. It seemed he had become the spokesman of the group. 'He was found here. He died of summat strange,' he said, emphasising the mystery of it. Colin regarded Amalric with a sneer. 'He might 'ave died from a bang on the 'ead. See – there's blood on his beard.'

'You mean murdered?' said Amalric.

'Aye, and you had a grievance against him. We've all heard you an' your missus arguin' about 'im. Wattle and daub don't hide much noise.'

'That's evil talk, Colin Scarthe,' intervened Father Luke. 'Go fetch the physician,' he said to no one in particular. 'He'll know. I saw him earlier going up to the Manor House.'

'Physicians, pah! Nowt but well-paid charlatans,' commented Colin, almost inaudibly.

Silence descended on the group. The miller, freed of his mill duties but with a face as white as his dusty clothing, set off up the hill.

After a while, Thurston arrived with his satchel. The miller puffed behind him.

'Is someone injured?'

'No, physician, dead. 'Appen murdered,' said Colin, before anyone else could answer.

Thurston peered at the corpse. 'Ah,' he said. 'Bring me a long stick.'

A man hacked a stick from a willow. Thurston poked the body and drew back the beard to expose Wyler's neck. 'I can't imagine that anyone would want to get close enough to murder this man,' he said. 'See his neck? It's swollen with buboes; his hands are black. His corpse stinks. You know as well as I what this man died of. He was probably too ill to travel far after he'd been in the village, and sought shelter.' Then he thought a moment. 'Where is his cart? The mule that pulled it? Where are all his belongings?'

Amalric felt sickened at the thought of the filthy pedlar's goods being taken by the villagers. He looked at Thurston who was gazing about him, obviously with the same thought in mind. He saw rising anger in the physician's face.

'I saw it as I come to the mill this mornin',' said the miller as he pointed down the hill. Heads turned. Amalric saw the cart some distance away, partly hidden by bushes, with the old mule still in the shafts.

As Colin was about to speak again, Father Luke cut in. 'We need Lord de Horesby. We may need to inform Beverley magistrates.' Before action could be taken, the sound of snorting, hooves on impacted ground and the tinkling of bridles was heard. Two horses appeared. On one, a tired middle-aged man slumped in the saddle; on the other, a younger man, sitting erect. 'Ah, no need. Good day, Lord de Horesby, and to you, Master Reeve; we were just about to inform you of this er... incident.'

Amalric, by Father Luke's side, felt disdain for his brother, who always seemed to be there at awkward moments.

Lord de Horesby smiled. 'Good day to you all. We heard the commotion as we approached and feared trouble. We've been away for a while in King's-Town on Hull and Beverley. What is the reason for this gathering?' He looked about him. 'Is that Wyler the pedlar? Dead?' He paused for a moment. 'The village will have to deal with his body. I'll inform the Beverley magistrate.'

Edwin took over from his lord, oozing authority. 'Yes, we've come now from Beverley. The magistrate there knew that after Wyler left York, pestilence and death followed him. They feared for the safety of Warren Horesby folk. However, they were too late to inform you of his arrival here, but made preparations to turn him away from their own gates, with advice for him to be confined outside King's-Town on Hull when he arrived there, accused of murder. I recall our own physician once advised the Beverley magistrates of the preventative course they should take in case of pestilence.'

'Yes, but my advice was only ever partly heeded,' said Thurston defensively. 'The Beverley magistrates should have prevented him from stopping *here* before taking their own preventive measures. They knew his route. We've been badly dealt with. When in York less than a week ago, I heard about Wyler but arrived back here too late.'

Edwin gave the doctor an ingratiatingly sickly smile. 'So, as the man is here, dead, all that is irrelevant. And how he died is obvious. I see his swollen neck. What do you suggest, physician?' Edwin leaned forward in the saddle, demanding an answer. Amalric felt himself redden at his brother's arrogance.

Thurston scowled at this forcing of responsibility onto himself but did not hesitate. 'The body needs to be buried here untouched, simply pushed into a grave,' he said dispassionately. 'The cart must be burned and with it all its goods, including what may be thought to be valuable: they may also have the contagion. Cursed, if you like. All items that have been taken away from it already must be returned and burned, not left in houses.' There was a soft gasp, which he ignored. A few men and women left immediately. 'The mule can be set free. If any of you have a mind to steal it, leave the mangy thing to roam for some weeks.'

Amalric knew the old animal would be dead by then.

'Will it be a Christian burial for the pedlar?' asked a sexton.

All eyes turned to Father Luke, who for a moment didn't seem to have an answer. 'Well,' he said, clearly needing to think it through. 'He's most likely caused his own death by association with evil places and the committing of sins. He's caused the death of others, in ignorance, perhaps. When he is buried, I will say brief prayers over the grave.' He turned to the carpenter. 'Please construct a simple cross for him, with his name, so that those coming across it will know his fate and avoid the area. The ground here will not be consecrated so no decision on that will need to be made. God will metre his punishment.'

The carpenter nodded.

Edwin pulled on the reins and turned his horse, ready to leave.

Thurston moved quickly to his side. 'I was called to the manor this morning by your wife. Wyler stopped there and spoke to her and two of your sons on the day he arrived in the village. Go straight home. Do not delay.'

Amalric watched his brother sharply urge his horse to move.

Then he glanced at Lord de Horesby, who was gazing at the sad, disease-ravaged body of Wyler. The lord caught Amalric looking at him and sighed. Something of an understanding flashed between them, but neither he nor Amalric attempted to speak.

Folk started to wonder what to do next. Colin spoke loudly, anxious to voice their suspicions. 'The pestilence is in our village, brought by the Faceby family again – Master Amalric's son was the first to go.' He looked accusingly at Amalric, his mouth in a sneer.

'No!' said Thurston in his friend's defence. He pointed to the corpse. 'This man killed Bosa. He came uninvited. Children are usually dying much more quickly than grown men, but even now his contagion may linger and kill your children too, and yourselves. Go home and take all the precautions you did last time.'

A hand came to Amalric's shoulder. 'The poor old pedlar was a misguided soul in his final years,' said Father Luke quietly. 'No one really cared for him except lice, fleas and a mule. His mind was addled. I'm struggling to feel right about his burial; I truly don't know the Church's view on this. He seems to me to have been a careless, unthinking man, but to judge him as a murderer? I'll leave that to God. God's vengeance follows the real sinner – it is a fact.'

Thurston had his own opinion. 'He *was* a murderer in my view. It's getting clearer that people who avoid washing, or who frequent sordid, stinking places with rotting meat and human ordure in the street are prone to pestilence and spread it in their own ignorant, pompous foolishness to the really innocent. We must not let people like the pedlar roam free. Facing *that* fact is essential for physic doctors like me.'

Amalric, as he had with the Great Pestilence before, knew that he was witnessing the clash of Christianity, physic and ignorance.

Amalric and Father Luke kept Thurston company as he watched to make sure the grave-digging and fiery disposal of the cart and goods were adequate, and the mule harried away deep into the wood. Thurston's distrust of the villagers' diligence would, on a less serious occasion, have amused Amalric.

The flames gave rise to a mood of celebration, especially when the alewife brought jugs of ale. 'Come now, 'tis my finest; low prices today, pay me later.' It became a festival. A raucous wake. Amalric turned to walk away.

'No stomach for death, eh, Master Glazier?' Colin was by his side, slurring his speech, his chin wet with ale. Liquid splashed from a large beaker in his hand. 'We're giving the old devil a right good chase to purgatory. He might even go straight to hell.'

Amalric glared at him. With Thurston and Father Luke, he left the scene in silence, leaving Colin sneering and staggering.

Feeling downcast, Amalric opened the door of his home. Through fire smoke, he saw Nesta flinging a shawl around her shoulders. The cloth was thin and smooth. The colours glowed glass-like even through the smoke. Silk! His horror overcame him. He rushed to her and dragged the shawl away, twisting her finger as he did so.

'Where did you get this?' he said, holding the soft cloth bunched in his fist under her nose.

Nesta rubbed her hand. 'Amalric! You've hurt me.'

'Nesta, the shawl?'

Her reply was hesitant. 'It's been in the box in the loft that I brought from home.'

'Nesta, you're lying to me.' Anger engulfed him. 'Your family never had the money for something like this!' he shouted. 'And anyway, it's beyond our station. Is it from Wyler's cart? Did you get it this morning when gathering mushrooms before the crowd assembled? Did you steal it? And what's this?' On the table was a small pottery phial. 'Not frankincense and myrrh tincture? Nesta, you've disobeyed me.' He grabbed the phial and rushed out of the house and threw it high over the garden into the brook beyond. He heard it splinter on a stone.

He went back into the house feeling weak. What had he done

in his anger? 'Nesta, I was impetuous. I'm sorry. I understand why you needed to…'

'Am!' Nesta's face was red; her eyes flashed wildly, and her response was venomous. 'You still see me as your servant, to do your biddin', to obey. I understand that too! But I am *not* your servant. I am your wife!'

He felt the blood leave his own face and his life begin to unravel.

Amalric watched the village fall into silence. The boy to whom Wyler had spoken after Bosa, died. Then four children over the following week, then more. Everything stopped. Heartbreak hung like Wyler's soiled brocade over the huddled, trapped homes. More children were stolen away, as if the devil crept in at night and took their souls while they slept. A few adults died too, parents of the lost children, mostly. The verger's cart trundled to a new pestilence pit in the church graveyard.

Between Amalric and Nesta, something, too, had died.

The house door clattered as only Edwin could make it. Amalric raised his heavy eyes and failed to disguise his annoyance.

'What do you want, Edwin? I'm in no mood to…'

'I come to seek consolation.' His voice cracked.

'Then you should be across the road in church.'

'No, I need to be here… with family. I've been to Matilde, I was always closer to her than to you, but she'll not let me into her house for fear of the pestilence.'

Amalric sighed and looked more closely at his brother. He'd never before seen him in such a state. His beard was unclipped. His lank, dark hair, tinged with grey at his temples, hung straight and greasy; it clung to his neck inside the collar of his open leather jerkin. Underneath, a fine linen undergarment showed creased and unwashed, as if slept in. His boots dropped dried mud onto Nesta's brushed, compacted soil floor. His face was pale, and his mouth trembled.

'Brother, are you ill? What ails you?'

'My heart is ill. My two youngest boys have died of the

pestilence. Only Robert and Walter remain; they are well, the Lord be praised.'

Amalric couldn't help a sudden flow of sorrow and sympathy, despite his own loss. 'Oh, no! My nephews.' What could he say? For once, the brothers hugged and cried together. 'And Clara?'

'She's well.'

Amalric raised his hand to the servant girl, who understood the silent message. Beakers of ale were poured. 'This is your strongest ale,' she said, and left the huge jug on the table.

Nesta came into the house with Hendric and Istrid. All three moved silently. Amalric watched his brother nod to Nesta and couldn't decide whether it meant something or nothing. Edwin barely glanced at his niece and nephew and kept his distance from them.

Amalric treasured the rare, precious brotherly moments together; he suspected it would never happen again.

Finally, the second pestilence drifted out of East Yorkshire. Amalric was thankful that the villagers hadn't pursued the cruel accusations of Colin Scarthe. This time, they were able to freely blame Wyler for its arrival.

However, Amalric felt his life had changed again. After his survival of the Great Pestilence, despite lingering grief, his life had felt special, favoured; he'd had a good, healthy wife who'd delivered three perfectly normal children and his artisan work rendered him a free man. Now, after the pestilence's recurrence and the death of his youngest child, he became like other villagers, weighed down by loss, and a strong feeling that life was not as it ought to be. He well understood the discontent that began to emerge within the village.

Chapter Ten

1363 Warren Horesby

Two years after the second pestilence, the loss of village children was keenly felt. Remaining ones had to do as best they could to find friends. Hendric developed an uneasy friendship with Cuthbert and his uncle Edwin's sons, Robert and Walter. It bothered Amalric.

One warm day when their parents did not require them to work, Amalric watched the lads walk past his workshop with long sticks and pails. They jostled noisily with each other, pushing and shouting, nearly bumping into an old widow as she struggled to walk with a sack of flour. Amalric rushed out to help the woman as she almost tottered over. He shouted to the boys to watch what they were doing in future, and help the old folk. But his shouts were ignored as they ran towards the mill pond.

Amalric carried the bag of flour for the woman to her home up the hill. She thanked him profusely for helping, but it had been no hardship; of late, his glass work excited no interest in him, his only commission being a simple coloured window for a small church a few miles away containing a traditional, haloed St Peter, standing with a blank expression. Like many others, the church wished to look back in style rather than forward. It was dull work and he was glad to leave it for a while.

'Hello, Am. Perhaps you might help *me*.' It was Nesta returning from the well, a pail of water in each hand.

Amalric turned, neither happy nor sad to see her. He took

her pails. 'I've just seen Hendric with Cuthbert and Edwin's two boys going to the mill pond, probably to fish for minnows and newts. They nearly knocked an old woman down. He's getting to be too much like them. They're bad company.'

'Aye. I agree. But I don't know how to handle him. He's nearly as tall as me.'

Nesta and Amalric had reached common ground: concern for their son. They talked about it back home, seated at the table. They were amicable. The sun shone through the open shutters and lit dust motes. Birdsong filled the unusually warm outside air. Bees hummed. Amalric reached out for Nesta's hand and she let him take it. It was an acknowledgement of their coming to terms with Bosa's death, and beginning anew to deal with shared problems, as they had in the days of their young love. And, like those days, they moved off to the sleep room.

Amalric woke from Nesta's arms to a furious banging at the door. He quickly dressed and found Mistress Yarrow standing with Hendric and Cuthbert, both dripping wet and her own skirts soaked. Behind her, Edwin's boys were laughing as they ran up the road.

'Master Faceby, your son pushed Cuthbert into the mill pond.' She held both boys by clothing at the back of the neck as if they were heavy wet washing.

'I did not!'

'You did!'

Both boys struggled. 'If I'd not been passing, Cuthbert would have drowned. He can't swim. I had to drag him out. This will not do. You will have to control your son better.'

Amalric felt a sense of injustice somewhere in this. 'So why is *my* boy wet through if he did the pushing?'

Hendric began to look rather grey. 'Robert and Walter pushed me into Cuthbert and he fell in, and then I overbalanced and fell in,' he said as he retched.

'Thank you, Mistress Yarrow. I'll see to this.' Amalric grabbed Hendric, pulled him in and slammed the door. He dragged him through to the back garden. 'Take off your clothing.'

Nesta, having heard it all, followed. 'Put your fingers down the back of your throat to make yourself sick,' she said. Hendric spewed up green-looking water with pondweed and other indescribable things. 'Now go an' lie down for a while,' she said sharply. 'We'll speak later.'

Amalric was annoyed at Nesta's interference with their son's chastising and was ready to convey his displeasure as Hendric climbed up the shaking loft ladder – but was too late.

'It's about time you saw to repairs of that ladder, Am. You can spare time away from the workshop. After all, the window sales are poor.'

Amalric felt a fault line in their fragile new contentment. 'I think those boys of Edwin's somehow made the accident happen. They were larking. They know Hendric merely tolerates 'em, and Cuthbert's a dullard. Like as not, they conspired to push both of 'em in.'

'Oh,' said Nesta. 'I don't think they'd do that. That's cruel.'

'Next time they could be larking on thin ice. Children've been lost under ice before.' Amalric felt tension rise in him. His heart raced.

'Now you're going too far.'

'No, you are. Why do you defend Edwin's boys? You know how malicious that family can be.'

'Maybe, but let's face it,' Nesta's voice raised, 'you don't have much time for your own children, so you're not likely to think much of your brother's. Always in your workshop!'

Amalric's feelings swirled out of control. 'Well, it worries me that Hendric has a look of Edwin and sometimes he lacks care for others, such as the old widow!'

Silence.

'What do you mean?' Nesta asked calmly.

'Hendric is too much like my brother.'

'What?'

Amalric floundered. Unrestrained words tumbled out. 'I sometimes wonder if Hendric is *really* mine.'

'Am!'

He saw Nesta's eyes widen but nothing would stop this now. It was horribly selfish, he knew, but he had to clear his mind. 'Well, there was that time way back when Edwin tried to ravish you. Mother always thought you might have tempted him. Maybe on another occasion you and he...'

It was a moment fused like paint on glass in Amalric's memory; a young, drunken Edwin had tried to have his way with Nesta, who was then a family servant. Amalric had been overcome with a surge of love for her and hate for his brother. He had attacked Edwin and won. It remained a bitter source of contention between the brothers.

Nesta's hands went to her hips. Her head tossed. 'So – it's your dead mother's word against mine? You believe I've been unfaithful.'

'No – yes – maybe he... then why does Hendric look like Edwin and have a streak that reminds me of him?'

'Am!' she shouted. 'I don't know! It happens.' Her pointing finger was under his nose. 'And as far as anything else goes, tell me why Mistress Yarrow always wants to help here in our home. I've seen the admiring looks you give her.'

'I can't abide the woman.'

'I don't believe you!' Nesta's foot stamped, raising the dust from the impacted floor.

And so it went on...

Amalric could not even remember what was said. It was one allegation after another. Years of petty problems, frustration and hurt gathered into a storm. With red eyes, he sought out his friend, the doctor of physic.

'Am, my friend, sometimes you behave like a dolt. Of course he has a look of your brother. You're all of the same family. It happens that way – the same ears, or nose. I'm sure Nesta has never strayed.'

Amalric felt defensive. 'She's a fell girl and was our servant. Edwin's always believed that servants are lesser beings and there to simply labour. The Great Pestilence changed all that for me… allowed me to marry her.'

'Nesta would not go with him I'm certain of it. Matilde would have had an inkling and told me. And anyway, Nesta has a simple, unquestioning faith; she would not disobey the Church.'

'No. She would not,' said Amalric, without conviction. When he painted faces on glass, he studied the emotions that would alter a mouth, the eyes. It was his trade. When he looked at Hendric's eyes, he saw Edwin.

A combination of unusually warm, clear nights and Nesta's coolness towards him led Amalric to moon-gaze. Thurston spoke so frequently of celestial bodies that he thought he'd spend his lonely nights observing one. He found the familiar face in the star-laden sky fascinating. Lately he'd tracked its waxing and waning over one and one-half cycles, likening it to a perfect disc of imperfect opaque white glass, twirling slowly to catch the light. Nesta ignored his new passion, sticking to her own view that whatever it was, it roguishly governed women's cycles.

Early one cloudless morning, Amalric went outside to see the full round disc hanging still against the lightening sky. As he gazed, he became aware of retching sounds coming from the back garden and recalled Hendric's cure after falling in the mill pond. He followed the noise and saw Nesta looking pale and sweating in the dew-wet garden.

'Nesta, are you ill? I heard noises. Have you been sick?'

'Don't look so concerned, husband,' she said cynically. 'What did you expect?'

A realisation dawned. 'But you wanted me, that afternoon.'

Nesta looked contrite. 'Aye. I suppose I did, and at what cost? This, my fourth child, may cost me my life, Am. I *am* cursed.'

He stood in shocked silence. 'Well, the sickness seems common enough in the first few weeks so maybe all will be well.'

Nesta's sickness did not cease; it went on and on. Matilde and

Thurston grew worried. Nesta began to fail.

'Am, brother, a quiet moment,' said Matilde as she peered through the unshuttered window of the workshop. Hendric was disobediently bending bits of precious lead cames into strange shapes. Amalric glanced with annoyance at his son, put down his tools and joined his sister outside.

'Thurston and I are very concerned at Nesta's deteriorating condition. It is the child that is causing her puking illness.'

'A devil child?' A thousand fears assaulted Amalric.

'It's a thing that sometimes happens. All I know is we can do nothing for her. All our concoctions for puking are to no avail. There is, though, one thing *I* might be able to do for her, but Thurston must not know.'

'You mean rid her of the child?'

Matilde nodded. 'I have a recipe using willow, tansy, ivy, parsley – all things that no one would suspect if they were seen in our physic room. I also have some ergot.'

'No, Mat, stop!' He hardly recognised the scheming woman before him. 'It's too late. The child already has a soul. Father Luke said so. But it's not old enough to survive outside the womb. It would be evil to... You would be charged with murder if found out. You would be damned to hell. Our mother never did such a thing, and she was a better midwife even than you.' Matilde gasped. 'Mat, I'm sorry. I only know she refused to do the same for Myrtle Ashe's daughter, and it likely led to you adopting Beatrix.'

Matilde looked broken. Her head fell even more to one side. 'Oh, I don't know what I was thinking! I just want to help. I love Nesta as a sister. She'll die if we don't do something. It's all I can think of. She believes she's cursed. She risked her life for me when I suffered from the pestilence, caring for me – I want to do the same for her.' Tears gathered in Matilde's eyes.

'And leave Thurston and Beatrix? Because if you were found out, that's what it would mean.'

'They would be cared for by Mistress Yarrow.'

The shared thought of Thurston, the slightly absent-minded,

untidy doctor, being bossed about constantly by the indomitably efficient woman brought a wan smile to them both.

'You are right, of course, Am, but I feel I've failed Nesta.'

Amalric went into the house. Istrid and Hendric were out. It was silent. The smell of puke mingled with lavender. Bed linen washed by Mistress Yarrow lay neatly in a pile on the family table, her generosity made knowingly obvious. Amalric made his way into the sleep room. Nesta lay exhausted on the straw mattress, a wooden bowl at her side. He lowered himself down beside her and heaved her up a little so that she could nestle in his arms.

Her face was ashen. 'Am, I was never adulterous. I couldn't be.'

'Shush now.'

'No, Am. I must tell you. When you fought with Edwin over me, we were all so young. Since then, I've seen a look in his eye, but that was lust for the servant girl I was, not for me now.' She took a gasping breath as if trying to capture more air than was available. 'Am, I never, never wanted him.' She gasped again. 'I only ever wanted you.'

Amalric felt her sag. What a fool he'd been. Nesta had been a poor fell-girl whose only option for survival had been as a servant. His mother had railed against their obvious attraction, not knowing that changes in society, wrought by the Great Pestilence, would allow him to go his own way. In that moment, his suspicions were glossed over, hidden by his pure love of her.

A few days later, Nesta died with the child nestled within her. The church service was tenderly conducted by Father Luke and afterwards she was laid at the edge of the graveyard where her soul could wander unimpeded back to the fells. Amalric found himself deeply regretting he had never been with Nesta to her home.

'Amalric, I must speak with you.' It was Father Luke. 'Come, let us sit in the church porch. The sun is on it and the stone is warm.' They sat for a few moments, absorbing the heat. 'I heard Nesta's confession before she died, and while I cannot divulge her secrets, she asked me to say she was ever loyal to you. She had a deep faith. She would never go against it, willingly.'

Never *willingly*? Why did he add that? Amalric was plunged back into his suspicions. His pure love remained flawed, like a sheet of glass, weakened where pulled out too thin.

Chapter Eleven

1364 Warren Horesby

After Nesta died, Amalric spent most of his time sitting morosely in the gloomy house. He hardly touched window work and only just managed to scrape together the manorial rent and church dues. A dark cloud enveloped him.

Mistress Yarrow once more took the opportunity to be essential to the Faceby home. Her caring for Amalric and his children was at first tolerable; Amalric appreciated her tall, elegant figure drifting through his home, and her spirit of efficiency. But gradually her efficiency became ferocious, and while she was cloyingly sympathetic to him, she ignored the grief of his two children and instead criticised their attempts to help — saying Istrid did not care for the milk cow, pig, hens or bees properly, or organise the servant girl to sweep the floor or wash the clothing clean enough, and Hendric didn't help their lad at the strips and with their few sheep, or bring in vegetables from the garden before they rotted. Amalric saw only darkness and ignored their plight. However, strangely, one person made a small impact on his gloom — Colin Scarthe.

Having Mistress Yarrow in the Faceby home was an encouragement for her brother to call. With obsequious malevolence, the man unwittingly roused Amalric by playing on his love of glass.

'Good day to you, Master Faceby, sir,' Colin said smarmily one morning through a tangled beard as he peered over the sill into the house.

Amalric, annoyed, went to the door and stood face to face with him. He wondered if the beard was infested with more lice than that of the average peasant and couldn't help but glance at it, instinct telling him much was moving in there.

'I'm off to York soon,' Colin said. 'Got work on the minster's new east end. Three years since the foundation stone laid and goin' on a pace. Seems they wanted to build it way, way back but the Great Pestilence come, killed their master mason and put paid to it.' He feigned regret. Colin's face drew stinkingly closer to Amalric's. 'It'll 'ave a big east window.' His arms stretched out. 'Bigger than any known. You'd like that, wouldn't ya, Master Faceby? Workin' on a window like that? 'Ave you 'eard about it?'

Amalric listened but he was beginning to feel an urge to punch Colin on his mangy chin. Of course he knew about the window. Nowadays he would prefer not to know. Before the Great Pestilence, his father had spoken often of how the stonework of the window might look: the transoms, the mullions, the tracery, and how pictures in coloured glass would fit into the curved spaces. It had been an exciting prospect for his father and himself. They were sure they'd get a commission to be part of the glazing team, working on site in the minster workshop against the great thick walls, chatting with all the artisans – the stonemasons, the lead smelters, the carpenters, the blacksmiths – all looking at shapes and measurements together. Then the disease had ravaged his life; his dream became as indefinite as smoke.

'I'll take our young Cuthbert, my sister's son, with me. The lad needs work. He could start with some labourin'.'

The urge to punch became stronger. Amalric's hands shook. He checked himself.

'His mother'll then be free to marry if she wants to.' Colin grinned idiotically. Amalric had had enough. With more reaction than he'd felt for some time, he slammed the door in the coarse man's face, hoping he'd broken his nose.

The day after, Noah caught and killed a rabbit. Amalric watched as, gently holding it in his mouth, the dog padded into the house and dropped it in front of Istrid. The girl beamed with delight at the food offering. Amalric too began to smile. But Mistress Yarrow pushed Istrid and Noah to one side, bent at her slim waist and grabbed the rabbit from the floor. She slapped the little carcass on the table and immediately instructed Istrid to prepare it for the pot. Istrid became tearful. The woman stood over her, decrying every pull and cut of the still warm skin and bone.

Seeing his daughter weeping and his dog waiting for praise that did not come caused something to uncurl within Amalric and a small glow of light to penetrate his dark mood.

The following morning he waited for Mistress Yarrow. She walked into the Faceby home without knocking as usual. Amalric was drawing a replacement square of glass for Meaux Abbey on a board. Raking sunbeams caught the woman's elegance; amber highlights glinted in wisps of hair attractively escaping her wimple, clean clothes fitted close to her waist tastefully flattering her figure, while neatly rolled sleeves indicated her efficiency. On one hip she carried a pile of folded clothing, as she might have carried a child. It was provocative.

'Here's your washing, Master Faceby.' She looked at him through dark lashes.

He hesitated to respond. Her careful beauty was affecting and he had reason to be grateful; she had left Thurston and Matilde's chores whenever she could to keep his home sparklingly clean.

'Thank you, Mistress Yarrow, I'm grateful for your help but I and my children can get by admirably on our own now. I'm sure my sister needs you more than we do.'

'Nothing but being neighbourly, Master Faceby,' she said curtly, clearly not expecting dismissal. 'Mistress Thurston doesn't always need me nowadays; I have spare time because I'm not allowed to clean in the physic room.' She glanced to one side and the other as if looking to make sure they were alone, and lowered her voice. 'Sometimes, I wonder about the work that goes on in there. Some say it's devil's work. I don't believe it is, of course. It's just that other people don't understand and talk. I try to convince them otherwise, but…'

Amalric was shocked at her conspiratorial tone and disloyalty, then reasoned it was a ploy to get him to open up to her. She leaned towards him; a herby, floral perfume engulfed him.

She dropped the pile of linen on the table next to the drawing. The top sheet slipped and skimmed his drawing board, causing lines to smudge, and slid to the floor.

'Master Faceby, I'll be honest with you. You're a widower with a young lad and lass. I'm free. Your business is failing. You need a helpmeet.'

Normal though it was for men in his position to re-wed, he knew his heart had been too wounded by frequent loss to cope with this woman's commanding nature. He needed softness in a companion. Amalric stood and faced her with his arms out defensively but she moved towards him, seemingly believing he wanted to hug her. Realising his ghastly mistake, Amalric stepped back, nudging a pile of baskets behind him on the floor.

She touched his arm.

'No, no, mistress!'

He stepped further back and fell indecorously onto the baskets.

'No! I'm sorry, I can have no other wife.'

She towered over him, an exemplar of womanly grandeur.

'I'm grateful for your help with household matters, but…'

Mistress Yarrow glared at him.

'I'm not in need of a wife… *just yet*,' he said, letting her down lightly. He scrambled to his feet, annoyed at his own weakness. He could not look at her.

'The labouring in York will suit my brother but not my son,' she said at length. Her tone was cold. 'I'm sure Cuthbert will return to Warren Horesby someday.'

He glanced at her and she stared back, forcing him to consider her abstruse plea for employment for her son. He remained silent; Cuthbert was not a lad to employ lightly.

Mistress Yarrow, seemingly irritated at the lack of an answer, and a woman scorned, turned on her heel and stalked away. Amalric watched her go. One true thing she had said — his glazing business was failing. It wasn't even worth employing an assistant; the only reliable glass work was dreary maintenance at nearby Meaux Abbey.

Several days after Amalric's confrontation with Mistress Yarrow, a messenger from the Benedictine nun's priory at Nunburnholme called with a request. He was to visit the prioress to discuss coloured glass for the east window of the priory church. Both excitement and apprehension mounted in him. Grief still haunted him. Would the nuns want something conventional or something more creative? If the latter, would his dark grief return and stultify his imagination?

'Tell the prioress I will be honoured,' he said to the messenger, without the confidence he knew he would need. 'I'll straightway pack stuff to measure up and accompany you back on the overnight journey.'

Some weeks later, Amalric stood in his own workshop, sweating with anxiety. He'd almost finished the panels for Nunburnholme Priory, but the last two most important ones were posing an insurmountable problem; his inspiration felt trapped, locked away.

The window was divided into three slim lancet shapes, the centre one being the tallest, separated by two slender stone mullions. The designs for each window were split into manageably sized panels that could be drawn full size onto the workshop table.

Till now, all had gone well. After many discussions and pleasant afternoons with the prioress, Mother Ruth, Amalric's sketch on a small board for the whole window had been presented to her. It was not conventional. Though too small for fine detail, she had gazed at it for such a painfully long time that he'd feared he might be accused of heresy, or blasphemy, or some such thing. But Mother Ruth had plainly adored the image of the Virgin Mary standing in a pose clearly affected by the weight of the child she was holding, a realistic pose, not a pose that curved the body into an unnatural S-shape, as was the fashion. She greatly approved that the Christ child was childlike, rather than the usual small man. She had wanted a real mother and child for her nuns. The prioress agreed to everything. Boyed up by her enthusiasm, Amalric promised that in the finished window, both the Virgin and child's faces would have an unearthly, spiritual beauty.

It was these two latter pledges that Amalric had trouble keeping. He felt the weight of Mother Ruth's trust. He realised he'd made a boastful and stupid claim.

Now, in his workshop weeks later, most panels were finished. Their flowers and draping of the Virgin's lower body created in glass were impeccable – but the drawing for the last panel was only partly done; Amalric was beset with the difficulty of showing both divinity and humanity in the faces of the mother and child. The full-size working drawing, called the cartoon, of the Virgin's upper body holding her child was on the white table but the faces were featureless, smudged, lead point ovals. He could not complete the drawing well enough to begin cutting glass.

Amalric slumped on a low stool and cupped his hands around Noah's head to nuzzle it, seeking comfort.

The door creaked open. Hendric put his head tentatively around the door. Beatrix was by his side.

'Da, you're tired. Let me help you.'

'Aye. Come in, lad. Hello, lass.' Amalric's suspicions of Hendric's conception had been pushed to one side and he'd nurtured a good manly relationship with his growing son. Beatrix was always welcome.

'You can't manage this alone, Da. You should have set up a workshop at Nunburnholme Priory and maybe had lay workers to help.'

Amalric smiled. 'Aye, that sounds well enough, but I didn't

want to leave you and Istrid coping by yourselves.' What he didn't want to say was that he'd found Mother Ruth's company too seductively pleasant to allow himself to wallow in it. It was safer to work at home. 'It's just this last panel… all the leading up and soldering for yon panels has tired me.' He nodded to lead-edged panels, mosaics of colour, leaning against the wall. 'I'm a mite stuck on this last one's drawing. See, I can't get it right.' He pointed to where the Virgin's face and her child should be. 'I can't fill 'em except with the grey of my rubbed-out mistakes. All I see in this space is little Bosa, and in this one, your mother.'

Grief had crept back and was compromising his work. He regretted speaking so openly to his young son. He too must feel the loss of his mother and his angelic little brother, but Hendric's face showed no sign of emotion. Amalric was suddenly reminded of Edwin. There was just the hint of the same indifferent look when confronted by another's pain. It shocked him. He slumped back onto the stool.

'Da, let me help. You need an assistant. I could start an apprenticeship, be expert at leading up and installing windows. I might not be very good at drawing but I can help with the heavy work. We can employ a second village lad for our farm strips and sheep so I can be here. If Nunburnholme Priory leads to more work, you could employ a glazing assistant.'

Hendric's youthful optimism warmed his father. 'Aye. That would be reet good.' He noticed Beatrix looking intently at the drawing. 'See, lass, my head's full of sheep's wool. I can't get this final panel right and the window is promised to Nunburnholme Priory ready for St Mary's Day.'[8]

'Uncle, would you let me try to finish it?'

Amalric felt strangely defeated. His shoulders sagged. 'Aye, lass, have a go. Keep to those areas and don't smudge the rest, and don't go outside them lines. I'm going across to the church now. Come, Noah.' He saw Hendric grin widely at Beatrix.

---

[8] St Mary's Day is 15th August.

Chapter Twelve

The church was so close and so familiar that it felt like stepping into a room of his own. It was still early in the day and the morning sun spread the colours of the east window across the floor and on Father Luke, kneeling before the altar muttering his Latin prayers. Amalric sat on the ledge opposite his favourite saint. As usual, the cold struck through his thin tunic to his backside and gave him more human thoughts than divine. The arrowed St Edmund offered no advice for such inconsequential discomfort.

Father Luke rose. 'Hello, Amalric. What ails you? Your countenance is gloomy.'

'Father, when I made the east window for this church, the Great Pestilence had passed and our survival was sad but joyous at the same time. I'd lost many in my family.'

'I know of your losses then, Am. Your mother, father, twin brother and sister. I too lost many brethren at Meaux Abbey. It was hard to face the aftermath.'

'Aye.' Amalric sighed. 'I recovered by pushing it out of my mind. I was young and ambitious and in love with Nesta. I'd no problem drawing the faces of the divine, the Virgin Mary...'

'Ah, and the angel Gabriel sent by God to tell her she would be with child – the lovely window here before us. But now... what ails you?'

'Now I'm so different. I lost Bosa. I lost my Nesta and our unborn child. It stops me finding the faces of the divine. I've stupidly given an important drawing job to my young niece. The hope that sustained me before is gone. I've become like "dust and ashes".'

'Mm, you are suffering like Job.[9] It *will* lead to good.'

'So we are told.'

Luke ignored the cynical remark. 'As a Cistercian, I cannot comment on the art of coloured-glass windows, but it seems to me that when you made the window in this church, it fitted well with the state of your heart at that time. Perhaps your new window for Nunburnholme Priory doesn't fit too well with your heart at present.' The priest gave Amalric an unnerving, questioning look. 'As we get older, I also feel the difficulties of my faith. It doesn't come easier, but harder as our human experiences and our questionings increase. You will find your path, Amalric. Take help from others. Guide the young.'

Priests had always seen into his soul, like Thurston could see into his body. *Guide the young.*

That night, despite Father Luke's assurance, Amalric tossed and turned, tortured by thoughts of his betrayal of the trusting nuns; horrifyingly, he'd let the task of drawing go to an untrained person, and a lass at that! It would be easy enough to cover her work with wet white chalk again, but what if she'd carelessly destroyed the rest of it? He couldn't face redrawing the whole panel, and how could he speak to Thurston and Matilde if he really upset their Beatrix? He agonised all night.

As soon as there was sufficient daylight, he went to the workshop and opened the shutters, not daring to look at the table. Stalling for time, he lingered to look at the back garden. It was bathed in golden light. Noah's nose was deep in undergrowth with his tail upright. The chickens clucked and pecked, with their amber feathers glowing. The pig grunted. The milk cow chewed relentlessly. A jackdaw settled on the little kiln, which stood safely away from the house, with a pile of fuel ready to fire the next lot of paint on glass. Then the bird hopped and flew to the privy roof, causing the little hut to teeter with age. It was the only one in the village set over water, built by Old Elias

---

[9] Job 42:6, KJV.

over a channel cut from the Ripple Brook. The powerful village stinks of subsistence life and ordure wafted over all this and assailed him, tempered by the moist fragrance of the closer herb garden as birds and small animals blundered through the stalks. Somewhere beyond, something disturbed a flock of geese. He turned from the window space and willed himself to look over to the table.

The smudged grey of before now looked white with firm, dark lines clearly defining shapes to be filled with glass. He moved closer and gasped. Inside the shapes, lines thinly drawn with lead point formed the most beautiful faces of the Virgin Mary and her child he had ever seen. Mary's eyes were focused as if to heaven, the nose not exactly straight but with character, the mouth with a knowing tip upwards of the sides. Sadness and happiness mingled. The edges of a silk-thin veil skimmed her forehead and random curls peeped from beneath.

The Christ child was a true baby, gazing at his mother. Divinity and humanity were combined as Amalric had never seen them before. All was drawn with such skill that the transposing of the lines onto glass would be easily achieved. It was truly beautiful – spiritual.

Amalric dropped onto a stool. The window drawing was done. Seeing such ability, he became aware that his own skill was insufficient for him to ever achieve his dream. Was this how ambition worked? If you didn't achieve your goal when young, would someone snatch it from you as you aged? But that was ridiculous, he reasoned. He wasn't *so* aged, and Beatrix wasn't snatching, she was simply talented.

Amalric went to work at once, choosing pale, flesh-coloured glass for the Virgin's face and the naked Christ child. He carefully traced Beatrix's drawing onto it with a fine-hair brush. As he loaded the pieces of glass into his garden kiln to fix the paint, he realised he could not claim to be the master of such beauty.

'Ah, Hendric, my son, and Beatrix.' Amalric had seen them though the workshop window. 'Come in and see.' The final panel had been leaded together and was laid on the table. Amalric held it up so that light shone through it. 'What can you see?'

'A beautiful glass panel, Da,' Hendric said.

Beatrix peered for a few moments, then, 'Oh, Uncle!' burst out from her. Around the edge of the shapes containing the Virgin's face and the child was tiny writing: *Beatrix Thurston, facit 1364.*

'Thurston, before I take the glass panels to Nunburnholme Priory, I want you to see the final panel.'

Amalric and his friend had both been at the manor for separate reasons and met as they left through the great front door. It slammed behind them, causing the lion-head knocker to clank unnervingly as if pleased to be rid of them.

'How are my nephews?' Amalric guessed Thurston had been summoned for the benefit of the children. Edwin and Clara lived with the fear of losing their remaining two boys. It would put an end to Edwin's aspirations of their marrying well and raising the family even more in society. Amalric knew future wives had already been marked out.

'Robert and Walter are unwell, again. But nothing bad. The lads are not of strong constitution, nor very brave. Their mother panders to them. It's not the pestilence returned, thank the Lord. I fear it may come again, though. I'm told it simmers in far eastern lands.'

'I saw my brother today about the villagers' rents. Lord de Horesby has passed over the full running of the estate to him. The man has never recovered since his losses from the Great Pestilence. To lose his wife and all his sons, leaving but his daughter, Clara, is a terrible thing. He's aged beyond his years. Edwin has taken full advantage of him. I fear for the future of the village folk and the land they farm.'

'Edwin will manage the estate well enough, but he will care little for the suffering of others,' agreed Thurston.

'Well, my friend, at least we can all rely on you in our hours of bodily suffering,' said Amalric without sarcasm. 'Even the poorest. It helps us all to know that.'

'I can only hope to cure the body, not men's lives, nor their souls.'

'I cannot cure anything.'

'Ah, but my friend, you heal with beauty. And I must talk with you about that. I believe my Beatrix has done some drawing for you. Matilde and I can't get out of her exactly what it was but she has since been dreamy; but maybe she's just being a young girl – definitely not my area of expertise. That's more in Matilde's line; being the village midwife has given her more insights into females than a mere man can ever know.'

They both smiled.

'Look,' said Amalric. 'Why don't we collect Matilde from your home and go to my workshop where you can both see what Beatrix has done? I'm carting the window panels to Nunburnholme tomorrow, so it will have to be today.'

In the workshop, Matilde stood with her hand to her mouth. 'Oh, Am, why did you let my Beatrix do such a thing? It's not fitting for a woman. I'm teaching her to be a midwife. You've used her ill.'

The panel was on the table, leaning on a wooden frame holding it against the light. 'No, Mat, I would never use her badly. It was her choice.' Amalric looked at Thurston to defend him.

'Good wife, she has drawn an exquisite face. It's beautiful. Spiritual.'

'Yes, a mother's face with her child!'

Then Amalric understood. Matilde was disfigured, and here was their adopted child portraying the perfect mother. 'Sister, I don't think Beatrix meant… I didn't think… but look, she's so talented. It's the Virgin, the perfect woman. Christ's mother. The child too is perfect.'

'They are of God. You shouldn't make images like that so… human.'

'But…'

'Anyway, making windows and healing don't mix!' Matilde

spat out.

Thurston interrupted. 'But of course they do.'

'No.' Matilde's eyes flashed wildly. 'What I'm teaching her will fit in with being a wife. This talent will not.' She lifted her fist as if to impulsively push it through the panel.

'No, Matilde!' Amalric put himself between the table and his sister, a picture of a smashed window and blood in his mind. She thumped her brother's chest instead. Thurston pulled her gently away.

Matilde stood contrite, her tears flowing in a stream that Amalric recognised as years of pent-up despair. Through them she gulped her fear.

'Am, I'm afraid of this new thing my girl has found within herself. I'm not her real mother and she will be lost to me.'

'Nonsense, Mat,' said Amalric. 'She loves you, and nothing is better than that. Give her the freedom to enjoy both her skills. It'll not be wasted. One day you may be grateful for her interests.' Amalric realised that Thurston was surprisingly lost for words and unable to comfort his wife. For a brief moment he felt he had a deeper insight than the physician. 'I'm sorry. Go now,' he said and abruptly pushed them out. 'I've to pack up the glass for Nunburnholme.'

'Uncle Amalric? May I come in?' Beatrix was at the workshop door the following day.

'Yes, lass, of course.' He waited patiently, wet cloth in hand, as she shifted from foot to foot. He saw her eyes roam over the sharp edges of thin vertical sheets of glass in the racks with their colours waiting to be discovered in sunlight, the large white table now damp with cleansing ale and waiting for new work, and finally, crates on the floor packed with the window panels for Nunburnholme Priory, their lids ready to be nailed down.

Beatrix had been awakened to the beauty and potential of glass. He knew it. He felt it. But it had caused confusion in her and, yes, despondency. How could she, an emerging young woman, cope with healing *and* glass work, both her talents and loves? She was pretty too. Her mother had taught her the careful use of unguents to keep her hair and skin soft. He had noticed that young men, especially Hendric and Cuthbert, watched her as she moved about the village.

Finally, Beatrix was able to speak. 'When I drew the face for the Virgin Mary and baby, it made me happy in a way I hadn't known before. I really liked doing it. I got lost in it. It was like speaking without a voice to someone not of this world. Learning from them. Do you know what I mean?'

'I certainly do.'

'It was like painting a picture of someone I knew but couldn't see. I know Ma and Da are happy when they heal someone and I want to be like them, but I also want to make windows like you. I'm muddled. I'm making mother sad. Hendric said to talk to you. He said you'd understand and help me.'

So Hendric *did* have some appreciation of others' needs, unlike Edwin. 'Well, I can't go against your parents' wishes, and in any case women don't, as a rule, make windows for a living.' Amalric chuckled at the ridiculousness of it and then checked himself; his niece was earnest. 'Let's see, then, Hendric is now my apprentice. When you've free time, you can join us. Work together sometime.' He paused. 'But… we mustn't do anything that your parents disapprove of. Go now and put the idea to them. Your mother is the one who really needs to be persuaded.'

Beatrix was overjoyed. 'Oh, Uncle Amalric, you understand me just as Hendric said you would.'

In that moment, Amalric saw her love for Hendric begin to open like a flower in her young heart.

The nuns of Nunburnholme Priory were pleased with their Virgin Mary window and wanted more. Amalric accepted their commission to fill the small window spaces around the priory church nave. However, he still preferred to work in his small workshop in Warren Horesby rather than set up more conveniently at the priory. Hendric could not understand it.

Working with both Hendric and Beatrix was joyous. Between them, Amalric and Beatrix created designs of twisted vines and other plants that surrounded the priory, along with birds which the nuns fed. Mother Ruth was always on hand to advise on flowers: ones that were symbolic or were mentioned in the Bible. Those that had healing properties interested Beatrix. One or two windows had figures of saints, both male and female; Amalric delighted in creating their faces with character: smiles, grimaces, bent noses. One, St Hilda, had a long plait of pale hair and grey eyes. Without realising it, he'd made a portrait of Nesta.

Beatrix made one smallish window for a very special place in the church, entirely on her own. It showed a lily, the flower symbolising the Virgin Mary.

Hendric became skilled at measuring and inserting windows. His ability to work with complicated stone shapes increased almost daily, and he delighted in restoring damaged windows elsewhere in the priory.

Amalric had seldom been so happy.

Chapter Thirteen

The journey: A stop at Nunburnholme Priory

'Da, wake up. We're at the turn-off.'

Noah barked into wakefulness.

'We're almost there, Da. We're at the Saxon cross.'

Amalric looked up sleepily. It took him a while to move from dreams of the past to the present. He shook his head to clear it as best he could and saw Erika off the glazier cart, fingering an image on the stone. 'It's wonderfully carved!' she called excitedly.

The priory approach was pleasant; at the verges, the path was clear of fallen branches and stones; bushes and trees were trimmed. A soft, late-afternoon sun raked the path and lent an autumnal closeness to the last part of the day's journey.

Erika remained walking, as if her young legs were itching for exercise. 'Isn't the cross back there beautiful, Elder?' said Erika, approaching the litter.

'Aye, lass. It is.' Amalric approved of the special name she had for him. 'Elder' overcame the complicated nature of their family relationship, and described him; the oldest man in the family.

'You know, Elder, when I see things like that cross, I want to make beautiful things. I adore your glass work and would be like you, but Mother still expects me to be a manor-wife, and Grandmother Beatrix keeps teaching me about healing.'

'Well, you'll find your way as well as any woman I know.'

Amalric felt his age. Once he'd been an adolescent with a passion for coloured glass. But a manor-born woman with artistic aspirations? It was unlikely they'd be realised. His own grand dream had been like smoke through a thatched roof: twisting through life's obstacles, escaping into the air, drifting thin and shapeless, at the mercy of the wind, ever upwards, finally apologising to God for lack of stamina. He hoped for something better for her.

A high stone wall loomed ahead. The litter stopped at a large oak double gate. George pulled on a bell rope and almost immediately a small door opened within one of the gates. He stepped inside. After a moment, the two halves creaked open, one pulled by George and the other by a nun. The horses resumed their regular trot. Ahead, through the gate, was the vary-coloured limestone of Nunburnholme Priory. Caught by the low sun, the shadows of the rough surface made intriguing patterns on the walls. Amalric felt his heartbeat quicken.

The nun was clothed in a black habit with a coarse, dun-coloured, sleeveless working overgarment on top. A dark cloth was wrapped around her head and chin. Her hand shaded her eyes as she watched the procession enter. She was obviously surprised to see such a decorated litter.

She turned to George. 'My goodness, sir, underneath the fancy, do you have sickness in the litter?' Her young face showed concern.

George answered. 'No, sister, the litter is for my wife's grandfather, who has poor legs. We're from Warren Horesby journeying to York and desire lodgings for the night.'

'Well, you are all welcome to Nunburnholme. Follow me. I will take you to the guest hall where your needs will be met. We expected visitors with the happenings in York, but you are the first to come looking for lodgings. Come.'

The nun turned her back on them. Her long habit moved elegantly around her.

The cart, litter and horses clattered to the priory precincts. Amalric gazed around. It was many years since he'd last been here. He found his memory had increased the size of everything. It was now, in this fresh reality, smaller than he remembered, but looked prosperous. The priory church, too, was certainly smaller than the more recently visited church of Meaux Abbey. It was of the usual cross shape and he could tell from outside that his coloured windows had been well cared for. Their surfaces were clean and sparkling. The moss growing on damp edges of lead cames was little. He remembered that his designs contained the small things that spoke of women. He hoped to see the windows from inside once more before he left.

Istrid and Ava helped Amalric from the litter. He was stiff and struggled to make his legs do what he wanted. He took his sticks. Noah dropped to the ground and though immediately hugged by Erika, pulled away to pad over to Father Everard's donkey. Dorkas dipped her head to him. After the exchange, Noah went back to his master.

The nun accompanied Amalric to the hall. He noticed a high-born refinement about her as she put her arm into the crook of his to steady him. It was pleasant.

'You may sit by the fire, sir, to warm yourself and your dog while the others are guided to their accommodation.'

'Thank you. Is Mother Ruth still your prioress?' he asked as he lowered himself to a seat by the hearth.

'She is, but aged, like yourself, sir.'

'Would it be possible to see her?'

'I'll tell her. Who shall I say is here?'

'Amalric, master glazier. She'll know me.'

'Master Amalric Faceby!' A small, bent, elderly nun pattered through the door at the bottom of the broad stone staircase. She wore no veil; her slightly trailing habit indicated her shortening frame, and wide soft shoes, her painful feet. Her face was full of joy as she approached. 'Don't get up, my friend,' she said, and put her hand on Amalric's shoulder to curtail his effort to stand. 'No ceremony, please. I hoped you would call here. I know Master Thornton the glazier and have heard of your desire to be in York.'

Her knowledge of his journey was a surprise. He lifted her hand from his shoulder and put it to his lips. The hand was warm but thin with bony nodules at the joints. 'Mother Ruth! I see you have led a life of toil since I last saw you. Your hands are evidence of that. How do you fare? Come, sit and tell me about yourself.'

Amalric pushed Noah gently to one side to make room. The dog sniffed the folds of the nun's habit and she responded by rubbing the yielding ears. 'What a lovely creature you are.' Noah tilted his head to one side.

Amalric noticed his old friend's once pure black habit had turned dark grey from its long-time pummelling at the laundry, but it was her bare head that intrigued him. Once shaven and never seen, it now revealed short, thin grey hair in little curls which, despite her facial wrinkles, gave her a young, elfin look. 'Have you cast off the veil?'

'Nay, Amalric. I plead old age. My scalp is too tender to shave, and the veil makes me itch so much I sometimes drag it off in temper. I had just done that when I heard of your arrival. I was so thrilled that I did not think to put it back on.' Her smile was mischievous.

Amalric smiled too. He looked more closely at her face and saw the downy hair on her chin, the once stark blue eyes turned pale grey, freckles merged to larger brown blemishes. A short silence fell; Amalric's memory travelled swiftly back to the past but he knew it held too much sentiment to linger there: secrets best kept. He felt his heart race. He suspected that Mother Ruth was experiencing similar. She spoke abruptly as if to stop remembering.

'Has your family gone to settle in their cells?'

'Aye. They have. They're all tired so I suspect they'll eat in their rooms and retire early. I slept most of the time on the journey and am not ready to sleep.'

'They'll be well cared for, as will the horses. The stables are next to the guest hall. Our hosteller is efficient.'

'The priory looks successful.'

'Aye, it is, but I'm only prioress in name now – I'm too old to be astute enough to keep it solvent. We have several young nuns who have come with good donations from their families, and I have a deputy with a business head on her shoulders. Thank the Lord. You met her at the door, I think.' Amalric nodded. 'The abbot has allowed me a suite of rooms of my own and I'm kept there in modest luxury. I pass the time well. In the cloister I help train young novitiates and in church I seek the Lord in the silence and gain inspiration from your windows.'

'My windows?'

'You must see them again before you go.'

'I installed them a long time ago when I was much younger and first met you. I remember coming to you feeling very out of sorts; I'd lost Bosa to the pestilence and recently Nesta with our unborn child.'

'Aye, I too was out of sorts. When the second pestilence came in 1361 our prioress died when away visiting the priory at Haltemprice. I had to become prioress. There was no one more suitable. I became proud and pompously believed God wanted to save me and my sisters rather than have us help those beyond our gates – at least until there was no risk of contagion. We confined ourselves to the priory and glorified God for saving us. Then I learned that outside our gate, very many people had suffered and died. I could not believe our sins were less than those who'd endured so pitifully, and felt guilty that I'd denied them Christian charity. I was distraught at my failure. But then, I saw the light, so to speak, and sought God through beauty – a Benedictine concept I'd forgotten. You came and gave us magnificent windows. It redeemed me. We invited all people in to see them, allowing God's light to penetrate their souls. I trusted you to work well for us… and you did. Never since have we turned away the sick.'

Amalric was moved by Mother Ruth's confession. 'I too was searching for redemption and found it with you. I'd failed my son and then my wife and unborn child.' He sighed. 'With the first window I stupidly promised you more than I could achieve.

I had to reconcile myself to using my niece Beatrix's talent. She drew the Virgin and Child's faces beautifully. It was a hard lesson for me – accepting the skill of someone else.'

'We must never underestimate how much we can inspire others – for good or evil. You were the initial inspiration, I'm sure. And to see talent in others is a talent itself.'

'Aye,' said Amalric thoughtfully. 'I eventually accepted Beatrix's help with images suitable for a house of women. Remember how you and I had to argue against the abbot for colourful flowers and birds in saints' windows... and won, to his annoyance?'

'Yes, we did,' she chuckled. 'I think it was then that the abbot *really* saw me as a stubborn woman who could keep the priory safe.'

'Being here comforted me.'

'We comforted each other. Life for a headstrong nun in the prime of life was hard.'

'And also for a young man without a wife.'

Again a short silence fell. With easy memory, he recalled she had once been lax about her clothing, letting her summer habit slip open at the neck. It had revealed a perfume, a mix of incense and roses: her church and her garden. His hands had strayed onto the whiteness of skin that was never touched by the sun. Her response had been warm, giving, breathlessly excited.

She smiled at him. 'God is forgiving. I found contentment in Him.'

'I loved you.' Amalric found himself looking deeply into Mother Ruth's eyes. Pale ones gazed back – only for a moment, but long enough to see in them the same sentiment. He knew it had been right, all those years ago, to make the windows at his home rather than set up a workshop here with overnight stays as Hendric had wanted him to do. It would have been hard to stifle earthly passions that may have surfaced in the evening quiet of the perfumed cloister garden. And if discovered, there would have been a devastating confrontation with the ecclesiastical rules that governed both their lives.

He took both her hands in his. The firelight flickered, highlighting the old nun's deep wrinkles.

As if reading his thoughts, Ruth spoke softly. 'We were both lonely at that time and young enough to feel a smouldering desire for each other. We did right not to meet alone again.'

'Aye, we did.'

'And after all these long years, we can still cherish a loving friendship.'

Amalric found himself longing to hold her, to put his own rough cheek next to hers. His love for this nun had been different from his feelings for Nesta: older, wiser, less questioning. He fondled the soft, thin, yielding smoothness of Noah's ear distractedly.

Mother Ruth straightened. She spoke with a lighter tone. 'But your windows, Amalric, they still inspire me, and all the nuns. I gaze at them for hours. You must see them tomorrow.'

The outside door of the guest hall opened abruptly and a blast of cool evening air entered. Someone outside pulled the door shut. Amalric turned from Mother Ruth to see Edwin standing there, slowly and laboriously stripping off his gloves.

'Edwin!' Amalric was shocked to see his brother there, and even more so by his weary movements and the failure of dim light to hide his pale yellow face above the immaculate short white beard.

At Edwin's side, the dog they had seen earlier stood shivering. Noah leapt up into alertness and took wary steps forward to sniff the animal. He stopped as Edwin's dog bared her teeth and growled indecisively, lacking true menace. Pulling on her lead, she crept towards Noah, who was unmoved by the trembling animal before him.

'Noah, here,' cried Amalric sharply.

Noah retreated to his master, and the other to Edwin, who took his horse whip from under his arm and gave her a sharp whack. The dog whimpered and cowered. 'Kati here is a weak dog,' he explained.

Noah looked up at Amalric as if perplexed by the cruelty

he'd witnessed.

Mother Ruth tried to remain calm. 'Master Edwin Faceby, are you seeking shelter?' Her voice wavered.

Amalric felt mildly surprised; Mother Ruth knew his brother! But it made sense. He would have called here on his many trips to York in his younger days, often to roam the more dubious Snickelways.

'I am,' replied Edwin. 'Where's the hosteller? I could do with a flagon of ale.' He stared at the prioress. 'My, you're looking fine without your veil, Mother.' Edwin's sarcasm cut through the tense atmosphere.

Mother Ruth put her hand to her head, her face pinking with embarrassment. 'I'll find the hosteller,' she said with a downturned mouth, and slithered off.

'Brother! Has your own old age encouraged no respect for those of similar account? And a nun at that!'

Edwin dropped to a bench. The fashionable hunting clothes did not disguise his thinning body underneath, despite the protective padding of the leather.

Amalric felt annoyed but concerned too. His tone softened. 'Why are you here, brother?'

'I'm going just a little north to hunt. My friend's hunting lands are good. He's been granted a chase – fifteen dogs and breeding more. You know it's my passion. I may meet you at your next stopping place when I've bagged the largest stag. There's one that for years I've hoped the dogs would bring to bay and this time they will. My two boys are with me, stabling the horses now. It's a great occasion. It rather outplays your own, I fear. I'll take Robert's son, George, with me; we need younger men. You'll manage fair enough without him. My ageing boys and I are a mite sluggish in the saddle from time to time.'

Edwin's face had the all too familiar challenge about it. Amalric recalled their youth, the rivalry; Edwin always reaching for higher status while he, Amalric, sought the challenges of an artistic trade. Now, old age was an inconvenience for Edwin, not a barrier. Amalric reluctantly admired such an attitude but as usual felt let down, less important in the scheme of life.

'Take George with *you* and leave us a man down when we may need protection?'

'Fear not, brother, there's too many on the road for you to be fearful of bandits.'

The hosteller came through the inner door carrying a tray of refreshments. At his side was Mother Ruth, her head covered with a veil.

Edwin grabbed a beaker and slurped beer. As it dripped down his beard, he turned to Amalric and grinned. 'I'll maybe see you in York, eh, brother, after the kill?'

Amalric did not reply.

Edwin picked a small lump of cheese from the wooden platter, had second thoughts and dropped it back, leaving it in crumbs. He then staggered off up the stone staircase to the guest rooms.

Mother Ruth laid a hand on Amalric's arm. 'My friend, we have seen your brother here before. We are well practised in curbing his excesses. He has always been... er... interested in young women, even in his old age. We've been careful of the girls we take in here. They come from respectable families. All are anxious to follow the faith and accept strict celibacy. I assume you'll be stopping at Wilberfoss Priory? Well, your brother has spent nights there too – many more than here. The present prioress there is not strict. Many of the nuns come from backgrounds where they've been forced into the Church against their natures. It's a sad fact that girls of high-status families have only two ways to go in life: a good marriage or the nunnery – even if they have no faith persuasion. Girls from artisan families have far better choices. Girls like your daughter, Istrid, and niece, Beatrix.' Mother Ruth smiled her approval of such lives. 'Even if they are without a husband, they can be fulfilled in occupational ways.'

Amalric nodded agreement.

'Some of the nuns at Wilberfoss hugely resent being forced

into convent life. They long for the marriage bed and can settle to little else. The prioress there is already on a warning from Archbishop Bowett about her excesses and defects. She's facing a visitation this coming year.'

Amalric was following every word. He knew what she was trying to say and suspected what was coming next.

'My dear friend. Be careful of your brother. His wish for dominion over women and his evil intent for you will likely out. Poor man. He has no other choice. God has made him thus. But God has also made you thus.' She opened her palms towards him as if giving a gift. 'Make sure you reconcile yourselves before time on earth has run out.'

People had frequently warned him about his wayward brother. Yet to see him tonight… in a nunnery… there was something pathetic about his weariness, his colour, the way he could not eat the cheese.

Amalric was up early the following morning and left the guest hall before food was put out. The day was lightening with a gold autumn mist. Noah was by his side, springing with pent-up energy. 'Off with you, lad. Have a run. I'm going to the church.'

The cold struck through to Amalric's bones as he sat on stone at the back of the church with a blanket around his shoulders. How on earth did nuns cope with Yorkshire inclemency? But of course, he knew. Their worship of the God they loved, His Son and His Son's mother kept them warm.

He listened to the intonations of the sisters' worship and followed the Latin with pleasure. Both he and his sister had been educated at Meaux Abbey: his father's reward for looking after the windows. It had set them apart from the other villagers. For Matilde, it had meant spurning the village dolts and marrying Thurston, a doctor of physic. For himself, it had meant understanding his father's manuscript about window-making, copied from that of the monk Theophilus. It gave him the ability to write Latin phrases from the Bible onto window glass. Edwin had refused the bookish education.

When the nuns' worship came to an end, Mother Ruth

approached from the sanctuary area. She was more bent than the previous evening, her feet shuffled and she had a walking stick in each hand. Her brow was moist and her mouth grimaced with effort and pain. Amalric was alarmed.

'No need for you to look at me so, old friend,' she said. 'I'm like this every morning. It takes a long time for me to loosen. I'm much better by evening. I rather think that my life would be better if I could live it top to bottom, front to back, swap sunrise for sunset.' She smiled. 'Come into the sanctuary and remind yourself of your east window in the first light of day.'

Misty sunlight shone gently through the window, spreading soft colours around the sanctuary.

'There, Amalric, it's beautiful, is it not?'

Beatrix's faces of the mother and child made him catch his breath.

'So human but so divine. This window has been central to our worship for nearly forty-five years now. Many have seen it.'

The door of the church opened. Beatrix and Erika walked down the nave.

'Oh, please excuse us, Mother Ruth. I hope only to show the windows to my granddaughter before we leave.'

Erika's eyes were large with wonderment as they darted around the building.

Mother Ruth held out a hand and Erika unconsciously put her own into it. 'Come, my child, see the beautiful artisan work of your relatives. We'll work our way around the walls and end at the east window.'

Amalric could see that Erika was entranced. At the east window, he watched as she was allowed to climb onto a stool to look more closely at the Virgin and child. He saw Erika's eyes wander over the sparkling glass. He knew that she was considering all the things that such a glass window offered: the beauty of transparent colour, the use of imperfections for texture, the artistry of cutting coloured shapes and joining them to make recognisable people and objects, the painted details, and the way that such a window expressed the faith and told its stories. Then something that Erika did instinctively moved Amalric's heart: she tapped the glass with her fingernail, felt its surface and followed the cames with the flat of her finger. Then she put her finger to her nose. As well as seeing, she was hearing, feeling and smelling the window. In that moment Amalric had no doubt, she was a lass who understood glass. He turned to Beatrix. They smiled and shared the revelation.

Erika jumped from the stool, her face aglow.

'Now, come into the crypt,' Mother Ruth said. 'There's a small window that's placed just above the level of the outside ground. It's behind the altar. Only when the sun is low, like now, does it light up. It's my special place where I find peace enough in the early morning to talk with Jesus and His mother.'

Beatrix turned to Amalric and whispered, 'She's taking her to the crypt to see my lily!'

Mother Ruth took Amalric, Beatrix and Erika to break their fast in the guest hall. Afterwards, refreshed and ready to face the day, they made their way to the priory precincts where Istrid and Ava were getting ready to leave. Warmed by a pleasant sun, the early morning mist had drifted away. Istrid patted and shuffled the cushions on the litter. Ava heaved bags onto the glazier cart. Father Everard appeared around the corner of the church, yawning and sleepily leading Dorkas. The donkey's head was up, her ears alert and her large black eyes watched Noah running playfully ahead.

'I said my prayers sheltered under the trees by the fish pond,' the priest said to Mother Ruth as he took a woollen blanket from around his shoulders and passed it to her. 'It was so relaxing, this blanket was so warm, I dozed off. I was more tired than I realised. You have a lovely plot here, Mother, you keep it well. I shall come again when I next pass on my way to the Cistercian House at York.'

'You will be more than welcome.'

Amalric looked around, searchingly. Mother Ruth guessed the reason.

'Your brother was not seen to break his fast in the guest hall.

Presumably he left before the sun had even begun to rise. Your nephew, George, too, has gone. I expect you'll see them at Wilberfoss,' she said.

Amalric looked towards George's wife. Ava shrugged her shoulders.

'Da,' called Istrid. 'Time to get into the litter. Come. We must be at our next stop before the day is out.'

Mother Ruth touched his arm. 'Two lay brothers will accompany you to Wilberfoss Priory for safety. They endure the manly tasks for which our female strength is insufficient and will enjoy a day of travel in the countryside. God speed, Amalric, my dear friend. May He bless you.' Mother Ruth's face was radiant in the early light, and her eyes moist. 'Here are some scraps from last evening's meal for Noah.'

On hearing his name, Noah's nose lifted. His eyes grew wide with excitement.

'Not now, boy. Later.' Amalric took Mother Ruth's hand and gently squeezed it. 'Thank you. You may see me on the return from York.'

'Aye. I hope so. Go now. See, my young deputy is waiting to see you off.'

Father Everard came to his side. 'I'll help you into the litter, Master Amalric.'

Realising they would struggle, the young nun directed them to a high stone mounting block near the pathway. While Istrid moved the horses and litter to it, the nun took Amalric's arm and explained as they slowly walked that the occasional passing knight was grateful for an easy means to mount his huge destrier. Amalric ascended feeling pleasantly superior.

As they moved off, the nun called, 'Wait!' She disappeared and returned with a set of short wooden steps.

'Take these, Master Faceby. They'll be available for you when you need to ascend and descend from the litter. You can return them when you wish.' She dropped them into the glazier cart and waved the party off.

Amalric settled into the litter. The little anxiety he had for his brother had been more than compensated for by the kindness they had all received from the nuns. They deserved the large portion of coins from his purse he'd left for them.

To shouts of 'Safe journey!' the little procession moved off with one of the lay brothers at the front and the other at the rear. Ava and Erika steered the glazier cart, followed by Beatrix on the palfrey. The litter came next with Father Everard on Dorkas next to it, dozing, with his legs hanging loosely either side. Noah padded restlessly and annoyingly on the litter cushions, constantly looking over the side then padding back to Amalric. After a while he started barking furiously.

'Alright boy, jump off, do what you have to do,' said Amalric.

Noah leapt down to the ground and speedily sped out of sight. Looking over the litter side, Amalric was amazed to see him return with a sandal dangling from a strap in his mouth. The dog went straight to Dorkas, who abruptly stopped. Father Everard was jolted into a dazed wakefulness. Amalric heaved himself higher and saw that the priest's foot nearest to him had no sandal, only a thick, rough-sewn, red winter-weight sock with thinning wool at the end of his substantial big toe.

Everyone laughed. It was so good. Noah thoroughly enjoyed the praise he received from his master for his rescue work. Mother Ruth's titbits were liberally fed to him but his real prize, it seemed to Amalric, was to walk with Dorkas. He wandered through her legs as she trod carefully, often bending down to nose him out of the way to safety.

The procession settled into a steady pace. Amalric was relieved to find he was better at tolerating the nauseating sway. The sun was climbing higher and would eventually be shaded by the litter's fabric roof, but for now, it was low in the south-east and dappled through the roadside vegetation with a pleasant slanting warmth. Around him, autumnal leaves hung delicately from skeletal stems and became almost transparent, like amber glass with sunlight behind. It would be a long day. Time to doze.

Part Two
Unrest

~~~~~~

Chapter Fourteen

1368 Warren Horesby

Amalric ran his fingers over hard amber undulations. The glass sheet was the topmost in a crate of new glass delivered from King's-Town on Hull. All the colours of the rainbow were waiting to be unpacked but he was tired and needed a rest. His reputation had grown since installing windows at Nunburnholme Priory, and with seven years without recurrence of the pestilence, there was a new confidence for beautifying churches and even manor houses.

He went outside and leaned against the workshop wall with hands tucked into the bib of his leather apron. He liked to watch people come and go. The entire village seemed to pass his home over a few days, as well as pilgrims and ordinary travellers seeking a quiet route from Hull to Meaux Abbey, Beverley and, less often, York. It was pleasant to pass the time of day with them.

Mistress Yarrow passed by frequently, saying no more than 'Good day', but this morning she stopped. 'It looks as though you and Hendric need help. I can see overwork written under your eyes.'

Amalric winced.

'Cuthbert will be returning from York. Nearly four years he's been there. The labouring job doesn't suit him any more, as I predicted. He wants more than just heaving stones up ladders. They'll not apprentice him as carver.'

That doesn't surprise me, thought Amalric.

'I'll send him to you when he arrives. You can teach him glazing.'

Horror flowed into Amalric. 'But Mistress Yarrow…' What could he say? It seemed that the woman was still intent on getting her son into his workshop and herself into his home. There were too many people around for him to cause a scene, and in any case, she allowed no time for him to respond.

'He'll live with my brother, Colin, at Dunghill – *he's* coming back too. His wife is ailing. Anyway, I must hurry. Mistress Matilde is busy. Pots and phials everywhere. It seems the doctor suspects another bout of the pestilence.'

One or two people were in hearing distance of the word *pestilence* but paid scant regard. Amalric knew they were of the opinion that the physician often fussed over nothing much and, having seen no signs of a new outbreak, the word had become like water dribbling from duck's feathers.

Seven days later, Cuthbert arrived in the workshop, brimming with confidence, thick fingers and no aptitude for glass work. Hendric, though, was pleased to have a work companion, all childhood disagreements forgotten. Beatrix had an unusually large number of pregnancies to deal with and was away from glass work for a while. Amalric kept moderately calm so long as he was spared acrimony.

Amalric's main problem was Mistress Yarrow. He grew tired of her admiration for her son and the constant tales of his prowess with the bow and arrow, practised every Sunday after church, and offers of work from knights. Amalric wished he'd take up an offer and go, but his mother's insistence that he stay with the glazing work meant *she* was still anxious to be part of the Faceby home. Amalric had no choice but to passively endure her and her son.

Two moons later, an overcast sky threatened rain, but inside Amalric's workshop it was cosy; an unnecessary fire played in the little raised hearth: soft colours reflected from the window glass and straw decorations hung from coloured woollen strings strung from rafters.

Amalric poured ale into Thurston's horn beaker as they sat at the table. ''Tis excellent news, my friend,' he said with a broad grin, 'and not before time.' He picked a morsel from a bowl on the table, which contained nuts, seeds and dried fruit, all scattered prettily with dried sweet-violet petals. 'Istrid and I thought this would be a good place for 'em to celebrate, bein' as how their love grew in this place.'

'I couldn't agree more.' Thurston took a long draught. 'My word, the alewife has made a good meadowsweet brew.'

Noah sniffed around, disruptively whining his disappointment at the dog-unfriendly food, until Istrid took it upon herself to nudge him outside. At the door, she looked up the hill.

'Here come the couple,' she called back into the house, 'hand in hand, and with Matilde by their side. My, they look grand. They are in their best clothes; Hendric's wearing a new close-fitting jacket and Beatrix the new surcote her mother made – it shows off her good figure.' Then Istrid's hands went to her cheeks. 'Oh, Mistress Yarrow and Cuthbert are close behind them.'

'No! Why do they come?' Amalric asked. 'Have they been invited?'

'I don't think so – *I* haven't told anyone. It's been secret until today.' Istrid bit her bottom lip.

They waited apprehensively.

At the door, Matilde pushed in front of Beatrix and Hendric and stood frowning. 'Mistress Yarrow and Cuthbert joined us as we walked down the hill,' she said, conveying both her innocence and annoyance. 'I had to tell them where we were going but not why, and they insisted on coming to pass the time of day with us.'

Ignoring the visitors at her back, Beatrix looked over her mother's shoulder. 'Oh, Istrid, you've made it lovely in here,' she said cheerfully.

Almost in unison Amalric, Istrid and Thurston said, 'Well, we *had* to celebrate.' They all laughed.

Meanwhile, Mistress Yarrow had craned her neck to see into the room and was looking questioningly at the festive food and drink.

'Come in,' said Istrid with a defeated look. 'We're celebrating my brother's betrothal to Beatrix.' She looked directly at Mistress Yarrow.

The other woman's brows drew together and then one eyebrow was raised. She was clearly shocked. 'But she favoured Cuthbert. They've been seen walking together.'

Her son also looked stunned. His breathing increased. Muscles bulged in his tight sleeves as he fisted his hands. His calves, twice as thick as Hendric's, stiffened in his tight hose.

'I never gave him that idea,' responded Beatrix. 'We've walked alone around the village sometimes and to Meaux Abbey once or twice to collect some of their special medicinal plants for Father. After all, we grew up together like brother and sister. I suppose the gossips at the well made more of it.'

'I heard there was kissing,' said Mistress Yarrow.

Beatrix's face reddened. 'It was only sisterly affection. We grew up together,' she repeated.

Cuthbert revived. 'I didn't see it as sisterly.'

'You certainly went too far on one occasion.'

'You slapped me – playfully, I thought.'

'Not playfully. You were lecherous!' Now Beatrix was close to tears.

Amalric watched anxiously and saw anger rising in Cuthbert as he struggled with Beatrix's accusation. The lad could look unnervingly tight-bound at times, ready to break into a furious rage at any moment. Hendric just looked bewildered, while Thurston's face had a stern expression.

Mistress Yarrow moved to the side of her son and held his wrist. 'Son, it's best to stay calm.'

Cuthbert's face moved unnervingly. ''Tis the glass she loves, Mother, not Hendric!' His tone was caustic. ''Tis the glass that is her passion. Like it, she's brittle and cold; sharp when broken.'

Amalric was astonished at the piercing elegance of the lad's talk. It showed an imagination he'd hitherto not seen, but his words were going too far. 'Now, lad...' he ventured.

Cuthbert ignored him. 'Hendric will give her glass and colour, not money and jewels. She'll grind glass and put it into her nostrums; fool the sick, make folk ill so they'll pay for her services. Even now, she drops colour into 'em to make 'em prettier to use. She'll work for the devil. Maybe she does already.'

Silence fell like a stone in the village well: plunging deep. Amalric recognised an accusation of no less than being in league with the devil. How could the lad lay such a claim? He saw his niece pale almost to the white of his workshop table.

Cuthbert's anger suddenly released in a flurry of exaggerated movements, like a display of knightly combat. His arms flayed, his fists sought a target. The women backed away. Amalric felt a mixture of fear and bravado, a desire to both protect and hurt. He looked at Thurston; *his* whole life was based on healing, not harming; he was wide-eyed. What was he feeling?

Then Amalric saw Cuthbert's eyes rest on the poker leaning on the wall by the hearth and watched with horror as he lunged for it. Cuthbert brandished the poker above his head, catching the woollen strings and bringing them down upon himself. He tugged to get free, littering the floor with bits of wool and straw.

Amalric moved towards the lad, not knowing what to do next, but Hendric had recovered and pushed his father out of the way. Dancing swiftly to and fro to avoid the poker as it swung heavily towards him, Hendric finally trapped Cuthbert between the table and the coloured window. The poker crashed onto the white table, missing Hendric's hand by the width of a mouse tail. Cuthbert rapidly swung it back, where it clinked into contact with the glass. He spun round towards the sound. A horrible expression contorted his face and Amalric knew in an instant what he would do. The poker was thrust vehemently at individual glass shapes in a stabbing, killing frenzy. Pieces fell out onto the ground outside. In a few moments, lead cames were grotesquely distorted and left empty of glass. Amalric's stomach contents rose into his throat.

Outside, Noah barked furiously at the falling shards. Hendric tried hard to pull Cuthbert back but the lad's manic strength, forged by archery, was too much for him and he pulled himself away from Hendric and crashed through the open door to the outside. Hendric followed closely and halted him by grabbing his collar. His work with heavy glass windows had given him a moderately strong arm too; he whisked Cuthbert round so that his adversary lost his balance, giving time for a hefty punch in the face. Cuthbert fell to the ground, dazed, with his nose starting to pour blood. Hendric once more grabbed the collar, lifting Cuthbert's head from the ground ready to punch him again.

'No, Hendric, son, leave him be now.' Amalric had come outside to alleviate his nausea and had seen it all. 'He knows enough how we feel about him.' A drizzle started and he shivered.

Hendric's fist hovered but he let go of the collar and Cuthbert's head hit the hard ground.

'Da, you're too soft. This man has broken something precious of yours.'

'Aye, an' he wanted somethin' precious of yours. Your betrothed.' Further words failed Amalric as something about the scene brought back his imaginings of his own brother with Nesta. 'Leave him be. He knows how we feel. Don't make things worse by either words or actions. Let it go. He's the one at fault.'

'Da, why must you always be so weak when it comes to

trouble?'

Amalric suddenly felt a wave of anger towards his son; uncomfortable with the truth he'd uttered. 'Just go to Beatrix! She'll need you.'

Hendric shrugged and went inside. He bumped past Thurston. The physician looked at his servant's son on the damp soil, still dazed, with drizzle causing dark patches to grow on his clothes and nasal blood to wash down his chin. Thurston's expression had become implacable; he turned to walk up the hill into a thickening cloud of moisture.

The drizzle became cold, splashing rain. Through it, Amalric could hear female voices becoming more strident, coming from his workshop. The door opened. Mistress Yarrow rapidly exited as if pushed. It slammed behind her and clicked secure. She went to her son, who was struggling to stand.

'Let's get you to your uncle Colin's,' she said loud enough for Amalric to hear. Her wimple began to drip and her hem sagged into a puddle. She heaved on Cuthbert's arm; he stood unsteadily.

Amalric watched them stagger up the hill, splashing through a muddy stream that had started to run down from the top of the village. They veered off indistinctly onto the side road to Dunghill. He sighed, knowing that there would be recriminations. He looked at the shattered window. Rain poured down the thatch and dribbled onto the twisted cames from where it fell like drops of pure, clear glass. What had once been a Christmas scene, with shepherds, sheep and an angel, was lost. All that remained intact was the angel, swinging precariously on a thin, stretched came, as if in flight.

The door clicked open. Matilde came out of the workshop with Istrid's comforting arm about her and, like Thurston, they went up the hill, to her home.

Amalric went back inside. The betrothed couple were still there. Beatrix's face was wet with tears.

'Oh, Uncle, this is all my fault. I spurned Cuthbert's advances; I really did. I didn't know he would react thus. I should have told him I was betrothed but it was a delicious secret. Oh, your beautiful window.'

Hendric put his hand to her shoulder. 'No matter, my love,' he said. 'Da won't mind, will you, Da? He'll make another. Come, let's take a walk.'

Beatrix looked at Amalric, and he nodded. 'Aye, lass. Go now.'

Then Amalric was alone, his workshop in disarray. *He won't mind. He'll make another.* His son had never really understood the passion for glass. He was an expert at putting glass into windows, but the artistry and the true love eluded him. Hendric would never understand that damage to such a window was damage to the person who'd made it. In that regard, Hendric was more like Edwin. Amalric realised that for all of Cuthbert's aggressive behaviour and evil barbs, he had recognised the love of glass in Beatrix, and the story he'd invented showed something of a creative mind. But to say she worked with the devil was unforgivable and loaded with threat.

The following day, Beatrix stood in front of the shattered window with Amalric. '*Will* you make another, Uncle?'

'Nay, lass. I was an apprentice when I made it. I've changed. Best to let it go.' He pulled the white angel from the twisted leading. 'I'll keep this, though. I'll put a new came around it and look at it from time to time to stop me being too proud. It'll be a talisman.'

'What will you do with the space? Please make another. I can help you.'

'Nay, lass. You'll soon be a wife. Our Hendric has a house and smallholding in mind. One of them that stayed empty after the last pestilence. You'll have your work cut out if you're to make it a home, carry on with the healing work and have your own babies. I'll repair with colourless glass. It'll suffice.'

'Aye. I suppose.' She smiled but suddenly her face took on a horrified look. 'Oh, Uncle, what if Cuthbert spreads it around that I'm a devil-worker?'

'Well, there's not much fear of that, love,' he said without conviction.

'But people are superstitious, and what he said about me and the potions – if people believe that…?'

'Nay, lass. People have more sense.'

Chapter Fifteen

The house door rattled open to the early morning light and Istrid, who had just come from the well, set her pails on the floor with a splash. Ripping off her shawl, she yelled to her little servant, 'Get these into the corner!' The lass scurried to do her bidding. 'Da, there's talk at the well about Beatrix and what she does with glass. There's speak of the devil. You know how stupid some of them women can be, reacting before they think. They're fearful that she messes with physic potions, adding glass, and half of 'em are threatening to ransack her mother and father's store of curatives… now!'

'This needs Father Luke. I'll fetch him at once. He'll be at prayer.'

On hearing Amalric's news, the priest annoyingly insisted on finishing his prayers. 'Shall I tell Thurston?' Amalric asked before he continued.

'No. The conflict of physic with the Church is bad enough. The devil is my business, not his.'

Amalric and Istrid went up the hill.

Mistress Yarrow was at the well, talking to a group around her. She saw them arrive and raised her voice. 'Oh, dear me, I would never have believed it of Beatrix!' Her voice took on an obsequious tone. 'Of course, though I work for them, I have no access to the physic room where the curatives are made up and so cannot give an opinion.'

Istrid responded angrily, while pushing up her sleeves. 'Not give an opinion! Today's gossip is *all* to do with *your* opinion.' She turned to the assembled women. 'What has she said – that her son Cuthbert was spurned by Beatrix when she had goaded him on? And that the lass adulterates ointments in secret, with glass and mysterious colours? And perhaps a snide remark about the devil?' Her bosom heaved. Several women nodded. 'I thought so – and her kept like a lady's servant by the soft-hearted doctor and Matilde. And…' she breathed, '… Beatrix, my friend, as kind a lass as any, who would not even harm an animal.' She moved towards Mistress Yarrow, pushing sleeves further up her arm, ready for a fight. 'Mistress Yarrow! Explain yourself!'

Amalric was both amused and concerned. Along with the women, he backed slightly away, leaving Mistress Yarrow and Istrid standing alone.

Father Luke arrived in a flurry of swirling habit and then stood by, still and silent. Amalric hoped he would step in to cool the situation, but he seemed to be letting the women work through it themselves.

Mistress Yarrow began to grovel. 'Well, Istrid, I know Beatrix is your friend and she's a grand lass, but my Cuthbert is an honest lad, and knows what goes on in that physic room. We've lived there a long time. He's been in there with Beatrix and seen her mixin' stuff more often than her mother.'

Father Luke at last intervened… calmly. 'Mistress Yarrow, what are you saying?'

She hesitated. 'Well, er, things go into those medicines which none of these women know anything about,' she said, waving a hand collectively over the crowd. 'Then they use 'em on their children, their menfolk and themselves.'

'And what goes into them that *you* know about?'

'My Cuthbert says…'

'What is it *you* say?' interrupted the priest.

Mistress Yarrow dipped her head. 'Er… glass is mixed in.'

'Glass, is it? Now, why would Beatrix do that? Have you seen it put in, or found any?'

'Er…'

An arm came out from the crowd and a finger pointed at

135

Mistress Yarrow. A voice followed. 'Aye, *she* said t'were the devil what made the lass do it!'

Father Luke raised both hands with palms towards the women. 'Enough! There is a way to solve this.' He turned to Amalric. 'Master Faceby, on oath, how would you add glass into an ointment or lotion?'

Amalric felt the weight that his testimony would hold. He didn't like this situation which had ultimately arisen from his spurning of Mistress Yarrow and then his niece's similar spurning of her son. 'Well, I suppose it would have to be ground up finely before being added to the mixture.'

'Would coloured glass change the colour of the lotion? Meld into it, as it were, not be identified as glass?'

'You would see coloured *bits* in both a lotion and an ointment. Colourless glass of course would not be seen so well. It would be gritty, though.'

'Thank you, and would it make a person ill if rubbed on or swallowed?'

'I don't know. Physician Thurston would know.'

'Then we have two reasons to go to his physic room: to examine the mixtures and see Master Thurston on oath about the danger.' Father Luke pointed. 'You, you and you come with me. Mistress Yarrow, you come too, and Master Faceby.'

The little group walked further up the hill to Thurston's home. The crowd followed and gathered near the building. Istrid stood at the front. Father Luke went straightway to the physic room door and walked in without knocking. The three randomly chosen women followed. Amalric and Mistress Yarrow stood in the doorway.

Amalric saw utter amazement on the women's faces as they glanced at tables crammed with heavy wooden mixing bowls, pots and mortars, pestles and spoons, knives, bottles, phials and fresh herbs. Dried herbs were hanging from the ceiling; leeches were swimming in bowls; manuscripts were piled in a corner. A plethora of pleasing aromas wafted around.

'I wondered how long it would take,' said Matilde, standing

at a bench beside her daughter. She glared at the tall figure of Mistress Yarrow.

Thurston appeared from an inner doorway. 'What…?'

The priest ignored him and waved his hand over the room and said to the three women, 'Choose any unguent, tincture or powder and examine it. Look for pieces of glass. Feel for grittiness. Look for evidence of colourings.'

Thurston breathed in and was about to speak, but Amalric, reading his thoughts, glanced at him and almost imperceptibly shook his head.

Father Luke remained dispassionate with his approach. 'I'm sorry, physician, but by my authority as a priest I must investigate devil worship.'

Amalric watched as this infringement of his friend's privacy and status was carried out. Thurston's face became puce; Amalric thought he might explode. Matilde was stony-faced. Beatrix's lips quivered as she held back tears. Father Luke remained unmoved.

The women delightedly took the linen tops off pots and with fingers poked inside, stirred up the leeches in their bowls, shook bottles and poured out the contents of some and tasted them. Amalric prayed desperately that none were poisonous.

'Now, search all around to find evidence of small glass pieces in table cracks, on the floor, hidden in cupboards; glass grounds left in the stacked mortars, for instance,' further demanded the priest.

The women obviously enjoyed their task. It was rare to have such an opportunity to invade a high-up's privacy; to turn the class structure upside down. Before the Great Pestilence this would never have been allowed.

No glass was found.

'Master Thurston, on oath with God, would ground-up glass or other colours in your medications be harmful?'

'Father Luke, our colours are merely derived from medicinal plants; sweet-violet petals, for instance. Glass would indeed be harmful – it would cut the insides. No doctor of physic would do such a thing. I would soon lose my registration. I would also lose it if I allowed a household member, such as my daughter, to be so cruel. I am on oath, not only to God but in my allegiance to the great Hippocrates and Aristotle, to save life and do no harm, to the great Galen whose methods I follow.'

Amalric smiled to himself. More often than not, Thurston argued against many of the ancient ways of doing things, but harm anyone – never.

Father Luke went outside and everyone in the physic room followed him. The priest closed the door and stood in front of it. He motioned Mistress Yarrow and Beatrix to stand before him. A muttering arose in the crowd and he raised a hand for quietness. The sun shone, the air was clear. Amalric saw a man in complete control of the situation.

The priest, familiar with talking to crowds, spoke so that his voice carried to the back of the gathering. 'My investigation is complete.' He turned to Mistress Yarrow. 'Mistress Yarrow, as you have suggested that Beatrix is working immorally with the devil, you may persist and put your case to a Church court. You will have to prove that she is doing so. It can be expensive.' He turned to Beatrix. 'On the other hand, you, Beatrix, may accuse Mistress Yarrow and her son of slander and she will have to deny it. This too will be in a Church court and expensive.' He faced the crowd. 'It all hangs on whether the devil was involved and whether it can be proven that glass or other obnoxious material was added to curatives. Nothing has been found.'

A silence fell. Father Luke put his hands inside the sleeves of his habit and raised his head as if to heaven. Amalric smiled to himself once more. Father Luke was play acting; he had seen such a thing done by wayfaring players in Beverley. He seemed to be appealing to God for confirmation of his actions and looked as though he was getting it. He lowered his head and looked at the crowd, then from Mistress Yarrow to Beatrix.

'From your silence, I assume that neither of you wishes to take accusations further?'

Beatrix nodded tearfully. Mistress Yarrow only raised her

chin defiantly.

Amalric felt relieved. Thurston looked at the priest with admiration. Matilde and Beatrix visibly sagged and Istrid unrolled her sleeves. The village women sighed with disappointment and started to gather the jugs and pails they had cast to the floor in their excitement.

Mistress Yarrow stood alone in front of the physic room. Amalric looked on as Thurston went to speak with her.

'I think you know what you should do now,' Thurston said softly.

'Aye. I'll go. As it turns out, my brother needs help. His wife is severely ill and he can't afford a physician.'

'You know I will help them if there is illness.'

'Pah! I know enough to ease her pain.'

Matilde went to stand by her husband. 'I can hardly believe you've been a help and companion all these years and yet have betrayed us so badly, and simply over the lust of your son who could not get what he wanted. You are a bitter woman.'

'Aye. I am. The wars and pestilence have deprived many women of a man. I wished to be married but being denied it, I had to seek a livelihood in your family. It's at an end. My son's talent is in his right arm. He'll gain work in the king's service. His grandfather's memory is still well respected.'

She turned abruptly away, swishing her skirt to the side; it emphasised her waist and long legs. She walked into their home to collect her belongings with her shoulders back and her head up. It took only a little while before she came out with a wrapped bundle. Amalric was moved to say something, anything, but before he could, she turned to him.

'Master Faceby, you will regret my going. Your household and business would have prospered with me to help run it. I lov... could have loved you.'

He watched her skirt swirl again as she walked towards the turn-off to Dunghill. It seemed to him she maintained her elegance no matter what, and yes, she would have fought hard to improve his lot. Not for the first time had the contradictions within life struck him.

Istrid was nearby. 'Oh, Da, I saw the look in your eye. She's a hard woman, and you are soft. As her husband, your life would be miserable.'

'Aye, but lass, *you* shouldn't be lookin' after only me. You'll needs marry sometime. I should have taken a wife a while back.'

'I would have so hated a woman like that in our home. I'm content to be housekeeper.'

'There must be someone that's lit a bit o' candle in your heart.'

'No, Da. Marriage is not for me. Who needs a dolt of a husband? Mistress Yarrow is right; good men are hard to find. I'll be content to help keep your glass business going with good food and comfort for you.'

Amalric grasped her round the shoulders. 'Reet-oh, lass.'

Istrid smiled mischievously. 'And you'd best be on your guard. You're still a good catch.' Amalric laughed until he thought his chest would burst.

Chapter Sixteen

1369 Warren Horesby
Spring

Over the following months, Cuthbert and Mistress Yarrow occupied Amalric's thoughts less and less. Life settled into a happier pattern.

The wedding of his son to his adopted niece had been a joyous occasion, and though he hardly dared admit it, the sorrow in his chest became less noticeable. This was partly because he could think of no one he would rather have had marry his son than Beatrix. It also brought him closer to Thurston – they were now like brothers. And with the employment of a village lad, Nathan, to help with glass work, he had more time to enjoy the relationships.

Amalric knocked on the door of his sister's and Thurston's home and walked into the house, uninvited but always welcome. Beatrix was poring over pictures in a manuscript, singing to herself:

> My love is like a golden apple,
> Sweet and juicy laden,
> His arms enfold me, firm the flesh,
> I am his chosen maiden.

'Oh Uncle Amalric!'

'Songs of love, eh? You look happy.'

'I am, Uncle.' Her smile was captivating. Her hair shone like a frizzy halo about her head. 'Today, I'm drawing in Father's physic manuscript.'

Thurston came into the room, smiling. 'Beatrix is helping me.' His mood was light, jocular even. 'Her drawing skills are greater than mine. Look, I've written about the pestilence. Copies of the finished manuscript will be made at Meaux Abbey ready for new physic doctors when the pestilence comes again. I've described the disease and now I need some drawings. Matilde knows all about the disease and is instructing Beatrix in the signs so she can draw images in the margins; buboes and the like.' He leaned over the table. 'She already has a leg with a bubo in the groin.' He put his face to the parchment and then drew it away with his eyes screwed, seemingly to focus on the drawing.

Amalric looked at the image. 'Ee, if it weren't so gruesome, I'd put it in my windows.'

'Don't forget the rash, the bloody cough, and blackness,' said Thurston, pulling a comic face and wringing his hands to indicate grisly detail.

Beatrix put her hands on her hips in mock anger. 'I could get on and do that if you two took your noses out the pages and stopped being so rib-ticklin'.'

Amalric enjoyed sharing the academic enthusiasm. These days his friend was more often morose and short-tempered.

Matilde walked in with a pot of freshly made ink. She too smiled. 'Go, go both of you. If this ink spills on the parchment, both writing and pictures'll be lost. Go. I've seen enough of the pestilence, my love,' she said to Thurston, 'to know what she ought to draw.' Matilde put down the ink pot on the table and picked up her broom, pretending to sweep them out of the door. She smiled good-naturedly at the two middle-aged men. 'Go. Drink yourselves into peace. The alewife has a new barley brew which should please you both.'

The thought of a barley brew was enticing; Amalric and Thurston heaved themselves from the smoke of indoors and interest in the manuscript, and went into the fresh air.

Sitting outside the tavern, they both held beakers of barley ale. Amalric's legs splayed out in front of him under his worn leather apron and Thurston's legs crossed under his threadbare woollen robe. As usual, they found a satisfaction in watching life move around them. Everyone who walked the road squelched animal droppings. This day, villagers were returning home after driving animals to summer grazing or tending sodden fields and woods; some had been to Beverley market on horseback; an ox cart trundled heavily, flattening ruts of soil and creating new ones. Two pilgrims hobbled through on blistered feet. Several small children were being carried or dragged along by frustrated mothers or older siblings.

'At last, the number of children is picking up after that last bout of pestilence,' said Thurston.

The silent sky above them was a soft grey/blue with a sun that lacked intensity. Charcoal clouds menacingly tipped the western horizon.

Amalric felt his mood changing. 'Thurston, back in your home, you said *when* the pestilence comes again.'

'Aye. Maybe sooner than we expect.' The physician dropped his head and spoke into his beaker. 'It will only take one ship with the disease on board for us to be engulfed in it again. I've heard that a few days ago, a ship arrived in King's-Town on Hull harbour. There was illness of some sort aboard and it wasn't allowed to dock. Not one person was allowed off, but bodies were thrown overboard and later rose to the surface, bloated and black. I'm not saying that this event signals the pestilence – it's a common enough sight, shipboard diseases are rife – but it's out there, over the sea. It worries me that folk no longer fear it. And if it attacks children again…'

'Aye, many folk are more concerned about the fashion that arrives on those ships than death – maybe a fine surcote acts as compensation.' Amalric thought of his brother. He and Clara had started to wear cloaks lined with the soft underbelly fur of rabbits. The warren behind his house was being exploited for such things; consequently, there were fewer rabbits for food. Mistress Yarrow had predicted it on the day she had come into his home asking him to marry her. He shivered. 'Each year,

143

spring seems colder than the year before.'

'That's because we're getting older.'

'Well, look in your cup and wallow in the beauty and taste of golden bubbles.'

Thurston lifted his head back. His eyes were unsmiling. 'I can't tell one bubble from the next, Am.'

'What?'

'My eyesight is failing. I can see the distance but not close. I have difficulty making a diagnosis these days. I can't sort out planetary conjunctions from my charts and I can't tell one type of spot from another. I can't even find a good vein to bleed, and you know how much store people put on that. Worst of all, I can hardly read my notes on diseases. The manuscript Beatrix is working on today will be my last. Also, times are changing; cutting will be a skill required by more and more physic doctors. I'm all for it but good eyes are needed. Ale bubbles are just a blur to me.'

Amalric was astonished. The loss of that piercing gaze which saw through to the very bones of a person would be a catastrophe.

'At night, I panic. I fear I won't be able to fulfil my ambition to find a cure for the pestilence.'

Amalric understood what a dream meant, the passion of it, the hope. His friend's repressed bitterness was palpable.

'I've dreamt of finding out why such diseases spread. Religious men like Father Luke are sticking to their theory, but *I'm* sure that it's not all to do with God's wrath. Other faiths, good men, have studied the contagion, talked of causes such as miasmas. Their words, like my Christian ones, are respected in physic circles.'

The charcoal clouds had advanced and loomed overhead. With a flash and a clap, large spots of rain clattered down.

There was a noise in the workshop. A rummaging. Amalric slowly opened the door and moved his head around it, fearing a thief or a trapped bird. He saw Beatrix.

'Ee, lass, what are you doing?'

'Oh! Uncle Amalric.'

'Have you been crying?'

'Yes. Father is going blind. He can't see things close to. He can't see his charts. He's angry with himself all the time.'

'Aye, I know, lass, but what are you looking for in here?'

'Forgive me, Uncle, for not asking you, but I'm distraught. You know those little squashed round glass discs you sometimes fire onto window glass? Well, when they're on the table, if you lift them slightly away, they make the marks on the table look bigger – scratches, the woodgrain and such. I wondered if they may be useful for Father. I wasn't going to steal them.'

'Yes, I know them.'

'Hendric said he'd help me to look.' At that moment Hendric passed outside the window space. Not seeing his father, he blew a kiss to Beatrix. Her cheeks blushed and she glanced guiltily at her uncle, but Amalric was pleased to know their love was not only surviving but growing.

'Did you find any, Beat?' Hendric said as he entered. 'Oh, hello, Da.'

Amalric rummaged among a box of small glass pieces. They found the discs. Some were coloured, some colourless – it was the latter they needed.

'Let's take them to Father.'

In the physic room, Amalric watched Thurston peer at writing in his manuscript through a small glass disc.

'Yes. I can see. It's bigger but wavy.'

'Here,' said Beatrix excitedly. 'Try this. The surface is smoother.'

'No, I can't see with that one. Nor that. Oh, that's so much better – better with my right eye than my left.' He picked up another disc and held it to his left eye and looked at the manuscript through it. 'It's odd. This one is better for my left eye. I can only deduce that my eyesight is different in each eye. Where did you get these, Beat?'

'They're mine,' said Amalric grinning. 'I fuse them onto glass with heat so they look like jewels, such as on crowns, but I've never noticed they make things look bigger.'

'I heard of this when I was at Oxford. About a hundred years ago, a master there was studying glass and light. Bacon, his name was. I wasn't very interested in that sort of thing and never considered it in relation to my own eyesight, which was good then. I believe aids for eyesight are used in Venice and Florence. But in our backwater, there's no such thing.'

'Oh! What if...?'

Thurston, Amalric and Hendric looked at Beatrix. They all recognised her facial expression.

'She's got an idea,' said Hendric.

'We could go to a glass blower and ask him to make some small discs of different thicknesses, arched on each side...'

'*Convexus*, I believe it's called,' interrupted Thurston.

'... arched on each side,' said Beatrix firmly.

Amalric grinned at the minor conflict. He knew his niece favoured the use of common language rather than Latin to explain something scholastic. It vexed her father but pleased her mother, everyday language being more understandable for ordinary folk.

Beatrix continued. 'He could grind them down until the surface is absolutely smooth and a perfect dome on each side. Then, Father, you could pick the best one for each eye. I could surround each one with lead cames, join them with lead and then you could balance them on your nose, or somehow attach a handle. That's difficult, though, lead is so soft. Perhaps attach twine to go around your head or handles around your ears.'

Amalric felt the joy of invention. His niece was already deep in thought about how she could bring her idea to fruition. What was it Matilde, her mother, had said – making windows and healing don't mix? Now she would see they did. 'There's a glass blower in Beverley,' he offered.

Amalric and Thurston went to Beverley. The blower was skilled at making everyday drinking vessels and physic pee-flasks, and luckily, the challenge of smooth, domed discs appealed to him.

Two visits to the town and the choice of several discs resulted in the purchase of two, one for each eye, enabling Thurston to see much better. Amalric also bought two elegant wine beakers: a late wedding gift for Beatrix and Hendric.

Thurston was delighted. 'When my Beatrix has sorted out how to keep these close to my eyes when I'm working, what shall we call them, Am? Occularies, perhaps?'

'Or maybe eye-windows?'

Back in Warren Horesby, Father Luke declared the discs a miracle. 'The monks in Meaux scriptorium would be glad to have such things; some work with their noses practically touching the parchment, others an arm's length away!'

'I'm sure Beatrix could offer advice,' said Amalric with more than a little hint of pride. 'She has a way with both glass and healing.'

Chapter Seventeen

1369 Summer

Matilde stomped through the door of her married daughter's home and closed it rapidly. Fire smoke wafted.

'Mother!' said Beatrix, blinking.

Matilde, sweating from the afternoon's humidity, wiped her forehead with the edge of her wimple. She ignored her brother sitting at the table with a new window design in front of him. 'Is your father here? He's not in his physic room. He went to Meaux Abbey scriptorium early this morning. He wanted to show the monks his occularies and ask them to copy his manuscript. I hoped he'd be back by now.'

'No, Ma. What's your anger about?'

'A messenger came to say I was needed at Dunghill for a case of chickenpox. The woman was said to be pregnant as well. I went, of course, it's nowt but a shortish walk, though I hate the place, what with all the rubbish they collect and pile up in great heaps. The flies! Great black things. Ugh! When I got there, I couldn't find the house. I asked for its whereabouts, but no one knew of the family. I saw Colin Scarthe lingering by the roadside grinning and then knew it was a hoax. That nephew of his, Cuthbert, was with him – both looked flushed and puffy round the gills. They beckoned to me. "Where's your lass? Is she not come with you to help?"' she mimicked Colin.

Amalric listened intently. He saw Beatrix blanch and put her hand to her abdomen.

Matilde continued, 'I wouldn't go near 'em; they frightened

me. They looked angry, wild. I feared and so ran down the street away from 'em and returned here the back way through the woods.'

'Oh, Ma. Cuthbert still bears me a grudge. Was he wearing a knight's livery?'

'Aye, he was.'

'Then he'll be gone soon. Back to his master.'

Amalric had listened intently. The Scarthes! Fear struck his chest.

Beatrix put an arm around her mother's shoulder. 'Come, sit by the fire. Get warm. You look nithered. Take no heed of 'em. Cuthbert's still not married. He's such a bitter man, no woman'll have him; the women at the well often say so.'

Amalric butted in. 'Aye, and his father must still resent me.'

'Colin's wife bore the brunt of her husband's ill behaviour until she died,' said Beatrix. 'How Mistress Yarrow copes with her brother now, I don't know.'

'Well, she's a strong woman. She looked after this family well enough when you were a child, Beatrix. "Cleanliness is next to godliness," she always said.' Matilde impersonated the way the other woman would put hands on hips; Amalric felt it to be eerily comic. 'She'd not let me forget it, with all her washing and sweeping. I still respect her for that.'

'Aye,' said Amalric, a little wistfully. 'Her brother has used her ill.'

A dull clomping of hooves on the grass verge came from outside and a shadow crossed the open shutter. Thurston entered. Even in the shade of the doorway, it was obvious to Amalric that his face was ashen.

'Matilde, my love, I've been home, but as you were absent, I assumed you to be here.' The physician saw his friend and nodded a greeting. 'It's come again – the third time. I heard at Meaux that the pestilence is in King's-Town on Hull. The town is suffering very badly, as badly as the first time. I believe Cuthbert was with his knight there; I hope he hasn't gone home to Dunghill, that miasmic hell-hole! If he has, we mustn't let anyone from there come here. We must try to avoid the spread.'

Horror flooded his wife's face. 'Are you sure it's the pestilence?' she asked. 'Only I was told there was chickenpox there – in Dunghill. It was false. Cuthbert was there.' Matilde reiterated her story.

'You did right to ignore them, Mat. It's better…'

A sudden hammering on the door stopped Thurston's talk. Alert with suspicion, Amalric rushed towards it but Matilde intercepted him and opened the door. Standing there grinning was a red-faced Cuthbert dressed in a knight's colourful livery, and behind him, his uncle, Colin Scarthe. Further back, running down the road, Amalric saw Mistress Yarrow, breathlessly shouting, 'Stop. You must! Don't do this devil's work!' Her wimple fell to her shoulders and then to the ground. Amalric recognised a contradiction – she was denouncing devilry in her *own* family.

It was too late. Cuthbert spat into Matilde's face and grinned. 'Oops, sorry, it should have been Beatrix.'

Matilde jumped in horror and raised her hand to her cheek to finger off the spittle. She turned up her nose at the slimy, foul-smelling, sticky substance. Thurston rushed to the door and pushed his wife and Amalric to one side. He took up his friend's walking stick from beside the door. Cuthbert backed away, but not before Thurston had time to hit him on the neck between his jaw and shoulder with the length of the stick. Cuthbert screamed and raised his hands to a large, angry swelling on his neck. He fell at Colin's feet, howling. His uncle kicked him aside to free himself to likewise spit. But Thurston was quicker and pushed him away with the end of the walking stick.

Amalric watched, alarmed, and in raking sunlight saw sweat highlighted on Colin's brow. On the ground, Cuthbert moved weakly, his neck bulging, trying to raise himself.

Mistress Yarrow arrived, with greying hair splayed dripping to her waist. Breathlessly she wailed, 'Oh no. I'm sorry. I'm sorry. I'm sorry.' Tears wet her face. Never had Amalric seen her in such a state.

'Take them away, woman,' shouted Thurston, 'before I'm tempted to beat all life out of them.'

Amalric knew he meant it. Since the betrothal incident, Thurston's heart had begun to harden. Cuthbert raised himself and all three staggered off.

Thurston turned to Beatrix. 'Take your mother away and see to her with all the curatives needed. Spare nothing that might do some good.'

'Thurston, my dear,' his wife spoke calmly. 'I've had more foul body fluids on me than I care to remember. I've recovered from the pestilence on one occasion and avoided it on another. I can't believe the good Lord will have me suffer now.'

Amalric was concerned at Matilde's strange resignation.

'But even so,' said Thurston, also remaining excessively calm, 'when you are clean, go to Father Luke and see what he can offer.'

'Ah, physician!' Father Luke had obviously seen the commotion from afar and appeared at the door. 'So now you are saying, when all else fails, try faith. A turnaround for you, I think.'

Thurston smiled wanly. 'Yes, you've caught me out. I'm extremely worried, Father. Cuthbert and Colin Scarthe have all the signs of pestilence. Cuthbert spat at Matilde. Foul substance from the lungs.'

'Then I'll speak with your wife. If the worst should happen, she will not die unshriven; her passage through purgatory will be short.'

They were coldly talking of death! The thought of his sister confessing her sins, preparing herself for death, nearly broke Amalric's heart; the pain of it was real.

Amalric, Thurston and Father Luke met together to discuss the threat of disease to the village. Amalric felt daunted by the knowledge and determination of the other two men. He added little.

'We need to close down the village,' said the priest, 'but we need Lord de Horesby's permission to do that. I fear Master Edwin will be too lazy to organise it.'

The accusatory tone surprised Amalric; the pestilence's return seemed to be giving rise to bitterness in these, his most gentle of friends.

Thurston became the competent physician, but his resentment showed. 'We will demand it. The Scarthes have put us at severe risk, damn them, and we must try to avoid further contact.'

Father Luke nodded agreement. 'Aye. Their act was, at least, attempted murder. They could face hell for eternity.'

Thurston ignored the priest's prophecy and considered more earthly consequences. 'I hope our village folk have not been to Dunghill recently to dump their rubbish. The miasmas are horrendous and the place constantly buzzes and squeaks with pernicious insects and rodents.'

Amalric thought of Mistress Yarrow and how she must be tormented almost beyond reason every day with the filth of the place.

The seriousness of the situation eventually filtered through the villagers' complacency. Alerted to the familiar danger, they prepared to exist on what their own gardens provided, or work alone at the strips. Lord de Horesby forced Edwin to organise clearing the old road skirting the village, so that travellers would pass, albeit with some difficulty, around rather than through it. Father Luke held services outside the church and had a new pestilence pit dug. Thurston lived alone to avoid taking contagion into Warren Horesby while he attended the pestilential sick of Dunghill and elsewhere; Lord de Horesby was only too pleased to allow him to use the bare little cottage inside the manor gate.

As always, Thurston's confidant was Amalric, and in quiet moments they would sit some distance apart outside the cottage, chatting.

'I diligently peer at old manuscripts through my occularies, and fill up new ones. Cleanliness of body and clothing seem important, as is wearing a mouth and nose mask stuffed with sweet-smelling herbs. But I have no proof. I totally discount superstitious nonsense – dried frog, bats' ears and so on. I've ceased bleedings. Often the supposed cure is worse than the disease. I've concluded that many people will catch it and a few will not. For the unfortunates, I have no cure, just something to ease their passing.'

'But more bothers you.'

'Am, I fear for Matilde. She was so ill in the Great Pestilence. Piercing her buboes was the worst thing I've ever had to do. I was in love with her and hated harming her, yet I wanted to do everything I could to save her. When I look back, I feel that we were all so young. What is it now, some twenty years? I was elated at first that I'd cured her but then horrified by her disability that resulted. The truth is, although like us she's survived the pestilences twice now, I fear she may be too weak to cope with another. Oh, Am, Mat works too hard with her healing. She's thin, eats little and is in a woman's difficult years.'

'Could she suffer? It's been days since she was spat at.'

'Am, I don't know,' Thurston said with force. 'I don't know. I'm frightened. This illness changes slightly with each return. There's been coughs and no coughs, unbearable throat pain then none, puking blood then none. Sometimes people have caught it from someone else in a day, another time in two weeks. But always buboes and black flesh have appeared.'

Amalric felt fear and uncertainty hovering over Warren Horesby as everyone waited for someone to become ill. But sunrises passed without a hint of disease. The spittle that had been the death knell for little Bosa in the pestilence of 1361 didn't seem to have the same effect on Matilde. It seemed as if she and the rest of the villagers had been spared. Most of them saw it as a miracle; God's mercy as a return for their diligence.

Amalric worried less and less about his sister and the villagers, but more and more about his own work. Who would want to think of coloured windows when pestilence peered through them once more? Bit by bit, his dream was being eroded. He knew too that Beatrix would be disappointed not to while away a few hours in his workshop. Thurston insisted she be alone most of the time, away from possible contagion, not least because she was with child.

On the eleventh day after the spittle landed on Matilde's face, Amalric and Hendric were in the workshop sorting colours for a new window. Line drawings took up half the space of the table, small pieces of coloured glass the other half. The day was heavy, hot and humid. The sky was a thin grey. Nothing stirred. Noah lay panting outside, his water bowl empty.

'I'll bring water for you, lad,' called Amalric. He was pouring it when Beatrix rushed up to him. She was unkempt, her eyes bloodshot, her face worked with distress.

'Mother has died,' she said. 'I must fetch Father Luke.'

Hendric heard. Together he and his father asked in unison, 'The pestilence?'

Without answering, Beatrix ran, heedless of her swelling abdomen, to the church, her skirts catching against long, dry, wilting grass. Hendric followed her.

Amalric sagged onto a stool by the doorway. His beloved sister, gone. Somehow expected; somehow not expected. He watched as, in the waving heat, three figures seemed to glide out of the church door, under the yew tree, through the gate and up the hill. He felt compelled to follow and struggled on his scarred legs faster than for many months. Noah trotted after him.

At the doctor's home he found Matilde slouched silently in a chair in the physic room. Noah sniffed the hem of her gown and whined. Beatrix threw herself into her uncle's arms.

Thurston stood by his wife's side, tears streaming down his ashen face. 'She found a lump in her groin and armpit when she awoke. Death came to her too soon. Quietly. Beatrix *must* stay away from her body.'

Amalric once more recognised the reasoning of the doctor. It would soon enough be replaced by deep grief. He guided Beatrix away.

Father Luke did what a priest had to do at such times with a little pot of oil and prayers. Istrid, alone, risked her own life preparing her aunt for burial. Matilde was unceremoniously laid in the newly dug pit in the church grounds that had gapingly awaited its first occupant. Amalric stood on the edge, comforted by thinking she would be there to welcome others. Who knew, he could be heading there himself soon? Thurston stood far off, his face like carved stone. Beatrix too stood safely aside, weeping.

A few days later, Amalric learned she had lost her child.

Eventually, the pestilence left the area and, surprisingly, had not been as rampant as expected. The Warren Horesby villagers had avoided it by simply staying at home and not going to unsavoury places where it was known to be. Dunghill, however, lost many, including Mistress Yarrow's son, Cuthbert, and brother, Colin. Amalric wondered if her stern composure had finally cracked – he felt sorrow for her.

Like other survivors, Amalric praised God for a further deliverance from the pestilence's clutches. But his relief was soon overcome by new anxieties when heavy rains came. Water ran down Warren Horesby's street like a river, bringing with it stones and branches, and small dead animals; it came within inches of his home at the front and also at the back when the Ripple Brook broke its banks. Farming land became a quagmire. Crops suffered from blight. Animals began to suffer a murrain. The pestilence pit swilled with black water; Amalric alerted Father Luke and they worked hard to fill part of it in before Matilde's corpse rose as a spectre, causing an outrage.

A meagre autumn and winter loomed ahead for Warren Horesby. The villagers shifted from gratitude to God for overlooking their sins to the realisation that they had not escaped His wrath at all. They became angry. Among the tavern drinkers, as seeds of grain rotted on the stalks, Amalric saw seeds of doubt in the Church sown among the peasants. Father Luke prayed an apology for their sins excessively, but trust in the Church had already begun to crack. The villagers began to mutter opinions contrary to the authorities over them.

New wounding had opened scars of grief in Amalric, paining his chest. Hendric had done his best to be optimistic in the face of his father's misery, but they were struggling to maintain a supply of work; in fact, they were barely surviving. Hendric decided to go to Beverley with Nathan, their workshop assistant, to see how things were going on with new building work at the minster; glaziers might be needed. After all, the Faceby name was well known there for repairs to the windows.

Amalric was glad to be alone in the workshop. The village was silent. Warm air drifted in through the open door, gifting his nose with sad, sharp autumnal odours: fallen leaves, rotting plants, mushrooms, woodsmoke. As if aware that his master needed cheering, Noah sniffed at the corners of the room and was surprised by the sudden emergence of a mouse from the daub. It disappeared rapidly back. The dog amusingly tried to fit his nose into the hole, without success, then clawed at it, finally pushing his paw into the darkness. He withdrew it, and downward ears registered comic disappointment.

'They're wilier than you, lad,' smiled Amalric. Mice had always played a part in the continuation of life. Carrying on, regardless of other traumas.

'Hello, Uncle Amalric.' Beatrix's shadow appeared in the doorway. 'I waited till Hendric had left and you were alone. Uncle, I need your advice.'

Amalric looked up, a little annoyed at having his reverie disturbed. 'Oh, not a husband-and-wife tiff,' he said, and inwardly groaned. He had thought Beatrix was beginning to pick up, but today she looked pale and drawn. His annoyance disappeared. Losing her mother and child had been hard for her. 'What is it, lass? Here, sit down.' He pulled a stool from under the table.

'No, Uncle, not a tiff.'

She sat and he saw she was clasping a small phial in her hands.

'I was feeling a little better today and so I decided to tidy up our physic room. Da is asleep, being very down, so I started with his mess first. His apothecary cupboard was a jumble. I noticed a phial of his special pain-relief potion was missing – you know how precious the phials are and I always save them when empty. Father never gets round to it, he's so disorganised. But this time, I didn't think much of it as he'd probably broken it and thrown it out. Then when I came to Ma's childbirth stuff, I found this.' Her eyes appealed for understanding as she held up an empty phial. 'See, the stopper is loose. It was hidden among women's potions in Mother's cupboard, where Father would never look.'

'Oh, aye?'

'It's father's pain-relieving potion! See, there's a tiny drop left in the bottom.'

Amalric screwed his eyes to see it through the wavy, discoloured glass. 'Ma must have stored it.'

'I don't understand the importance of that.' Her uncle was now impatient to know the point she was making. 'Just tell me, lass.'

'I think Mother killed herself, Uncle. This is Father's missing phial of pain-relief potion. I think she drank as much as she could when the buboes came, and before it took effect, put the phial in her cupboard hoping no one would suspect what she'd done. Then she took herself to the chair and let it overwhelm her, hoping Da would think she'd died of the pestilence.'

Amalric felt himself freeze, unable to connect with the news. Beatrix hovered in front of him, her face wet and her nose dripping. Then the full realisation dawned – his sister had chosen her only way out. Her survival from the Great Pestilence had left its mark and she could not face it again.

'What shall I do, Uncle? To kill oneself is a dreadful sin. Though she's buried in the pestilence pit, it's consecrated ground. What will it mean? Re-bury her? Confiscate her goods and chattels? There are laws, aren't there? Do we have to tell Father Luke?'

'Shush, lass. No need to panic. Here, let's 'ave a drink of ale and think.' He bent to pick up a jug keeping cool in the shadows.

'Beatrix, my dear, maybe this was the right thing for your mother. She suffered a great deal the first time, more than twenty years ago. She was too weak this time to face it all again.'

'But suicide. She'll be damned for ever.'

'It was a ghastly thought. Amalric tried to alleviate the horror. 'Well, for one thing, your father won't know she killed herself. Another is that Father Luke had already given her the Last Rites.'

'Aha. My daughter and friend drinking the hours away?' Thurston was at the doorway.

'Da! What are you doing here?'

'I woke and sought you. Seeing your cleaning task in its early stages and not finding you, I guessed you would be here. It's natural to find solace with one who also mourns. But what's amiss, you both look unusually perturbed? What's that you have there?'

Amalric put his hand over his niece's on her lap, the one clasping the phial. Truth was always of the utmost importance to Thurston. 'Beatrix has a concern. She's in a reet muddle. She's found an empty phial of your pain-reliever among the childbirth jars and phials.'

Thurston leaned with his hands on the table. White chalk dust from the edge rubbed off onto his robe. He patted it, spreading more. His expression was unreadable. He dropped his head to his chest. 'So... you are surmising that she killed herself?' he said quietly. 'Well, she did.'

Amalric and Beatrix did not respond.

'She did,' Thurston repeated emphatically. He turned away from the table. His long gown gave him the elegance of a professional man, but its worn and grubby condition showed something else. Amalric saw the physician who was unassailable on the surface but who was spent inside.

'Did you think that I would not know my wife?' His tone was cold. 'Did you think that as a physician I would not see the signs: her imbalanced humours, sweating, headache, soreness in her neck, under her arms, groin, blood streaking her pee. I consulted the planetary chart. But I saw it chiefly in her eyes. After suffering the Great Pestilence, I knew she could not bear it again. I'd noticed a few days before that a phial of my pain-relief concoction was missing.' He looked at his daughter. 'You see, I'm not so disorganised as you think. I ignored it. It was that which killed her, I'm sure of it. Hippocrates urged physic doctors to do no harm, but which was the greater harm for Matilde? As physicians do, I studied theology before physic and know what taking one's own life means in the eyes of the Church. *I* understand the body as a shell God has given us which must be considered along with the soul. I have no evidence of life after death, only evidence of the pains of life, so I work only with those. My sorrow is that I let my own wife deal with her anguish alone, sparing me of blame.'

For a while, the three of them sat in bewildered silence, then Thurston said, 'I'll go and find Father Luke. It'll be up to him whether he informs the magistrate, or bishop; whichever he chooses.'

Amalric and Beatrix watched as Thurston walked over to the church and disappeared into the porch. While awaiting his return, they aimlessly prepared the table for a new window. More chalk dust was sprinkled on the surface and drops of water added to give a firm, smooth surface for drawing. Amalric felt an ache of creativity; his next saint would have a face that showed an understanding of both body and soul pain. It would be seen in screwed eyes, a furrowed brow and downturned mouth. It may likely be an angry face. Jesus could be angry in His pain; why not a saint?

Thurston returned, drooped onto the stool and put his face in his hands. Tears fell between his fingers. 'Father Luke is a kind man. As no one saw Matilde take the poison, there's no proof she intended to kill herself. He said he'd visit her at the pestilence pit at night when he would not be seen, pray over her and sprinkle holy water. The church grounds hold all types of people, he said, Matilde would be an asset, no matter the manner of her death. He is an honest man and let slip he may, in time, regret his benevolence should the Church authorities find out and disapprove. But things are bad *now* – he said – death may claim any of us unexpectedly and we would all wish for compassion. He said these days, suicide is not rare and God alone will punish as He sees fit. He is forgiving. I hope Father Luke's right. Strangely, I left feeling sorry for *him* – his role is a hard one.'

Chapter Eighteen

Amalric stood at the bottom of Warren Horesby village by the mill, squinting through lightly clouded sunlight at cultivated strips, coppiced woods and grazing land. He was resting from a 'leg-stretcher' to loosen his burn scars. Multiple shades of green formed a background to red silken poppies, purple-blue cornflowers, sparkling yellow buttercups, dandelions, fluffy meadowsweet and others forming a riot of summer colour. Butterflies danced over them. Buzzing sounds came from every direction. Two skylarks sang high above. Creamy grain swayed plump on stalks; there would be a good harvest this year. The pestilence had not been known in noteworthy intensity for eight years. Village unrest had settled to an indistinct, tolerable tension. Glazing commissions had levelled enough to keep body and soul together. Amalric felt happy, almost melting into his surroundings. Most wonderful for him was that Beatrix had finally safely given birth to healthy twins a few months before, a boy and a girl. It was of course sad that Matilde had not known her grandchildren, and Beatrix had felt acutely the loss of her loving support.

Whistling a tune, Amalric continued his walk, joining the main path where he saw his friend on horseback.

'Ee, you look grand, Thurston. A new robe, eh? And blood red. A reet venerable physic man. It matches them tired eyes,' Amalric beamed.

His friend grinned back. 'Aye. Like your grey tunic matches the shadows under yours.' They clasped hands. 'I'm returning from days in King's-Town on Hull where I collected it among other physic things transported from Oxford.'

'Well, it's a fine garment.'

'Aye, well, my other was threadbare as you well know, and badly stained. These days I must look the part so that my research into the pestilence will bear credence. A physician in an old threadbare, stained robe gives a message of failure, while a crisp, modern one spells success. Would that I had the money it indicates I ought to have.'

'You should ask more for your services and not give away some treatments for free.'

'I can't, Am. Good health means able to work; bad health means sinking into poverty, even starvation. And there's many around not recovered from recent near starvation.'

'You're a good Christian, Thurston.'

'You know my work doesn't entirely support that. I can't pay much heed to the soul when the body rots around a person. Though I agree that the soul needs attention to prevent adulterations of the body.'

'I detect you're feeling just a little uncomfortable in your blood-red garment. You're a mite pensive.'

'Well, I had to bow to the trend. Red is a sign of my profession, especially now that cutting, or surgery, has become a challenge.' Thurston rubbed sweat from his brow. 'I'm a mite warm in this fine wool. I see flowers are open at their greatest; high noon is a poor time to be travelling in such a garment on a hot day.'

'Father, Father!' The shout came from Beatrix as she breathlessly ran to them, her figure still buxom after the twins' birth. Thank goodness, I've found you.' Her face glowed with exertion and a twinkling expression. They were instantly cheered with pleasant curiosity.

'Beat, my dear – what is it that causes you to come running with such a face?' said Thurston indulgently.

Beatrix bent with her hands on her knees to get her breath through laughter.

'There is a traveller at the tavern; his two servants are asking for help with an ailment of his.' She glanced at her father's garment and smiled perceptively. 'He might be wealthy. He's on a journey on horseback northward from London and has developed a great furuncle. He's heard of you.'

Amalric's smile instantly fell into open-mouthed horror. A bubo? The pestilence? No! Not again. He looked at Thurston. His friend seemed unmoved.

'Oh, yes?' Thurston appeared to know what was to follow. 'Where is this lesion?'

'On his fundament.' Her mischievous smile grew large. 'It's too embarrassing for him to let *me* deal with it. I've put him into your physic room at home.'

Thurston turned to his friend and put a hand on his shoulder. 'Fear not, Am, 'twill be but an eruption caused by his backside rubbing too long in the saddle, or a fistula – something a little more complicated. Common in travelling folk. So... he's wealthier than a pilgrim, Beat?'

'I believe him to be a king's man, from the embroidery on his tunic. He has a couple of servants with him. He says he'll pay any amount to be rid of the pain and discomfort.'

'Ah, so many say that, and once the healing is done, they think again. However, luckily, my new robe will impress,' Thurston said sarcastically. 'He will have to stay a few days while the obnoxious matter draws to the surface and can be lanced. Or maybe it's the kind of thing that requires "surgery".' He winked at Amalric. 'Come, Beatrix, let's go to do the job. You may make the poultices for me if we need them.'

Amalric watched his friend and niece go up the road together. How he loved them.

'The fellow is well known in court circles,' said Edwin to Amalric the following day as they chatted by the manor gate. Amalric's Latin skills had been required to decipher official papers, but Edwin's interests lay more in future possibilities than present paperwork. 'It'll be good for me to have a contact at court.'

'Mm. I expect you've been toadying.' Amalric was disappointed that the traveller lodged at the manor rather than the tavern. On the other hand, Edwin would hear only dull tales of London's fashionable elite, while tavern talk with the man's servants would be far more enlightening.

Edwin feigned hurt. 'Come, come, brother, I'm attending to his needs, that is all: a comfortable guest room, fine foods, wine. I keep the fire going because he shivers with a fever. I'm generous in that regard.'

'But you did the toadying?'

'Yes. I'm the host, after all.' Edwin quickly changed the subject. 'His clothes are very fine. The fashion news is most interesting. Long toes on shoes have been seen overseas – for such as me. I must speak with the Beverley cobblers.'

'So Warren Horesby's Jake Cobbler will not be good enough?' At this inference of disloyalty to the village, Amalric gleefully observed Edwin's lips curl. 'Anyway, of more concern to me… the traveller's servants say that trouble is brewing down south, what with crippling taxes for war, the Church being too rich, grasping landowners… Such talk will breed discontent up *here*. Artisans and peasants are losing out. It's not reet. Folk are fed up with strugglin'.'

'Aye, well, brother, you'll do alright with your windows. There's ever more monastery churches wanting bigger windows.' Edwin's face took on the callous aspect that so riled Amalric.

'That's as maybe. But for me, only repair work at Meaux Abbey, though Hendric keeps trying for work at Beverley Minster. Most contracts are still for parish churches where the poorer folk want some beauty. I'm happy with that.'

'Happy! Beauty? Pah! That's talk too grandiose. What use is beauty to the peasant?'

The doom painting in Warren Horesby church flashed into Amalric's mind: sinners falling to hell, the righteous being carried up to heaven. Rich and poor — all being judged equally. Everyone deserved some beauty in their lives, not only the rich. 'Lord de Horesby keeps Clara and you in fine clothes, he pays you to keep up his hunting land and woods, breed fine animals and gather rents. You *take*, Edwin, and seldom give back to those beneath you. Most of our villagers have been near to starving many times. Some still are. Can't you see that?'

Edwin was unaffected by Amalric's tirade. 'Do I hear a note of jealousy?' he said with a smirk.

'You do not. I've no need of fashion nor great wealth.' But in his heart, Amalric recognised his own tinge of envy. He still loved coloured glass passionately, but it saddened him that large coloured windows were increasingly being seen as a statement of wealth, their beauty sometimes inconsequential. In any case, he simply did not have the money to enlarge his business to cope with such extravagance.

'I've lately been hearing about the great window that was installed in Gloucester Abbey some years after the Great Pestilence, filling the wall behind the high altar. With your attitude, it seems to me you'll never work on such a thing. Was that not once a dream of yours?'

Amalric suddenly felt a hot, crushing disappointment. He'd recently heard that work on the new east end of York Minster had been stopped through lack of funds and who knew what other troubles. It inexplicably bothered him. How was it that Edwin could use words like a dagger? He turned away from his brother and left him standing at the gate. Amalric felt as if he was bleeding.

Less than a moon's cycle after his arrival, the king's travelling man, Master Geoffrey, was outside the tavern with Thurston and Beatrix, sitting at a table in the sun with a jug of ale beside them. He sat with one buttock taking most of his weight, but his face showed little sign of discomfort. Amalric walked to meet them. Three loaded horses grazed on the green with two servants lolling idly by. Noah went to sniff the horses, who snorted with condescension.

'Come, Amalric, this is Master Geoffrey,' said Thurston, smiling and indicating the travelling man.

He's been paid, thought Amalric; either that or Geoffrey is a scholar. Thurston was always cheered by chatting with educated men.

Geoffrey stood politely to greet Amalric and then sat back on the bench, cautiously positioning himself. The king's golden embroidered emblem shimmered on his tunic. He started to speak.

Amalric failed to understand the courtly accent, so unlike the Yorkshire brogue. 'I'm sorry – I didn't get wha…'

'Ah, *I'm* sorry. I'm being most impolite. My London voice is not easily recognised up here. I'm a poet by talent and inclination and can slip easily into several ways of speaking.' Geoffrey cleared his throat and changed his accent. 'Poetry pays nowt to speak of but I have connections and am travelling on a king's commission. Your friend has healed me, almost, thanks be. And this young woman who I believe to be your niece has dressed my wound with amazing skill. She knows more of me than most women, save my wife.' He tipped his head back and laughed. 'While up in these parts, I decided to go to York; a sort of pilgrimage to St William's tomb. The northern saints interest me as much as the southern ones. If I had been able to bear it that far, I would have prayed at his tomb to be healed, but as it was…'

Thurston sighed theatrically, 'Your pain and discomfort were so much that you had to put your faith in physic instead. When the Church fails, physic is a good second best.'

Amalric was amused by the age-old argument.

'Nay, physician. Your name has spread. Your honest nature is refreshing. Many doctors of physic see money before healing. I may write about them one day.' He turned to Amalric. 'And your trade too, is poetry of sorts, I hear. Your niece has been telling me of your windows with much enthusiasm, and your passion for coloured glass. I would like to have seen the east end of York Minster. I believe there is to be a huge window, but work has been held up and shows no sign of starting again. Possibly troubled finances.'

More about large windows! Amalric made himself keep calm. 'Yes. I make coloured windows. Beatrix helps me when she can.' He looked fondly at his niece.

'She speaks most poetically about them. She's described the colours to me most beautifully. It has stirred me.' He looked up to the sky as if inspired: '"Phoebus her mass of tresses with a gleam / Had dyed in burnish from his golden stream",'[10] he said in a courtly, exaggerated manner – his arms extended as if greeting a maiden.

Amalric and Thurston looked blankly at Geoffrey, but Beatrix's eyes were fixed intently on him.

'Oh, Master Geoffrey. That's beautiful.'

'Well, don't you lose sight of your talents, my dear girl.' Amalric had the odd feeling that this comment was actually aimed at him. 'God-given talents are valuable.'

Amalric wondered what that meant, but before he had the opportunity to ask, Geoffrey stood to leave.

'Goodbye – I'm grateful. I'll remember you, physician, and your blood-red robe, and you, woman of healing and glass, and you, poet of colour.'

---

[10] Geoffrey Chaucer, 'The Physician's Tale', *The Canterbury Tales* (Nevill Coghill, trans; Penguin Classics 2003).

Chapter Nineteen

1378 Warren Horesby
Early autumn

Amalric approached Michaelmas with settled feelings. The harvesting was finished, and the villagers' dues had been paid to the Church and manor. Starvation would be held at bay. The days were shortening. It would soon be time to hunker down, with food stocks in lofts and joints of meat hanging from rafters to catch smoke rising from constant central fires. Wood, peat and dry cowpats would be stored for fuel. Cows would be brought into living areas to provide heat when necessary. Soon the end of the yearly cycle and the start of another would be celebrated; the painted St Michael weighing souls on the church west wall would be feted, with fairs and jollity in abundance.

Amalric stood outside Beatrix's back door in sunshine, leaning on his walking stick, watching little Ava and Asa. He felt immensely proud of them. Although twins, they were clearly individuals. Asa favoured Hendric in looks and Ava her mother, with wild blonde hair.

'Your Istrid should be back soon with the cart,' called Beatrix from inside. 'She's promised to bring me some fresh pies from the market. They'll make a change from old vegetables and dried-up chicken. Will you stay to eat, Uncle?'

'Aye, lass. How could I refuse a Beverley pie?'

'Oh, Uncle, it's so good to have the harvest put away. Father says he knows of no pestilence anywhere up here in the north. We can feel confident of getting through the winter.'

'Da, Beat, are you there?' The returning Istrid called through the doorway. She dropped from the cart and delved into a sack. 'The pies were fresh out of the oven. They smell wonderful. The twins'll love them.'

Amalric helped his daughter unload the cart. Beatrix made a hot herb drink for them all and they sat to eat. After each market visit, Istrid poured out news, which generally required a few days before Amalric had absorbed it all.

'It seems the French recently invaded southern England without much success. The papacy is to split so we have two popes: one in Rome, one in Avignon... and the Scots are raiding again. It's being said that this time, they may get as far as here.'

Amalric considered what had been said. He viewed southern problems and those of the Church with equanimity; both could be thought about another day... but the Scots – that was much more serious. Such raids had gone on for years, but usually further north. Now, with such a good harvest and fine weather, maybe they would be tempted to foray as far as Warren Horesby. His equanimity was shaken.

Two weeks later, boys dashed down the hill, slithering on melting hoar frost, their arms flailing and fear in their voices as they shouted a warning that 'strange men' were heading for the village. Amalric was alarmed. On this chill but fine day, most of the Warren Horesby men were at their strips, on manor land or in the forest. Even the miller had left his boy in charge. Both Father Luke and Thurston were at Meaux Abbey. For once, he wished for his brother's presence, but Edwin was away in York.

Amalric hurried up the hill. Apprehension had swept through the women. They'd gathered their small children and girls in doorways. Young boys hovered in front of their homes, unsure of their manly responsibilities. The alewife stood outside the tavern with Beatrix next to her. At the green, the only man besides himself was Joshua Smith, the blacksmith and churchwarden, holding a heavy hammer, moving nervously from foot to foot. Amalric pondered the ineffectiveness of his own workshop poker in his hand; all his other tools were with

Hendric and Nathan at a church down the valley where they were fitting a window. Istrid came to her father's side with her broom. Noah stood by their feet, alert.

Eventually, the frosty silence was broken by snorting and clomping sounds. Six horses, their heads down and breath forming misty clouds around them, entered the top of the village and continued to the green.

Amalric could not identify their livery. The men looked rough, fierce and weary. Two or three had clothing spattered with blood, all with vast amounts of mud. One, with black greasy hair and sweating brow, had a roughly bandaged leg, wet with a filthy discharge which, even at the distance, emitted a necrotic stench with every movement. His shoeless, blue swollen foot hung limply below. A metal cradle was swung over his horse's side containing smoking contents.

'King Alfred's cakes!' Amalric involuntarily blurted out, recognising smouldering lumps of fungus. 'Oh, Lord, help us.'[11]

The leader, a tall, thick-boned man, with an abundant mane of red hair and a profuse, curling beard, turned his head to follow the noise. Amalric involuntarily stepped back. The man leaned forward, making it easier to see how his thick, multicoloured woollen garment folded around him, securely held with a thick belt. Into this was tucked a sword. Slung over his shoulder and tied to his saddle was a prodigious array of other weaponry. He spoke to Amalric, but his words were meaningless. While her father and the villagers stood perplexed, Istrid stepped forward with one defiant hand on her hip and the other holding her broom vertically like a fighting staff.

'We cannot understand a word you say.'

The redhead looked at her, seemingly shocked by her

---

[11] King Alfred's cakes is the common name of a fungus found on trees. It has the appearance of burned bread buns and the name was possibly inspired by the legend of King Alfred burning the cakes he was supposed to be minding. When set alight, the fungus will smoulder for a sufficiently long time to enable the transportation of fire when travelling, even in wet conditions.

boldness. The one with the smouldering fungus looked on lecherously, but the redhead turned angrily to him.

'Come away, lass,' whispered Amalric, behind his daughter.

Just then, Lord de Horesby came stumbling down from the manor. An open fur-lined cloak flapped over his sleep garment. 'What are you doing here?' he said, raising leather-gloved hands in protest.

The man with the smouldering fungus picked a stick with a bulbous end from a pouch in his saddle and put it to the metal cradle. It burst into flame. He stood on his good leg in the stirrup and threatened to throw it at the tavern. 'Food,' he cried loudly.

The alewife screamed. Small children burst into tears.

Lord de Horesby rushed forward. 'There's no need for that,' he said, appealing to the man. 'You'll only spoil the ale you might have had.'

The man nodded agreement and flung the torch onto the low-hanging roof of a cottage nearby, instead. The thatch smoked. A young woman rushed in and came out with a baby before flames took hold.

'Get water,' cried Joshua Smith to some young boys. It was to no avail; the heather thatch burst into flame. Rodents, insects and birds emerged through the grey crackling billows. Heather thatch of many seasons began to fall inside the walls. The raiders roared with malicious laughter. Amalric found his mind returning to the scene in church: devils silhouetted against the flames and smoke of hell. He also recalled way back, rushing into the choking smoke and dropping flames of his own home to save his father's valuable Theophilus manuscript. His chest tightened and his scarred legs felt the flames again.

He nauseously watched raiders drop from their saddles and walk around the women, leering, touching, blowing kisses and rubbing their own bellies to indicate hunger and worse. They got back on their horses, their weapons ready to create more havoc.

Lord de Horesby called to the redhead. 'Stop them! We can

give you food. For the Lord's sake, stop them!'

The redhead leaned towards him in his saddle. 'Aye, for the Lord's sake.' He then spoke slowly, apparently hoping to make himself understood. 'If you'll feed us noo, we'll be awa.' Amalric could not comprehend this man and felt as cold in his bones as the raiders seemed to be in their hearts.

Noah barked hysterically towards the man with the fungus. Amalric knew the strange stench of the man was the cause. The man picked up a smouldering lump from the cradle with his bare hands, viciously kicked his horse forward and threw it. It landed on Noah's back. The dog dashed wildly around in circles yapping, trying to rid himself of the lump which stuck to his hair. The man laughed.

Even through the smell of the flaming house, Noah's burning hair and blistering flesh hit Amalric's nose like a whirlwind. He yelled obscenities and ran to his dog, ready with bare hands to pull off the smoking lump and put out the little flames now getting a stronger hold of the ginger hair – anything to stop the dog's pain.

Suddenly, someone else's hands pushed him away. 'You need those hands, man!' a voice said, and pulled off the fungus with leather-gloved hands. The alewife brought a flagon of ale and poured it over Noah's back. He sagged down and lay whining. A luxurious fur-lined cloak was thrown over him. Amalric sat and put the dog's head on his lap. He rocked back and forth as a torrent of tears, released from years of suppression, poured from his closed eyes.

The redheaded raider sat on his horse in silence, watching the scene. He raised a hand and glared at his men to prevent them from disturbing it.

The crowd of women and children and the blacksmith were silent.

Istrid, with wet face, glared at the redhead and threw her broom in front of him but said nothing. Instead, she went to her father. 'See, Da, Beatrix has gone to prepare her father's physic room. She'll heal Noah.'

Lord de Horesby knelt by Amalric, shivering in his nightshirt, his eyes pink.

The redhead watched. 'It's only a dog!' he said.

Istrid spun round to him, her expression venomous. 'Have you no idea what it means to love?'

The redhead did not answer. Instead, he dropped from his horse and went to Noah. He pushed Amalric away, who fell onto Lord de Horesby. A gasp arose from the villagers. The redhead's five other men stood alert and aggressive.

Amalric was horrified. 'No, no, please!' He keenly felt his own feebleness.

The redhead lifted a hand to quiet him. Then he picked up the dog. Noah whined. Amalric could not bear to look.

'Da, it's fine. Look.' The redhead's men were still sitting on their horses but gazed open-mouthed as they watched their leader carry Noah to Beatrix, who stood waiting at the physic room door. Amalric staggered quickly to catch up so he could hold his dog's flopping paw.

Lord de Horesby also followed. They arrived as the redhead came back out of the door having deposited Noah. Lord de Horesby spoke to him.

'These villagers have no defence against you. They have nothing to give you. I'll feed your men at my manor. It's up to you and them whether you take more from me.' His tone was resigned but he added, 'The church is down the hill, should you need it.'

'Aye. I need a kirk. Sins tae confess. Parched soul.'

Amalric took no heed of the redhead's attempt to communicate and went inside to his dog.

While Beatrix attended to Noah, Amalric listened to the clamour of the raiders feuding among themselves as they made their way up the hill to the manor. Then he carried the bandaged Noah home. A bed was made for him by the fire. Amalric settled him and Istrid put a glass of warm ale in front of her father. She was unusually quiet.

'What happened, lass, when I left with Noah? I expected the

village to be ravaged.'

'The raiders went to the manor, had their fill of food and wine, took some valuables, smashed some glass windows and vessels, and rode off.'

'Just rode off?'

'Aye. Not with their leader, though. He's named as Douglas Redhead. He went to the church and then towards Beverley, leaving his men to go their own way, back north.'

When Thurston returned from Meaux Abbey, he expressed surprise. 'Our village got off lightly. The monks said the raiders have left a wake of burned villages and death all the way from the border to here. They even tried to attack the abbey a few days ago, but the monks saw them off with their own weapon inventions. Going back north, eh?'

'Aye. Our Istrid says five went up north and one to Beverley.'

'Well, it may be the last we see of them. I've heard that York has the pestilence bad again.'

'Oh, no. We've been clear of it for years.'

'It seems it came out of nowhere this time. It's usually moved from south to north, but I'm wondering if this time it's come from the north with the raiders. Did any of them look ill, have coughs?'

'They looked weak, weary, and several were spattered with blood; one had a nasty reeking leg wound.' Amalric saw his physic friend's eyes narrow as he took in the magnitude of what he'd heard.

'It'll come here again, Am, for the fourth time. This new pestilence is even more virulent. We may have it for a year or more.' He stared at Noah, sleeping by the fire. 'It might even affect animals. Don't let your dog roam more than necessary, though with his burn, he'll not want to stray far.'

'Well, at least we have the fairs and jollities to look forward to. We always have a good time at Michaelmas.'

'No, Am. No. The pestilence is too close. Gatherings are far too dangerous. There must be none.' Thurston's voice was raised. He could not remain calm. 'Surely, you've not forgotten how the pestilence spreads among people. I've told you many, many times of my observations of this disease.'

Amalric was silent for a while. Like other villagers, he found it easy to take note of the physician's words when things seemed logical, but increasingly difficult when such logic was forced on to an already hard life. He shrugged his shoulders.

The whole of Yorkshire suffered badly from the pestilence for a whole year. Warren Horesby agonised and grieved. The very old and young accounted for most of the deaths. The burial pit where Matilde lay was filled. Amalric felt yet another contradiction that through the grief of others, he had been consoled; Matilde was not now alone. Maybe *she* found redemption through using her healing skills to comfort the souls now alongside her.

Amalric and those he loved disgruntledly took Thurston's advice to keep away from crowds and gatherings, and survived.

Noah too, survived his burns; Amalric remembered Nesta's treatment of his own burns with maggots and had not feared them when they appeared under the dark, leathery patch of burned skin on the dog's back; they cleansed his wound.

Chapter Twenty

1380 Warren Horesby

At the manor gate, Amalric looked back at the fine building which, he admitted, Edwin had done a good job of maintaining. This day, he'd been asked to repair a damaged window. His brother had been thankfully absent. It had been a rare joy easing lead cames, bent by the force of gales, back into shape and inserting new, small squares of colourless glass – all with the sun warming his hands. Turning to the view of Warren Horesby, his light mood waned; the village had a sad muteness about it. Many homes stood empty; some in ruin. Where once smoke billowed from every cottage fire, creating a grey, wafting veil in the valley, now smoke filtered through far fewer thatched roofs.

He walked down the hill with Noah blissfully sniffing animal droppings. Ahead, he saw Thurston talking to Father Luke.

'Good morrow, both of you. I've just been told by a manor servant that an old man, Oxford taught, was directed to the tavern a short while ago to partake of refreshment. You might like to meet him. We could all go there together for a tipple. You both may enjoy some fresh, learned conversation.' He grinned mischievously. His friends would certainly enjoy seeing a fresh, educated face in the village. He hoped it would cheer them. Many folk passed through, but few could discourse the equal of Thurston and Father Luke.

Father Luke responded by speeding off. 'I'll just have to say noon prayers. I'll say them quickly.'

Thurston beamed with anticipation and he and Amalric walked down the hill together.

A heavy horse with bulging panniers munched dry grass from a patch at the side of the tavern. Sitting outside on a rough bench with a beaker in his hand, a jug of ale and a platter of cheese and bread on a small table by his side, sat a man whose grimy, well-worn scholar's cap tipped to one side on long, white hair. His hair and beard fell untidily onto dark, bedraggled clothing, dusty from travel.

Thurston was the first to greet the stranger. 'Hello, sir. I hear you are of Oxford.'

'I am,' replied the stranger, 'though of late, Lutterworth. And you sir, from your red garb, you are a physician?'

'Yes, an Oxford graduate too.'

Sharp grey eyes above a large aquiline nose pierced Thurston's own. 'Ah, one of those threatened by the rising skills of cutting men. Separating flesh from body often cures, I hear.'

Amalric had expected a southern brogue like Thurston's own, but there was definitely a northern inflection.

Thurston appeared taken aback by the bluntness of this man. 'My name is Thurston... and yours?'

'Ah, Thurston of Oxford. I've heard of you. Have *you* heard of John of Arderne, one of these rising... er... surgeons? You needs watch out. Pee-tasting, bleeding, humours and planets haven't all the answers.' His smile mocked.

'And you?' asked Thurston, bristling a little at the abstruse challenge, but all the same making strong eye-to-eye contact. 'Are *you* John of Arderne? I've had cause to study his treatment for fistula.'

'No. John Wyclif, theologian. They say I've radical ideas, to put it bluntly.'

'Yes, I can believe that!' Thurston had ice in his tone.

Amalric, standing behind Thurston, was enjoying this clash of scholars. Unexpectedly, the bearded face relaxed and smiled.

'I'm journeying home to Hipswell, near Richmond. A rare visit to my family and an escape from my detractors. This may be my last time there. I'm getting too old to travel. After Scottish raiders and pestilence, I'm not certain who's still alive. A cousin, maybe. Mm... I'd like to discuss the pestilence with you.'

The sound of sandals crunching on dry soil alerted Wyclif. 'Ah, who is this in clerical garb?'

Amalric, who till now had been ignored, his artisan status obviously of little interest to the scholar, spoke up. 'It's Father Luke, our village priest,' he said, expecting this to add more fuel to the academic fire.

'Cistercian, I see from his robe. A favourite of popes gone by. High standards.' Wyclif's eyes narrowed. 'Good day to you, Father. I'm John Wyclif.'

Father Luke stopped. 'John Wyclif? *The* John Wyclif?'

'I am. No doubt you've heard of me and my views on the Church.'

'I know they were condemned by the pope. I've read your tracts. You have unorthodox views of the eucharist and you disapprove of teaching by clerics, even the pope. Yet you are a cleric yourself.'

'Yes. Correct, but I take the Bible as the only source that can be relied upon. Not that of popes and other clerics.'

'I don't like your unorthodoxy,' said Father Luke. 'Nearly fourteen hundred years we've had popes, from St Peter himself.'

Amalric could see Father Luke was discomforted. This meeting had perhaps been a mistake. Luke, unlike Thurston, did not have the emotional resilience required when challenged by such a man.

'Well, I'm going further,' said Wyclif, seemingly enjoying the consternation he was causing. 'I wish to translate the Bible from Latin into common spoken language.'

At this, Father Luke became red-faced. He sharply raised a hand to halt the uncomfortable words. A beaker was in danger of being knocked over. Amalric feared a deep conflict between the two theologians. 'Shall we order more ale? Alewife!' he called, before an answer came.

'You mean the lowest peasant should be able to read the

good book and make up his own mind?' persisted Father Luke.

'I do, if he can indeed read. At the very least, it should be read to him in his own language.'

'But it has been in Latin since St Jerome translated it from ancient time. You are no saint, sir!' Father Luke, who'd been standing till now, sank onto a bench.

Wyclif calmly took a long draught of ale that had been laid before him by the buxom alewife, and allowed his statement to sink in. He turned to Amalric and cast his eyes over the leather apron and scarred fingers. 'What is *your* trade?'

'Amalric Faceby, sir, coloured glass window-maker. I read Latin.' He said the latter in defence of the common man for whose soul they seemed to be arguing. 'I write Bible words within the windows.'

'Not so common an artisan, then? Have you seen the work of young John Thornton of Coventry? Lutterworth is not so far from Coventry. I'm frequently in the church there, and though I abhor many of the practices of the clergy, including beautifying worship, I'm drawn to the truth of the young man's depiction of Bible characters – he seems to get to the heart of the common man. Real faces.'

Amalric was astonished at this turnaround in the conversation and was immediately interested. '*I* try to depict real faces.'

Wyclif put his hand up dismissively to silence Amalric. 'Mm. Well, I believe York Minster had planned a big window but funds for it are absent.'

The York window again! Amalric wondered if it would always haunt him. He felt rejected, like a child.

Wyclif looked to Father Luke to carry on the religious discourse, but Amalric saw Luke's face disturbingly turn from red to purple and his hands twist together in agitation.

'Better take your priest friend back to his church,' Wyclif said imperiously to Amalric. 'He's not so strong as I thought he was.'

Thurston nodded agreement. He too had developed unconventional ideas of physic, and Amalric knew he would delight in Wyclif's arguments. With Father Luke removed, the increasingly tense atmosphere would burst and calm like an ale bubble.

'Do you follow Aristotle? Did he have a view on pestilences?' were the last words Amalric heard as he accompanied Father Luke down the hill in silence.

The priest disappeared into the church without comment. Amalric felt oddly alone and suddenly aware that, with the words of the stranger, daily life was about to change. He was glad when Noah trotted towards him from the roadside undergrowth expecting his ears to be rubbed and the burned patch gently touched.

The day after meeting John Wyclif, Amalric looked out towards the church. After a recent downpour, the yew tree shone with cleanliness and deep colour; a symbol of the Church and permanence. The church gate was open, swinging from the wattle fence. 'Come, Noah, let's have a stroll and see who's in there.'

The porch was warm with collected sunshine, but beyond the open oak door, the building was cool. After the glare of sunshine, Amalric had to accustom himself to the dimness. Eventually, St Edmund and all the other painted images emerged as if from hiding.

A low muttering sound came from a kneeling figure in front of the altar: Father Luke at prayer. Amalric sat and waited. After a few minutes the priest raised himself and turned.

'Ah! Good morning, Amalric.' His face seemed to sag; his eyes were red-rimmed, his expression doleful.

'Luke, what ails you?'

'We've long been friends, Amalric.'

'What do you mean?'

Luke settled himself on the stone bench beside his friend. 'Am, my time here has been wonderful. I've almost been part of your family, but the priest in me is saying it's time to go. I can no longer help this village with an honest heart. Rest assured, I'll always pray for you.' Luke gathered his thoughts.

'About one hundred and fifty years ago the pope declared Cistercians to be of the highest standard, as Master Wyclif said, a truly efficient order held up as an example to others. Austere. But things have changed. Now some Cistercians decorate their churches and make lots of money from wool and produce. Worse, there is more than one pope; how can *that* be tolerated?

'And the world we live in is changing too, especially since the pestilences: peasants demand more return for their work, landowners disallow the use of common land in favour of wool, young women flagrantly bare their necks and young men lack discretion with their tight hose. The knights happily go off to kill. We have all sinned mightily, Amalric. God's pestilence lurks to punish our sins, again and again. People know the Church is helpless.'

'Oh, Luke.' Amalric was perturbed by this outpouring of distress. What could he say to a man of deep faith?

The priest went on. 'I feel the beginnings of dissent, even in this village. I know for certain rebellion is simmering in Beverley. When I was recently at Meaux Abbey, news from their community in Beverley was of meetings in the marketplace with lots of shouting about landlords and taxes, loss of common land. There is a threat that Beverley men will meet with York men. They are fired up by news of rogue Kentish men.'

'But to be fair, Luke,' Amalric interrupted, 'we *are* being bled dry by taxes. We pay far too much for the king to wage war in France, a land we don't know.'

'Aye, true, Am. But I feel the tension in my bones. It frightens me. That man Wyclif was my last straw. Encouraging uneducated peasants to think for themselves with regard to their faith! The prospect of the most holy of books open for all to read is an abomination! My views do not accord with those of the village. I believe my life may be at stake. Driven men are quick to draw their weapons, even though they're only scythes, sickles and pruning knives.'

'Nay, Luke. Not a priest. That would be a monstrous crime.'

'Aye, well, I'm going before I find out. I'd steer clear of

Beverley, if I were you.'

'I can't. Hendric is seeking work there.'

'So be it.' Father Luke began to bite his bottom lip, and his expression softened. 'Am, I must say, even as a Cistercian, I can appreciate the beauty of your work and see it as a route to the soul. The only thing of any sense that Wyclif said, and which you should heed, is that there is a glass man in Coventry with new ways of looking into the human soul with his depictions of real men. Your own work has shown such ways. Do not deviate, tempted by lesser work.'

Amalric was astounded at the slackening of Cistercian values. 'Luke, I don't know what to say. I'll miss you. You've stayed some thirty years after the Great Pestilence, when you were only supposed to tide the village over, and you have bent to our ways. But before you leave, forgive me just one question.'

'Aye – go on.'

'Way back, you said Nesta would never do anything wrong "willingly". What did you mean by that?'

'Ah… that we all do things that cause our conscience to suffer in later life. Things that under different circumstances we would not do "willingly". That is all.'

The priest's gaze had the familiar looking-into-the-soul aspect about it. Amalric felt uncomfortable and knew there would not be a satisfying answer.

'That is all passed, Amalric. Forget and forgive. And forgive me, I'm an ageing man unable to bend any more, too set in my ways to fully understand the turmoil of the souls in this village. I need the calm of the cloister. Your brother will see you right with a new priest.'

Amalric was not so sure.

Amalric stood by the church gate with Noah at his side and watched his friend, Father Luke, walk away up the road, a sack of his small, lowly possessions slung over his shoulder. His Cistercian habit of undyed wool swung from side to side with the gait of a tired, ageing man. A few folk waved as he passed them. Amalric felt a restlessness in the air.

Unrest or no, there was glass cutting to be done. Precious blue glass was on the table, laid over a drawing of St John the Baptist: a small window for a small church. Blue for the sky. The glass had to be cut with a heated cutting tool and the edges trimmed with a grozing iron.

The little hearth had been brought to life with bellows. When the cutting tool was hot enough, he applied the metal tip to the glass, ready to follow the drawn black line underneath. He pressed too hard and a crack spread across the sheet of glass like fragile pond ice. It was expensive glass and now the profits would be negligible. He angrily pushed the broken pieces to one side and sat heavily on a stool.

Small jobs and an unfulfilled dream were not how he had wanted his life's work to be. He looked at the face he'd drawn on the table, that of the saint who had suffered in the desert and then baptised Christ. In the sun-beaten, emaciated face with tired eyes, Amalric saw the insignificance of his own ambition against the significance of this man. It became clear to Amalric that his own life had been about what he aspired to be, rather than what he was. He had to face the fact that his inadequate business sense and stubborn refusal to follow conventional styles was not up to achieving more than a small window for a small church. John had set Jesus on His path. Maybe the purpose of his own life was to set others on a path, denying his own dreams. He threw down his tools and decided to go across the road to the church.

'Noah! Come, lad!' The dog appeared.

In desultory mood, Amalric stood in the nave. He would miss Father Luke. Without a priest, how would he be able to communicate with God? Would a new priest arrive soon? Had Edwin even bothered to try to find one?

The little birds twittered and flew about the rafters, unconcerned; Noah eyed them with mild curiosity. The east window glass glowed with subdued colour while the colourless glass squares of a south nave window caught a burst of sunshine. Maybe if he could make a further coloured window for this church at his own expense, it might cheer himself and the villagers. He could use up some of the cut-off pieces he kept in tubs, too small for larger windows.

'Good day, my son.'

Amalric spun round to see a middle-aged man in a grey habit. Under his paunch was a rope belt with three knots in the hanging end: the Franciscan symbols of poverty, chastity and obedience.

'Ah. I've startled you. I am employed by Lord de Horesby's reeve, Master Edwin Faceby, to serve this parish... er... temporarily. And you are?'

Amalric looked askance at the friar, not caring for the tone of superiority in his voice. 'Good morrow to you. I'm Amalric Faceby, master glazier, the reeve's brother. I own the business across the road.'

'I'm Friar Swale, named after the river near my home – from the Franciscan friary in York.' His expectant gaze was unnerving.

'Welcome, Friar Swale. Father Luke has been replaced sooner than I expected.' Amalric sought for words. 'Er... I was just wondering if sometime I might make a new coloured window for the nave here.'

'Would it be costly?'

'No. It would be at my own expense.'

'Mm. As you wish. If the villagers want it, I cannot object; church buildings are not my concern. I'm off to make a tour of the village.' He skirted around Noah, who stared benignly at him. 'I don't care for dogs. Good day.' He swept out.

The encounter left Amalric feeling faintly perplexed. The Franciscan order generally preferred to work among the poor in towns. He'd heard the order was facing difficulties within its organisation and wondered if Friar Swale was something of an outcast, seeking obscurity for a while. And there was yet another contradiction; should a friar so dedicated to life and nature dislike a harmless pet dog?

Chapter Twenty-one

1381 Warren Horesby
Spring

'Mornin', son.' Amalric put down the bellows as Hendric arrived at the workshop after two days away in Beverley. 'Istrid tells me there was trouble at the tavern last evenin'. She heard about it at the well.'

'Aye, Da. There's no secrets at that well. It's amazin' what them women find out.' They both smiled. 'I was with cousin Robert slakin' my thirst after the journey home.'

Amalric immediately felt troubled. Robert, Edwin's eldest son, even in his middle years was a troublemaker.

'Robert was deep in his cups and started talking about peasants gettin' above themselves. It nearly ended in a brawl.'

'Aye. It's best to stay out of it.'

'Trouble is, Da, with bein' in the middle, we free artisans are viewed with suspicion from both sides. Sometimes I support one side an' then the other. I say too much.'

Amalric nodded agreement; it was a hard position to be in. Hendric's slightly bruised cheek was evidence of that.

'Anyway, Da, I've some good news. I've secured a south window repair at Beverley Minster.'

'That's reet good, lad. There's a lot of work there, especially with the new-build at the west end, but it's like getting blood out of limestone to get a contract. Well done. You may be able to afford a treat for them twins o' yours.' But at the back of his mind was Father Luke's warning – stay away from Beverley.

The April sun had not yet risen as Amalric, Hendric and Beatrix set off on horseback to Beverley, with Noah barking his disappointment at being left behind. The horse panniers were loaded with white boards, various-sized measuring rods, plumblines, lead point, compasses and other tools. Beatrix had a pannier containing Istrid's food for the day, and room to spare for her shopping requests.

Amalric pondered as they rode on how much more window shapes could change, but he felt confident that glass would be fit for the challenge. Glaziers were forever as inventive as architects. But there was a contradiction – while the great churches and monasteries found rich patrons to commission monumental extensions and windows, poverty lurked around them everywhere.

'Ah, there's the crossroads and the sanctuary cross,' said Amalric. 'Not far to go now. It's a good place to stop and eat. See, a soft grassy bank to sit on and a perfume of bluebells coming from yon glade. They're a mite early this year.'

Hendric slid off his saddle. 'I always get a bit nervous when I see that cross. It makes me think of the reasons a man may want to plead sanctuary. Beverley pulls 'em in, being the only church for miles what'll grant it for murderers and their like.'

'Aye, but it's a Christian duty. Their patron, St John, will no doubt approve,' his father replied, while eyeing his niece rummaging in a pannier. Salted pork, pickled vegetables and bread appeared from cloths. 'Ee, women know how to pack food for travellin'!'

'The cross gives me the shivers too,' said Beatrix. 'I won't be moving far from the market today. I've heard there's unrest.'

'You'll be safe enough at the market' love,' said Hendric, with fondness in his eyes. You might find a bit of somethin' for yourself – a fine bit of cloth, and p'raps somethin' for the twins.'

Beatrix smiled her appreciation then tipped her head. 'What's that noise? Is that a crowd coming near?'

Coming towards them from another road was a crowd of figures: a plethora of short tunics, leather aprons, hoods, scythes and sickles carried over shoulders, staffs held by thick hands and bare, muscled arms. There were women with worn features, coarse wimples with straw hats over them, skirts tucked in belts and rolled sleeves. The procession ignored the little party at the cross and went on the road to Beverley in a rabble of angry voices.

'Oh, Hendric!' cried Beatrix. 'Where are they from? I think we should go home.'

'Nonsense. They're nowt to do with us.' Hendric was clearly confident there was nothing to worry about.

As they rode into Beverley, Amalric, Hendric and Beatrix felt a tension. Folk they had seen on the road stood around on corners; groups chatted furtively. Amalric once more recalled Father Luke's warning.

They entered the minster precinct and left their horses with a stable boy. Amalric and Hendric slung satchels from the panniers over their shoulders; long measuring sticks poked out of the corners. Beatrix took shopping bags.

Scaffolding sprawled over much of the building. 'It looks as if the whole minster is inside a wooden cage,' commented Beatrix.

'Aye. Old parts of the minster are being repaired and a new west end built.' Amalric walked around scrutinising the poles. 'They look a bit weak to me, Hendric, especially those on the south side where they've been fully exposed to last summer's sun as well as winter's frost. This scaffolding's been used before, too; you can see where ropes have worn it. Our window is high up, a'top it all.'

'Oh, Da, you've just an old man's caution,' Hendric quipped.

'And look, there's wool bales all around the walls, between the scaffold poles, ready to load and be sent off. It's too busy around 'ere for safe work.'

Hendric's eyes sparkled. 'Nay, Da, it's lively.'

Amalric ignored his son's excitement. 'We'll go to the west end first to see how it's coming along. It'll be good to get an idea of the fancy stonework it'll have.'

New towers for the west end were rising from foundations; their fresh limestone walls glinted in the sunlight. Nearby, protected by a canopy of wood, was the masons' dusty workshop. Most men wore a cloth covering their nose and mouth. To one side, masons refined quarried stone into precisely cut ashlars. To the other side, stone was being carved artfully into more complicated shapes. An ugly gargoyle's head glared menacingly open-mouthed at them.

Amalric sought out the master mason. He spied a stocky, thickset man wearing a fine-quality leather apron and cap. 'Good morning, master mason. I'm Amalric Faceby, master glazier. This is my son, a glass-fitting craftsman, and his wife. I'm eager to know if designs are being sought for the coloured glass that will no doubt be required for your new window openings.'

'It's *assistant* master mason,' said the mason, pulling down his facecloth. 'I can't help you, I'm afraid. Not my concern.' He put down his tool and held out his hand. 'Call me Arnold. I'm known as Arnold the Mason, Arnold Mason if you like.'

Another man chipping away at a block nearby without a mask looked up. One eye peered at them, the other was a scarred depression. His mouth drooped open and wet. Amalric recognised the face of the gargoyle. 'You'd best be away,' the mason mumbled. ''Tis naught but trouble here today.'

'That's Jack,' said Arnold. 'He's proud of his stone portrait, done by himself while starin' at his reflection in dark glass. He lost his eye when his chisel broke and flew just as he hammered it a year or two back. Been bad-mouthed ever since. But he's right. Don't hang around here today.'

'Well, we've come to measure up a window on the south side, so we won't be in your way,' said Hendric.

'No. Not here, there's trouble brewin'…' Arnold started to say but Jack intervened.

'Aye, be gone. Gerroff.' He waved his arms in annoyance.

Amalric became nervous. He put his arms about Beatrix's and Hendric's backs and shuffled them away.

'Oh, Da, don't fret. It'll be nothing to concern us.' Hendric was cheerful and eager to get on with their job. 'I'm going outside to look at the opening we've to fill. We may need the master mason's advice if the stonework's not up to scratch. You look from inside, and I'll meet you up top.'

Amalric nodded and watched his son jauntily walk off, knowing that climbing scaffold always gave him a thrill.

Chapter Twenty-two

Amalric and Beatrix entered the minster through the west-end scaffolding. It was eerily silent. Usually there was singing, or the chanting of prayers, and robed figures scurrying in slithery sandals looking busy but never doing a job that Amalric could identify. Today, only the soft clinking sound of the masons chiselling could be heard, and the inevitable bird chatter. They walked down the nave. Amalric pointed to one side.

'See that, Beat, through the pillars? Remember the sanctuary cross? Well, that's the stone chair where they ask for sanctuary once they're in here.'

'From something such as murder?'

'Aye, and other crimes. Sometimes it's folk who're oppressed, or wrongly accused.'

'And do they get it, sanctuary?'

'Aye. Usually.'

'Usually?'

'Aye, well, it's safe enough when a person sits on it, but they have to get off at some point; that's when they get caught and maybe it's sanctuary no more.' Amalric peered further. 'Hey-up, there's somebody in it. He's got red hair.'

'Oh, leave him be, Uncle.'

'Aye, lass, Hendric'll be at the window checkin' it. Come, let's make our way there. I hope the masons have done the stone-edge repairs well. They almost look too busy. Eventually there'll be a large window with coloured glass,' Amalric said wistfully.

'Will you seek work on it, Uncle?'

'I'd like to. I only asked Arnold Mason about it on the off-chance, but the minster's master of works has made it plain he only wants his own Beverley glaziers. He's not keen on outsiders. His name is John Flitch. He's been here for some years. I've come across him many times before now.'

'Outsiders? We live only hours away!'

'Well, to him that's outside. Faceby and Son is alright for simple glazing jobs like today when he needs Hendric's technical skills, but for coloured glass he likes to keep his own style; even draws the design for the glaziers.'

A shuffling sound was heard. 'See, he's coming now. I'll show you what I mean,' her uncle said, winking.

A man wearing an outdoor cloak approached. 'Good day, Master Faceby. You have just caught me. Ready to start?'

'Good day, Master Flitch. Aye, ready to measure up, but I'm a little concerned about the scaffolding outside. It looks weak, weathered.'

'Nonsense. It's fine. It'll last till your job is done.'

'And the west end? The masons seem to be getting along fine. No doubt you have the glazing planned. Will you be needing Faceby and Son for that in due course?'

'Maybe. There'll be some technical skill required. The architect has drawn some complicated tracery.'

'And for the coloured glass?' pursued Amalric. 'Will you be employing artisans from outside the town?'

The response was icy. 'The Chapter is happy with my minster glaziers. We don't need others to help. Thank you.'

'I was just wondering if you were considering any ingenious new designs, only I have many ideas that involve a new style...' Amalric smiled benevolently.

Master Flitch was curt. 'There is nothing wrong with the style I shall use. It's tried and tested, and everyone can understand the depictions of the Bible. There's no need to... to...'

'Be new?'

'Yes. No need. It sounds to me as if you've been influenced by that young upstart John Thornton from Coventry, with his grotesque peasant faces. They're not suitable for Bible figures.'

Amalric was momentarily quietened. It was the mention of John Thornton again. He had obviously struck an uncomfortable chord with Flitch. 'Have you met the young man? I have not.'

'I have. Recently.' Flitch straightened himself and took a deep breath of impatience. 'The young upstart! You need to stay clear of him and his dangerous ideas.' His finger wagged in front of Amalric's face. 'You'd best get on with your measuring. Goodbye.'

'Uncle!' exclaimed Beatrix with a conspiratorial smile, as they watched Master Flitch walk down the nave. 'You might have lost us today's job.'

'Pompous ass. He needs Hendric's expertise so won't get rid of us, but he sees no excitement in new ways. Coloured glass is a window on the Bible; the windows he wants to see are a closed manuscript.' Amalric felt a sudden regard for John Wyclif.

Amalric and Beatrix looked at the scaffolding inside the minster. It was in fair condition despite some wear and tear, but was not suffering from exposure to the biting winds, rain and sun that had caused much deterioration to the outside scaffolding. The poles felt substantial and firm when Amalric grasped them. He put his leg on the first rung of the ladder; his tight burn scars painfully stretched. His legs ached in bed at night; he could no longer climb scaffold like a squirrel.

'Come and sit, Uncle. I have father's salve for you in my satchel, thinking you may need it. Let me massage it into your scars. It'll help.'

'Thank you, lass. I won't say no.' He loosened his hose and Beatrix gently massaged his legs, softening the taut skin.

'You know, when I speak to people like Flitch I become sad. Bible people *were* real people. I try to make them so in my windows, but not everyone wants reality. They deny what has been learned through bad times; the pestilences have changed so much. We should grasp the opportunity to start afresh and reveal hidden truths.'

'Well, Uncle, your windows are dotted around the county giving out your message. It's up to others to take note.' Beatrix looked steadily into her uncle's eyes. She had somehow adopted her father's ability to see beyond the flesh. Amalric knew, in that instant, she was aware of how he longed to make a large window full of things he believed in, and also how it was drifting away.

She helped him adjust his hose. 'Come now, up the ladders you go. Hendric is probably up there on the other side already. I'm going to the market for Istrid's provisions. She wants herrings.'

High up on the top platform standing before the empty window space, Amalric was surprised not to see Hendric already on the outside platform before him, peering through. He usually climbed rapidly. After a short while, he was relieved to see his son's cheerful face appear over the stone sill. The sunlight caught his maturing features. His hair, tied into a tail, moved with the breeze as if on strings.

'I've just been chatting to a fellow below,' he said. 'Apparently, there's trouble in the minster; something to do with the Archbishop of York exceeding his boundaries and making demands that the canons can't agree to; they're loyal to the pope, and are a royal foundation anyway, and feel they've no allegiance to the archbishop. It's nothing to bother us so long as they pay us. But there's trouble in the town as well. Townsfolk, villagers, peasants and artisans are all up in arms wanting to change the governance of the town: a monopoly and privateering bunch, it seems. And they're complaining about ever higher tax payments. The archbishop has been appealed to, to help. I wouldn't want to be him; he's in the middle. It seems one great muddle. I can't understand such matters. It's best ignored.'

Amalric wasn't so sure. It sounded like a small fire in a dry forest; one gust of wind and it would be an inferno. 'Let's get on with our job and go home.'

Hendric ran his fingers over the edges of the window space. 'The masons have done a fine job replacing edging stones.

They've cut good grooves for us to slide glass into. I could do it myself, but I don't want trouble with their guild. I need to decide where to put metal bars; the glass'll have to be attached firmly to 'em; there'll be ferocious winds up here. They were too loose afore; that's what damaged the last glass, flapping back and forth. What's it like from your side?'

'Good,' Amalric answered. 'I'll measure up. We need to get the curves right.'

Crisp edges to the stonework made the task of measuring easy, and Amalric effortlessly drew the stonework shape onto a piece of thin, whitewashed wood. He whistled as he worked, happy to be high above the town stink where he could see over the landscape, now greening up well for summer. The sky was cloudless. All was so quiet, apart from the soft hiss of the breeze, that even the masons' clinking noise was not heard rising up from their workshop.

'Whoa!' called Hendric, as the faint noise of many shouting voices suddenly sounded.

Amalric looked out and saw his son's hands grasping the wooden scaffold rail. 'What's wrong?'

Hendric was looking down beyond the precinct. 'That stream of men and women we saw on the road are coming towards the minster. They've been joined by others. It's a much bigger crowd. They look angry. Somethin's wound 'em up. Their leader looks like… yes, it is. It's that Jack fellow, the one-eyed mason. He's got a hammer.'

A shuffling noise inside suddenly alerted Amalric to movement below. He looked down. Ministers with sacks slung over their shoulders were walking past, heading for the south door.

A voice called to them, 'This isn't the answer. You could be excommunicated.'

One turned and bumped into the scaffold. 'We can't serve more than one master: we're leaving. Going to London!' he shouted back.

Amalric grabbed hold of an upright as the poles wobbled

precariously around him. When it settled, he looked over to Hendric in a panic.

'What can you see?'

'The rebels have invaded the precinct. They're near the south door.'

'They'll meet the ministers from inside. Have you time to get down?'

'No, they're just about here.'

The crowd noise increased. There was a bumping and cracking of wood. Hendric's head disappeared from the sill, followed by a scream.

Amalric leaned forwards as far as he could. Some of the scaffold had fallen away.

'Hendric!' Amalric's call was lost in a tumult of voices and further cracking of wood. It was impossible to see through the maze of broken wooden poles. He speedily descended and limped through the nave.

Chapter Twenty-three

'Hey! Master of the burned dog!' The voice came from the sanctuary chair as Amalric struggled towards the south door. A thickset figure stood in front of it, not daring to let go of the chair arm. There was a lot of red hair and beard.

'Douglas?' Was it really the Scotsman? What was he doing here? 'I must find my son; he's fallen from the scaffold!' Now was not the time to have sympathy for a rebel Scot.

At the door, a figure in a habit stood alone, wringing his hands, loudly wailing his abandonment. Outside was mayhem. Protestors and clergy mingled in a raucous sea of long robes and short tunics. Workmen's tools flashed in the sunlight – sickles, poles, hammers, the occasional sword. Hendric was nowhere to be seen. Amalric had expected to see his splattered body on the stone pavement, but in the turmoil he couldn't even see the ground. He turned around, looking all over as the crowd surged around him. Had someone carried his son away?

'My son! My son! Have you seen…'

A voice that was not his son's called through the melee. 'Over here!' It came from beside the minster wall where Arnold Mason was waving frantically at him. Amalric pushed his way over. Hendric was splayed on top of a bale with Arnold pulling splintered poles off him. Fear engulfed Amalric. Was his son dead? He struggled through the crowd towards the bale, but felt his hood being grabbed by someone.

'No, this way, man. Join us.' It was Jack, his face leering threateningly. 'Follow me.'

Amalric loosened his hood so that it came away in Jack's

hand. Now free, he forced his way to his son. Arnold had cleared the poles and was holding the lad's hand. When he saw Amalric, he let go and slid into the crowd.

Hendric's right leg dangled over the edge of the bale; the foot's position was strange. His hose was growing tighter as the limb swelled.

'Dear Lord, it's agony! Da, help me.'

His father put an arm under his son's shoulders and cradled his head, then sought the satchel on his shoulder. He realised he'd left both their satchels in the church and so had nothing to help: no ale. Oh, why had Arnold left so rapidly?

His son slipped into unconsciousness. Redness seeped from somewhere under him. Some of it soaked into the soft dun-coloured wool, leaving the rest to trickle in two thin streams down the side of the bale. The crowd tumbled away in an ecstasy of rage, emptying the precinct as quickly as they had filled it. Amalric, hugging his son, had never felt so alone, so helpless.

'Here they are, mistress.' It was Arnold with Beatrix.

'Oh, Uncle! Are you alright?' The anxious face of Beatrix appeared. Her eyes scanned her husband as she spoke. Amalric nodded, dumb with shock.

'Sir,' said Arnold softly. 'I apologise for leaving you alone. I'd seen your son's wife go to the market and knew the crowd would go there. I needed to be there before them, to find her.'

'We must find out what his injuries are!' Beatrix muttered to herself.

Amalric's eyes passed from his son back to her. Gradually he saw that, trained by Thurston and her mother, she was able to push her feelings aside. He began to calm.

'Obviously he has broken his leg,' she said. 'Both lower bones near the ankle. Fortunately, the skin above them is not broken; that would have made things much worse. But the bleeding from his back? Mm, which to deal with first? The blood is not very much, though it could be soaking into the wool and thus hiding the amount.' She gently slid one hand under his back. 'I feel a wound but it's not as large as I dreaded. I feared a piece of wood might be embedded.' She withdrew her bloodied hand and wiped it on her gown. 'He has fainted so it's perhaps better that I straighten the leg... Arnold, would you please fetch my uncle's tools from the nave?'

Amalric roused himself. 'My tools and Hendric's are on the scaffold. High up, I'm afraid.'

'Never fear, sir. I am as a squirrel.'

When Arnold returned with the satchels of tools, Beatrix took two long measuring rods and laid them to one side. She took out a large piece of clean rag, normally used to tear into pieces to sparkle up a newly installed window, and tore it into long strips. Then she took a splinter of wood, wrapped cloth around it and put it between Hendric's teeth. 'That will prevent him from biting his tongue if he should come round. Now... Uncle and Arnold... hold Hendric firm by putting your arms under his armpits. Hold him still against my pulling. Ready?'

They nodded.

Beatrix took hold of Hendric's foot and gently moved it into a position where she could put her hands around it. Grasping firmly, she shouted 'Now!' and pulled steadily. Hendric screamed out of his faintness and descended again. The wooden splint fell from his mouth. The leg became straighter.

'Let go of him slowly, both of you. Now come here, Arnold, and hold the foot in this position while I tie the measuring rods to his leg to prevent the bones from moving and to keep it as straight as possible. I'll also tie both legs together.'

That done, she said to them, 'Now, we need to turn him over onto his side so I may see his back. Arnold, please help my uncle gently pull him over while I support his leg.' Hendric screamed again as his body was pulled over. Beatrix examined his back, tearing shirt fabric to see better. 'That's a relief. There's a gash on his back but it's not deep.' She took off her shawl and, holding the cloth to the wound, passed the long length of the shawl under his body to tie it tightly around his chest. 'There, that should stop the bleeding until I can deal with it at home.'

Hendric was once more on his back.

Beatrix had been calm but now Amalric saw she was starting to shake. 'Eh, lass, you could do with a hot drink. Come, sit on one of these 'ere bales for a moment.'

Arnold took Amalric's hint. 'I'll go and heat up some ale in the masons' workshop.'

When he returned, Amalric was holding his son's head. Beatrix sat, still shaking.

'Here, drink this. There's beakers for you all,' said Arnold. He put a cloak around Beatrix and one over Hendric. 'We use these when we are on the scaffold to keep the cold at bay.'

'I don't know how we'll return home,' said Amalric into his ale.

'I can take Hendric in a mason's cart,' said Arnold. 'We've one for small stones. It's big enough for him to lie down and for Mistress here to be by his side. It's dusty but the cloths used to cover the stone will keep him warm. We can tie their horses to it. But it'll be a slow, jolting ride. I'll have a word with the merchant who owns these bales. The top one is spoiled with blood; we could use some of it to pack round the lad.'

Beatrix nodded acceptance and there was pleasure in Arnold's eyes.

A sudden 'Psst!' made all three turn to the noise which came from behind stacked bales further away, and which barely hid the bulk of a man. He crept warily from behind them and revealed himself disguised in a monk's habit that was too tight. The length failed to hide bare, hairy legs, and the hood, a bush of red hair and beard. There was no way this man could be mistaken for a monk; for another thing, he stank mightily.

Amalric strangled a hysterical laugh. 'You! Douglas Redhead. Aren't you seeking sanctuary?'

Arnold, too, held in laughter. 'He's been here these last few days. With no one left in the minster to protect his claim to sanctuary, if the mob sees him and remembers his part in the Scottish raids, they'll act first and have sense later. His head'll surely be a game ball or on a spike at the gate. He could have

Hendric's horse if you care to have him with us, riding behind if the stink is too bad.'

Douglas, seemingly sensing compassion, broke into an astonishingly large smile. It oddly cheered them all and, without further thought, Amalric and Beatrix agreed.

The journey was hard. Douglas' strength proved to be very useful for moving stones and branches out of the way of the lumbering wheels. Beatrix was anxious to get the shocked Hendric home to give him some of her father's special potion. He was clearly in great pain, screaming with every jolt.

Back in Warren Horesby, Hendric was settled into the care of Thurston, with Beatrix and the twins fussing around him.

At the Faceby home, Amalric was surprised to see that Istrid's reaction to Douglas was curiously accepting. She immediately sent the filthy man into the back garden with a pail of tepid water to strip and wash.

Amalric and Arnold hunched by the fire with a stew pot bubbling above it. The fire glow, along with a beaker of ale, was soothing, but Amalric was forced to reflect on this latest event; climbing scaffolding for high windows would now be a problem; both he *and* his son would be lame.

'I fear this will alter my business,' he admitted to Arnold. 'Hendric's skill lies mainly in fitting and repairing. Much of that requires scaffolding.'

'Aye, I'm about Hendric's age and we masons have the same problems. It's one thing carving on the ground, but another getting pieces up to the highest point. We do some carving up top. And there's all these new ideas with curves and corners and fancy bits. I've lost a few men.'

Istrid came from outside and disturbed their talk.

'Ah, here's my daughter to serve her stew. Come to our table, Arnold,' said Amalric. 'It's reet good food. Just like her mother made.'

Istrid put a platter of bread, bowls of stew and spoons on the table and immediately left them. Armed with sheep shears and a rush light, she went back to the garden, calling as she went,

'I'm resolved to rid him of his lice and stink. That red hair and beard will have to go!'

Arnold finished his ale with a great gulp and peered hungrily at the full bowls. He took one. 'Ee, it looks good.' He sniffed the steam. 'I wish I had someone to give me food like this.'

'You've no wife?'

'No. She died last year in childbirth. It's hard for women. She was young, not strong. She'd had many childhood illnesses and near starvation when a child. She bled. The child did not survive.' Arnold's hands shook.

'Aye. I lost my Nesta and child with the puking sickness. It makes you angry.'

'I'm still angry, and that's what spurred me to join the protesters. There're too many taxes. I couldn't give my wife the good food she needed, despite my good job. The master of works is a mean man. He filches money that he should give to the men.'

A silence fell as each man slurped his stew. Then Amalric laid his wooden spoon in the empty bowl. 'I'm sorry you had to miss the excitement by looking after us.'

'Don't be. I've no real heart for rebellion. That mix today will likely end in disaster – clergy walking out because they don't want interference from the archbishop, and peasants and free men appealing to the same archbishop to fight for them. Too much tax. You can't win against the Church and king. I'm glad to be out of it. I'm sorry that your son fell foul of it all.'

'Beatrix will sort him. She's a good healer. Her adoptive father is a physic doctor. My great friend.'

'Aye, she seems a great lass,' said Arnold. Shouting and clatterings came from the garden, interrupting his interest. Istrid's voice rose above it. Arnold smiled. 'It sounds as though Douglas won't have his hair cut.'

'Oh yes, he will,' laughed Amalric.

Chapter Twenty-four

1382 Warren Horesby
Late summer

The Beverley uprising had spread to York, where even religious houses were attacked; Friar Swale left for his Franciscan mother community there. Amalric suspected he had sympathy for the rebels, which rather contradicted his services to Lord de Horesby and especially Edwin.

Word came that a horrendous uprising had taken place in London, where several factions had met and caused mayhem and death, even killing clergy. Amalric feared for his village but, for once, Lord de Horesby ignored the advice of Edwin to deal heavily with likely miscreants, and maintained a calm and benevolent course that defused early signs of hostility. Normal life teetered. Things simmered at high heat for more than a year.

During that time, Amalric pushed wider social problems to one side and bemoaned ones closer to home. Hendric was a huge source of anxiety. Broken bones often resulted in black, putrefying limbs that had to be hacked off before death ensued. He watched to see if his son would be a cripple with a crutch – or worse, pushing himself around on a little wheeled cart at ground level.

For glazing, there was the problem of no expert help in the workshop, even if sizeable commissions came in – which they didn't. Amalric even gave up his plan to make his second coloured window for Warren Horesby church in order to save enough glass for a small window, should one be requested. But no request came. Amalric faced the fact that life's current hardships provided little incentive for village churches to embark upon schemes to beautify worship. Settling down to life as it was, meagre and without inspiration, was the only way to be content. A glimmer of hope turned out to be in the form of Douglas with down-to-earth practical help.

Eventually Friar Swale came back, conducting services in 'God's open air', which was not satisfactory; the covering of soil on the pestilence pit had once again become too shallow owing to wind and rain so that its stink, in hot sun, pervaded the graveyard. Services were constantly hampered by flies, congregants wafting them away. Something had to be done. Douglas was the answer.

Amalric leaned on the church fence with a smiling Istrid, watching Douglas as he layered soil on the pestilence pit with muscular ease. In just over one year, Douglas had changed from being a wanted man to a generous helper. He'd been both a weaponed, brutish marauder and an idiotic clown disguised as a monk. Another of life's contradictions.

'Well, lass, you've a good man there.' He recognised his daughter's first-ever sign of romantic love. 'You clearly adore him.'

'Work outside here suits him. He's happy with animals and the garden, and odd jobs.'

'And mostly sleeps in the barn,' Amalric added, with a smile. 'I can hardly believe he's not recognised as a raiding Scot.'

'In his heart, he never was one. He was just trying to survive. When I persuaded him to cut his red hair and beard, the sun brought his freckles out and I realised he had Uncle Thurston's colouring.'

'Then you taught him to speak more Northumbrian than Scottish borders...'

She nodded. 'Yes. He's lucky the villagers think he's a northern relative of their physician.'

'You did well. Thurston seems happy enough to have a bulky relative whose abilities are useful. It amuses him no end!'

'I've asked Douglas to marry me, Da.'

It was no revelation that his strong daughter had seen fit to do the asking. 'He's said yes?'

'Yes. But we won't leave here.'

'So no more sleeping in the barn for him?' her father said, with a smile.

Hendric mended. His foot was a little twisted and stiff but he was able to climb scaffolding with care. Faceby and Son was able to work again, but it only trickled in. Even the once regular maintenance work at Meaux Abbey had dried up. It thus came as a surprise to have a message from Amalric's old friend there, Father Luke, with a commission for replacement glass in *all* the clerestory windows of the abbey church, and repairs as necessary to the remainder. A new abbot, William of Scarborough, had apparently come forward with a large donation.

Amalric was exhilarated; this could mean up to two years' work for his modest workshop. He hoped the glass would be coloured, but was not surprised to be told it was to emphasise Cistercian values.

Father Luke apologetically explained, 'The abbot requires the leading to be geometric to match the floor tiles: straight or circular, clear and unadulterated by colour, paintwork to be grey tones only, no silver stain. This will allow God's pure constant light to shine through, showing His controlled design for the world and how everything links into everything else.'

An almost imperceptible sigh passed through Amalric's lips.

'My old friend, I know it's not what you would wish; no figures especially, but that's not the way of this monastery. Our rules on such things were laid down way back. Here we still strictly abide by them. I can appreciate that it will go against what you love to do, but it will be a sacrifice for God. I'm sure you can do it.'

Amalric wondered if his old friend and the abbot *really* knew how hard it would be. Not following his own heart with colour and natural shapes would be only one of the glazing problems;

each interwoven, geometrically correct pattern had to be meticulously interpreted in glass; one piece slightly out of shape when leaded would send the whole panel out of true. It was too finicky, too lacking in spontaneous creativity to be exciting, and would take too long to make. But yes, sacrifices had to be made for God from time to time. And it would pay. The only creative concession would be an emblem in the bottom right-hand corner of each window, a painted feather, a reminder of church birds flying heavenwards, and the words *Faceby and Son*.

Father Luke's face became cheery. 'We'll source and order all the glass for you. Just tell us what you need, and we'll store it here at the abbey. You may work both here and in Warren Horesby, but some of our lay brothers, when on pilgrimage to France, were taught the art of window-making and will be on hand to help. And, of course, there'll be ale and good food to see you through.' The monk smiled broadly. 'And I'll be able to converse with you, my friend.'

1384 Meaux Abbey

It was a fine, warm day. Amalric was glad to be going to Meaux Abbey to install the last window. It was ready to be hauled up to the high clerestory. The job had been long and hard – one and a half years – sweltering in summer when the glass slipped out of sweating fingers and freezing in winter when they were too stiff to grasp it, difficulties enhanced by the exact geometric shapes required. Amalric had been almost driven insane by circles, straight lines, interlocking curves – all perfect! All fitting into thin lancet window spaces with pointed arches. All matching the same design in floor tiles. However, the hard work was to be rewarded by a satisfactory amount of money and, hopefully, an enhanced reputation.

'You look peaky, son.' Amalric was surprised to see Hendric, who had entered the workshop, steadying himself by the table. His son had coped well till now, climbing scaffolding with a stiff ankle but firm leg muscles.

'I'm fine, Da. Just a little too much to drink last evenin' with my cousins. Robert ordered a flagon of strong wine. The servant who brought it looked as though he'd had a taste of the stuff himself: a bit green round the gills, he was. Anyway, I took no notice and swigged a huge beaker of it.' He belched loudly. 'I didn't suspect it might be too potent for me.' He belched again and swayed. 'I'm more used to our alewife's strong barley ale; I admit I should have been wary.'

'Aye, well… them sons of Edwin as old as they are'll be the death of you. They act like lads. But we've the last glass to put in today so we need an early start.'

The workshop door banged open. 'Uncle, don't let him go. He's not well.'

'It's just a wine-head, Beatrix,' replied Amalric, as Hendric swayed a little more. 'He'll get over it on the ride to Meaux. At least the light will last till late evenin' so he'll be able to take his time. And you know I can't climb to help, because of my legs. I'm prone to cramps these days which leave me unable to move.'

'Are both of you ignoring the fact that the pestilence has been seen as close as Beverley's filthy Snickelways? Hendric was in the town a few days ago. Father says it's only a matter of time before it becomes a contagion again.'

Amalric had forgotten.

'Look at him. His eyes are red. Are you hot? Have you any lumps?' Beatrix started to pull Hendric's collar away to look at his neck. He knocked her hand away angrily.

'Bea, stop it! I had red wine last night. It was ferocious. Never again – my head's like a clatterin' mill wheel. Go home. I'll see you when the window is finished. Da and I *have* to go to Meaux today.'

'Aye, lass. It's a must. The monks have been holding their services in the Chapter House long enough, just so we can work. The scaffolding needs to come down. The lay brothers'll have brought the window out of the abbey workshops. They've helped with so many other windows, they know exactly what to do and when. We can't let 'em down.'

In truth, Amalric simply wanted to be done with the commission and look forward to midsummer's day. His work had been of the finest, he knew that, but he had no pride in the originality of it.

'Then I'll go with you. I also know exactly what to do.'

There was no stopping Beatrix. In a short time, she returned with her travel cloak and a bundle that was excessively large. Amalric suspected she'd packed extra clothing for herself in order to climb the scaffold. He knew she'd hope to have the opportunity to help insert the glass into the stone frame and experience the thrill of seeing it lit by high sunlight.

'Come, then, let's get on the cart.'

Istrid was there to see them off. 'You look a bit wan, brother,' she said, and raised a hand to his forehead. Again, he knocked it away.

'I'm fine. I'm improving already. You women'll be the death of me. I'll rest on the cart.'

Amalric noted with disquiet the repeated word *death*, but Istrid and Beatrix simply looked at each other, confirming the stubbornness of men. He inexplicably felt the need for his dog. 'Come, Noah.' Noah clambered onto the cart.

Chapter Twenty-five

The journey to Meaux was better than they had expected. The recent purchase of a good horse and well-made small cart made the journey for Amalric easier, but Hendric found the rolling and bumping on the pitted road increased his headache. He walked for most of the journey. Noah, too, refused to ride and walked twice as far, running to the overgrown sides of the path, leaping after the red squirrels, mice and other inhabitants of the hedgerows as they skittered out of the way. Occasionally he would look up at his master with floppy ears and raised tail, panting joyfully and exhibiting a few feathers around his mouth, which indicated a struggle but no catch.

Hendric improved as his wine-head drifted away, leaving just a dull residual ache. His father, though, noticed that he'd pulled his hood partly over his eyes as if the sunlight hurt them.

The little party arrived at the abbey and met with other people both delivering goods and taking others away: great sacks of wool for spinning, and vegetables. Amalric had persuaded Noah to ride so he'd be out of danger. He stood with front paws on the edge of the cart, barking at every horse, mule and donkey and lifting his snout to new stinks. They clattered over the bridge and passed through the abbey precinct, amazed as usual at the amount of activity therein. Beatrix dropped from the cart with her bundle as it slowed down. She'd seen a friend.

'I'll just have a quick chat to Maria and will see you in the church.'

Hendric's hood was still low as they entered the abbey church through a small door set within the huge oak one at the west end. Light poured through the new, clear, colourless glass windows. Amalric stood and remembered. There was always something to jog his memory in this great space: his learning as a boy together with his elder sister, Matilde, both sitting in the shade of the cloister with water dribbling in the little fish pool, birds singing and the smell of herbs wafting, the monks' eagerness to teach about faith and the logical Latin language. He recalled his father's friendship with Abbot Hugh and the earthquake in spring 1349 that had shaken all their bones and presaged the Great Pestilence of summer. Father Luke, a young man then like himself, had been one of the very few survivors of the disease.

Scaffolding had been erected both inside and out, with ropes and pulleys to heave each leaded window panel up to the window space. In the stone surround, rebates had been cut for the window to slide into and be made firm with soft putty of Amalric's own recipe. Metal bars had been placed across the open space, passing from one side to the other. To these, copper ties soldered onto the lead cames would grip the bars to hold the glass totally secure. Amalric felt, after all, it was a fine achievement and an honour to make glass windows for these austere, efficient monks.

He stood with hands on hips, weighing up the scaffolding as he had done for every window. Since Hendric's fall from the scaffolding at Beverley Minster, safety had become an obsession. Here, logs passed through holes in the wall horizontally so that both inside and outside, vertical scaffolding was held to them securely. Flat wooden platforms were attached at intervals with ladders giving access to them and, finally, the high windows. A further platform held by ropes and pulleys was designed to carry the heavy glass panels up to the top.

'It looks safe to me. These Meaux brothers certainly know what they're doing.'

A small group of brothers, standing by ready to help, nodded at the appreciation. Two visiting nuns watched with interest.

Indistinct plain chant echoed from the Chapter House and

sun shone through the south windows and reflected off the tall limestone pillars and golden-coloured encaustic floor tiles. The immersion in warm sunlight and enveloping muted sounds warmed Amalric's heart.

'Right, son, let's get on with this.'

Hendric looked up out of his hood and screwed his eyes against the glare. 'Aye, Da.'

'Son, maybe it's not a good day for you to fit the windows.'

'I'm fine, Da,' Hendric said sharply.

Beatrix appeared. She'd changed her clothing and was wearing her husband's spare hose and sleeveless leather jerkin and shirt. Despite her age, her figure looked good: the laces of the jerkin tightened it into her waist, her legs looked slim and her arms muscular and strong. She posed provocatively. It was enough to cause Hendric to lift his head and smile. A soft gasp came from the lay brothers. The nuns smiled. Amalric looked apologetically at them.

Beatrix grinned and gave her husband a playful tap at the side of his head. He winced. She ignored it. 'There's work to do. So… you'll let me help?'

'Aye. Come on.' Hendric took his wife's hand and led her to the lowest ladder, allowing her to go first. Noah stood by. Hendric rubbed him behind the ears and the dog's eyes never left the two of them as they climbed higher, even though he had to move back to keep them in view.

Amalric worked below. He took glass panels that would form the complete window from their protective wooden cases and put them onto the flat rectangle of the lift, securing them with twine.

'Ready, Da, tell the brothers to haul away,' shouted Hendric from above. Both he and Beatrix were positioned to steady the ropes of the lift as it rose to prevent the platform swinging. Amalric and a lay brother hauled on the ropes from below. Greased pulleys groaned into action.

The lift reached the level of the top platform, with Hendric and Beatrix ready to pull it in. Beatrix grabbed a rope. Hendric leaned forward to grasp another, but his arm raised and stopped in mid-air. He looked down, then stood perfectly still. Amalric could see that his face was the colour of the limestone wall, but at that distance it was hard to make out his expression. He saw Beatrix let go of her rope to reach her husband. The lift started to waver. It tilted. The glass moved forward a little under its own weight, slipping under the twine. The brothers tried to steady the lift from below, but its sway gained momentum. Then Hendric himself began to sway. Beatrix reached out further, leaning precariously, but couldn't even touch him. Hendric swayed more. In an instant he fell, crashing onto the lift, causing it to tilt further. Both he and the glass slid off.

Sunlight from windows flashed off the glass panel as, like a sail, it glided down. Hendric, with flailing limbs, followed. Amalric, absurdly, he thought later when he relived the scene, realised that figures falling to hell on the west wall of Warren Horesby church had probably been inspired by such a fall. An indescribable sound from the tiled floor indicated Hendric's last moments of life, and the window's destruction. Then all was still. Even Noah, at first, stood motionless, but quickly recovered and was the first living thing to go to Hendric, picking his way over glass shards and empty lead cames. He nudged Hendric's unmoving hand and sat down beside him.

Amalric looked up to the platform, hoping this was an ageing man's fearful imagining and expecting to see his son there; but only Beatrix stood on the platform, holding a rope, statue still. He then looked down at his son. Amalric had been at a scene like this before, when his father had struggled with Edwin over a box of money. Edwin had pushed his father, whose head had smashed on the hearth. Blood seeped in the same way it was seeping now from Hendric's head.

Anger in Amalric's mind allowed no room for sorrow in his heart. As anonymous arms in a monk's habit went around him, he shrugged them off and limped as quickly as he could from the church. Noah left Hendric and followed. They found themselves in the cloister accepting a beaker of thin ale and a bowl of water from a monk.

Beatrix then appeared, supported by the two visiting nuns, her manly clothes streaked with blood. Amalric knew she had cradled her husband's head just as he had cradled his father's. The nuns encouraged her to sit, but she ignored them and stood in front of him.

'Just now,' she said with suffocating difficulty, 'when I held him, I saw a bubo in his neck and one in his armpit. 'Twas the pestilence. I told you! I told you!' She turned, tears streaming down her face, and went to sit in the furthest corner of the cloister, her head in her hands and a nun's arms around her.

Amalric couldn't blame her for the outpouring. The pestilence had struck again and changed his life. The ever-present lump of sorrow in his chest which had become a part of his life took over from anger, rose into his throat and came out in a huge wail. It echoed around the cloister. Noah jumped at the noise, then put his head in his master's lap and allowed tears to fall on his tousled hair.

A monk sat quietly at Amalric's side. It was some time before he recognised Father Luke.

'Why, Luke?' They were the only words he could utter. They embodied every question he had.

'Because God allows it.'

'I've little left to cope with God now. I'm getting old and infirm and crushed by circumstance.'

'Well, in God's eyes, what little you cope with now may be enough. Come to the fire in the refectory, my friend, you need stronger ale.'

Chapter Twenty-six

1385 Warren Horesby

'Ah, Master Faceby, how are you today?'

The voice came from Warren Horesby church sanctuary, dispelling Amalric's hope of peace and prayer. It was easier to pray here alone than in services with the unfathomable mystery of the eucharist, and fidgeting folk anxious to get away to their fires, or crops, or animals. He was also weary of Istrid's fussing over him, which channelled her own grief at the loss of her brother. On this day, early in the morning and still dull with sleep, he cared not to answer the voice.

'"Tis but a normal question, my friend, given the fragility of man. Praise God we've not had a contagion since the death of your son, some months ago now. How is his wife, Beatrix?'

'Good day to you, Friar Swale,' said Amalric morosely. He'd not expected the friar to be in the church and his callous comment was like a cold knife cutting through hard butter. Hendric had been buried at Meaux by brave monks on the day of his death to avoid contagion, so there was not even a grave nearby for him to mourn over. Also, Beatrix was on his mind. She'd not suffered the pestilence, but they'd not spoken since Hendric's death. He could hardly endure to be reminded of her denunciation.

The friar had a satchel and was obviously on his way out of the building. Amalric saw that his girth had increased markedly since his arrival.

'I was with your brother last evening.' A whiff of wine wafted over to Amalric. 'We had a long chat. Giving consolation. He feels the loss of your son, his nephew, very much. In that you are equal.'

Amalric half-smiled. No... they were not equal. Even if Edwin had been Hendric's father, he could never have loved him as much as he, Amalric, could. To Edwin, people were valued for what they could give him, never for selfless love.

'I've spent time with him in the falcon field. Such beautiful birds. Flying up heavenwards.'

'I prefer birds to be free,' responded Amalric, as a twittering came from the roof beams.

'Yes. Well, I must go up to the manor again today. I've promised to speak to some peasants on behalf of your brother. It seems they are restless and may cause trouble. They worry unnecessarily and must realise our system of agriculture has to change.'

Amalric looked with disbelief at this friar who was not an ordained priest, as Father Luke had been, but nevertheless a friar of the Franciscan order. As far as he knew, the simple itinerant order was meant to care for the souls of the poor in the growing towns and diminishing villages, and not so much for the wealthier manor elite, especially not the reeve. Amalric had always admired the order, but this man seemed a complex example.

'I must go,' said the friar.

Amalric followed Friar Swale out of the church and slowly wandered down the path to the gate, where he leaned, crossing his arms on top, watching him stride up the hill. Noah slumped to the ground, his head on his front paws. As Friar Swale disappeared, Amalric's eyes turned to focus idly on his home across the way. The thatch needed a little attention but, in all, Douglas was a huge help with the maintenance. Wattle and daub walls had recently been repaired, as had shutters. At the left end, the barn had not looked so clean and secure for years. At the right, in his workshop, the glass window sparkled – that was unusual. His interest intensified. Since its coloured predecessor had been knocked out by Cuthbert, he'd not had the heart to clean the plain window that had replaced it. He'd not even been in the workshop for at least two moons. It was hard to remember. The next moment he was across the road.

The door creaked as he peered around the edge. Noah pushed his way inside. Light fell on the cold hearth: the ash looked fresh. Thin cutting irons lay tidily on the hearth edge. Turning to the table, grozing irons and remnants of lead cames lay next to a smallish structure formed of three square panels of glass, each side the length of a large man's foot. They were joined together to make three upright vertical sides and one open side of a square. He was shocked, intrigued.

On looking closer, he saw the glass was mostly colourless with beautiful drawn images; some with a little yellow stain. Small pieces of coloured glass formed a decorative edge to the whole, with glass jewels done exactly as his Theophilus manuscript described.

He picked up the three-sided object and held it to the light. It was utterly beautiful. It illustrated Creation: the right-hand panel was the sky, with clouds, birds, a crescent moon; the left represented the sea with fish, seaweed, shells and bubbles formed of glass imperfections; the central panel was the earth with wheat, flowers, a butterfly, a snail, a tiny mouse and a spider's web that caught the light like strands of silk. His artist's eye immediately recognised the painter's hand.

The door creaked open. Beatrix's surprised face appeared.

'Oh, Uncle Amalric – I'm surprised to see you here. You've found my… I'm sorry, but…'

'No need to be sorry, Beat. This is beautiful. What's it for?'

'It's to surround a candle. The light will shine through all three sides. I thought it might be useful to put in the window to advertise your business, or for our church, or for us to sit in front of and think our own thoughts and remember Hendric.'

'It's truly a work of art, Beatrix. You have a great talent.' He felt ashamed. 'Look – I'm sorry. What can I say about the day Hendric died? I know how much you loved him. And you had twins to think about.'

'Uncle, I was angry, but now my thoughts are clearer. I know Hendric would have gone up the scaffold, whether you asked him or not. He loved the work. You didn't want to deny him. But I failed to save him from falling. I needed to blame someone. Making this candle-holder is my atonement. Glass was part of his life, and installing your beautiful creations was a great joy to him. Putting some love into glass is like still loving him. Can you understand that?'

'Indeed, I can. But tell me, how did I not know you were making this beautiful thing? Why didn't you tell me?'

'You were too deep in grief to notice, Uncle Am.'

Part Three
Reconciliation

~~~~~~

Chapter Twenty-seven

1388 Warren Horesby

Lost in thought in his workshop, Amalric was aroused when Noah barked at a shadow falling across the workshop window.

'Ho there, Master Glazier. Are you in there?'

Amalric peered round the door. It was early afternoon and frost was threatening.

'Lord de Horesby! Dismount, sir, and come into my workshop. I'll come to help. You can tie up to the ring by the door.'

'Ooh, my bones are fixed, having come back from the journey to Beverley,' said the old man, as he stiffly hoisted a leg over and slid from his horse into Amalric's steadying arms. 'Your brother and I have been to my lawyer there. Edwin's gone back to the manor. I wanted a word with you.'

'Come in and sit by the hearth, sir. You must be cold. It's rather dusty, I fear.'

'No matter. I can't be doing with fuss these days.' He flopped onto a stool. 'A beaker of ale would be more relevant.'

Amalric obliged from a jug under the table. As he poured, Lord de Horesby noticed the candle-holder.

'That's beautiful.'

'My niece made it two or three years ago. For her dead husband. I'm thinking of leaving it in the church where more can see it.'

'Ah, a woman working in glass, eh? It has a woman's touch. Whatever next?'

'What can I do for you, sir?' Amalric scrutinised the old man's face, seeking clues to account for this visit.

'A moment to loosen up, if you please.' Lord de Horesby enjoyed a gulp of ale and stretched his arms and legs. 'You know, Master Faceby, I cannot understand why a few of us in this village – me, you, Dr Thurston, your brother, for instance – have not suffered the pestilence when our loved ones have passed away at a mere nod to it. And I'm the oldest survivor among us and even now suffer few infirmities – except for stiffness getting on and off horses! I can't abide to ride in Clara's litter!' He thought for a moment. 'Now then, I've seen my lawyer today, as I said. To make my will. When I die, my manor estate will go to my daughter, Clara. Edwin will, of course, still be responsible for the upkeep of the estate until his death.'

Amalric felt his mouth involuntarily turn down.

'Now come, Master Faceby, Edwin is a good manager, yet I know he has a ruthless streak. My main worry is that he'll turn too much land over to deer for hunting, and sheep, though he's not alone in his ideas. The market for wool is expanding and it's hard to resist. I fear for the peasants. Men will soon be working only for wages and ask more and more. It may mean the end of serfdom. Trust will be lost between landowners and those who work for them. To be fair, as you know, returns of the pestilence have caused so many to die that there are not enough men to work the land. More and more women seem to be taking on work, to say nothing of voraciously seeking husbands.' He chuckled.

Amalric sighed agreement, finding the remark

uncomfortable. He'd not seen Mistress Yarrow for a long time.

'From Clara, the estate will go to my great-grandson, George, with Edwin to guide him, thus bypassing Clara and Edwin's sons. You may think that strange; George is young now, but despite his inherited faults, I already see he is the only one with enough ability and discernment to carry on the… But you don't need to know the detail.'

Amalric was mildly amused that Edwin would not actually be left the estate, but failed to see where this was leading.

Lord de Horesby smiled and put a hand on Amalric's shoulder. 'My will has something for you. When I die, it dictates that you, *you* personally, make a window in memory of the de Horesby family for our church. I will leave the design to you, my friend. All I ask is that it's colourful and will honour my name. There will be money for it.'

Such trust! A thrill ran through Amalric like a cool stream on a hot day. Another window for the church at last. 'Ee, that would be reet good. May it include a portrait of you?'

'It may.'

'Then I'll draw a portrait of you in preparation… now.'

'I'm not about to die yet! After death will do.'

'It will not! The face of life is what needs to be celebrated, not the face of death.' Amalric grabbed a white board and immediately set about drawing the grizzled face. The light was low but the shadowed undulations brought out character, and Amalric delighted in the task.

'Perhaps you could neaten my beard, and don't forget the Horesby ring.' A large emerald glinted from his index finger. 'Or the dint in my forehead; it's been there all my life since my nurse dropped me. It would not be me without it.'

Fate stepped into Lord de Horesby's life a mere half-moon after visiting Amalric. Thurston brought the news straightway.

'He fell when dismounting his horse. The ground was hard with frost. He broke an arm and a leg and sustained a severe bump on his head. He never regained consciousness. I was with him two days before he slipped away.'

An uncomfortable suspicion grew in Amalric. 'Who'd been helping him dismount?' he asked of Thurston. The reply was as expected: Edwin.

'Now, Am, you cannot accuse your brother of murder. Even Edwin wouldn't... There was absolutely no evidence. The man's bones were old and fragile, more than you know.'

'What did Father Swale have to say?'

'Nothing about the fall. He's comforting Clara and Edwin.'

'I bet he is.'

Chapter Twenty-eight

Amalric deeply felt the loss of old Lord de Horesby. In the church, after his funeral, Amalric asked St Edmund to intercede for the safe deliverance of Lord de Horesby's soul. He'd been a sad man since his wife and sons had died in the first Great Pestilence, his lineage and wealth being no match for lost happiness. Way back, some years after the Norman invasion, his family had been granted land which had included a great rabbit warren. The rabbits had been a source of food for the village which had grown up around it and become known as Warren Horesby. Lord de Horesby had contributed land and finance to the foundation of nearby Meaux Abbey. The village had benefited greatly from his benevolence. What would become of it now?

Edwin stood at the glazing workshop door, arrogantly turning down his lips at the mosaic of coloured glass pieces on the chalk-white table, a weak sun glinting on them.

Amalric instinctively knew why his brother was here. 'So, Lord de Horesby's will has been read? Am I to make a memorial window for the church?'

'No.' Edwin tugged at his silk scarf. 'I've decided to use the money for a plaque instead. I've a sculptor already commissioned.'

'A young, untrained one, I suppose. Cheaper than a window?' It was upsetting but not surprising. Nothing Edwin did was a shock any more.

Amalric felt cold and colourless at the sudden arrival of winter.

People walked dolefully through the village wrapped in layers of dull, heavy clothes to keep out the bitter weather. Vegetation was brown. Clouds settled low and grey like an old wool blanket, shutting out the sun. Amalric felt the loss of colour and became convinced that he should make the de Horesby window as promised, but at his own expense.

His racks held a few sheets of coloured glass, and rather more small pieces were in tubs. If he was careful how he cut, it might go far.

Even if he had the money, he pondered, he doubted whether much coloured glass would be available; pestilences, wars with France and trade restrictions had all had an effect. The King's-Town on Hull warehouses were largely empty. Architectural trends for large windows too were eating up whatever coloured glass was available. Artisans like himself had often to resort to silver stain for yellowish shading, or a subtle colour change such as blue to green. His father had helped to pioneer it. The trouble was, many new windows now had yellow as the dominant colour and Amalric disliked its excessive use.

Then there was the issue of style. He was determined not to pander to present taste; in faces, for instance, the eyes were often large and the brows high: a window on the soul perhaps, but not a window on personality.

Amalric pushed mundane difficulties of his craft away and thought only of how he could use what glass he had for the new window. He felt rejuvenated and was in no mood to compromise his own artistic ability, nor the old man's individuality. He even dared to think that the inscription could be in the common language, not Latin. The power of artistic freedom surged through him.

He decided to go to the church to choose a window space. Inside, all was silent save for the gentle whistle of cold air through gaps in the windows and doorway. The birds made no sound. Dried leaves and droppings of small creatures scattered the floor tiles. Amalric was warm with excitement even though his breath misted in the cold nave. A suitable window was one in the south wall opposite St Edmund. Its Saxon original had been a small arched shape, open to the elements until his own grandfather had enlarged it into three lancets, divided by two narrow vertical stone transoms. The central one was about the height of a small man; the other two, shorter and all filled with brittle, greenish glass. Amalric considered a design.

It was unlikely that the wardens and villagers would object to his plan, and Friar Swale had shown little care for what happened to the fabric of the church. The defiant confidence that Amalric felt was new and thrilling.

Back in the workshop, with his imagination buzzing, Amalric set about drawing his design. Often, he found himself leafing through his father's old precious Theophilus manuscript. Over the years it had been his guide, telling him all he needed to know about window-making. Now it was a comfort, anchoring him to his trade. Eventually, he was ready to make the first full-size drawing on the table.

Only hunger kept him from his task. The only person he cared to talk to, besides giving instructions to Nathan, his assistant, was Joshua Smith, the churchwarden and blacksmith. He made the soft lead cames for Amalric and hammered white-hot iron into fixing bars for the window. They had both agreed to do all the work without payment. If the villagers cared enough to give money to help – well, that would be appreciated.

Amalric's joy on completing the first panel was almost indescribable. It contained the lower half of Lord de Horesby's body.

'Ee, Master Faceby, that's grand,' said Joshua. 'You've captured the kernel of the man in his feet and hem of his garment alone. That's just how he stood, with the weight on one foot and the other turned out a bit. Best we start to think about how to fit it securely into the space.'

'Aye,' responded Amalric. 'I ought to be finding a mason to make good the window reveals. The stone is a mite spalled. I need it looking at by a good 'un. There's one in Beverley. We've enough money to pay 'im.'

'Beatrix, lass, I need to speak with you.' Amalric's niece was sweeping out her house. She stopped. Her eyes didn't smile at him. He'd recently noticed that her usual jollity had left her, leaving her morose.

'Ee, lass, you don't look so merry today. The healing work not going well?'

'It's alright, Uncle, but since the last pestilence there's been fewer folk around to be ill. Them that were unscathed were fit, and still are. There's babies on the way, of course, what'll help village numbers eventually. Then I'll be pulled out with work 'cos they'll all arrive about the same time, but at the moment... Anyway, it gives me more time with Ava. She likes to help me. Asa spends a lot of time with his Grandfather Thurston. I think he'll want to go to Oxford for physic.' She smiled wanly and slumped on her broom.

'Beatrix, lass, I've nearly finished the new window for the village church.'

'Oh, Uncle. I'd love to help you.'

'Aye, well, you can be an assistant to me again when you're spare, but meantime, I've a little jaunt for you. I need new badger and hog-hair brushes. I wonder if you'd go to Beverley for me. There's a few folk travelling from the tavern tomorrow and stayin' for a couple of days to do their shoppin'. You could go with 'em. It's safer. I know our Istrid needs stuff and she'd be happy to look after the twins. Go on old Betsy. An' there's somethin' else. I need to speak to that Beverley mason we met, way back, for repairs to the stone of the window. Maybe you'd seek him out. What was his name now?'

'Arnold,' she said excitedly, then checked her enthusiasm.

He thrilled that she seemed embarrassed to have answered so rapidly. 'Would you ask him to come?'

'Oh, yes, Uncle.'

'Then go, lass.'

'Uncle!'

Amalric was outside his door, pulling up stalks of climbing weeds that had died over winter and threatened to resurrect.

'Beatrix! Let me sit on this bench. Ee, lass it's good to see you. You look reet well.' She was flushed. 'You saw Arnold, then.'

She laughed. 'Yes, I did. He'll come to see you shortly.'

The church window panels leaned against the south nave wall. At intervals, little threads of copper could be seen, soldered to the cames ready to be wound round Joshua's bars.

Arnold Mason stepped down from his ladder. 'There, Master Faceby, the stonework is repaired, new grooves are cut to take the glass, and the stone is sound.'

'And I've checked that the bars are firm for the copper ties,' said Joshua. 'It's all ready for the glass to be put in. Then your putty, and it'll be done.'

'Your window will be safe for years,' said Arnold. 'I'll stay to help lift the panels for you tomorrow. An early start should see it done in one day.' He saw Amalric's outstretched hand. 'Nay, I don't want your money. My work here has been a delight.'

The next day, by late afternoon, the three men stood back to take in the full view of the new window. The sun was beginning to set and slanted through the glass, catching important imperfections. Amalric felt that, along with nearly all his glass, he had put nearly all his heart into the window.

Lord de Horesby's image filled the centre lancet, and the two lancets on either side had the green land and distant hills of East Yorkshire. Included, small as if in the distance, was Horesby manor house and the farmed land around it. Summer leaves decorated the outer edges of the window so that the whole was seen as if looked at through trees. But it was Lord de Horesby's figure that first drew the eye.

'Oh, Master Faceby,' said Arnold. 'That's the most wonderful window I've ever seen. The man still lives!'

Beatrix grasped her uncle's arm and stood with tears running down her cheeks.

Amalric felt something indescribable. He had put all that he remembered of the old man into this window, but looking at it now, it was as if some other hand had guided him. He was amazed at his own talent.

Lord de Horesby's image stood as firm, as if he had real feet on the ground. His long, dark blue robe hung with folds indicated by linear streaks in the glass. His hands emerged from the robe displaying the Horesby gold ring with its large emerald; a small raised dome of green glass. A white collar tipped the neck of his robe. But it was his face that demanded most attention. The wrinkled neck, the thin white beard and hair, the depression on the forehead from the childhood accident. The modelling of the nose with imperfections, and loose skin surrounding the eyes were all remarkable. He was sad and kind at the same time.

The writing at the bottom said in local language, *Praise God for the life of Lord de Horesby of Warren Horesby. Died 1388. Remembered and revered. Suffered many hardships and pestilences with his villagers.* A feather at the bottom right was combined with the words, *Amalric Faceby, Glazier.*

Amalric was the last to leave the church. Entering at the same time was a young sculptor pushing a low cart on which rested a stone plaque. The lad mumbled something about setting it up tomorrow; Amalric barely glanced at him.

The next day was a clearing day in the workshop after the installation of the window. By midday Nathan was sweeping behind the door, when suddenly it shot open. His broom caught his face and sent him staggering backwards. Amalric caught him just before he fell. Noah barked in panic. Edwin barged in, his staff brandished like a weapon, followed by Friar Swale looking red-faced and troubled.

'Brother, what do you mean by installing that window?'

Amalric had a headache following the celebrations of the evening before; a joyous, raucous affair at the tavern with Thurston, Arnold, Joshua and bucolic villagers.

'Window? Ah, window in the church. Which one?' he said derisively. 'There's the east window, north windows, south windows – one of which I installed only yesterday…'

'Don't bandy with me. You know what I mean. You have the effrontery to make a memorial window without telling me.'

'Effrontery, eh? Is that what I have? Well, well.' Amalric was enjoying this.

'Yes. You have deliberately disobeyed me. I told you I was arranging a memorial plaque for Lord de Horesby, and obviously nothing else was required.'

'A memorial plaque! Pah! Is that what you call it? A meagre bit of stone with bad carving by a lad who probably can't spell either Latin or English – a memorial to a great family and a great man. A family who will be lost to memory if you have your own way.' He waved his hand in hopelessness. 'You want money and space for your own cold stone memorial, I suppose – a big one in the north-east corner. You and Clara, feet resting on a hound, maybe a book in your stone hand to indicate intelligence.'

'Now, gentlemen.' Friar Swale lifted his hands from where they rested on his corpulent belly and held them up, pleading for reconciliation. He was ignored.

'The window must go.'

'Go! Over my dead body!' Amalric had not felt so much uncomplicated anger rising for years. He felt revived. Alive.

'You know you should have had my permission. You did not. I would not have sanctioned it. It's unnecessary and not er… biblical. Is it, Brother Swale?'

'Well, er…'

'Yes, I should have had the permission of the Lord of the Manor – well, I did.' Amalric knew he had the upper hand. 'It just so happens it was before he died.'

Edwin tipped his staff toward his brother. 'You well know my superior position with this manor. My wife is…'

Friar Swale intervened. 'Now, gentlemen, gentlemen. In my view, the window is… er… I… er…' The friar was obviously out of his depth with this problem combining art, the Church and manorial rights.

'Nathan?' Amalric saw the lad holding his sleeve to a nose dripping copious amounts of blood. He threw him a cleaning cloth from the table. 'Nathan, use this and go to the forge. Tell Joshua what's happening here.' The lad rushed out, holding the cloth to his nose before Edwin could stop him.

Edwin turned his indignation on to the friar. 'Come now, Friar, what say you of this glazier flagrantly using the church to make money on a new window without permission?' He looked at Amalric. 'I expect you hope to be paid for this out of my lord's will.'

'Well, I really have no obj...' said Friar Swale, trying to answer Edwin.

'It was all at my own expense,' said Amalric, 'and the wardens and villagers have a say too as to what goes into their church; they pay enough for it with their tithes. And look at your friar, here, he's doing rather well out of those, judging by his belly!'

The friar's face turned puce. Edwin looked unable to contain his anger; his staff swung menacingly. Amalric became nervous. If Edwin went to the church, his new, very best window would be at risk. One prod at it with the staff would ruin it. There was no glass left for repairs.

Edwin turned abruptly to leave, but looked surprised to see Thurston and Arnold standing at the door, side by side. To Amalric they looked comical, but to Edwin it meant more aggravation. Amalric hoped that Thurston would be as perceptive and calm as usual, despite the signs of an ale-head in his puffy but twinkling eyes.

'Good day to you all,' said the physician with a hint of mockery. 'Are you conversing about Master Faceby's new window? The master mason and I have just been to see it in mid-morning light. It is remarkably fine.'

'It is the finest I've seen in all my travels,' said Arnold. 'It will be of great repute.'

'Indeed,' continued Thurston, now disarmingly. 'It is to your great credit, Master Edwin, as the new manor-lord consort, and you, Friar Swale, as the minister of the church, that you agreed to it. Together with the... er... stone plaque, the... er... name will not be forgotten.'

Arnold sniggered.

Amalric was relieved to see a group of people coming down the hill and going towards the church. Nathan was with them, his face streaked with nasal blood. 'Master Faceby!' he called. 'The villagers have come to save the window. The blacksmith gathered 'em up.'

A sizeable group of both men and women went to stand defiantly with folded arms at the church porch. Joshua Smith stood in front with muscled arms folded and thick legs splayed, accompanied by Douglas Redhead: a formidable duo. Amalric was highly amused. On the surface, the mood of the villagers was good-humoured, but Edwin's face paled.

There was no doubt that Amalric had won. Once, long ago, after the Great Pestilence, when he had made the east window for the church, the villagers had not understood the beauty of coloured glass, nor its power to tell the Christian story. At that time, painted walls and woodwork had been enough to guide them. Now, years later, they had begun to appreciate the artistic splendour of glass, added to which, the new window would honour all their friends and relatives who had died from the dreadful pestilences, focused on the image of one man, their manorial lord.

This was not lost on Edwin. He turned to Friar Swale and said grudgingly, 'It will stay.' The friar nodded but held back as Edwin turned to walk away.

'You know, Master Amalric, I believe you are of the opinion that I spend too much time at the manor. Well, just think on – my order helps not only the poor and downtrodden, but also the rich and unwise.'

Amalric felt contrite.

'Friar! Come!' Edwin called. 'A jug of ale at the manor, I think, for us both.'

The villagers followed Edwin and Friar Swale, their tension breaking into laughter. Joshua slapped Douglas on the back. 'A jug of ale at the tavern, I think, for us both,' he said mockingly. They walked up the hill, chuckling.

Thurston and Arnold stood with broad grins.

'All reet, what else is there to say?' asked Amalric.

Arnold spoke, gleefully. 'We saw the young lad of a make-believe mason in the church erecting his memorial plaque. Sadly, we had to tell him he'd made a mistake. The appalling writing said, *To the glory of God and in memory of Lord de Horsefly!*'

Chapter Twenty-nine

1394 Warren Horesby

Coloured glass had become more available, but it was still hard for village churches to contemplate the expense of it, and while Amalric's work had been reduced to mainly colourless glass, his fears for the future could not compare with those of his friend; Thurston had agonised over the possibility of another bout of pestilence, the fifth. He told Amalric it simmered like the contents of a cooking pot. It would take only more fuel added to the fire to make it boil over. That had eventually come in the form of a reckless journeyman, a carpenter, moving from a stricken area in the south to work on a screen in York Minster. York boiled over.

Few townsfolk had gardens sufficient to allow them to subsist, and thus the disease penetrated viciously into almost every home, tavern, shop and warehouse. Amalric had no idea of the details, but he saw dread in Thurston's eyes as he isolated himself once again from Warren Horesby in the cottage by the manor gate. Amalric frequently watched him from a distance as he left it to offer advice, treat the sick as best he could and record the manifestations of the pestilence's terrible return. Thurston had forewarned the Warren Horesby villagers and they hunkered down to survive on self-sufficiency. Even so, many became ill, being insufficiently prepared. The graveyard was enlarged and another pit dug, helped by Douglas, and as before, Amalric watched the dead bounce daily on the sexton's handcart to a communal rest across the road and into the church grounds.

For almost two years, Thurston worked between the triangle of York, Beverley and King's-Town on Hull. It was a terrible outbreak. At the end of it, he told Amalric that the pestilence pits in York held the bones of eleven thousand folk.

Warren Horesby had weakened; one-third of the people had disappeared and their homes were left empty; the pestilence pit stank again, farm strips were choked with weeds, the mill ground a poor crop sluggishly, and its pond was clogged with strings of green slime. Sheep survived on their own. The church roof leaked and soaked surviving villagers as they gave thanks for their deliverance, but leaks were of no concern to Friar Swale. Yet Amalric found it in his heart to forgive him; the friar had served poor, sick villagers in their agony in a way that had surprised him. The friar had been, after all, faithful to his calling and lucky to survive his closeness to the contagion. It was true, God moved in mysterious ways.

On a sunny but blustery late winter day, with the pestilence behind them, Thurston and Amalric sat outside the tavern holding thick cloaks around themselves. The village was silent, unkempt and morose.

Amalric looked to the north. 'When them clouds get here, we'll have to leave: they're full o' rain.'

The alewife served them an insignificant ale. She had lost much weight and had a glum countenance. Thurston handed her more coins than was necessary and watched her nod thanks and hobble away.

'Poor woman,' he remarked. 'She lost a husband and three children. Pitiful, it was. All that remains for her is her tenancy of this place, and that could be taken from her at any moment if your brother sees fit to install a man. I feel guilty to be alive but blessed that my children are alive. Ava has an aptitude for healing but her air of carefree innocence worries me. Asa's doing well at Oxford, one of the youngest. He wants to research the pestilence for his thesis.'

Amalric knew that there would be nothing better to buck up his friend's sagging spirits than a discourse over his grandson's academic work. He listened intently until the rain came.

1395

Spring evidenced, bringing a sense of hopefulness and colour to Warren Horesby. Amalric whistled cheerfully in his workshop, then stopped and stared with disbelief at Edwin's grandson, looking nervously at him through the open doorway. 'George! What are you doing here? Is something wrong at the manor?' As far as he could recall, George had never set foot inside the workshop.

Nathan, the glazier assistant, looked at the young man quizzically, apparently amazed at his tight, striped hose, fitted jacket and long-toed shoes. Amalric was amused to see the shoes; the style had recently become popular in England, some years after Edwin's knowing of them abroad. Apparently, some were so long they needed strings tied from the toe to the calf to keep the flapping ends from bringing the wearer indecently down to earth. George's were not so extreme. His brimmed hat, though, had long streamers which seemed to have no purpose whatsoever except to entertain dogs. Noah snapped at them excitedly.

Amalric held back a grin with tight lips. 'What can I do for you?' he said pleasantly.

George nudged Noah away with his foot. 'Grandfather Edwin has sent me to tell you a window has cracked and fallen out. You must come; it's cold in the main hall.'

'So you're taking his messages, are you, lad? Well, welcome, it's good to…'

George suddenly, without the politeness of a goodbye, left the workshop rapidly. Amalric realised he'd seen Ava walk past the open door, dreamily swinging an empty flour sack from its twisted multicoloured closing string, presumably going to the mill.

'Not staying for a beaker of ale, then?' called Amalric after him.

Amalric mused on the situation. Ava was a comely lass who'd eschewed the village lads, considering them dolts, making her one of the oldest village maids. This warm, late spring day, she looked particularly attractive in a clean, white overgarment, pulled in at the waist to prevent it flapping, but which served to emphasise her curvaceous figure. Her fuzz of light blonde, unruly hair was fastened up and left uncovered, exposing her neck. Amalric was reminded of Father Luke's dismay some time back at the lewd fashions — bare skin, tight hose and such – of young people, and found the little scene playing out before him interesting.

He was joined at the window by Noah. The dog stood on his back legs with front paws on the windowsill looking out. Amalric stood relaxed, leaning on the sill. Ava touched George's hat and seemed to be mocking him flirtatiously. She put the sack under her arm and stood with hands on her hips, laughing. George was obviously not amused.

Amalric was enjoying the little playlet and put his hand to Noah's soft neck. Simultaneously, George put out a hand to Ava's neck and stroked it. The gesture had the appearance of mild flattery, but then he put his mouth to her ear. Ava recoiled and slapped his cheek, just as a maiden would be required to do after a trifling seduction attempt. Amalric expected George to skip away with merriment, shouting endearments. It was what he would have done when a young man. But George's face became deep pink. His mouth moved inaudibly. Ava looked affronted, turned sharply and walked determinedly downhill.

George stood for a moment with tight lips and clasped fists, seemingly not knowing what to do next. He looked up and down the road; no one else was about. He set off towards the mill, following Ava.

Amalric became alarmed. This was not how the scene should have played out. His imagination began working excessively; George was of Edwin's lineage, with *love* learned crudely in Snickelways and dark taverns. Amalric knew he had to intervene. He must follow George. But he had stood still too long. His legs would not move and held him in cramps. He groaned in agony and fell to the ground below the window. He sat and rubbed them, earnestly trying to bring back life to his legs, but the pains would not go away. Noah barked concern.

The agonising knots in his calves kept him on the ground for longer than he wished. When they finally began to unravel and he was able to stand by grasping the windowsill, he saw George walking back up the hill. His clothes were mildly untidy, as if he had done some moderately strenuous work. Little else seemed amiss, except that he walked rapidly ahead with his ridiculous hat in his hand, crumpled and with the streamers flowing. Noah made to go outside, tempted to run to them.

'Noah, no!' shouted Amalric.

George turned, and wild eyes met Amalric's for an instant.

Now really alarmed, Amalric, with tender legs, gingerly staggered down the hill to find Ava. He met her coming towards him unsteadily, her overgarment grass-stained. Her head was down and her eyes were hidden by a fall of hair. She had no flour sack.

'Ee, lass, what's 'appened? You look in a reet mess.'

'Nothing,' she replied sharply. 'Nothing!'

Amalric watched his granddaughter walk with difficulty up the hill, grasping her skirts closely to her. The road was empty and she met no one. He went down towards the mill, and in a copse, found a flour sack.

Time passed and Amalric heard nothing about the incident. He expected the matter to be too sensitive to raise and could only assume that whatever had happened in the copse by the mill had passed without dire consequences.

Chapter Thirty

Amalric heard that after almost twenty years without funds, stonework on the east window of York Minster would soon resume. His mood was diffident. Thoughts about it and the opportunities he once might have had were pointless and painful. His racks were almost empty of glass, and he had no work contracted. His regular visit to check on the Meaux Abbey windows had been recent so there was no excuse for a pleasant ride out. The uncomfortable truth was that he'd recently neglected the village responsibilities his artisan status required. He decided now was a good time to revive them. The matter was becoming serious; the mill pond needed clearing of weeds and, being at the opposite end of the village to the manor, it had not come to Edwin's attention. Left alone through summer and into autumn it would become a disaster. It meant a visit to the manor, and he didn't look forward to it.

Strolling up the hill, he noticed Beatrix in her doorway.

'It's good to see you, lass. Where've you been recently? You look peaky. Have you been ill?' His legs ached from the walk and he was glad to stop. Negotiating the increasing ruts and stones was hard work.

'Uncle! Please come in for a rest. I need to speak with you.'

Amalric dipped his head under the doorway lintel and went into the main room. Summer flowers decorated the table. Unusually, these were drooping and old. He flopped onto a chair, the only one that had a well-carved, shaped seat which fitted his buttocks just right, and the back leaned at a comfortable angle. It was an old family chair, a man's chair in a woman's home. He liked that.

'This is a good chair. I remember the man who made such fine work. It was Briskin Carpenter. He died in the Great Pestilence. His son never managed the same skill. Too young, he was, to have had a good apprenticeship. Good only for coffins. Then he left to go travellin'. Not heard of him since. Nice lad.'

'Uncle Amalric, Ava is to be married.'

'Married!' He was astonished. 'Who to? I didn't know she was even courtin'.'

Beatrix looked down at her apron and removed an invisible fleck. He then had the fluttering in his chest he knew to be apprehension of something known while still unknown.

'She is with child and is beginning to show.'

Amalric was dumbfounded. He knew instinctively it must have been that day in the copse when he had said nothing about what he'd seen. He stared at his niece.

'To George?' It had slipped out.

'Yes, Uncle. You guessed right. George. I heard her crying when she realised about the child. It wasn't the first time she'd cried recently. This time, I forced her to tell me what was wrong.' Beatrix looked at her uncle quizzically. 'You don't seem surprised it's George. Do you know something?'

What could he say? 'Only that George is known to be a mite, shall we say, lecherous. But he's young still. I've not seen much of the lad, but I wouldn't trust him.'

'It's not what Ava wanted, I know, but you know how difficult it is to prove that anything is amiss with such a relationship. He forced himself on her, she says, but how can that be proven when pregnancy is always seen as proof that the woman was complicit? I've seen much of these problems. Anyway, Ava hopes to bring the child to birth. She's doing nothing to jeopardise that. Oh, Uncle, Hendric would have been beside himself with anger, were he alive to see it.'

'Aye, he would. And isn't George too closely related to Ava? There's laws about such things.'

'Friar Swale said, very disapprovingly, that he was prepared to accept the relationship. I'm not sure how he views my own bastard origin in the mix – he remained silent on that.'

'What does Thurston have to say?'

'Oh, Uncle, I've never seen Father so angry. He's at the manor now. I won't burden you with more, Uncle. We just want to avoid village gossip, though heaven knows the women round the well will have something to say when the marriage is announced. George is… is happy about the marriage.'

Blood was rising in Amalric's head.

'Uncle? Your face is full of anger.' Beatrix grasped his arm as if to restrain him, but he pulled away.

'Aye, well… I was on my way to the manor on village business and must continue.'

Amalric sped up the road to the manor, his paining legs forgotten. Thurston was on his way down from there. Amalric was taken aback by his friend's demeanour. 'My friend, you look as though your world's fallen apart.'

'And you look ready to kill someone. I'm guessing you've seen Beatrix.'

'I have.'

'Well, it's all arranged. Ava will marry George in one week, before she has time to show much more. They'll live at the manor, but part of the bargain I've managed to get agreed is that I'll make fit an empty village cottage for Ava and the baby's use at my expense. I've asked Douglas to look one or two over for me. The one chosen will have to be cleaned of all pestilential debris. There's not one that a person has not died within of the disease. I'll bequeath it to her.'

'Aye, they'll be full of muck. No doubt my Istrid will help.' Amalric took hold of Thurston's shoulder. 'All may be well, my friend.'

'My aim, Am, is for her to have a cottage of her own to bring the child up should things go bad with George. I fear for her life. If he beats her, I want her to have a retreat of her own.'

Leaving Thurston, Amalric limped on to the manor. He

pushed ferociously on the large oak door; the lion-head knocker reacted loudly. He forced himself past a bemused servant and stomped into the great hall, loudly demanding of another servant, 'Fetch Master Edwin. I have business.' The man ran off, his clogs clattering on the stone floor, and disappeared behind a curtain that cut off a passageway.

Amalric looked around; things had changed since Lord de Horesby had died. There was little evidence of the old man's parsimonious habits. Edwin had clearly availed himself of the finer things in life. A fire played in the central hearth, extravagantly piled high with logs. Six chairs, clearly made by Briskin Carpenter fifty or more years ago and brought out of storage, were neatly placed around a large table. Flowers were arranged in a fine pottery jug in the centre of the table, reflecting their colours in the polished surface, and good, carved wooden bowls held dried fruits and nuts. Two deep-bowled, rimmed, pewter plates, each with a sharp pointed knife laid upon it, indicated a forthcoming meal. Next to them stood two fine glass drinking beakers, no doubt from the far East.

Edwin appeared from the curtain, adjusting his hose and with a noisome stink wafting from behind him. He pulled a long overtunic from a hook on the wall and slipped into the sleeveless garment with stately effect.

'Ho, brother. First the clever doctor and now the fool. Well, I've made myself comfortable in the privy, and so I have time for you before I eat. Is it manor business or something more personal?'

Amalric was incensed by the sneering expression and voice, the neat beard with black and white coarse whiskers, the fancy hair with straight-cut fringe, the colourful clothing and especially the emerald de Horesby ring on an index finger. 'The mill pond is clogged. It needs clearing,' he said in monotone.

'Really? I'll get someone to see to it. Next item.'

'The next item is your grandson.' Ascending emotion caused Amalric's voice to rise. 'I know what has happened to Ava. The trait has run through you to your sons and their sons. You say

I'm a fool; well, it doesn't take a fool to understand that this is no amicable and natural union. It was forced.'

'Can you prove it?'

Amalric knew he couldn't. Suspicion was not enough.

Edwin went on, 'Ava is a comely girl, broad of hip. She'll bear the child well. Good breeding stock, eh, Am? I'm delighted — a great-grandchild at my young age. Well, younger than you, anyway. To live long enough to have a great-grandchild is almost a miracle, for us both, don't you agree? One day, Ava will make a good mistress of this manor house.' He picked up a glass beaker and ran his finger over gold decoration. 'She'll drink like a princess from fine, pure glass such as this.' He held it up to the light. 'See – no imperfections.'

Amalric knew this was a snide remark aimed at his use of imperfections in glass for windows. The effect was to further incense him. Edwin ran a spittle-dampened finger around the rim of the vessel. A high-pitched ringing sound ensued.

'Ah, the sound of purity – unsullied, like a maiden.'

At this, Amalric could no longer hold himself in. Fury burst from him. He knocked Edwin to one side and clumsily grasped a knife from the table. The jug toppled over. Flowers and water spewed over the smooth surface. The glass drinking vessel dropped from Edwin's hand to the floor and shattered. Hundreds of glass pieces, like salt chopped from a block, crunched under their feet as Amalric advanced forward with the knife while Edwin retreated. The knife grew closer to Edwin's neck. All Amalric could focus on was a little drop of blood that began flowing slowly onto the point.

An arm pulled at his elbow.

'Thank the saints we got here in time.'

The voice was Thurston's, but it was another's hand that pulled at him – larger, younger, ginger and hairy.

'I grew afraid of the look on your face, Am, and came back with Douglas Redhead.' The Scot towered above them. 'We are old men, me, you and Edwin. Cease this attack. Do you want your grey head to blacken on the posts in Beverley? His taunting

240

is meaningless. It will do no good. What's done is done.'

Amalric was sickened at the thought of what he might have done. The knife clattered to the floor. He noticed that Edwin was trying to hide the shaking that had resulted from the attack by making a firm effort to pull his luxurious tunic tightly around him. He looked rather pathetic.

Amalric felt as heavy as a boulder. His legs were hardly able to move. The repeated hurt and reconciliations with Edwin and his family wearied him beyond measure. Thurston and Douglas took him by the arms and ushered him away.

'Well, brother,' Edwin called from the big oak door as he watched the three men walk away from the building. 'The child will at least be a Faceby.'

Chapter Thirty-one

1396 Warren Horesby

Amalric looked at the thriving child in the Faceby family crib and softly touched the small cheek. 'Your little Erika is adorable,' he said. 'Born at Christmas, eh? Such babies are special.'

He was in Ava's cottage. Months back, Istrid had spent much time with pails of water, cleansing herbs and her broom, removing every dubious piece of debris, including all identified and unidentified animal droppings, dead insects, mice and birds. Thurston had employed village thatchers to put up a new heather thatch; Douglas had repaired wattle and daub. The grandson of Briskin Carpenter, recently returned to his family home, had made passable new shutters for the windows. Fresh soil had been impacted onto the floor. The furious activity had resulted in a cosy home.

'This is where I'm happy, Uncle. I'm so grateful to Grandfather Thurston, but I fear he has little money left. He pays for a living-in servant. I see little of George's parents; Robert and his wife are often away hunting and brushing up longbow skills. Grandfather Edwin likes to see Erika and me at the manor house. He thinks I will eventually be mistress there and sends me to Clara to learn… though she is ailing and a most unhappy woman. The family pays scant regard to faith, but I shall be an avid supporter of Warren Horesby church.'

Amalric sensed a great unhappiness in the girl. He hoped her faith would help her to relieve it. 'And how is George treating you?'

It was an audacious question, but Ava looked tired; her blonde, curly hair hung limp. She was obsessed with her child, but rarely mentioned her husband.

'George is not taken with Erika, I'm afraid. He wanted a son. Even before the birth, he'd persuaded his father to purchase a young falcon and a young fine-bred pony to grow up with the child. I'm a disappointment. He longs only for a son.'

Amalric was not at all surprised at George's attitude. Edwin's household had always reeked of overbearing masculinity. Though what father wouldn't want a son? But Amalric himself was charmed by the sweet baby girl. The women he'd known within his family had been strong, fulfilling the roles of housewives, mothers and healers. Women had talents that emerged in moments of crisis, or slowly so that you didn't know they were there until they had gone. He wondered what talents this baby girl would have. Would they be suppressed by society's expectations and laws, or would she be allowed some freedom to pursue her dreams? He knew how unfulfilled dreams could trouble one's life.

'Ee, lass. But he looks after you reet well – I hope?'

'He doesn't beat me, if that's what you mean. I do what I must do to be his wife. Hopefully I'll give him a son one day. Never fear, I'll bring Erika to see you often, Uncle.'

The Yorkshire sky was deep blue. Halfway through tidying his workshop, Amalric was resting on a bench outside the workshop with Noah at his feet. All was bathed in autumnal-silent warmth. As he looked up the hill, he saw Ava coming down. On her hip, held there by a knotted shawl over one shoulder, was little Erika. Noah, too, saw them and bounded to greet them. He sniffed the child and was rewarded with a tiny hand coming out of its restraints and waggling fingers at him. Amalric felt his smile reach almost from ear to ear.

'Hello, Uncle, I thought Erika might like to see some sparkling glass. As young as she is, she tires me with her curiosity. Now she's started crawling, I can hardly keep her in my sight.'

Amalric stood and shook his legs one at a time to loosen them. 'Come in, lass, come in. Take the weight off your feet. That bairn of yours is a healthy, heavy package.'

Ava still looked tired. She was not the happy, carefree girl she had once been. He went to a wooden box and rummaged inside and pulled out small, smooth blobs of glass. Erika was immediately interested but her mother firmly held her.

'Your mother is quite right to hold you back, little one. If they fall, they may break. My old hands can cope with sharp edges, but not yours.' He held a piece into the light. 'Look at what sunshine can do.' Reflected colour shot onto the white table. The child suddenly leaned forward, reaching out to touch the otherworldly splash of luminous blue. Her mother almost dropped her and bent forward to take her weight. As she did so, Ava caught sight of something in the corner of the workshop. It was a flour sack with its colourful twisted tie hanging loose. There followed a moment when Amalric knew she was realising what he would have seen from the open door on her dreadful day.

'You know, don't you?' Ava's eyes blazed as she looked him full in the face. 'You know what happened to me. You never said anything, but you knew. You could have helped.'

Amalric felt distraught. 'I couldn't have done anything. I tried. I saw him follow you. My legs cramped – I fell.'

But Ava was in no mood to listen. Tears gushed. 'I expect it went round the tavern. Everyone in the village must know.'

'Of course not! I told no one!'

Ava rapidly secured Erika and left. Amalric stood at the workshop door with Noah, bereft, watching their hurried progress up the hill.

It was dusk when Thurston arrived. 'I guessed I'd still find you here. This workshop is an extension of you.'

'Aye, Thurston, you've always understood me.'

'And you me, right from the time we met at Meaux Abbey when I was studying a manuscript looking for cures for the

Great Pestilence. You told me of your father's precious Theophilus manuscript on the art of glass. It was our similar ways of learning our own trades.'

'You've seen Ava, haven't you?'

'I have. Am...' Thurston hesitated. 'Whatever happened that day, I know you would have prevented it if you were able. I believe the worst thing you did was to keep the flour sack where it could be seen.' He smiled compassionately. 'Old friend, Ava will eventually realise she misjudged you. It was a shock seeing the sack. It brought everything back. Beatrix is looking after her now. Women understand each other.'

1397

'I've not seen your Ava for more than a year and three moons,' said Amalric, regrettably, to Thurston. 'How's the little one doing?'

'Erika is fine. She's a strong little thing and has coped so far with her childhood illnesses without much bother,' said Thurston. 'Ava too is well. She's having a small chapel built in the grounds of the manor. It's nearly finished.'

'Aye, I've seen it from a distance. How did she get the money to do it? I can't imagine any of the family would pay for such a thing.'

Thurston smiled. 'Ava has become a strong woman in her bitterness. She had Clara on her side and threatened to go into a convent if she couldn't have her way. It was a risk. Beatrix was distraught, wondering what would happen to Erika. I believe Edwin in particular was eager to give in to her demand.'

Amalric smiled. 'Well, well! I think I'll pay a visit to the chapel to see Ava; it may offer the chance for us to break our silence.'

Chapter Thirty-two

He was nervous, walking slowly with the excuse that it would keep his legs from tiring. Noah padded in long grass, catching the dew in his hair as his nature forced him to investigate interesting scents. It was a crisp day and the cool late autumn breeze on Amalric's face was a delight after the smoke of the morning fire. The low sun raked over houses, illuminating the thatch but still keeping the less savoury aspects of village life under the overhang in shadowy obscurity: piles of chopped wood, water barrels, animal dung, privy soil and piles of rubbish saved just in case the stuff could be used again. The pestilences had left a legacy of keeping what could be kept.

At the top of the hill, Amalric stood with fisted hands on his waist to get his breath. Before him, sheep grazed, flecked against dull grass. Further on, skeletal trees, preserving their marrow for winter, crowded the valley and rose out onto the edge of the uplands. It was a sparse beauty. At any time, this scene could change to frozen whiteness. Amalric sighed at the transience of it and hoped the coming winter would see God's kindness. He turned onto the manor path and pushed open the gate with an effort. Once it had hardly ever been closed, but now the heavy gate was always shut; nowadays, people seemed more protective of what they owned.

The stone manor was imposing, its roof tiles shiny with moisture. To the left was a small, rectangular building of fresh-cut stone, also with a tiled roof.

He moved tentatively towards it and walked around. In the south wall near to its western end was a door space without a door, and a small, glassless window space to the right of it. Another small window space was high up on the west gable, a third was low at the east end. Through the latter, a flickering light could be seen. The glazier in Amalric couldn't help but momentarily weigh up the possibility of inserting coloured glass in them, but he immediately discounted the idea and went through the low door space. A cloud of sweet-smelling incense and beeswax hit his nose. Noah sneezed. Facing away from them was Ava, kneeling. Her long gown splayed behind her from narrow shoulders onto the rough stone floor. Light crept around her figure from, Amalric assumed, a candle on the floor in front of her where an altar should have been.

Ava turned at the unexpected noise and recognised him even through the dimness. 'Oh, Uncle!' She stood, revealing a beeswax candle and a bronze cross on a rectangle of tiles.

Amalric was shocked. Deep shadows, enhanced by the candle-light, shaped her taut, pinched face. 'I'm sorry. I didn't mean to bother...'

'It's no matter. I expected you to come. You must want a commission for the windows.'

'Ee, lass, no. I just wanted to...' The sharpness of her response was hurtful.

'I'm sorry.' She sounded contrite. Her shoulders dropped. 'Will you come to the manor house for a warm drink?'

'No, lass.' It was hard to steady his voice. 'It's just that it's been a long time since we talked, and I thought this might be a place to mend us. I'm sorry for what I failed to do for you.' There, it was out; blurted, as the pressure finally broke through long-held restraint. Tears formed. He held them back with a sniff.

'Oh, Uncle. It's I who should be sorry. I was unhappy and it was a relief to be able to outwardly blame someone rather than myself. I was a silly girl. Let's forget it. See, here is a stool. Please sit to help your legs.'

'Thanks, lass.'

'My only happiness now is Erika, and that's tainted with

fear.'

'Oh?'

'Small though she is, George's grandfather Edwin is pressing for a suitor. George too. I've not been able to have another child yet, so they wish to secure the future. They have someone in mind. A lord somebody or other. It appals me. Erika is still in her baby years. I'm distraught.'

'So... you're turning to faith.'

'Yes. I shall make it my business to find good priests for the village if necessary. Friar Swale shows no sign of leaving yet, and he is a good man. He helps me.'

Amalric made no comment.

'Uncle, I need this place of my own to pray, away from the gaudiness of the village church. Oh, I don't mean your windows, but the wall paintings. They seem to look down on me and clamour with their fading colours and forebodings. This place will give me peace when it's finished. The walls will be bare stone. The altar will be stone, I hope, with candles and incense.'

Amalric was more concerned for Ava's physical well-being than for her faith. 'But you'll have cold air coming in them windows. You don't look strong enough to face a bitter winter.'

'*I'm* strong enough. But there *is* sickness in the manor. A coughing disease is going through the men of the family. My father-in-law, Robert, and his brother, Walter, suffer from it, but not badly yet. Grandfather Edwin has it too. The men spit on the floor for anyone to tread in and sometimes I see blood in it. They expect me to ignore it. They've no doubt picked the sickness up when gambling, or from loose women in vile places. Goodness knows what else their foul bodies hide. They are filthy beasts. My husband, George, is well. Clara is the most ill – she doesn't cough, but I think she's grown weak with unhappiness. Grandfather Thurston is never asked to attend these days and so is unaware of my misery.'

'Oh, Ava.'

'I've kept it quiet so far and escaped to the cottage Grandfather Thurston procured for me. You must all have thought I was being aloof. But in this little chapel, I will be able to be myself and seek the truth.' Tears started to drip down her cheeks.

'And Erika?'

'I keep her away from them as much as I can. These days, I seldom have her at the manor. I'd rather she was with my mother.'

Amalric had no words.

'Uncle?' Ava said tentatively. 'You're right about the windows. Would you be interested in a small commission?'

'Now, you don't have to please me.'

'I'm not. But advise me, for although I'm happy to make some sacrifices regarding comfort, I don't think I could pray adequately if I was freezing to death.'

Amalric saw a glimmer of a smile. 'Well, winter's coming on so I'd best hurry. How about keeping it simple by filling the windows with clear, colourless glass except the one at the east? It's small.' He stopped to think. His tongue felt the grey whiskers curling around his lips. 'How about a clear glass star against a blue background, like God's pure light appearing out of the sky? A sign, like at Bethlehem. No charge. A gift.'

Ava put up her hands to her open mouth. It was obvious to Amalric that an unaccustomed emotion had taken her by surprise. 'Oh, that would be just perfect!'

'Arnold Mason in Beverley might find you a spare stone for an altar fine enough for your cross.'

Amalric's heart felt light. Opening the gate to leave was easier than when he had arrived. Walking down the hill he whistled happily, his tune only wavering when a rut had to be negotiated or when Noah darted unexpectedly in front of him chasing a squirrel or other rodent.

Amalric mused on his meeting with Ava. It had solved something. Brought a flash of happiness. Her chapel windows would be in before the new year's bitterly cold gales hit East Yorkshire. It would be a labour of love.

So unusual was his state of mind that, entering his home, he bumped his head hard on the low lintel. All his life in the same building and still he forgot to drop his head! Through flashing lights, he saw Istrid by the central fire; his mother and Nesta had stood in the same spot with the same wooden spoon, stirring the same pot. Their images merged. He rubbed his head. It hurt and he still felt a little dazed. He blinked to clear his eyes and a shadow of someone sitting by the fire became evident. A man dressed in poor peasant clothing was chatting to Istrid as she stirred. They both looked up at his groan.

'Oh you'll have a bump there,' said Istrid, as she went to a cupboard, 'Da, this is Aldred. He's from a hamlet in the hills.'

'Oh, aye?' He wasn't very interested; his head thumped.

'My mother's hamlet. This is Mother's brother's grandson. He's a relative of ours.'

'Nesta's hamlet?' Amalric's mixed emotions took him by surprise. 'I never met your family. I'm sorry, lad.' He put out a hand to the stranger who was short, thickset and had nearly reached manhood. His heavy, straight, mouse-blond hair, light-freckled face and cheeky, alert expression was reminiscent of Nesta. Amalric gulped. 'What are you doing here? You're welcome, of course.'

Istrid put a dab of arnica unguent on his forehead. It felt cool.

'I wanted to meet my family. I never met Aunt Nesta, but I believe she was a servant in this household before she married you, Master Faceby.'

Guilt swept over Amalric. In truth, Nesta's utterly humble beginnings had caused him to think of her as his possession, remembering that he'd rarely thought of her as part of a loving family and certainly never thought to ask her father for her hand in marriage, or visit her family home.

Aldred seemed oblivious to Amalric's inner turmoil. 'I believe you've suffered badly from the pestilences in this village. They all passed by our hamlet until some years ago when it came with a vengeance and saw off just about everyone in their homes. I was left an orphan, a mere babe. I was found by a priest in a barn with animals, and rats gnawing at my toes. See, one is missing.' He displayed a scarred foot. 'I was taken to Swine Priory.'

'Just like Beatrix,' interrupted Istrid.

'I grew up there and was well schooled. I helped with building repairs for my keep; only now, I really need to be away from the nuns with their suffocating love. I'm on my way today to be a Cistercian lay brother at Meaux Abbey.' A half-empty sack of possessions was by his side. 'I may take Holy Orders, but I'm not sure.'

'I know it well,' said Amalric. 'There'll be much to occupy you.'

'Yes. I want to look at new things. I'm interested in how they use the power of water, and their work with metals. I can read Latin, so I want to see how they're copying books. Some of the monks use occularies to read; Aunt Istrid has told me they were invented in your workshop. It's all very interesting.' Aldred's eyes shone with enthusiasm.

'Not so much faith, as faith in what is to come, eh?'

Aldred seemed a little embarrassed. 'Well… I want to invent things.'

'I'm sure you'll do well. How did you know we were here?'

'The nuns knew my aunt Nesta. It seems she kept in touch with them after leaving your doorstep-child with them. It was they who found I still had relatives in Warren Horesby. They had also seen some of your windows in churches. You're quite famous.'

Amalric, Istrid and Aldred chatted amiably over Istrid's meal. Noah, too, had taken a shine to the lad and sat with his head on Aldred's lap as he talked.

'Well, next time we see you, lad, you'll be attired in a… er… light-coloured habit, is it? Not a good choice, in my view, around here, on account of the mud.' Amalric felt old and his forehead hurt; the different long woollen habits of the many types of religious orders confused him.

Chapter Thirty-three

'It looks more like a unicorn than a stag! That's mischievous of you.'

Nine-year-old Erika giggled at Amalric's laughing criticism of her drawing. Noah too joined in the hilarity by nosing the drawing board, attempting to tip it. Nathan leaned on his assistant's broom, smiling.

Earlier, Erika had appeared breathless at the workshop door, her blonde curls like a quivering halo, asking dramatically for sanctuary; her mother, Ava, had attempted to drag her into the manor meat kitchen with its hanging animal corpses and stink of blood, for a lesson on preparing meat. Amalric had been only too pleased to grant it; risking the wrath of her mother was worth the little lass' jovial presence.

'Oh, look, here comes Grandma Beatrix.' Erika had glanced through the open shutters. 'She's running. What's amiss?'

Beatrix clattered through the door.

'Ee, lass, you look all hot and bothered. What's up?' said Amalric. 'A woman of your years shouldn't be running down the hill like that. You've got a bit too much weight on should you fall.'

Beatrix stood, panting, with hands on hips. 'Uncle, you get more blunt as you age.'

Amalric looked blank. Erika giggled.

'A man calling at the tavern has brought a message from

Arnold Mason.' She drew breath. 'Arnold was at York dealing with stonework at the minster with, would you believe, John Thornton! He's signed the glazing contract for York Minster's east window.'

'John Thornton?' So many times that name had been mentioned.

'Yes. John Thornton. Both are stayin' at Meaux Abbey overnight on their way to Coventry. Arnold has persuaded him to call here for refreshment tomorrow – to us, your workshop – afore they go on to Haltemprice Abbey, for their next overnight stop.'

Amalric was agog at the news. 'Well, it seems at last the window will be made.'

'Oh, Uncle, John Thornton, here! And him the most famous glazier in England,' said Beatrix.

'Aye, and you must be with me when he comes.'

Erika's eyes widened; she'd heard talk of this man too. She stood, clattering her board to the floor, narrowly missing Noah's nose. 'Oh, Elder, may *I* meet him?' she said, suddenly full of excitement.

He bent to her. 'Very well, but first, my lass, help Nathan get this workshop tidy. You can clear up the bits of glass I've been too tired to shift. Mind those pretty little fingers, though. We don't want 'em scarred.'

Erika could hardly wait. 'I'll do it now.'

'Beatrix, go see our Istrid and ask her to get some ale and food in for Master Thornton.'

Always, these two women reminded him of Bible women, Martha and Mary, one practical, one thoughtful.[12]

The day after, the workshop had an air of enthusiasm about it that Amalric had thought long gone. Standing among its tidiness, he felt apprehensive. 'I've no glass work here to show Master Thornton... but we could show your candle-holder.'

'Oh, Uncle, no,' said Beatrix. 'He won't be interested in my

---

[12] See Luke 10:38-42.

work. It's small and pointless. Anyway, it's you who has ambition, not me.'

'Nay, lass, my ambition is nowt but an empty dream now. I'm old. You're still capable, though. Erika, go across to the church and fetch your grandmother's candle-holder.'

Erika ran off.

'Uncle, she may drop it.'

'Nay, lass, glass is too precious to her to be careless with it.'

'Come in, sir.' Amalric stood back from the door, surprised to see a stocky figure shorter than himself despite his own increasingly bent back. The rugged face grinned at him.

'Master Amalric. At last. Good day.' His voice had the brogue of the flatter lands of middle England. 'I'm grateful to Arnold Mason here for bringing me to meet you.'

Noah sniffed the visitors, found them without interest and pushed his way outside.

Beatrix emerged from the shadows of the workshop, and Amalric clearly saw Erika noting her grandmother's eyes skim over John Thornton to rest on Arnold behind him. She grinned at Amalric mischievously. He suspected that, young as she was, she sensed romance.

Beatrix caught Erika's grinning face and ushered her to fetch ale and food from Istrid in the house.

'Ah, but this is wonderful.' The famous glazier's eyes wandered over the few pieces of glass in the racks, and his flattened hand roamed over the great white table. 'You know, I long to be back in a little workshop like this, with the warmth of the small hearth and my own tools, all the glass to hand and my home next door, with a single assistant or apprentice...' he looked at Nathan hovering in a corner, 'instead of a troublesome clutch of them. Good tavern ale to refresh me and the fundamental noises and stinks of the village. Now, most of my life is spent in big towns,' his mouth turned down, 'where life is fraught and big churches make constant demands and changes to my designs. And the ferocious, merciless stinks, well...'

'What did you mean when you said you were meeting me *at last?*'

John Thornton settled himself on a stool and leaned forward on the table. 'I came through here many years ago. The pestilence was raging and I feared to stop, but I felt I needed to take confession. I went into the church. There I saw your wonderful east window, done when you were a young man, I believe. The Cistercian priest there, one trained to disdain decoration, truly admired it. I was astounded. It was the faces. The angel telling Mary she was to have a child. It inspired me, Master Amalric.'

Amalric could hardly believe what he was hearing.

'Your use of imperfections in the glass to add feature and texture was so… original. Arnold took me to the church again today before coming here, and I saw your second window. It's a masterpiece. The face of the old man has life. I'm in awe of your work.'

Amalric was astonished. 'I don't know what to say.'

There was banging at the workshop door. Nathan opened it to find Erika having kicked at it and with arms holding a platter of bread, cheese, cold meat and herbs. She put it onto the table with an exaggerated 'phew!' and helped Beatrix lay out the meal.

While waiting, Thornton's eyes scanned the room and rested on the hearth. 'Ah, what is that?'

Erika put down some bread and darted to the candle-holder. She lifted it onto the table at the side of the cheese. Her face beamed proudly. 'It's my grandmother's. She made it. Look, it has bubbles.'

'Aye, she did. Beatrix here made it,' echoed Amalric.

Thornton took a piece of cheese and peered at the detail of the glass while eating. 'It's Creation, yes?' Bits of crumbly cheese fell. 'It makes me smile. It's wonderful. I like your little details of spider and web, butterfly, birds, fish. I like the bubbles.' He smiled at Beatrix. 'You know, you could sell such things to manor houses as small encouragements to prayer.'

Beatrix had no time to respond; Erika placed a drawing of

her own on the table under the master glazier's nose. 'This is mine. I drew it. *I'm* going to learn how to make windows.'

He scrutinised her drawing of a unicorn. 'And so you should, with skill like this. It's mystical! What a talented family you are.'

More food was taken. Ale was poured.

'The window I'm designing for York Minster is partly about Creation, from the Old Testament, but also the book of Revelation from the New Testament – the beginning and end of days – appropriate after so many pestilences. Do you have any plans for future windows?'

'No.' Amalric was keen to explain his abrupt answer. 'We have only a little glass in stock. The pestilences have hit us hard over the years. As you see, I'm very aged and infirm now. My son died – he fitted all the windows. His wife, Beatrix, here, she's also my adopted niece as it happens, and has a village healing and midwifery practice to keep up. She has little time for windows, though I encourage her.'

Thornton looked thoughtful. 'So… your glazing ambitions have died? You must revive them. I may be able to help in a small way. I've planned and drawn much of the York east window, three hundred panels in all, but some are still to do. I could leave you with the size and subject of two shapes left to fill, and you could design their content, send them to me small scale and, after I've approved them, perhaps actually make them here. You see, I need to outsource some work; the minster workshop won't cope with the amount to do and the time to do it in. My contract states I must finish just over three years from now. There would be a small remuneration for you. Arnold Mason here will be doing work in both York and Beverley; send your drawings to him and he will see I get them.'

Amalric had no words.

'If you wish, before I leave here I'll show you my designs. I have sketches of them in my satchel.'

Amalric looked around for Beatrix, but she and Arnold had both disappeared.

'They're outside,' said Erika, '*I'd* like to hear about the window, though.'

Master Thornton spread parchments on the table. Erika held down the curled edges. Laid before them were pictures and details illustrating parts of the Bible.

At the pointed top of the window was God, then below in the tracery shapes was the company of heaven: angels, prophets, saints. Below these, where the tracery ended and the window lights became tall and narrow, were scenes of the Creation and the Garden of Eden as told in the book of Genesis, and other Old Testament stories. Below them, visionary events recorded in the New Testament book of Revelation. Finally, at the bottom of the window were depicted earthly people of faith: popes, bishops, kings.

It would be a massive window. Erika was hardly able to breathe for the delights in front of her. For Amalric, the expressive faces attracted him most: the imperfect noses, the furrowed brows, the open mouths and, best of all, focused, seeing eyes. Some faces were angelic; some ordinary. Some happy; some sad.

'What do you think, Uncle,' Beatrix asked later, 'about seeing faces drawn similar to yours in Master Thornton's drawings? Do you envy him, wish your own dream had come true in the same way?'

'Nay, lass. I've concluded in my old age that our dreams are not for us alone, but to be shared. I'm past my three score years and ten now. Maybe a shared dream is of much more value in the eyes of God. We're all different, with different talents. Mine have been but small achievements. Our inspirations all come from an earlier source. Each of us plays a part. Remember that poet who came to Warren Horesby?'

'I do: the one with the sore fundament?'

'He's since had a bit to say about the part we all play. Come to think of it, if your father hadn't healed him, he wouldn't be as famous as he is now.'

Chapter Thirty-four

Amalric worked hard to think of designs. The window shapes were unfamiliar and the window itself was so huge it was beyond his old mind to comprehend it. Inspiration was not coming to him. His heart beat strangely and he broke out into sweats merely thinking about the difficulties.

As he had so many times before, he sought comfort in the church. It would thankfully be empty since Friar Swale had returned to his Franciscan roots to aid the poor of York.

In the quiet, Amalric confronted the figure of St Edmund. Today, he looked disappointed with humankind, the wounding arrows affecting him no more than pimples. A great king before he was martyred, it looked as if his crown had ever so slightly slipped off the horizontal. Amalric had never noticed that before.

'Ah, Master Faceby!'

Amalric spun round. 'Eh?'

'I recognise you from another's description.'

The figure who approached wore a short black cloak over his shoulders. His hands were hidden in pale, long sleeves. Was he of the itinerant Dominican order of friars?

'I'm Friar Damian,' he said.

Had Ava found this man to replace Friar Swale?

'I'm new here, ready to help your village for a while; there are many poor folk.'

Amalric tried to think more tolerantly of him than he had of his predecessor.

'By the look on your face,' went on Friar Damian, 'I'm

assuming that St Edmund is not interceding sufficiently well for you.'

'It's not quite that, Friar. St Edmund is worn out by my pleas for help over the years. He can't help me now.'

'Ah, I was recently by chance in this church when a famous glazier and mason came to see your windows here. They mentioned your possible work for the new east window at York Minster. My friary is in York. I know well the windows of the minster, but they signify wealth that my order scorns, so I look at them when no one else is around.' His smile was broad and compassionate.

Amalric continued. 'I find the huge window beyond anything I've ever known. My workshop will cope with the individual panel sizes but my creativity is dead. I once had a dream to make a big window that kept my hope... and talent alive, but the pestilence has shattered it bit by bit over the years. I'm old. My hands have bony lumps. I fear I'll disappoint Master John Thornton.'

'But you've graced the church here with extraordinary windows, and I believe your niece, Beatrix, made the beautiful small candle receptacle that now resides on the windowsill over there where sun is even now shining through it. She will help?'

Amalric was surprised by this friar's knowledge, passed on by Ava, no doubt. 'Aye, but Beatrix too is ageing and has little time for glass now with her healing work to attend to.'

'Master Faceby, listen to me. As you see, I'm a Dominican. A great man of our order was Thomas Aquinas, an Italian – declared a saint some eighty years ago. He was a very practical man. Now, I know inspiration can need sadness or happiness to fuel it, but... if the sadness is so deep that your creativity is trapped within it, I believe St Thomas would say, seek something that has made you happy in the past, even if only a small, simple thing and even if only a little happy. It is a key to letting your despair escape. Give God that happiness that abides within you. Small works derived from happiness and love are works of greatness. They go to make an even greater whole.'

Amalric stared at Friar Damian, his mind opening up like a closed leaf in spring. 'Thank you, Friar.'

Amalric worked on designs with vigour. Beatrix popped in to help when she could. Erika, too, spent as much time as she dared with him, but Clara, Edwin's wife, had become bedridden and Ava's responsibilities in the manor household increased. Amalric feared for young Erika, recalling Ava's chilling words about a marriage suitor for her daughter.

St Edmund interceded on Amalric's behalf after all, working through Father Damian's words, so that inspiration flowed. In his old age, Amalric drew small-scale designs for possibly the biggest window in Christendom. With ink purchased from Meaux Abbey, his drawings for the two panels were on parchments rather than board for ease of transport. It was a new experience for Amalric to roll up the animal skins and see his designs disappear, then to feel unease and a temptation to unfasten the leather thong and unroll them, just to make sure they were still there.

He handed the packages to Beatrix who was to deliver them to Arnold Mason in Beverley.

'Safe journey, lass,' he said, as he patted the horse's behind. 'You'll have good company on the way to Beverley. Folk are waiting for you at the tavern and the weather looks dry. If it rains, protect them drawings as much as you can; they cost a lot in materials and time.' Need he say, don't let them out of your sight? He decided not to.

Istrid appeared with a pack of food. 'Here, food and drink for you, cousin. And get off Betsy and walk every now and then, you don't want them old bones to seize up.' She grinned.

Beatrix responded with a tap from her whip. 'Just watch yourself, *old* friend.'

Amalric smiled at his much-loved women and watched the horse set off up the hill to meet with travelling companions. Beatrix waved. Amalric hoped that, for her sake, Arnold Mason would be in Beverley to hand the drawings to. He would be a good man for her... and his drawings would then be safe.

Two days later, Beatrix was back in the workshop.

'Oh, Uncle Amalric,' she said.

He could not read her expression and he felt himself pale.

'We got as far as the sanctuary cross, and when we stopped to freshen up before entering Beverley town, we were waylaid by a group of brigands. They ransacked our satchels and panniers and stole our food.'

Amalric saw she was not harmed and his thoughts went immediately to his drawings. His heart raced.

'Fear not, your drawings are safe. One of the men demanded to know what the parchments were, so I unfastened the thong for them to see. I think they thought something precious was protected – well, it was. You should have seen their faces. I'm guessing they hadn't seen such things before. I had to explain how they were to be used. Honestly, Uncle, I was so scared; it was like sitting on the edge of a knife. I had to give them no excuse to tear up the parchment, they understood so little. Everyone in the group just stood and watched. In the end the men, four of them, just spat on the ground and gave them back to me. They rode off, their bellies full of Istrid's food. The folk in the group, though, were amazed at your drawings. They're safely in Arnold's workshop now, unharmed.'

Beatrix was excited by her adventure and her own bravado. Amalric felt his face regain colour. 'Well done, lass. And did you *see* Arnold?'

'No. He's in York.'

Her sad face lodged in Amalric's heart.

Chapter Thirty-five

1405 Early winter

'Hello, lass.' Amalric had just emerged from the church and seen Beatrix approaching the gate. Behind her, Erika was strolling languidly down the hill. 'I've just been tidying up the windows,' he continued, slightly surprised to see them. 'The sills were covered in mouse and bat droppings, much worse than the birds, and the glass was covered in cobwebs hangin' from the corners. Joshua Smith an' his wife swept a pile of stuff from the floor and altar. Hopefully it'll last afore we bring the greenery in for Christmas.'

Beatrix put up a hand to quiet him, waving away his concern for the church fabric. She was breathless but anxious to speak. 'Uncle! A traveller has passed on a message. Part of the central tower at York Minster has fallen. It was some days ago now. It seems that men of Arnold's team were passing by and some were injured. While they've had a bit of treatment, the wounds look ill. Arnold is bringing them here to be mended; there's nowhere in York for 'em, and anyway, they'll be nearer their home in Beverley. He'll be with 'em. They've been on the road for a couple of days and could be here tomorrow.' She breathed at last.

'Ee, lass, that were a breath-full.' He smiled at her, knowing her excitement was more than the excitement of healing. 'So, I expect you want to go to prepare. See our Istrid first for food for 'em, and I'll occupy the young 'un. It'll be better than sendin' her back to the manor.'

Erika heard and pouted. 'I'm not young!'

Amalric ignored her. 'Go an' pretty yourself up as well, Beat.' He knew his niece would not see this as an affront to her personal care, but an eagerness to have her please Arnold. He watched her almost bounce away.

Amalric turned to Erika. 'Now then, lass, come with me,' he said, and ushered her across the road to his workshop.

The girl was the epitome of boredom; her perky nature subdued. She flopped onto a stool.

'How about making a small, coloured plaque? We've just enough glass.' Erika's eyes widened. Her great-grandfather had hit on the one thing she was interested in. 'You can draw what you fancy.'

'I like flowers. I'll draw cornflowers. And I like poppies and buttercups.'

'So we have a colour scheme of blue, red and yellow. Then we'll need green leaves. It'll only be a small window because my glass stock is down to just shards, really, but I think we can manage one flower of each type. I have blue and red glass. For the yellow, we'll put silver stain on colourless glass, and for green, we'll try the stain on blue because yellow and blue make green.'

'I know that, Uncle.'

'I suppose you do. Can you remember what the flowers and leaves look like?'

'Yes, of course.'

'I guessed as much. Well, then, you'd better start drawing. I think I have…' he ran his finger along the rack, '… ah yes, here's a board for you to use.'

Nathan, the workshop assistant, hovered, eager to help, clearly buoyed by Erika's enthusiasm.

The next day, Amalric left Erika and Nathan in the workshop and hobbled up the hill with Noah to await the arrival of Arnold Mason and his injured workers. He found himself among folk excitedly chatting about the imminent ghoulish spectacle. He wanted none of it and went to stand with Thurston and Beatrix outside their home. Ava had come to help. He realised then that Thurston, like himself, was old, bent and tired. Beatrix, too, in her old working tunic, was ageing and weary. Only Ava, in a crisp apron, showed energy for hard work.

A drizzling rain began. A lumbering, squeaking sound and a mild shaking of the ground was heard before the origin of it appeared through the wet mist. One or two impatient boys went to meet it. A large two-ox cart, meant to carry huge stones, appeared around the bend at the top of the hill, driven by the fatigued Arnold. The boys were jumping up, trying to see its occupants. The flat of the cart had a great leather sheet covering humps made by bodies beneath. An exhausted but uninjured mason sat beside it, his role as carer obvious in the flasks of ale, blood-soaked bandages, and worse, around him. A constant moan came from beneath the sheet.

Alongside the cart, another person on horseback wafted his whip as if ridding himself of flies; he shouted to the leaping boys to 'Be off!' His black cloak over a rather grubby pale habit identified him as Friar Damian.

Arnold pulled the oxen to a halt at the level of Thurston's physic room. He climbed down stiffly from his rickety seat. 'The corner of the tower fell, bells, the lot,' he said. 'My men here were either trapped or hit by stones. One was killed outright. I couldn't get them cared for in York because it's rumoured that the pestilence is on the way and all the beds in the religious houses and elsewhere are empty, saved for the sick poor. The place is in a frenzy again. There's precious few folk left to do the caring this time. The place is a den of fright. Doors and shutters are closing at every turn. The roads are a confusion of carts and animals and people on foot. This cart was big enough to force our way through, thank the Lord. I'm glad to be out of it. These men are in sore need of help.'

Without being asked, Ava lifted her skirts and climbed onto the cart. She heaved at the leather sheet. It revealed a sorry sight. Four recumbent bodies lay dishevelled and damp. Dust mingled with dried blood on their flesh, hair and clothing. Filthy bandages covered obvious wounds. Their faces were caked in debris, their eyes sunken. Amalric felt a sense of hopelessness. He looked at Thurston, who shook his head. These men had been on the road too long. They were very cold and stank as if rotting. Ava sniffed wounds and prodded flesh. One moaned constantly. Amalric thought he recognised him.

'Friar Damian, why are you with these men?' asked Thurston.

'I was in the minster when the tower fell, having come from a visit to my friary to see how the new east end was progressing. Now part of the tower has fallen, I suppose work on that will stop again. The minster's once again open to the skies.'

Arnold interrupted Friar Damian. 'The friar has been a great help on the journey. We were approached by bandits, five of them, near Stamford Bridge. He said prayers over the injured as they approached. I took on the responsibility of lying. With a glum expression I informed 'em that these men were victims of the approaching new pestilence. One of the injured groaned at the right moment and coughed bloody spittle. The bandits were rapidly persuaded that it was the truth and fled like the devil from a cross. Friar Damian has assured me I will be forgiven for lying.' He glanced at Beatrix with a slight grin. She returned it.

Thurston interjected, looking up from his bent back with obvious impatience. 'We can learn more about the journey later. Ava, reveal the men to me and consult.'

The result was to have two of the injured taken to the doctor's home and two less injured to the tavern.

Later the next day, Amalric's curiosity got the better of him. He wanted to be sure that he'd correctly recognised one of the injured men and went to the physician's home. Female shouting and a man's raised blaspheming voice could be heard some distance before the building was reached. Thurston came out of the door at the very moment Amalric arrived.

'Ah, Am. Come with me to the tavern. I'm in urgent need of barley ale. I wish to wash the stink of errant pus from my nostrils and also give my ears a rest.' His occularies swung from a string around his neck.

Amalric caught an obnoxious whiff from his friend's long-working tunic which moved stiffly from side to side as they walked.

'This is no work for an old man. Cutting is for the young,' said Thurston.

'Cutting?'

They moved to a bench outside the tavern under a chestnut tree and gave the alewife their order. They sat in silence until it arrived.

Thurston took a long draught and held the almost empty beaker on his knee. 'Aye. Cutting. One of the men had to have an arm sawn off. It stank and was crackling and blistered with putrid gas. He would have died otherwise.' He finished off his ale in gulps. 'Ava abandoned all her manor ways and did whatever was needed. Beatrix is no young woman but she had the strength to saw bone. Your Istrid, too; she washed the man, kept water and cloths coming, dealt with the copious blood. It never fails to amaze me how strong in both spirit and muscle women can be.' Thurston shouted for more ale. 'You know, Am, old age is such a barrier to my work, to say nothing of my eyes. My body is elderly, of course, but my mind is also stuck in the past among the planets, bleedings and pee-tasting. I'm a man of pestilences, not cutting. It's young men who've been on the battlefields of France who've pushed forward new ideas. I've read of their works, mind you, and know their theories and intricacies of human flesh, but to cut into it… The thing is, with the raising of great buildings, there are more accidents. Some building sites have become even like battlefields. The only battles I've known are with the pestilence and I've lost each one.'

Amalric knew what Thurston meant. In his own field, he could no longer force his mind to think of whole, vast windows with myriads of figures like Thornton's. In the future they would be made by younger men who'd grown up with huge architecture, clambering around stone mullions, transoms and curving contours. For him, the pestilence had held back his own window creations; ordinary village folk had wanted designs that took them back to a known past, not an unsure future.

'How are the other men?'

'Good enough for homely care to heal their bruises and torn flesh. No broken bones.'

'May I ask the name of the one you've just attended? The one shouting.'

'Ah, the amputee. Jack, I think.'

'I thought I recognised him in the cart. Did he give you trouble?'

'Aye, he did. He's suffered injury before, which may account for his… er… belligerence. He has one eye only. When my mix of drugs wore off and the pain got to him, we had to get the master mason to hold him down, he would have otherwise killed one of the women. He'll need a lot of care if he's to survive. Do you know him?'

'I met him in Beverley, a stirrer of trouble if I recall.'

'That is so, but my Beatrix has a plan to calm him,' Thurston grinned.

Amalric was delighted to see a glimmer of the younger doctor.

Chapter Thirty-six

A week later, Beatrix almost dragged Amalric to the physician's home, telling him he would see a miracle. He peered through the open shutters and saw, highlighted by sunshine, a pale but very much alive Jack on a raised pallet, his shoulders lifted by pillows. His clean, grimacing, gargoyle face was shorn of its untidy whiskers and his damaged eye had a pad over it. One arm ended above the elbow; the other squirmed erratically, disturbing fresh bed covers. A bowl of broth was being held before him by an aged, scrawny but obviously active woman – Mistress Yarrow! Jack's one hand attempted to push the bowl away.

'I don't want it.'

'You will have it!' Mistress Yarrow's voice was insistent. 'You are a grumbling man. I'm not here for my own health but yours.'

'I don't want it!'

An empty spoon was tapped on Jack's forehead. 'You will have it!' He looked up at Mistress Yarrow with surprise in his one eye, opened his mouth and waited for her to fill the spoon and deposit its thick, nutritious contents into his toothless cavern.

'There. That's better.' Authority was well and truly in the hands of Mistress Yarrow.

Amalric turned away, with hands holding his mouth shut. When he was out of hearing distance, he let out a huge laugh. Beatrix joined him, lifting her apron to wipe tears from her eyes.

'Ee, lass, that's a reet tonic.'

'And there's more, Uncle.' Her cheeks became a high pink.

'Like Mistress Yarrow, I'm drawing close to my older years, but Arnold has asked me to be with him when the York window is finished. We'll live in Warren Horesby.'

Amalric felt his smile erupt again. 'Ee, lass, it does me reet good to have you happy.'

Jack's health continued to improve, but before he was well and able enough to live independently, Mistress Yarrow persuaded him to marry her. At the simple marriage service of the elderly couple, Amalric found himself suppressing a chuckle as Jack clearly enjoyed being dominated by a woman, saying constantly, 'Yes, my love,' and the shining face of Mistress Yarrow offered no doubt that having him under her control was ideal.

The excitement surrounding the tower fall diminished and Amalric had to face the reality that whatever the great window for York Minster had promised, a greater authority had acted otherwise. Plans for reconstruction of the east end, including the window, had been stopped – again. Way, way back, it had been halted by the Great Pestilence and death of the master mason. Then held up for twenty years owing to a lack of funds. Now the tower fall. No doubt, money for the Great East Window would be used up for the tower's rebuild. And, to make matters worse, Amalric had heard that the Archbishop of York had been accused of treason for participating in a rising against the king, and beheaded. How could the minster clergy recover after all that and put their minds to continue? Amalric could only assume that God was not pleased and that the work would never be completed. He knew without a doubt that the drawings he'd made, ready to be enlarged, would simply gather dust on a mason's workshop shelf in Beverley.

The evening sun was low and pink. It was unseasonably warm for winter. Amalric and Thurston had taken the opportunity to have a stroll, stopping by Amalric's home to sit on the bench outside with a flagon of ale at their feet and watch the evening gently fade to darkness. Noah nosed in nearby undergrowth as creatures either scurried away or emerged for the night.

Amalric looked closely at his friend. In the soft shadow, his pale face looked almost luminous. He'd conversed only a little on their stroll.

'Does something ail you? You look wan.' Amalric wondered if the latest vigorous treating of the sick had finally been too much for the old physician. He was now very thin and bowed. His ginger hair had long gone while freckles had proliferated on his face. To have survived so long and healed others so well was a miracle. He, Amalric, must also look changed; not the young man with black, flowing hair that in his mind he still was, but instead, old with receding white hair, thinly tied back because he could not be bothered to cut it. The truth of ageing was hard to take.

'I'm unwell. Very unwell. I cannot heal myself.'

Amalric's thoughts sharply turned back to his friend. 'You mean…'

'Aye, my friend. Fortunately, Ava found us a good man in Friar Damian. I'll be happy to speak with him and confess my sins.'

'You – speak with the friar about the afterlife?' This was surprising. 'I hope he stays long enough before you…'

'He will. Though he'll eventually leave here for his friary in York to attend the poor there. You look shocked. You see, Am, I'm not too unlike other men. I know that when medicine fails, I also need what faith can offer.'

Amalric frowned.

'I have a little time yet.' Thurston looked up at the sky. It was an endless deepening blue. 'We have survived five pestilences, you and I, but I won't be surviving any more. At least the latest feared bout has not arrived. I think York would have greatly succumbed, being still so ravaged.'

'Maybe we've seen the end of it.'

'Even so, its legacy will stalk the land. It has reminded us of the equality of all human beings. The new idea for painted or stone memorials for the wealthy showing a skeleton are grimly correct when they say, *What you are I once was, what I am you will be.* Mind you, the skeleton is usually depicted hopelessly incorrectly, especially the pelvis and ribcage; the sculptors have very little understanding. I must enlighten Arnold Mason before he's called to carve such a dismal abomination.'

'Thurston!' Even now, he would not let his healing interests rest. It was always amusing. With a smile, Amalric put his hand on that of his friend. 'A physic man to the end, eh, Thurston?'

'Aye. And you're a man of glass to the end, eh, Am?'

Thurston died. Amalric didn't want to linger over how he died, nor the pain of it. Friar Damian had been with him and, as far as Amalric knew, physic and Church had reached a truce. The congregation insisted he be buried in the church nave, a reminder to everyone of the selfless healing the community had received. The stone above him had carved on it the Latin epithet, *Medicus.*

Amalric felt devastated. The friend of his youth had gone. The friend who had always calmed him, who spoke good sense and had seen the real Amalric. They had been as brothers, especially since Hendric had married Beatrix. Thick dark shutters had slammed and shut out the sunlight of hope.

Despair racked Amalric. An ageing Noah sat at his feet. Soft ears flopped over his boots, and every now and then languid doggy eyes looked into his master's face. As ever, the dog made no demands of his master.

Beatrix sat in Amalric's workshop. Grey skies kept it dark. As so often in the past, it was at the table where despair was shared.

'My hope of being with Arnold is lost, Uncle. He will have to stay in York to help rebuild the minster tower. What time will be left for the two of us? York is a long journey away. He's ageing and I fear he may fall, like Hendric.'

Amalric remained silent.

'You know, Uncle, I sometimes think that my most peaceful moments have been when I've been working with glass, here. I love it, especially the drawing and painting – but such a life is not for a woman. I'm busy with healing, anyway, now Father is not here. But it drains me. So many young folk have left the village that child-birthing is now uncommon. All I see are people despairing of their crumbling bodies, pain that can't be alleviated, and stinking sores. And I don't enjoy cutting. One limb I have helped remove. I could not do it again. Women will never have the cutting art.'

'Lass! Women *can* carry on businesses when they're left alone.' Amalric felt too old to bear Beatrix's pain as well as his own. He spoke sharply. 'You're already getting known for the candle-holder. Think! You could make small devotional items for travellers: merchants and pilgrims. Use this workshop until you can be with Arnold Mason. Nathan will help; he asks little except food. And give Erika something to do with glass before her mother leads her into either marriage or a nunnery.'

Beatrix ignored his terseness. 'Sometimes I have to remind myself of Ava's brother, Asa. I so rarely see him; he's so tied up in Oxford. He has many of his Grandfather Thurston's manuscripts.'

Amalric softened. 'Ah, manuscripts. All my memories of your father began with old vellum pages. Who shall *I* pass my Theophilus on to?'

'Uncle, what will *you* do now that you have no hope of work in York?'

'Ah… the minster window was but the hope of a candle's last fluttering. I will do nothing. I'll let our Istrid pamper me to death and let Douglas do all the hard labour.'

Chapter Thirty-seven

'Awake, my friends...' A banging on the house door was followed by it swinging open. 'Why are you so doleful?'

Noah barked furiously at the man standing just inside the doorway, removing his leather cap and rubbing his curly hair, causing white dust to cloud out of it. The same dust ingrained the thick wool of his short, leather-belted tunic. On his shoulder, he carried a satchel from which poked two rolled parchments. His ruddy face was smiling.

Amalric left his comfort by the fire and struggled to the door. 'Arnold? What is this?'

'I'm sorry to be in such disarray, but time is short. It's work for you, my friend. John Thornton has asked me to deliver your drawings for glass panels back to you. He approves and needs 'em pretty sharpish. Work on the east window carries on – it's not been held up by the tower fall as much as we all thought. Thornton's installed much of the glass already. New glass will be delivered to you.'

'He still trusts me to do them?' Amalric was astounded.

'Aye, he does. He likes your two designs. "Give 'im the job if e's still alive," he told me. But lookin' at you now, sir, I'm not so sure. You look a mite weary.'

Amalric beamed. 'I'm alive alright, merely old. Go tell that niece of mine I'll need help.'

Arnold sped off to Beatrix, leaving Amalric looking

nervously at his hands; there was a new slight tremble and the swollen joints were stiff. He just needed to stave off the inevitable for a few moons. 'Please, St Edmund, ask the Lord to give time for my body to complete my art, and to honour Him,' he asked in the church later.

Istrid massaged her father's hands with healing oils, loosening them enough for him to copy his drawings onto the white table which was just big enough to make the panels. The young, steady hand of Erika transferred them to glass and she also became adept at cutting glass and chipping pieces into their final shape with a grozing iron. Joshua Smith was called on to make lead cames. Nathan was on hand to help lead-up, solder and fire on painted detail in the garden furnace. Beatrix helped when she could and, with Arnold, took the finished panels to the York Minster workshop. Douglas helped heave them onto the mason's cart. Amalric watched it rumble off. He'd experienced a joyous flare of hope, but now, with the clatter-rumble as his glass panels disappeared out of sight, he wondered ridiculously, as he had when Beatrix took his first drawings to Beverley, whether his work would still exist when it was out of his sight. Only when the glass panels were installed would he know they were safe.

Chapter Thirty-eight

Amalric woke with a start and shook his head to clear it of transparent coloured figures roaming excitedly over colourless glass, and falling down, down. He'd been deeply asleep when jolted by a sudden swing of the litter. The young Noah barked annoyance.

'Hold on, Da, we've turned onto the road towards Wilberfoss Priory and it's badly rutted. It's not been too bad on Ermine Street today; the Romans really knew what they were about, but now…'

Amalric clung on as his world swayed from side to side.

The sun shone weakly, but the approach to the priory was cheerless, unlike that of Nunburnholme. Weeds grew close to the edges of the track in great profusion. The perimeter wall ahead had small plants growing from gaps in the stonework, which Amalric knew would eventually destabilise the wall. I'm being too critical he thought. It will be good inside.

Istrid, however, was tutting. ''Tis showing a lack of good housekeeping. I can smell rotting vegetation, stagnant water, animal waste.' She was ever sensitive to the aroma of filth. 'Just look at the animal droppings. Many a peasant would be glad of that for their land or fire.'

Father Everard, riding at her side, turned down his mouth. Noah stood up in the litter and blissfully lifted his nose to the deliciously pungent air.

Amalric viewed the state of his surroundings with mounting disquiet. The horses' hooves squashed clumps of weeds on the approach. Trees overhung and branches dragged on the litter roof. They passed through an open gateway in the wall leading through to the precinct where cobbles were lifted by underlying roots.

The priory buildings rose before them, so like Nunburnholme in design, but inferior in upkeep. Wooden doors were rotting at the bottom from wetness; windows lacked glass panes.

Amalric watched Father Everard go to the large door of the priory and clang on a great knocker. A small, cupboard-like door opened within the larger one, revealing a pale face expectant of his request. The priest's plea for lodgings was granted with a nod, and a nun opened the door.

Father Everard brought the steps given them at Nunburnholme Priory to the side of the litter. Who was this priest? asked Amalric of himself.

'Come, Master Faceby, allow me to help you alight,' said the monk in a jocular tone. Amalric took his hand and, to find his footing on the step, looked down and on the ground saw Everard's bare feet in sandals. He'd obviously abandoned his red woollen socks to keep them out of mud. One toe was missing!

With a sudden realisation, Amalric blurted out, 'Of course, you're Aldred, you're my Nesta's relative! I've been puzzling who you are! Nesta's brother's grandson. You will have changed your name at ordination. Oh, lad!'

Everard looked surprised at the outburst. 'Oh, Master Amalric, did you not know me? I was unaware. I'm so sorry, it's my fault. I just assumed you'd remember me. I took the name Everard at ordination. Everild's Spring[13] was the name of our

---

[13] Everild's Spring is fictitious, but St Everild was a seventh-century Saxon woman who founded a convent in East Yorkshire.

hamlet. Everard is the masculine form of the local saint.'

Amalric felt joyous. He broke into a huge smile. 'It was stupid of me not to remember. An old man's failing, no doubt. It's such a relief to know.'

'Come, Da,' called Istrid. 'Don't spend time chatting, we need to get you inside. Take up your sticks.'

Amalric walked towards the guest hall, his legs stiff from sitting. The nun at the door stood drooping, drying red hands on her overtunic. He nodded thanks and was surprised to see she was quite young but had no plumpness of youth; her ill-fitting habit hung from bony shoulders. Her veil was lank. For Amalric, there was merely a nod, but for Noah, her eyes lit up with interest and she put out chilblained fingers to stroke the dog's snout. Noah leaned into her.

When they were all inside, warming by the meagre fire, the same silent nun brought ale and bread. Amalric asked if he might meet the prioress to pass on the good wishes of Mother Ruth. She nodded, but no one returned.

Later, Amalric, feeling quite awake, stayed before the priory guest house fire. It struggled to blaze up from damp logs, spitting heather and dried cow dung. Beatrix and a tutting Istrid were by his side. Ava was finding a bed that she and Erika could share. Father Everard was in the priory church saying his evening prayers. Noah slept on his master's feet.

Istrid's face had not lost its sign of disgust. 'I'm not sleeping in that bed I've just seen,' she said, as she tried to poke life into the embers. 'I fear bugs. The chamber is icy cold. A warm body'll be a heyday for 'em. I'll fetch straw mattresses and blankets from the litter we've brought from home. None of our things are going on the beds here. You can sleep in front of the fire, Da. I'll make a soft bed for you. I'll sleep in the chair.'

Amalric was always amazed at his daughter's practical sense. While it was common for travellers to have their own bedding, his daughter excelled. He looked at Beatrix and a knowing smile passed between them.

'I know you think I fuss, but it's for all our benefits. Being bug-bitten is no joke.'

Beatrix nodded. 'My father was always convinced insects spread disease. He'd observed it so. He kept dead ones in glass phials to remind himself of them. I loved the butterflies but hated the fleas, lice, ants, wasps, horseflies…'

'Well, it's only the itch that would bother me now,' said Amalric. 'I cannot think further to what it might result in.'

'That's why you have us, Da, to do your thinking for you.'

'And I'm reet glad!'

Amalric reached down to stroke Noah. The dog twitched in sleep, obviously enjoying a dreamy chase. Amalric felt a tinge of jealousy. What were fleas, lice and bedbugs to a dog?

Dusk began to permeate the guest hall and the silent nun lit rancid rush lights.

Then, as if repeating the events of the night before at Nunburnholme, the door was opened sharply. It smacked against the wall. Noah was shocked from his sleep and barked ferociously. Amalric, while staring at the fire, put his hand to quieten him and at the same time, even though he didn't see who it was that had entered, felt a sense of dread.

He turned from the fire to see two men dressed in a livery that he didn't recognise. They were struggling through the door with a pallet on which lay a crumpled figure covered in a muddy blanket. One hand lay exposed, hanging down, limp and oddly out of position. The fingers were swelling; too much to remove an emerald ring. The men bent to lower their bundle to the floor.

Beatrix was quick to react. 'Nay, lay him on the table,' she said as she swept horn beakers to the floor.

Istrid gaped. A third man followed, an anxious look on his face. He was holding the taught lead of a young dog. Noah moved towards her.

'Good day. I'm Lord de Montfrid's reeve. Are you Master Amalric Faceby?'

'I am.' Amalric's sense of dread increased.

'Sir, this is Master Edwin, your brother, I believe. He was

badly injured at the hunt. This is his dog, Kati,' he said as he tied the animal to a chair, relinquishing any further responsibility for her.

Noah tentatively crept further towards the quaking animal. 'Noah! Stay!'

Beatrix had already approached the injured figure, full of concern. 'Oh, my Lord!' she cried, as she lifted the blanket from the man's mud-splattered face. 'It *is* Uncle Edwin!' Her gaze went to his arm. 'Broken bone is jutting through the flesh.' She lifted it tenderly onto the pallet. Edwin screamed.

Amalric hobbled towards his brother. He saw the bone and the shine of fresh blood clots. Beatrix pulled the cloth that covered him further back and leaned her head to his chest.

'It ruttles,' she said hopelessly.

'Fetch prioress,' Edwin gasped through fluid-filled breath. The silent nun disappeared into the shadows.

'What happened?' asked Amalric of the reeve.

'We were after a great stag. Your brother here wanted to be in the forefront. I tried to dissuade him – he looked so ill, so old, sat uneasy in the saddle – but he would take no advice. We stalked the beast for hours and the dogs brought it to bay by the river. I ordered for rest until my master, Lord de Montfrid, arrived, but Master Edwin oddly charged in on his horse for a kill. The stag was having none of it and reacted with horns down. His horse reared and your brother fell off onto dogs and bracken, and then rolled to the mud and rocks by the river. The dogs then tore at the stag. Some went for *him* but we held them off. My master is blazingly angry. It's as much as I could do to bring your brother here – as he himself asked.'

'Umph!' was Amalric's only comment.

An elderly nun hurried in. She pushed aside Beatrix, who tottered, nearly falling. The nun's eyes moved over Edwin's body. She gently touched his arm and watched his chest rising spasmodically. She wiped the blood that trickled from his mouth and put a hand to his bruised cheek. Her own face crumpled. It was clear she knew that all was lost.

Amalric realised that Edwin was well known in these parts. He stood back with Istrid and Beatrix, feeling a stranger to his own brother. The silent nun had followed the prioress with a bowl of water and cloths. She covered Edwin with unbleached linen to hide the horror, leaving his head free. Blood quickly seeped through. With wet cloths, the prioress cleaned mud and blood from Edwin's face. Blood marked her habit. She cupped his face in her hands. Her veil slipped. She tenderly kissed his blue lips and tears streamed onto his pale lemon cheeks.

Istrid stared, shocked, unable to move. Beatrix's instincts were to help the injured man and Amalric found himself holding her back as she tried to go to him.

'Nay, lass, let the woman tend him. She must be the prioress. Your uncle asked for her.' Amalric's head felt as if it would burst. He thought of himself with Mother Ruth.

A hoarse voice called out. 'Brother, come.'

Amalric let go of Beatrix and limped to Edwin. With a clarity surprising to himself, he thought to go to the side with the good arm. He heard the ruttling sound of the damaged chest. The nun stood by, courageous in her dread.

Edwin reached out with his good arm to grab Amalric's wrist. 'Am, this woman... my true love. Had to keep secret. Many years. Forced to nunnery. Was young. Like me... always longed... different life. Now... I'm dying. She... in trouble. Priory excesses... defects. Archbishop to visit.'

Edwin desperately tightened his grip. Amalric felt a wave of revulsion; a brother's touch after decades of keeping distance! To have this secret so long; not to tell his own brother! But then, he had likewise not told Edwin of Mother Ruth.

'Speak for her, Am. Archbishop. She... maybe will... have to leave order. Cast out.'

Feelings of recrimination twisted by sudden understanding and love swept through Amalric like a storm. He gulped with emotion. 'Edwin – I'm old, cannot...'

'I'll stand by her, Uncle.' It was Istrid, at her uncle's Edwin's feet. 'I'll speak with Father Everard. Together we'll make a case.

If it fails, she'll never want for a home as long as I'm alive. She may come to me and Douglas.'

The nun simply looked at Istrid, emotion playing too strongly around her mouth to speak.

Edwin nodded and closed his eyes. After a few moments, he turned his head to the nun. 'Bury here. Happiest in all my life.' Then he turned to his brother. 'Am. York. Success. Too little. Gift for you.'

There it was again. The slight on his achievements, and a gift? Never. But a fleeting expression on Edwin's face — was it triumph? — caused something to rise in Amalric: a scene from the past seared on his memory like fired paint on glass.

The date of it was irrelevant. He'd seen Friar Swale hurrying up the hill to the manor with a little satchel over his shoulder and his habit flapping around his corpulent figure. Istrid had come down the hill with news that Clara, Edwin's wife, was dying. Compassion and brotherly concern had flowed into Amalric. He'd found his brother in the manor hall sitting at the big table, empty even of flowers, holding the little glass plaque Erika had made in Amalric's workshop. He'd looked up at Amalric and said it had been a gift from *their* Erika, given because she hoped the image of meadow flowers, blue, red and yellow, would give him solace. Amalric had asked if it had. 'No,' had been the cold reply.

After Clara had died, George had inherited the manor estate but ineffectively. His grandfather Edwin had remained reeve, still able to control it with an undeniable power. With Edwin gone, George, who seemed as reckless as all the progeny of Edwin, would have sole responsibility. Amalric despaired. It was all too much, all of it, everything, all the love and loss, insensitivity, callous disregard of others' lives. He stomped out into the fresh air... and cried and cried until he was spent.

A full moon glowed in a cloudless night sky, overpowering the net of stars. Amalric leaned against an oak tree, his face wet and legs trembling. By his side, Noah growled softly in response to cloppings and jinglings from shadowy figures coming into the precinct. Rush lighting brought out by servants lit two figures sagging in their saddles: Edwin's two sons, the ageing Robert and Walter. George followed, a little behind, alone.

Amalric urged Noah to be silent. He could not face these men, his nephews. Why were they so far behind Edwin's arrival? Yet he knew that even their father's imminent death would have the least importance if something distracted them on their way. Old Lord de Horesby had been right, the one hope for the estate's survival rested with George, and that, too, might be hopeless.

The silent nun appeared, carrying a stool in one hand, and in the other a beaker emitting a honeyed aroma. She touched his arm sympathetically and indicated that he should sit and drink.

'Why do you not speak?' Amalric asked.

She opened her mouth and pointed inside with her finger. In the shadowy moist interior, Amalric was sure there was no tongue. After everything today and over the years, this needed no response: no question, no expression of horror. It was how things were. The young nun silently slipped away and left him to his medicinal beverage.

The following morning, Amalric said a last goodbye to his brother. Edwin lay in the priory chapel, clean and surprisingly young-looking. He'd indeed been a handsome man. The emerald ring had gone, leaving a torn finger, and with it, it seemed, his brother's dominance. It was odd that now he could no longer utter pithy comments, Edwin seemed more affable. Never once had Amalric ever considered that Edwin would die before himself, and in the arms of a woman he truly loved, and be buried in the consecrated grounds of a godly house, a priory. Perhaps they were not so unlike, Amalric mused; he too had had his secret love.

Amalric put his hand to his side to stroke Noah, seeking the comfort of a warm, velvet ear and unquestioning love, but Noah was not there. He'd been distracted by rodent aromas and was working his way around the walls of the chapel. When he reached the door, it opened onto his nose and he shot back, barking furiously.

'Noah! Quiet.'

Sheepishly around the door came the silent nun pulling Edwin's dog, Kati, on a lead behind her. A narrow, soft leather collar had replaced the broad, spiked one. The dog had been groomed and was already looked fitter, no longer shaking. Her large, dark eyes widened as Noah moved towards her and sniffed her thin legs. She sniffed him. The nun put out a hand in apology, then patted Noah. She looked earnestly at Amalric and then held out the leather lead towards him. He nodded. The bitch was finely bred, so unlike the mix that had always been his own numerous Noahs. His present young Noah would soon grow to tolerate this new addition to their home. Maybe there would be pups. Yes, it was right that he should take the animal; it had been his brother's. Yet he couldn't bring himself to take the lead. The nun moved forward and thrust it to his hand, her face full of movement in her attempt to communicate. She was close enough for Amalric to detect something else beyond her pleading for him to take what was rightfully his. He saw it in her eyes. His heart nearly broke, such was the rush of sympathy he felt for her.

'No, sister, you keep her. She suits you well.'

The nun's face suffused with joy. She grasped his arm and nodded furiously. A rough cry came from her throat and tears to her eyes. She hugged the dog's neck. In the dust of the chapel floor she wrote, in local language, *I thank you for Kati.*

Amalric watched the preparations for the last part of the journey. The end of this day should see them in York. He wondered what was in store for Ava now, with her husband free to govern the estate.

'What's George doing today?' he asked of Istrid. 'Edwin's sons can surely see to his body. George may wish to go back to Warren Horesby.'

'Well, no matter what *he* does, Ava is determined to stay on this journey with us.'

'Aye, well, let's just set off, lass. This stay here's been

harrowing. I just want to move on.'

Annoyingly, Noah refused to settle. Amalric had the fleeting thought that maybe he would have liked a female doggy companion. Back in Warren Horesby, the Noahs had often wandered off into the night, to return with added vigour in the morning. But Amalric was sure of his decision to leave Kati behind. 'Go travel with your friend, Dorkas the donkey. That might help.' Noah leapt off the litter and shot forward. A moment later he was trotting in and out of Dorkas' legs, causing Father Everard's dangling feet to swing and make his seat uncertain. It was a comical site. The group laughed.

'Sorry, Father,' shouted Amalric.

The response was a friendly wave.

Amalric settled among the cushions, feeling more at peace, but he missed having the faithful Noah beside him… it was only a year ago that he'd been a puppy under a yew tree, yet his coming had signalled a momentous time. The litter swayed and Amalric felt himself dozing again.

Chapter Thirty-nine

1408
The journey: Arrival in York

'Stop dozing, Da,' said Istrid, turning around to face her father. 'We're almost there.' It was late in the afternoon and the sky was beginning to darken. 'Watch out from now; the road's getting a bit difficult with all the carts an' stuff.'

A multiple clanging of bells carried on the autumnal air confirmed their approach to the city of York. Amalric was determined to keep his eyes closed; his dozing had been almost without dreams as if he'd caught up with his past life. He felt surprisingly restful, and wished to enjoy the bells enhancing his somnambulant peace — while trying to ignore the displeasure of his swaying progress.

Suddenly, the litter rocked violently. Amalric opened his eyes to see a great ox had lumbered into the front horse. Istrid was valiantly pulling on the reins to calm the panicked beast and was shouting expletives he'd never previously heard her utter.

'Ee, I'm reet sorry, mistress,' the ox-driver said, holding up his arms defensively. 'I'm takin' him to market. He's a ruffian and I want rid of him. I hope yon mister is all reet.'

Amalric, still clinging desperately to the litter sides, raised one hand as if the experience had been nothing. 'I'm all reet,' he said, and grabbed Noah's collar for fear of losing him over the side in the melee. Istrid turned back to look at her father and beamed the joy of conquest.

Amalric was now fully alert. Ahead of him on the Walmgate

Road, he was surprised to see that stone had replaced much of the old Viking earth and palisade city walls. But of *no* surprise were the grassed mounds below the walls, indicating mass graves of pestilential dead. He'd last been here as a young man to apply for membership of the Glaziers' Guild just after the Great Pestilence, and he'd seen for the first time what horrors folk had faced. Since then, he'd learned, the city had suffered horribly again and again.

The Walmgate Bar was ahead. Amalric's little group bunched with all manner of folk and means of transport to get through the gate. He found it amazing to be funnelling through the tunnel of the new defensive barbican, noting the contrast between new lichen-free stone and the long-standing coloured lichens of the old archway. But even more arresting were leathered, time-blackened heads of criminals or those accused of treason stuck anonymously on poles; a strong warning to travellers harbouring evil intent.

Once inside the walls, a malodorous stink hit everyone's nose as they clattered over a bridge straddling a sluggish brown stream. It was clearly the depository of all human and animal liquid waste. At its banks, all sorts of solid waste lay in piles, buzzing with a black, shifting net of insects. Folk covered their noses and ineffectually wafted at flying things.

Ahead, carts of all sizes lumbered left and right in the peaks and troughs of dried mud and animal dung. One tipped to one side so much that overloaded items fell in front of disgruntled travellers and held everything up until it was cleared. Fancy litters, like the one Amalric was in, swayed in the horde. Dirty young lads darted among them trying to sell goods. "Ave a puddin' sir?' 'Fortify yourself, sir,' "Ave ya somewhere to stay? I know a place.'

Horses, donkeys, mules, dogs, people of all shapes and sizes, religious and foreign costumes. It was a full assault on Amalric's artistic senses. A jumble of images. A cacophony of sounds. Why were there so many people? He'd not expected this.

Finally, the repaired tower of the minster was seen above the crowded buildings. It was massive. Amalric's heart lurched. Soon he would see the window.

'Don't go down there,' shouted Father Everard from in front, as the litter was being pushed by the crowd down a left fork. 'It's the butchers down there.' Istrid made a huge effort to keep the lead horse to the right. A glance down the street provoked a memory; it was hard to forget! It was a narrow, stinking thoroughfare where the roofs overhung on each side, almost touching at the top so that the raw meat on stalls below was protected from the sun. The sound of chopping indicated the dismembering of beasts, and Amalric remembered blood and offal flowing into the gutters from sloping pavements, and butchers with absent fingers. He thought of Thurston and his hatred of the *miasmic muck*.

As they drew closer to the minster, it was clear why there were so many people jostling about.

'See, Da,' said Istrid, 'the celebrations are for the minster window.'

It was like a special saint's day. Flaming torches lit the scene as the evening gloom deepened: mummers on carts, jugglers, men and women on stilts, hot pies on sale from trays carried on heads, hot ale sold from huge pans resting over hot embers; ribbons were waved, small bells tinkled, wooden bird-scarers clapped, voices called and sang. Faces appeared over the litter side and it was hard to tell whether they wore a mask or had a visage distorted by disease. The young Noah stood with paws on the litter edge, shaking with the unfamiliarity of it all, and added to it with frenzied barking.

Amalric was apprehensive; he could only just see Ava and Erika behind him struggling to keep the glazier cart from tipping. Father Everard and his donkey were now nowhere to be seen. It was too much for Amalric's old head. He began to feel panic as his breath quickened and his chest cramped.

Then... the new east end of the minster rose above the melee. The clean, cream stonework was stark in the dusk. The window was enormous! A huge, pointed arch enclosed smaller pointed arches. From where the outer arch began to narrow to its point, the space was filled with tracery; a stonework maze of smaller shapes. The glass in it remained disappointingly dark, revealing nothing of coloured glass, only the occasional glitter from an undetectable light source. Amalric felt faint.

'Fear not, Master Faceby, we'll soon have you in warmth and peace with honeyed ale in your hands and a large bun to eat.' It was Friar Damian, with his hand on the edge of the litter. 'I made it my business to be visiting the Dominican friary to greet you. I'll guide your Istrid there.'

Amalric closed his eyes and gratefully settled back onto cushions, with his hands over his ears.

To Amalric's immense relief, the clamour died down and soon they were clattering over the stone paving of the friary. Istrid drove the litter up to a set of mounting steps, and lay brothers arrived to help him down. He was a little shaky and felt embarrassed at the care he needed.

In the large refectory, seated in a high-backed chair with cushions, again in front of a fire and alone except for Noah, Amalric at last began to feel himself relax… but he was not easy. Where was everyone else? He felt strangely deserted in this unfamiliar place. Even Noah was ignoring him, lying on warm tiles, exhausted from his new experiences.

At last, a grinning Friar Damian arrived, holding a small tray. On it were a large beaker of ale and a huge, freshly baked bun with expensive almonds scattered on top, still warm.

'This is our essential arrival gift for weary travellers to York. You must be in some distress after finding yourself in the middle of celebrations for the new window and the blessing tomorrow.'

The friar settled himself in a chair by Amalric's side. 'Now… I expect you're concerned for the other members of your party.' He leaned forward. 'Well, Istrid is seeing to the unloading and settling of your horses. Father Everard has gone to the Cistercian Monastery. Beatrix has gone to look at the overnight accommodation, which is monks' cells, sparse but clean – I'm sure she'll be satisfied enough to collapse on a bed, for she looked exhausted. And although it's late, Ava and Erika have gone to St Leonard's Hospital to see what charitable money they may be able to offer for the sick there; it's in a poor state since their resources were severely stretched in the last pestilence and they've not been able to recoup them. But... they still care admirably for the sick – lepers especially, and those with the coughing sickness.'

Amalric was comforted by Friar Damian's relating of his family's whereabouts. It felt homely. But news of Ava promising money from the manor estate?

'I fear for Ava,' he confided to the friar. 'I'm not sure she should be spending her husband, George's, inheritance.'

'Well, all I know is that she expects George to meet her there, at the hospital.'

Amalric could not imagine what this meant.

'Oh, and Friar Swale is here in York and told me that he will seek you out tomorrow.'

Amalric's mood, which had hitherto been lightening, plummeted. He was, of course, grieving for his brother, but he had also felt a lightness because of the removal of continuous rancour. Now it had suddenly returned with thoughts of George and Friar Swale.

Father Damian left him in peace by the fire. A female voice woke him from troubled dozing. Through half-closed eyes he saw Istrid by his side.

'All is settled, Da. We have sleep rooms. I'm exhausted. Friar Damian will see you to one.'

She left as Erika and Ava came through the door. Erika ran to his side, jolting him further from his doze. She looked pale.

'Oh, Elder – I've seen lepers.'

'My poor daughter has seen sights that have hit hard,' said Ava.

'They were so pitiful,' explained Erika. 'Without fingers and toes. Their faces looked thick and puffy. Some had no nose. Horrible!'

'Aye, I believe so.' Amalric had escaped seeing such horrors, but recalled Thurston visiting the hospital and being upset by the way the Church had cared for the soul well enough but little for his efforts to cure or research the cause of such a hideous disease. 'I hear you were to meet George there?' he probed.

'We did.' Ava was surprisingly calm. She said no more and left with Erika to go to bed.

The following morning was bright and clear. The sun beamed through the little window of Amalric's cell and woke him with warmth on his face. He took a moment to gather his thoughts and then a thrill gushed through him, the like of which he'd not experienced for a long time: he would see the Great East Window and Master John Thornton's exceptional art. Noah sensed excitement and jumped off his master's bed, stretched and then stood looking expectantly at him.

'Yes, lad, it will be a fine day.' Noah's head tipped to one side. He bent forward and stroked the dog's head. 'See, I'm tremblin' with excitement.'

Istrid knocked on the thin wooden door and entered. She seemed youthful, with the cheeky grin he loved to see. 'Ee, Da, it's lucky we don't have to be in the minster at sun-up: your hands are shakin' that much you'd be unable to dress. You'd have to go naked. York isn't ready for that! Noon is soon enough for you. Come, I'll help you get your hose on. Then we'll sort that grey hair so you look reet grand. There's no rush.'

'Aye, but I want to be there afore the crowds, lass, to see that east window with few folk around it. I don't want to be in a crush. I want to see it with both the eastern morning light and the noon light – mornin' glory shining through the colours and then, when the direct sun's off it, the detail.'

'Well, that's as maybe, but first I need to get you and Noah fed or else you'll faint away before you see anything. You'll be there early enough.'

Amalric felt like a little child. Istrid put her arms about him. It felt good to be loved. He would indulge her; as well as her concern for him, he knew she would find the tempting smells coming from the refectory hard to resist, so seldom did she wake to a meal prepared by someone else.

Beatrix joined them to break her fast, then Father Everard arrived to help steer them safely to the minster. Noah sniffed the hem of the monk's clean habit and whined.

'All in good time, lad. Dorkas is having a rest. She's not needed this morning.'

They approached the minster, walking the short distance from the friary. Folk were already lining the way in anticipation of seeing dignitaries on this special day. They stood back, allowing Amalric's group to walk down the centre of the road.

Amalric had to admit, his little party looked grand. He felt every bit the neatly turned-out venerable master glazier in his heavy cloak, walking slowly with two sticks. Istrid was by his side in a new, dark-blue travel garment. Beatrix was elegant in a long, green gown, and Father Everard lent ecclesiastical gravity. The young dog, trotting with head-up bewilderment in the middle of them, added just the right amount of humour. It amused Amalric to have folk speculate who they were and in response he waved regally to them. Istrid and Beatrix girlishly suppressed giggles.

They turned a corner. Before them was the new east end of the minster, a wall of glass and stone. The stone reflected the direct morning light and Amalric's squinting eyes went up and up. His head tipped back as far as his stiff neck would allow. He reckoned the window *must* be the largest in all Christendom. The morning sun picked out the stone mullions and curving tracery in high relief. The glass was not the dark mass it had been in the dusk of evening, but even so, had no colour of its own; its glory lay in its reflective properties and, for now, mirrored a white sky as clouds scudded across. Colour would be seen inside. Only the lead cames gave any indication of glories to come in the outlines of bodies, heads, haloes. The sight of it rendered both Amalric and his companions speechless, and all he could do was stand with an open mouth.

Inside, priests, lay brothers and canons scurried back and

forth, their sandals making slapping, sissing sounds on the shiny floor, ignoring Amalric and his little group. He felt small, standing in front of the window which soared above him – a huge weight of stone and glass. All at once, like a miracle, the morning sunshine burst unimpeded by clouds through the window, revealing a huge array of vibrant colour: red, blue, green, amber, purple, white. It glittered and glowed. Reflections poured onto the surrounding walls and floor. The brilliance of the early sun disguised detail, as he knew it would, but he could see that figures were everywhere. Amalric felt himself a mere beginner in front of the heroic masterpiece. Never had he felt so immensely lost in colour. The window spoke to his soul.

'It'll be a reet mess if it all falls out, given an earth tremble or two. It's too big.'

The voice shattered through Amalric's amazement. It came from a round-shouldered man passing by, wearing stone-dusty clothes. He lurched away towards the west end, dustily lost in sunbeams and dark shadows. Amalric stared after him.

'Take no notice of him.' It was Arnold. 'He's had to work hard, helping to finish the window stonework to settle the glass firmly. He's tired and going home. There's nothing that will move this window. It'll stand for a few hundred years. What do you think of it, Master Faceby?'

Amalric was glad to see the stone mason. Beatrix smiled broadly. Father Everard and Istrid greeted him warmly.

'Ah, Arnold. My words can never be enough to describe the magnificence.' Amalric looked at Beatrix for confirmation. She nodded. She was happy. Her eyes sparkled with more than just the glory of the window. It was good to know that in her declining years she would have a soul-meet.

Amalric, feeling lively and challenging, turned to Father Everard. 'What do *you* think of the window, Father?'

'All I can say is that times are changing, even for my Cistercian order. For me, the window carries within it all that the pestilences have made us consider about life and death. Each wave has felt as if we've been moving further to the end of days. I must admit, the beauty, expertise and audacity of this window will encourage me to further understand God's reflective light and His plan for us.'

'Well,' said Amalric, 'there's a window in here that will also encourage you to reflect on the past. It has five tall, thin lancets to it, each with Cistercian-derived decoration. It's about two hundred years old. I first saw it as a boy with my father.'

Arnold butted in. 'Let me show all of you around the minster while it's still quite empty. We can start at the window just mentioned. It's over there in the north transept.'

'I'd like to see the monkeys.' It was Erika. She and her mother had arrived. 'You've told me about them, Elder.'

'So I have. Let's look at them together.' He ushered her away to the nave. 'See here, lass, the monkeys are at a height easy to see.'

Erika peered at the monkey figures. 'I saw a real monkey yesterday at the fair. I felt sorry for it. It was like a little man chained to its master.'

'Well, these monkeys represent people. See, one is a physician. He holds a glass flask like the ones your mother's grandfather Thurston had.' Amalric remembered how Thurston had despised the depiction of a doctor as a monkey, holding the very recognisable jar used to contain the contents of a person's bladder, the colour, smell and taste of which could give a diagnosis. Unsure of the window's original message, Amalric could only understand it now as a slur on the inadequacy of physic doctors trying to cure the body while the Church concentrated on the soul. He wished in that moment he'd been able to make a window to honour physic doctors, to contradict this one. A window that showed how hard men like Thurston had worked in the pestilences.

'Ah, Master Faceby.' A voice boomed down the nave. It was Master John Thornton. He strode over to Amalric, looking very grand in new garments. 'I'm so pleased you're here.' He smiled at Erika. 'Look what I have here.' From below his cloak, he pulled out the little plaque that Erika had made and given to

Edwin as solace for losing his wife.

Amalric was astounded. 'Where did you get that?'

'I was given it by your brother a while back. He came to York to find me. I could see he was ill and grieving his wife. He'd recognised the talent of the young lass here and asked me to take her as an apprentice at my school in Coventry. I thought about it long and hard – I've never apprenticed a lass before – but then I agreed… if that's what she wants. She would be well looked after, lodging with my sister. Your brother has left sufficient money in his will, his lawyer has confirmed it.'

Amalric stood dumfounded. Erika sharply drew in her breath. John Thornton raised his eyebrows at her, awaiting a response. Amalric then understood that this was the gift Edwin had spoken of before his death.

Erika grinned with excitement and was finally able to say, 'Oh, yes, yes.' Then all that was against this most wonderful opportunity hit her. 'But Father will never let me…'

'Well, we'll see,' said Amalric, the hopelessness of it making him almost weep.

'Oh dear, you must excuse me,' said Thornton, seemingly sensing problems, 'I have things to do. Busy day.' He turned to move off but spoke to Erika first. 'There's a lot for you to take in, lass. Plenty of time. You can even wait a year. Think about it, eh?' He smiled amiably.

Just then, as if summoned, George came through the far west door. His proud gait was easy to recognise. Behind him were Friar Damian and Friar Swale. Amalric felt Erika clinging to his cloak and looked for her mother, but saw Ava deep in conversation with the others looking at a window far back.

'Elder, I can't…'

'Stay, lass. We'll have it out with him.' Amalric's heart felt like a stone sinking into a well. The day had been ruined – despair had banished hope.

George strode up. He looked every inch the grand estate owner in a tight green tunic, fine leather boots and black velvet cloak. The thought flickered through Amalric's mind that a gasp must have rippled through the crowd outside as the handsome man passed. The two friars hung behind, pretending to look at carving on a pillar but likely to be in hearing distance.

'Uncle Amalric,' George called good-humouredly, as he approached with an outstretched hand. The de Horesby emerald ring glinted. 'I needs speak with you.'

Amalric kept an arm around Erika and limply shook his hand.

'Uncle… er… Great-uncle, I know what you think of me. The time is short before the window blessing, but I must appraise you of my mind nowadays. Friar Swale…' They both looked around to see the friar unnecessarily running his hand over the pillar. 'Friar Swale worked hard to temper the overbearing traits nestling within my father and grandfather. He taught *me* philosophy and faith. *I* listened but *they* stubbornly refused to be anything other than what they had always been. However, with Grandfather Edwin's death, I've realised that even he'd mellowed a little. I've confessed many things to both Friars Swale and Damian.'

Amalric was growing impatient. It would soon be time for the blessing and he wanted a long look at the window before then. He found it difficult to follow George's words with their too-good-to-be-true quality. But George insisted on continuing.

'I've bestowed St Leonard's Hospital with an annual sum of money so that they may be better able to care for the sick. Ava's brother, Asa, will have a physic living there should he want it. I believe he's anxious to research illnesses like his Grandfather Thurston. I will care for the estate land, but cannot promise to hang on to the arable land when there are few to work it. I may have to have more sheep.'

George drew breath and peered at Amalric, who gave no reaction; it was a lot to take in.

'Truly, Great-uncle Amalric, I *am* reformed.'

Amalric pulled Erika to himself.

'And for my daughter,' he looked fondly at the trembling girl. 'She may forge ahead as a glazier whenever she chooses – but I still want her to marry well.'

Erika burst into tears, with relief or the fact that freedom was not entirely to be bestowed, Amalric couldn't tell.

The two friars approached, sensing the end of conversation. 'It's all true, Master Faceby,' said Friar Swale. Friar Damian nodded in agreement. 'You can't believe the task I had,' Friar Swale continued. 'Your brother was a hard man, but he lived long and I had time to give him a new perspective on life. He regretted many things.'

Amalric, too, regretted his own attitudes towards his brother *and* Friar Swale, but today was not the time to dwell on them.

Ava glided towards them, elegantly dressed in black. She seemed happy.

Ignoring Amalric and the priests, she said, 'Oh, George, I'm glad you're here.' She was breathless with eagerness. 'I went early this morning to St Leonard's Hospital. I've agreed with them to have a little hospital set up at our manor, at Warren Horesby. Their nuns will run it. We can put rooms aside at the manor for the sick, maybe build more. All of Grandfather's and Grandmother's physic equipment can be brought there. Mother's too. They'll use my chapel. Who knows, Asa may join us. Oh, George, I'm so excited. Thank you.'

Amalric saw a look on George's face he had never seen before. He did not know what it meant. 'Ava, I wonder if you would assist me to look at a particular window? It has healing elements you may be interested in.'

Standing below a nave window away from the little group, alone with Ava, Amalric spoke with concern. 'Look, lass, is George really a changed man? It seems imposs…'

'I don't know. His mood may be fleetingly softened by the death of his grandfather and thus his new control of the manor, but here in York, I've rapidly sorted all he agreed with lawyers so that if he turns back to his old self, things cannot be undone. I shall have my little hospital; my brother, Asa, will have a place to fulfil his physic ambitions and Erika will have her glass. We are safe, never fear.'

Chapter Forty

'Master Amalric!' It was John Thornton. 'We have but a short time before the blessing of the window. The clergy gather and the people will soon be let in. The sun has moved further to the south. Go to the window. I will join you shortly. Istrid is there waiting – you must be some distance away to be able to see it all.'

Amalric hobbled over, supported by Ava. He felt tired.

'Have a chair, Da. Come, sit.' Istrid motioned him to a wooden chair with arms and a padded seat placed in front of the window, but far enough back to give him a good view to the top. He obeyed her instinctively. 'There, now, throughout the blessing you'll see the window. No need to move further.'

Noah sat on the cold floor, alert, in front of his master. Istrid remained by his side and the others followed. Amalric was surrounded by those he loved.

They waited for John Thornton. The window detail was becoming quite clear, even to Amalric's old, poor-sighted eyes. He could see that figures were everywhere, their bodies held in movement and gesture. It was as if each part of the window was almost alive. The beginning and end of all things. The first and last days.

Amalric had the strange feeling that, for him, life was drawing to a conclusion. Beatrix would find happiness with Arnold Mason, Ava and George *may* be reconciled… but in any case, Ava would be fulfilled through her Christian charity. Istrid, too, was assured of companionship; Douglas, her husband, would tolerate her strictness and find her softer side. The

Wilberfoss prioress had consented to live with them should the bishop insist she leave the priory, and Istrid's relationship with her relative, Father Everard, showed signs of becoming like mother and son. Also... Noah had found a friend in Dorkas, the donkey.

And Erika...what about her? Amalric looked at his own gnarled hands, scarred with cuts from glass and now with swollen joints and shaking that had increased markedly since this last commission. He would make windows no more, but his little workshop would help Erika before she was apprenticed in Coventry – a lass of the new age after the pestilences, when a woman working on huge windows would not be so unusual.

'Ah, Master Faceby, I'm here at last. Let's have a look at the window.' John Thornton pointed. 'See the faces and how much they resemble some of your own? Seeing your windows at Warren Horesby gave me the confidence as a young man to do something different. I saw that you had been influenced by the Great Pestilence and I vowed, like you, to put emotion into faces. Now, about your own work. See, high up in the tracery, is the figure of a young girl, an angel.'

Amalric screwed his old eyes but saw only a blur. 'Aye, I see where you point, but it's so high I can't see clearly.' He thought of the occularies that Thurston had used to see things closer. If only he now had something to see far away.

'Well, I can assure you it is there.'

'It's Erika, with her halo of curly blonde hair. The young lass inspired me.'

'And a lot lower... there's your dog.'

Amalric made out the panel, but though he could not see the detail of what he had made, it remained glass-clear in his mind; Noah was drawn as a young dog, sleek, before his coat had become shaggy like all the other Noahs. He was standing at the prow of his namesake's boat, *Noah's Ark*,[14] with both front legs on the edge, turning his head back to look at his master. That's

---

[14] Genesis 6–8.

how it had always been – all the individual Noahs and himself going into the future.

'Being there, your dog will not be forgotten. It is a wonderful image,' said Master John Thornton.

That was it. Amalric knew he *had* after all, achieved his ambition – but not as he'd originally envisaged. Now he knew that dreams could be just too big for the time or place; someone or something else was in charge, deciding who should do what. Once, a lifetime ago, he'd wanted to make a huge window; it had been his dream – only it was not possible for a small glazing business struggling through five bouts of the pestilence to do such a thing. But… he had achieved two panels in a great window of a great Christian church. It was enough. His own love of glass would continue to influence others. He felt happy.

Yet, no matter how much he valued the moment, Amalric could not help but recall how the horrific pestilences had brought much else into question for himself, his family and friends: Thurston the doctor of physic, priests, monks and friars, the women in his life. Like himself, they had all tried so hard to keep their faith as harsh realities complicated day-to-day life. And his brother? And love? Well, he'd learned that true love survives doubt, and forgives. From Nesta he'd learned long ago that any type of love was too precious to toss away.

Here, in front of this window, he felt a kind of reconciliation: all the figures were equal, God's light shone and colour exploded through the glass onto walls, floor tiles, furniture and people. It was as if the sunlight itself held all the colours of heaven. Light was the first thing created and possibly held all the answers to all questions ever asked. Without light, there was complete darkness. Light was hope. Amalric had never felt closer to God.

Singing came from somewhere. Figures dressed in sumptuous clerical garb came down the aisle and gathered before the window.

Amalric reached out for Erika. 'Take this talisman, lass.' He pulled a glass angel from a pouch around his waist. 'It's from my first coloured window. It's yours now, to keep you safe. And use my Theophilus manuscript to guide you when you are a woman of glass.'

A pain made Amalric wince. It was chest cramp. It refused to sink into the depths and be lost as it usually did. He felt weightless. Something carried him. Up and up, he felt himself go to the very top of the window. The light was intense, surrounding a seated figure; God Himself.

Familiar Latin words were being spoken below. He'd learned them from the Meaux Abbey monks way, way, way back when a boy:

Videmus nunc per speculum ænigmate,
Tunc autem facie ad faciem

For now we see through a glass, darkly; but then face to face: now I know in part; but then shall I know even as also I am known.[15]

Somewhere below, a dog whined.

---

[15] 1 Corinthians 13:12, KJV.

Acknowledgements

I would like to thank my husband for his tolerance when I was busy at my computer, my daughter for being brave enough to read the first draft, my friends who caringly kept asking how I was getting on with my novel and, not least, the inspiration of Isca, a canine friend, to whom I am known as Carrot-Lady.

Also to stained-glass window-maker, Deborah Lowe of Todmorden, for her beautiful candle-holder which was the inspiration behind the one in my story.

To Instant Apostle for offering me a contract, and to Sheila Jacobs for her wise comments.